no good deed

No Good Deed © 2020 Emma Cole
All rights reserved.

This book is protected under Copyright Laws. Any unauthorized reprint or use of this material is prohibited. No part of this publication may be reproduced, distributed, or transmitted in any form or by any means, including photocopying, recording, or other electronic or mechanical methods without the prior written permission of the author, except in the case of brief quotations embodied in critical reviews and certain other non-commercial uses permitted by copyright law. For permission requests, please contact the author.

This is a work of fiction. All of the characters, organizations, and events portrayed in this story are either products of the author's imagination or are used fictitiously, and any resemblance to actual events, business establishments, locales, or persons, living or dead, is entirely coincidental.

Cover Art – Everly Yours Cover Design

playlist

Never Be the same
Camila Cabello

You Don't Own Me
Grace/G-Eazy

Bulletproof Love
Pierce the Veil

Safe Inside
James Arthur

25
The Pretty Reckless

Do it for Me
Rosenfeld

Black Sea
Natasha Blume

No Time to Die
Billie Eilish

I See Red
Everybody Loves an Outlaw

Nightmare
Halsey

Smoke and Mirrors
Jayn

Problem
Natasha Kills

Watch Me Burn
Michele Morrone

Alone
Alan Walker

Love is a Bitch
Two Feet

Dark Side.
Bishop Briggs.

Hit Me Like a Man
The Pretty Reckless

Shadows
Sabrina Carpenter

Own Me
Bulow

Get Free
Whissell

Ice Cream
Black Pink/Selena Gomez

Bad Bitch
Bebe Rexha/Ty Dolla Sign

Miss YOU!
CORPSE

Middle Finger
Bohnes

Pray.
Bebe Rexha

Born for This
The Score

Deep end
Ruelle

911
Elise

Cruel World
FJORA

Prisoner
Miley Cyrus/Dua Lipa

playlist

Numb
Sabrina Claudio

Blood//Water
Grandson

Warpath
Tim Halperin/Hidden Citizens

Fireworks
First Aid Kit

Break You Hard
Natalia Kills

Sociopath
Stay Loose/Bryce Fox

Broken Inside
Broken Iris

She Talks to Angels
The Black Crowes

Feral Love
Chelsea Wolfe

You Never Know
KNGDAVD

Serial Killer
Moncrieff/JUDGE

Fool
Nostalgia/Tyler Bates

I'm a Mess
Bebe Rexha

Authors Note

TRIGGER WARNING
Vulgar speech, explicit scenes, non/dubcon, drug use, violence, gore, and possibly a myriad of other aspects that may not be suitable for all readers may appear in this book.

REVIEWS
Please do consider leaving a review as it helps others determine if this is the right book for them. In addition to that, the more interest there is in a particular series, the more likely that it will get bumped up in the schedule. (If we don't know how you feel about a book/series, we don't know what you'd like to see next.)

PIRATING

Please don't be a pirate, it really does have an impact.
It is theft, so don't do it!

Dedicated to Murphy's Law, cuz seriously... Fuck that bitch.

Synopsis

My name was Eden Moretti.

After being betrayed by those I'd trusted, my life spiraled out of control. I lost my innocence and dreams in one fell swoop.

Now, I'm a junkie dancer who will do just about anything to earn a buck or get my next fix. When you're living off the books to stay hidden on the fringes between Carlotti and Finelli territory, anything means...anything.

The mafia lords and their heirs own this city. They fiercely protect their turf along with anything else they lay claim to. Murder, mayhem, and money are the driving forces behind the ruthless Families, and death comes swiftly to those who get in their way.

Tony, Vanni, Marco, and Santos are the heirs to the Carlotti Empire, one of the most prolific crime syndicates in NYC, and one of them was the catalyst for the wreckage my life had become.

Due to a budding war with another Family, our paths have crossed again. Except this time, I didn't have a chance to run. The Carlotti men I'd once trusted as boys, took me, but to what end?

To save me? Keep me? Kill me?

The Carlotti heirs don't know what they just took on, but I'll enjoy showing them exactly what I'm capable of. That is, if I don't wind up dead first.

***No Good Deed is a dark contemporary reverse harem romance. Content Warning: vulgar speech, explicit scenes, non/dubcon, drug use, violence, gore, and possibly a myriad of other aspects that may not be suitable for all readers.

**Recommended for 18+/Mature Readers due to content

"Find what you love and let it kill you..."
∼ *Charles Bukowski*

one
watch me burn
Eden

The burnt chemical taste hit the back of my throat as I inhaled tonight's drug of choice from the glass pipe I'd stashed in my locker. I held it as long as I could before exhaling, letting the smoky substance billow out of my mouth. The effects immediately fell over me, washing across my skin like a splash of cold water on a hot day. Heat crawled up my cheeks, and my body already felt lighter. As much as I hated smoking my drugs, it was all I had to get through this shit night. I needed tonight's take to afford my preferred choice. The higher my tolerance built, the harder it became to keep myself supplied.

It was getting nearly impossible to stomach taking my clothes off for the seedy nightlife skulking around Cherry Baby, the strip club where I worked. Not that it had ever been my first choice or particularly enjoyable, but it *was* better than taking my clothes off on the streets. And unfortunately, sometimes I still had to go the extra mile after they came off to make ends meet. But it was good money, and I had nothing else. No family or friends, nothing besides the club and roommates that were merely acquaintances. The drugs made my shit life tolerable, which was why I stayed strung out almost twenty-four seven. They also ate up a good portion of my earnings... My days and nights were a vicious, continuous cycle of supply and demand.

I took one last hit then stashed my pipe back in its hiding spot, hoping Slimy Sam, the piece of shit bouncer here, wouldn't find it and steal it from me. Again.

I walked over to one of the vanity mirrors and leaned against the tabletop. The bright lights and cheap fixtures were installed throughout the room, given to the girls here to hussy ourselves up for the clients. My dark eye makeup was starting to smear, giving my forest-green eyes a hollowed out appearance. Noticing the sunken contours of my once full cheeks, I groaned. I'd lost more weight in my face this month, and Danny was going to be pissed. Danny Savani was my boss, and even though this place wasn't the worst joint in the downtown area, it was definitely not the best either.

Cherry Baby wasn't a terrible place to work. You didn't get forced into doing anything, but there was a certain expectation of willingness required, and you didn't last long without it. It also wasn't somewhere frat boys or family men came with their buddies when they were playing hooky from their wives, not unless they stumbled in by accident. No, this was a place that served a darker clientele, the ones that were rougher around the edges, much like the club itself. The club was done in an eclectic mix of gaudy and modern decor, depending on which area you were in. Some parts had been renovated, mostly the areas that customers would see, or the secured areas. While others, like the dressing room and back hallways, had only had the minimum maintenance done in recent years.

One of the areas Danny *didn't* skimp was the entertainment. Without quality tits, ass, and at least a passably attractive face, he wouldn't pull the full houses that packed in nightly. He didn't play games, and he expected his girls to maintain their tip-top shape, or they got the boot. I was one of his highest earners and had worked here longer than the ever-revolving queue of girls that came through. Not many of the employees stuck it out a year, let alone seven. But if I didn't start remembering to eat, I'd be back to hooking on the streets. Trust me, it was much safer to entertain the crowd and service clients in the relative safety of the club, than in a john's car or on a piece of discarded cardboard in a dirty alley.

With a glance at the big clock on the wall

warning me my set was coming up, I hurried to fix my eye makeup and reapplied my signature black cherry lipstick. If anyone examined me closely, they'd see that I still looked blitzed out of my mind. Luckily for me, I'd done this shit long enough to fake it if I needed to, and their attention wouldn't be on my face if I did my job right. I quickly brushed through my long raven hair, smoothing down the flyaways, and made sure my fishnet thigh highs were situated just right. As soon as I finished, feeling I was as presentable as I was going to get, the door to the dressing room slammed open.

Sam, the slimy son of a bitch, stood in the doorway, his overly beefy hairy arms crossed over his bulging chest. The man looked like an ape but had half the IQ, I swear it had something to do with the 'supplements' he took for working out, but it wasn't like I had any room to point fingers. He was pissed tonight though, his pockmarked cheeks going taut as he clenched his teeth until his face settled into a scowl.

"You're late for your set. Get the fuck out there," he growled, throwing a sausage-sized thumb over his shoulder. "Boss has got some important guests that'll be requiring your services tonight, and they were promised a front row preview of the merchandise. Don't fuck this up for him."

I unwrapped a cherry lollipop, popping it into my mouth to hide the residual scent of chemicals on my breath. "Got it, Hulk. The boss won't be displeased."

Sam caught my arm as I tried to pass him, squeezing my bicep tighter than necessary. "Watch your fucking mouth. I got no problem with you frying your fucking brain, but I bet the boss will." I yanked my arm from his grasp. Surprisingly, he let go without issue. I guessed he was probably worried about leaving a mark and Danny finding out.

"I'll watch my mouth when you learn to stop touching me. Wouldn't wanna damage Danny's goods, now would ya?" I grinned at him, knowing damn well I'd won this round by the look of pure hatred on Sam's face. Any encounter with the man was about as pleasing as a cheese grater catching your skin because you were too lazy to use the food holder. Winning arguments with him was always a favorite pastime, especially since he was one of the few that had been here as long as me. If he didn't rub me the wrong way we might have even been friends.

Knowing I really did need to get in position before I missed my cue, I headed for the stage and tried not to stumble on my stiletto heels as I made my way out into the hall. My small window of coherency was depleting fast as the drugs started to fully kick in. With my tolerance getting higher, the time of lucidity was getting narrower with the heavier substance use I required. And I'd used up too much of it arguing with Sam.

The sickening aroma of stale beer, too much cheap perfume and cologne, and cigarettes hit me as I stepped out into the open club. It was packed tonight as usual, and not likely to empty 'til well into the early morning. Some of the girls were already doing their sets on the smaller stages set out along the floor, while others waited on tables and catered to the numerous partying patrons around the room.

The announcer's voice came on over the speakers, getting the crowd—and my would-be clients—ready for my appearance.

"Alright, gentlemen, get your wallets ready, it's time for tonight's headliner to come out. Our next dancer on the big stage is no divine being, but her body and moves will have you thanking God that she was created. Give it up for Angel!"

I held back the scoff I wanted to let out. If there was a God, he sure as hell wasn't watching over this place. Or me for that matter. I doubted even the devil would want to claim either one.

I softly rubbed a thumb over a small peony-shaped birthmark on my left wrist, a tradition I'd had as long as I could remember. I wasn't sure why it provided me a small sense of solace, but I believed it gave me luck in small doses. Enough to keep me surviving in this fucked up world.

Taking a deep breath in, I sashayed like the good little stripper they wanted me to be as I climbed the set of stairs to the stage in preparation of coming out of the hidden exit. I didn't pause, but kept going, heading straight for the spotlight that illuminated the pole. Pushing away the view of the clamoring customers around me, I instead focused on the feeling pulsing through my body and the fast-paced vulgar-worded song playing over the speakers. I rocked and swirled my body, using the pole as my crutch and lifeline to keep from falling on my ass as I performed. Roars of approval met my ears as the lace of my panties hit the glossy surface, the audience none the wiser to my state, and the bills floated around me as they were tossed onto the stage. All I had to get through now was the up-close and personal portion of the act, and I would be almost done with the evening.

Forcing my eyes to focus, I zeroed in on the two men in suits sitting just at the edge of the stage. Those suits were not the kind you find at a rent-a-tux. They were tailor made and obviously expensive, alerting me that these two were likely my clients for the night. I made sure to give them as much eye contact and full frontal views of my body as possible. As usual after using, my jaw was stiff, and if I wasn't careful I'd be unconsciously grinding my teeth and eventually I'd end up looking like the addict I was with fucked up or missing teeth. I forced my jaw to loosen and plastered a fake smile on my face as I continued. If I fucked this up, I was a goner.

The men lined up against the edge of the stage

seemed to love every second of what I gave, delivering an occasional smack to my ass when I ventured close enough or shouting *'Fuck yeah, baby!'* and *'Give us more!'* at me. The urge to vomit reared up, but I didn't have time to deal with an upset stomach, and I squashed it down before getting down on the floor for the eye-level portion of my routine. Tits hanging and ass up and swaying, I made my rounds as I periodically flashed my crotch and played with myself, mostly in front of the two I sure as hell hoped were my clients. It wouldn't do to fuck up and give overt attention to the wrong customers.

By the time my set ended, sweat coated my body, and my stomach *still* rolled with nausea. My pansy ass stomach needed to get with the program, sucking, fucking, or both was about to go down, and I'd be worse off if I ran out of the tiny bit I had left in my pipe. The men had turned to leave before I made it back through the hidden door, and I knew I'd only have a few minutes to freshen up. Either Danny or one of the other bouncers would make their inevitable appearance to escort me to the selected room.

I barely made it back to the dressing room bathroom and into a stall before dry heaving over the toilet. Fucking miserable, I went to the sink and rinsed my mouth before drinking straight from the tap in an effort to put something in my stomach. Using wet paper towels, I freshened up the best I could in the sink and felt marginally better afterward, enough to hopefully finish out the night, and went to my locker for mouthwash. I swiftly lit up my pipe, taking a bigger hit than last time to tide me over before filling my mouth with the rinse and swishing on the way back to the bathroom. A quick spit and another rinse with water to tame the minty aftertaste, and I headed out into the main dressing area to prepare for my clients.

I picked my way through the feather boas, scraps of lace masquerading as underwear, and the ever-present rainbow coating of glitter that could never be fully cleaned from the room as I made my way to the door. Bliss coursed through my body by the time I neared the T in the hall, one way leading to the area for private showings, AKA the brothel dens, and the other back to the stages and bar. Even the chipped paint and stains on the dingy cinderblock walls couldn't rouse the disgust they usually inspired in me. I ignored the looks of pity a few of the new girls aimed my way when they passed me on their way in from waiting tables. If they lasted a month, they'd be on their knees or bouncing on a dick right along with me, but that was usually when they balked and got their pink slips. *Must be nice to*

have the option to keep your integrity. Me? I liked food in my belly and the crappy apartment I could just barely afford after scoring from my dealer.

Sam waited at the split to escort me to the proper den, probably to make sure I didn't try to jet. Not that I would without my earnings from the set. My gas tank had been sucking fumes as I pulled into the back lot, the little orange light mocking me from the dash as it let me know that I was too strapped to make it back home without tonight's pay. Unless I wanted to walk... But if I attempted that, I'd be giving up the goods for free long before I made it to my block.

"You know, you could have just told me the room number, unless you're planning to watch from your hidey-hole again to yank one out. Better clear it with the boss though. You fuck up with his *guests*, and you'll join Mickey at whatever pig farm his pieces were sent to." My words sounded a bit slurred, even to me, but the burly man didn't seem to care, visibly paling at my reminder instead. All the long-timers, like me and Slimy Sam, witnessed what had happened when a group of recognizable high-rollers came in and Mickey, a new bouncer, had thought to hide in the passage that ran behind dens.

The club was originally a speakeasy, the dens the original party rooms, with cubbies featuring spy holes. That hall was supposed to be locked, and the cubbies stayed curtained off unless Danny wanted to gather dirt or make sure his merchandise wasn't being used for unpaid extras. It was cheaper than surveillance equipment yet still effective. Sam had the keys as it was his job to do the checks, but the boss had some people even he wouldn't fuck with. Those clients were usually touted as 'guests' and treated accordingly if you had any type of survival instinct, which the idiot opportunistic Mickey had lacked. Dumb fuck had had to be collected and deep cleaned out of one of the back rooms after the boss' guests came knocking when Mickey had tried to blackmail them.

I remembered the plastic totes he'd been carted out in, totes I'd had to help fill. The smell of death and fucking *meat* had been horrendous enough for the mere memory to nearly have me puking now. I'd been new back then. Definitely not innocent, as I'd been turning tricks on the street just to survive before Danny hired me, but I hadn't been an addict at that point. No, the drugs came later when I couldn't sleep. The nightmares and phantom scents were bad enough, but it was the terror that the same would happen to me that kept me startling awake at every noise. It affected my job performance and attracted Danny's attention, so when one of the other girls offered me something to calm down, I took it without question. Experimenting with what would dull the world but still allow me to function and fit into my budget, I started my descent into addiction.

By the time Danny figured out I was a junkie, my drug use was affecting my sets. I think some small amount of guilt kept him from firing me, but I'd been warned to tone it down at work and keep earning him money. Which led to needing at least a modicum of quality to the junk and higher prices. Which in turn led to being the resident cum dump that wouldn't turn down any request, barring a few things Danny himself put in place. He needed me whole and able to work, after all.

A sharp slap to my thigh brought me out of whatever space I'd drifted off to. I guess Slimy Sam finally noticed I'd topped up after my set.

"*You're* going to be the one that fucks this up if you don't lay off the pipe." My worry blazed a path through the haze. There'd be nothing I could do to stop him from breaking into my locker while I was occupied with cock-gobbling. If he took my pipe, I'd have to use a lightbulb again, and the old-fashioned ones were hard to come by nowadays. "Jesus fucking Christ, girl, where'd you go this time?"

With a good deal of effort, I made myself focus on Sam. "I got this. Just tell me which room," I said even as the effort to be lucid brought back the nausea. *Fuck, maybe I'm getting sick.* I couldn't afford to take time off. Before I could start to zone out on what I'd do if I got bad enough to need to stay home, Sam grabbed my arm and tugged me through the windowed door to a nicer section of the warren of corridors that made up the club. Here, the cinderblock walls were covered in faux velvet hangings, making a tawdry yet posher atmosphere than the employee halls.

I thought about struggling, but I was too worried I'd twist an ankle in my sky-high stilettos thanks to my inebriated state. "You know what'll happen if you walk into the wrong room. I thought you wanted to keep your job," the dick sneered down at me.

He wasn't wrong though. Clients tended to get pissed and demanded refunds if the debauchery they'd come for was interrupted. Refunds meant someone had to pay the difference, and that someone wouldn't be the house. I couldn't afford to cover even a basic blowie at this point. Not until I got my cut from tonight. Which reminded me...

"Hey, who collected my money tonight? If I get shorted again, I'm gonna cut a bitch." Usually, I'd collect my own bills off the stage and tally up with the house, but when I had clients that couldn't be kept waiting, one of the other girls was given the task so I could freshen up and be punctual. The last time, I'd made half of my usual, and that shit wasn't happening again. The club was full, and the audience had been generous.

"I had one of the other guys escort a newb straight to the cage." I breathed a sigh of relief at that; the cage was where all the money was taken to be tallied up, and it *did* have surveillance. "Straighten up and do your job, or I might just be able to convince the boss to let me have a turn." Sam's *very* short-lived nicety regarding my earnings was immediately squashed by the reminder that even as a whore I wouldn't let him have a go at me. *Slimy prick.* At least he turned my arm loose as we started passing doors with a cacophony of moans, grunts, and the bass of music filtering through them. The higher-priced rooms were soundproofed, though that could be a blessing or a curse, depending on the client.

"By the way," he said as we reached the V.I.P. room, "they requested some girl-on-girl action… I sent Trixie."

Other than a scathing glare, I couldn't do or say shit. He'd opened the door right as my nemesis' name tripped out of his jackass face. Knowing exactly that, he just smiled back at me as he used one meaty hand to shove me over the threshold, the other shutting the door behind me.

This is hell.

two
i'm a mess
Eden

I stumbled a few steps on the spiked heels before I caught my balance. I'd also caught the attention of the room's occupants, except for Trixie, whose bleach-blonde head was bobbing in the lap of one of the men from earlier. The clients sat on the booth in front of a makeshift stage, a table that was bolted to the floor. It was close enough to reach out and touch, but far enough away to fit a hooker on her knees. Mirrors ran across the wall above the booth, their reflection softened by the swirls of gold etched into them.

Other than his fly hanging open and his pants slightly lowered, the man Trixie serviced was fully dressed, as was his friend. They were of the typical coloring of this area, with dark hair and eyes, though one's skin tone was a bit swarthier than the other. From their kempt nails, appearance, and quality suits, I surmised they were made men or one of the local families' 'cousins.' A wannabe would be slick, but they tended toward off-the-rack wear. If these guys were slumming it, they would have dressed down, but not cheaply.

I took it all in at a glance, my mouth running dry at whatever game Danny was playing. They had better quality pussy at their beck and call, and I wanted far, far away from whatever these men were really here for. Not to say my cunt was sloppy or unclean. I worked hard not to catch anything, including feelings, but I wasn't even a bit refined. No, I was a wrong side of the tracks girl who got paid by the activity picked off a fucking laminated menu. Men wearing bespoke suits didn't need women like Trixie with obvious home bleach jobs or me in my dollar store lingerie; they could afford top-notch trophies along with all their accoutrements. Even under the high, I was embarrassed by my attire. I'd worn it to keep the spendier stuff used on stage from getting torn up, and now I came off like the back-room tramp I was. At least I'd had Mandy wax me in our little makeshift salon in the corner of the dressing room after our shift the night before last. No stubble here.

My eyes drifted back to the hands of the men. I only recognized the tailored suits because we knew to look out for them and make ourselves scarce if they showed up, not because I could tell what label was inside based on the cut or drapery or whatever the fuck it was called. No signet rings were present on his fingers, so not immediate circles, but the clothes still had me on edge. Cherry Baby sat in the midpoint between territories. Danny paid out the ass for the privilege of being in the neutral zone, so the lower initiates and wannabes from both the Carlotti and Finelli crews would come in, but never on the same night as the guys with actual power. Men like these never came in when we were open to the public. They'd occasionally use the club as a meeting place, but to be here tonight meant something was going—

"Hey, my dick isn't gonna suck itself. Get the fuck over here." The finger snap that accompanied the voice startled me out of my racing thoughts. All this shit was ruining my high.

Without protest, I sauntered across the room to the horseshoe-shaped booth and dropped to my knees in front of the man. Tossing my long dark hair behind one shoulder, I reached out to unfasten his trousers.

I peeked up from under lashes heavy with mascara and ran my tongue over my full lips, wetting them, as I deftly fished the man's dick out of his silky boxers. His eyes were dark, heavy-lidded, and shining with lustful anticipation— his mouth open enough that I could see the pink tip of his tongue tracing the edges of his ultra white top teeth. After a slight tug from me, he lifted his hips enough that I could reach his smooth balls. I wasn't sure if he was naturally almost hairless, but there wasn't much more than fuzz, a blessing in some cases.

Leaning in, my tongue darted out to swirl around the ruddy tip of an above average-sized dick before my jaw opened wide, allowing his length to tunnel straight to the back of my throat. With tried and true expertise, I sucked and licked him to the precipice as I tugged lightly on his delicate sack, murmuring soft moans timed to vibrate the head every time it nestled in my throat.

I wasn't even taking him all the way before he tapped out, dragging his dick from the suction of my swollen lips with a pop and a string of saliva trailing after it. Wiping the moisture off on my shoulder with a quick twist of my head, I shot a questioning gaze at my client.

"Did I do something wrong?" I nearly purred, hiding my frustration that he'd stopped me when I'd almost had him blowing his load. *Fuck, I nearly took it without a condom. Fucking tweaker move, Eden.* Berating myself, I tried to pay attention to the man while also attempting to catch sight of the bowl of condoms that was usually set out. Hopefully not cherry this time. Cute that they matched the name of the club, but the damn things burned my snatch, and washing the sickly sweet smell out of there was a nightmare. Not to mention the after-effects of using them with anal that didn't bear thinking about. It took more than a smidge of effort to abort my shudder.

"No," he answered sharply, patting my cheek just as I spied the bowl on a side table. He then reached over to grab a handful of Trixie's hair, pulling her off his friend, her face sweaty and lips swollen. "Jesus fuck, you suck at sucking. Angel had me about done within two minutes, and you've been hoovering Oscar's porker for ten minutes straight. Did you leave the man any skin?"

A glance at Oscar's shiny member revealed it was indeed a bit red, but it was also half-limp and still comparable in size to the stiffy I'd been servicing. I wondered if he had issues getting a full erection, some large men did, and alternately felt badly and a bit vindictive that Trixie was turning fifty shades of red from her efforts and consternation. I rarely had any trouble sucking a dick to full-mast. Hence another reason for our nemesis status— I was just plain better at everything.

"Get on the table, Hoover."

My smugness waned at the cueing of my least favorite part of the scheduled activities, at least the ones I knew about anyway. A stomach cramp nearly had me spewing on my client's polished loafers, and I beat back the urge with my will alone. I was starting to wonder if the nausea wasn't just from my hatred of whoring and being sick from forgetting to eat tonight, but if I'd actually gotten a bad batch. Not like I could ask for a refund or could afford to buy more yet—especially after splitting this take with Trixie. Even if two were more expensive, she didn't command the same rates I did, and Danny would make me split the take fifty-fifty as usual. His house, his rules, and an even split kept most everyone happy.

"My Angel, why don't you get on top." It wasn't a question, and his familiar caress of my cheek and possessive use of my name made my blood run cold. I wouldn't be any man's regular warm hole, not after my mom and— fuck, I needed another hit.

Shakily, I got to my feet, the man chivalrously helping me up. The very idea of it was laughably ironic. I was here because of his cash, not because he was my date. I didn't want to risk a smack or pissing him off, so I complied with his demand, stopping briefly to shrug the flimsy lingerie off before I climbed up on the table. With the spin of no-name's finger, I changed direction to straddle Trixie's head.

"You had first pick last time, Oscar. I'm choosing this time, and we can switch for the next round." *Next round? Oh, come the fuck on. Did they bring fucking boner pills?* I stifled my initial groan but balked when neither of them moved toward the condoms.

"Hey, you guys gotta glove up. Should have had them on already, but I forgot to mention it." I held the man's stare as I made my demand, refusing to back down. This was one area Danny wouldn't hesitate to intervene over, special guests or not. Can't sell tainted pussy.

"Danny Boy said all the girls are clean. Was he lying?" The man started to tuck his dick back in, and I could see my next score dissolving into the ether along with my job. If this cunt claimed I said Danny couldn't be trusted, my ass would be out of here without even collecting the night's earnings.

"No, no. We're clean, but we stay that way by insisting on protection." He hesitated but didn't quite look sold. I knew what *would* work though. "Plus, some chicks see a little baby batter oopsie as a ticket out of here with the right man." Trixie started to say something, but I sat on her face, smothering her with my crotch, and aimed a pointed glance at the shaved pink pussy under me. That instantly had the man stepping over to grab a few foil squares, tossing one to his partner who seemed to be having better luck stroking his own dick. I lifted up, letting Trixie breathe when she tapped out on my outer thigh. *Fucking idiot woman. Trying to get us screwed bareback. No way, you trashy whore.*

"I'm Arlo by the way. And I think you heard Pony Boy back there is Oscar." The ripping of the packets rasped through the room, sending relief coursing through my veins... until Arlo explained what they wanted. "Danny said muff diving isn't your favorite, but you'd do it with a smile if we brought party favors. Then he wouldn't have to charge me double to get your cooperation." My ears perked up at party favors, but my brows lowered into a frown at the lost money. *Fucking Danny.*

"Would you like to do the honors?" Arlo held the thankfully pale, non-cherry rubber out to me, making a tsking noise when I tried to reach for it. Instead of handing it over, he rubbed the lubricated latex over my lower lip. Getting the hint, I took it into my mouth, working it around until I knew I had it going in the proper direction before taking the tip of his erection between lips. I slowly went down on him, the condom unrolling down his shaft until he hit my throat, and with a slight gag, I took him in to the hilt.

"Shit, yes. Angel has a divine mouth, Oscar. You're in for a treat." *Bossy ass is gonna be in for a treat if he doesn't stop tickling my tonsils.*

Thankfully, he retreated, directing me to lick and suck at Trixie's sex while he fucked her unless I was sucking on him. I wasn't high enough to give it much effort, doing the bare minimum to pass for the 'girl-on-girl' request and earn my cash. More than anything else, it was because I couldn't stand the bitch the pussy was attached to. What girl hasn't experimented or at least thought about it?

Trixie, though, didn't have any such reservations. She went to town, nearly gnawing on my clit and nether lips in her zest. Her focus moved to just my clit as Oscar pressed against my opening without any warm up and started to cram it in. *Fucking Pony Boy was right, he's definitely hard now.* I might have whimpered by the time he hit bottom, cursing Danny again for setting this up when I was running low.

"Damn, Arlo, she's got a tight little pussy. It's gonna be wrecked by the time you get to it." Oscar punctuated his statement with a dark chuckle as he took a few rough, slamming thrusts before pulling out to fuck Trixie's face. The mirror that ran the length of the wall reflected the tawdry scene if you bothered to look. Shame ate at me, because look I did, and I debated bailing and cutting my losses.

As if he'd read my thoughts, Arlo suddenly held a little tray and short straw in front of my face. The skinny white line of powder beckoned me like a siren intent on sinking a ship. I ignored the tiny voice saying maybe I'd had enough for the night and snatched the straw like the lifeline it was before expertly pinching off one nostril and instantly inhaling the drug with the other. Arlo let out a devilish laugh and took the tray away, winking one dark eye at me as he wiped up the residue with a finger and smeared it on the tip of his condom-covered dick. Without hesitation, I wrapped my lips around it, removing all traces of my vice while giving him what he wanted.

When Trixie crept her long-nailed fingers toward the crack of my ass, I pinched and twisted a spot of skin on the inside of her thigh to deter her. A yelp sounded right before a slap to the wandering hands caught part of it, but I was grateful Oscar put a stop to it. "Hands off, Hoover, I'll personally stretch that ass later." And my ass clenched as Oscar instantly lost points on the attractive scale. *How much did they fucking pay for?* I wasn't sure how long I could handle this shit tonight, and I'd done zero prep for anal. I cringed internally at the thought, then for real as I gagged on a particularly deep thrust from Arlo.

The men continued alternating between fucking and getting sucked, and every time Arlo pulled out of Trixie, he'd lure me to take his cock in earnest with little bits of strategically placed powder. It wasn't the same as snorting or smoking it, but the cumulative effects of those bits paired with the line began to take me to my happy place. I didn't even care that my mascara tracked down my cheeks from all the face fucking-induced tears. I just wanted to stay blissed out until the deeds were done.

My stomach still twinged occasionally under it all, but it was easy to ignore for the time being. Until the door crashed open. Muffled shots dropped Arlo and Oscar, who had both been spit roasting me at the time. My body fell, still connected with theirs, as Oscar slumped over me and to then the side. My scream was choked off as my face was crammed into Arlo's groin, teeth scraping his dick, not that he would mind now. When we hit the floor, I was able to dislodge my mouth and take in Arlo's sightless eyes. Scrambling under the table and out from under half of Oscar's body, I saw that his eyes were just as vacant. My heart picked up double time when Trixie's scream was cut off with another pop and liquid started to trickle off the edge of the table to the floor in front of me. Directly in my line of sight was Oscar's groin, cock flaccid, the condom gone, likely dislodged in the fall.

"Get out here, bitch. If you make me come in there for you, I'll make it last." The harsh voice came from somewhere above a pair of wingtip shoes, polished to a high enough sheen that I could see my distorted reflection in them. No way was I going out there.

My dexterity and coordination were severely impaired from all the drugs, not that it would have mattered since I had nowhere to go when a hand reached under the table to jerk me out by my ankle hard enough that I slid across the floor. Briefly I saw Trixie's body still atop it, leaking blood and what I then discovered was piss.

"Fucking disgusting, man. Just shoot her and let's go deal with Danny. It reeks in here." I was too terrified to look up at the second speaker as I waited for the pain that I hoped would be brief. And then I'd join the cause of the barnyard smell of piss, shit, and blood that enveloped the room.

"No, I warned her. Better to make an example now than have to come back again." I huddled into my nakedness, crossing my arms as my teeth began to chatter.

The first voice was again closer than the second, and my chest seized as I started to hyperventilate. A hand grabbed a fistful of my hair, jerking me up to my knees, and my face was forced upward toward the irate man. Tears blurred my vision as I tried to beg for him to end it quickly.

"P-p-ple-ease," I hiccupped out past the wheezing breaths I was failing to get under control.

"Fuck, Tony, just put her out of her misery. She's a fucking junkied out mess anyway." But the man wasn't listening, instead he dragged me to my feet by his grip on my hair. My hands flew up to scratch at his in an attempt to stop him from ripping it out at the roots. I couldn't even screech because I couldn't fucking breathe.

"Tony, wait!"

My arm was seized in a second iron grip, my wrist twisted at an odd angle, putting an agonizing bind on the joints. Something was scrubbed over my face, clearing my eyes enough to recognize the features in front of me. The panicked voice I should have recognized faded as my body went rigid before starting to convulse uncontrollably. I'd barely made out, "It's *Eden,* Tony" before my stomach finally got its way and emptied itself as everything went black.

three
i see red

Tony

"It's Eden, Tony."

No. Fucking. Way. Giovanni's outburst had damn near stopped my heart from its current rapid adrenaline-induced pace. Eden *Fucking* Moretti. I wanted to laugh at such a ridiculous notion, that *this* drugged up whore could be the girl who still haunted our thoughts even after all these years, but the truth was plain as day, etched on the skin of her wrist. A peony-shaped discoloration that made up an unmistakably unique birthmark. The one definite identifier that *this* was the girl who'd gotten away from us.

"No. There has to be a mistake." As soon as the knee-jerk denial left my lips, the girl I held up spewed a waterfall of vomit everywhere and began to convulse violently. I dropped her in surprise and a bit of disgust, but my younger brother was swiftly at her side, kneeling next to her and holding her head to the side, so she wouldn't hit it on anything.

"Fuck! I think she's O.D.'ing. She's turning blue and clammy. We need to get her out of here," he insisted, putting his hands beneath her back and behind her knees to lift her once the convulsions stopped.

"That's not Eden, and we're not taking her fucking anywhere. Put her down, and we'll just end her right here," I ordered, pointing my pistol at her head.

Vanni turned so the gun was aimed at his back rather than her head, knowing I'd never intentionally harm him. "Don't even think about it, Tony. If you can look at that birthmark and seriously deny what you see, you're a fucking idiot. It's her."

I glared at him, both shocked and a bit pissed off that he'd dare to undermine my order. *I* was the next head of the Carlotti Family, the most powerful organization on the eastern seaboard. Yet there he was, defying me over this *hooker*.

"Look, let's get her some help and make sure. I know it's her. If I'm wrong, you're free to finish her off, but trust me, *please.*" My brother's eyes, so like my own, begged me to agree.

I couldn't believe this was happening, but he did have a point. I didn't want to accept that this frail waste of space creature in his arms was our Eden, but the birthmark was too much to ignore. At least if

I proved him wrong, I'd get to tell him *I told you so*. And that was something I didn't often get to say to my almost always rational brother.

I dropped my gun back to my side as a sense of unease filled me. *This is probably a fucking mistake.* "Fine. But know that I will *not* hesitate to end the bitch when you're wrong."

Giovanni shot me a satisfied grin, reminiscent of those he'd sported as a teen. Nothing made him happier than proving a point to get his way. "Got it, boss. Cover me while we get the fuck out of this hell hole?"

I nodded and held my gun at the ready as we left the blood-splattered room behind. Thankfully, the stupid Finelli boys, Oscar and Arlo, had paid enough money to be left alone. No one guarded the halls as we slipped out and made our way toward the back of the Cherry Baby club.

Vanni followed closely behind me, his grip tight on the would-be Eden. I thought we were home free when I saw the back door with the glaring exit sign above it. At least, until a large figure stepped out of a room, blocking our escape.

The burly man I knew to be named Sam, or some shit like that, from our occasional after hours visits to the place, drew his own gun and took up a defensive stance. "Who the fuck are you? Drop the girl, or I'll blow your fucking brains out. The club is neutral territory, and Angel belongs to us."

Recognition lit his face, then came the terror, but the idiot didn't lower his weapon. "Mr. Carlotti, let me get the boss, I'm sure this is a misunderstanding."

Just as the words left his mouth, I pulled the trigger. My bullet hit him square in the middle of his forehead, dropping him like a sack of bricks and leaving a spray of blood and bits of bone and gore plastered across the cement wall. "Yeah, sure you will," I snorted derisively. Someone should really tell Danny boy not to play his club's music so loudly. Honestly, we probably didn't even need the silencing muzzles on our guns. Other than the snag of a maybe-Eden, the night had gone smoothly and mostly according to plan.

I gave his body a kick as we stepped around it and out the door into the fresh, crisp air of the night. We'd parked the Audi right outside, making it easier for Vanni to slip into the backseat with "Angel" on his lap.

"Shit, we have to move, Tony. Her skin is bad, and she's shivering. I think she's getting worse." His panic pushed me into action. I jumped into the driver's seat, started the engine, and sped out of there as quickly as I dared without bringing undue attention to us. All we needed was to deal with the hassle of the police pulling us over.

"Is she breathing?" I asked, swerving through the traffic as fast as I could. Taking her to a hospital was out of the question. She'd have to see the doctor we kept on retainer for just this type of situation.

"Barely. Her body is still shaking pretty fucking badly, and her pulse is racing. I'll call Doc and get him on standby." He pulled out his phone, but I reached back and grabbed it from him.

"You make sure she stays alive, and I'll call the doc."

I connected my phone through the car speaker and rang Dr. Carlos Sorento, the man we brought all of our injured when they were down for the count. He was efficient and kept his mouth shut for a good price. My father would be pissed we'd used him for some cracked out stripper, but hopefully, I'd have a good reason for it. If she didn't turn out to be Eden, and he found out, it might be my brain that got the bullet.

The doc answered on the third ring. "Sir?"

"I've got an overdose coming to you. Cocaine for sure, but unsure of any other substances. Female, approximately five foot five, maybe one hundred pounds. Convulsions, vomiting, clammy skin, rapid heartbeat, and her complexion is turning a grayish-blue," I listed off to him, knowing he'd be better prepared with detailed info. *Shit.* I'd blown right through a stop sign, distracted by everything going on around me.

"Female, you say?" he asked with a curious and interested tone I didn't entirely like.

"I'll pay you extra to keep this between us," I replied, warning evident in my voice. "What do we do? We're ten minutes out."

"Is she breathing?" I glanced at Vanni in the mirror. He nodded.

"Yes. Barely."

"Good. Keep her breathing. If she vomits again, make sure her head is turned. That's about all you can do until you get her here and I can assess her so I can counteract her symptoms. If she remains unconscious, I may need to test her to see what else she might have taken."

"Good. Be there soon." I hung up the phone and focused on getting us there, winding through the dark streets toward home and away from the busy city. I swerved around other drivers, picking up speed the nearer we drew to the estate. "I'm going to fucking lose it if she's not Eden."

He let out a dark chuckle. *"You're* going to lose it? Just wait 'til Santos finds out." *Fuck. Santos.* The reason this girl meant anything to any of us at all.

Growing up in the Family could be tough, but I was always surrounded by my brother Giovanni, our cousin Marco, and our best friend since childhood, Santos. Santos was the one who'd met Eden first then introduced her to the rest of us. She'd been a bit of a wild card, sweeping all of us under her spell with just a bat of her lashes. Maria, her mother, had been hired by Santos' father, Rodrigo, after Santos' mother, Alina, died from cancer. He couldn't keep up with the house and found Maria to help with it. Among *other* things. Maria had quickly become not only a presence around the house, but a concubine in his bed. It wasn't until Eden turned fifteen that Maria brought her around to help. She bewitched Santos pretty quickly. Back then, he was a good kid with a soft heart that didn't often open up to people, but Eden knew how to bring out the best in all of us. She was lively and funny and took to being friends with everyone who was in Santos' life. We could tease her like one of the guys, to a point anyway. Marco was forever hitting on her, but she just seemed to shrug it off like she didn't notice. Santos did though, and if it wasn't for the fact that he knew Marco would never act on it, he'd have kicked his ass and then banned him from the house. I wasn't certain, but I think he'd known we all had a thing for the dark-haired girl. Her pouty lips that were a dusky rose without anything on them had featured more than once in a fantasy during alone time with a bottle of lotion. I'd accidentally walked in on her going down on Santos one time and had left before she noticed, but that image was burned into my brain in technicolor. I'd been jealous like crazy that she'd only had eyes for him, but I could never entertain being anything other than her friend.

But like in most stories, shit hit the fan. None of us really knew what happened, but one day Eden just disappeared. She'd left a letter for Santos telling him how much she hated him and her life. She told him not to look for her or contact her.

We'd soon discovered some of Alina's jewelry had gone missing, adding insult to injury for my long-time friend and to us. It was hard enough trying to understand why she'd suddenly left, but that news destroyed us. Santos' mother had been a wonderful person, and those jewels and some pictures were all her son had left of her.

After that, none of us were the same. Santos grew cold and threw himself further into the Family business under his father's wing. I hadn't wanted this life for him, but he'd refused to listen. I'd hoped he would've found something to do outside the Family, like a normal nine to five job, and maybe settle down with some kids. Vanni, Marco, and I were stuck in this life, being Carlotti blood, but Santos had a choice. Now, the man was a force to be reckoned with. He excelled at anything thrown at him and had quickly risen in the ranks as an enforcer. His brute strength and coldness worked well for a variety of jobs.

Which was why I was suddenly very afraid of what we were going to tell him. If this girl *was* Eden, he'd either have us throw her away, or he'd put a bullet in her himself.

"We say nothing until we know for sure," I barked at my brother, leaving no doubt in my order.

"The last thing we need is Santos off the rails." People and property tended to get broken when he went on a tear, sometimes him, sometimes not, but there was always a mess to clean up.

"Yeah. Probably best." A gargled choking sound met my ears, and Vanni cursed. "Shit! Shit! Shit! She's convulsing again! Are we almost there?"

Thankfully, we'd just made it to the estate.

"Be ready to jump out with her."

I pressed the remote as we rolled up to the iron barred entrance and ten-foot cobblestone walls that encased the property. The gates had barely finished opening before I was racing down the gravel road toward the left side of the manor that was my Family home. While my parents lived there and conducted the most private of Family matters at the manor, I chose to live in a guest home on the property. It was large enough that Giovanni and Marco lived with me, but Santos had a place a few miles away from the rest of us. He preferred the seclusion.

My car slid to a stop in front of the two-story house where the doc and Marco stood outside, waiting.

"Well, guess we have to tell Marco what's up," Vanni lamented, throwing open the door and climbing out of the car with the girl in his arms.

"Not it," I replied, rushing after him. Doc Carlos was quickly at Vanni's side, walking with him as they brought her into my home. Marco didn't follow them, choosing to stay in stride with me.

"What the fuck is going on? I heard Doc come barging in and setting up shop in the dining room. Who's the girl?"

His questions were fired off faster than my brain was allowing me to process. That, and I didn't want to be the one to answer them. While Santos would predictably go off to fuck something up, Marco was too unpredictable to guess what his reaction would be.

"Ask Vanni. It's his dumb idea." Marco threw me a questioning stare, but he knew better than to press the matter. He was a bit older than Giovanni and twice the handful. It was a wonder someone as fun-loving and vibrant as him could stomach the life we lived, but then I'd see him in action and the wonder would disappear. Our cousin might come off as a friendly face, but he was still someone not to cross.

We walked into the dining area and were met with the sight of this fragile woman splayed on her back across my dining room table. The doctor went through the motions of checking her vitals, writing everything down before pulling out an auto-injector and jabbing it into her thigh followed by a regular syringe that he tapped and carefully inserted into her arm. After a few minutes of nothing, Angel—I refused to call her Eden yet—let out a deep gasp but remained otherwise motionless.

"I've sedated her and given her medication to counteract the drugs. I'm going to set up a saline drip since she's severely dehydrated, and hopefully, she'll recover. We should move her to a bed or couch, so she'll be more comfortable. I'll keep an eye on her for the time being."

I nodded and motioned for Giovanni to pick the naked girl up. I wasn't touching her with the blood and who knew what else all over her, but Vanni had already been contaminated.

Marco jumped into action, following after. "I'll get her something to wear," he offered.

"Wait, get something to cover the bed, and a bucket, in case she starts puking again or God forbid loses control of her bladder." I shuddered and sympathized with Marco whose lip curled up in distaste. He turned to leave, and I added as an afterthought, "And something to clean her up a bit, too."

I waited for them to get her settled in the spare room, choosing that moment to walk over to my mini bar and fix a glass of whiskey. I drank it down in one go then filled another before going back to the dining room and taking a seat. My nerves were shot from the day that didn't seem to want to end and the prospect this girl could be Eden.

As much as I didn't want it to be her, the idea that it could be both excited and terrified me. Unbeknownst to Santos, I had also been hopelessly head over heels for that seventeen-year-old girl we all had gotten to know. It was so long ago and such a brief blip in the fabric of our lives, but it had been one of the biggest events in our shared history. One day she was there, and the next gone, leaving an Eden sized hole in our lives. It had been almost a decade since everything had gone down, yet it felt like yesterday. A war waged inside me about how we were going to tell Santos. His reaction was bound to be bad no matter what.

Stomping feet sounded down the hall before Marco pulled a chair out and sat down next to me. His face was a mask of shock.

"No fucking way," were his only words.

"Exactly what I said." See? I wasn't the only one in doubt.

"I just can't believe it's her. After all this time..." He trailed off, features going pensive and eyes distant. The drink I'd just taken got caught in my throat. I coughed, leveling him with an astonished stare. "You're joking. You seriously can't be swayed that quickly! After the way her mother was, do you think the real Eden would've ended up doing the same damn thing? Snorting drugs and giving away her pussy to any man who'd pay a good buck?"

For the first time in longer than I could remember, Marco threw me the angriest of glares, hazel eyes flashing with contempt.

"We have no idea what that girl went through to get to where she is. When I took my vows to this family, I swore I'd follow your lead 'til the end and never question the orders you gave me. But you being so blissfully ignorant of the evidence in front of you is insanity, Tony." He swept a hand through his shoulder-length dark hair and sighed. Marco wasn't one to bullshit me or go to bat for a cause he wasn't certain of. My cousin going against me meant he'd made up his mind, and it would cause a rift in our group if I didn't at least respect it.

"Open your eyes, man. That's Eden. That birthmark is no tattoo or scar. It's real, and it's in the same place it was all those years ago. It's not a trick of the light or a hallucination. That girl *is* Eden. Yes, she's got some fucked up life from what Vanni just filled me in on, but it's her. Look past the gauntness, the blood smears, and the fucked-up makeup, and you'll see her. I did, and I wasn't nearly as close to her as you and Santos were."

I had no reply. My men were turning against me on this, so sure of everything revolving around her, but I needed time. I needed to know for sure.

I threw back the rest of my drink, slammed the glass down on the table, and marched back to the spare room. Vanni sat in one of the chairs in the corner, watching as the doctor continued to manually monitor her vitals at her bedside. I took a deep breath and stalked over to the prone figure now dressed in one of Marco's overly large shirts that swallowed her tiny frame. The doctor ignored my presence as I leaned over her, my eyes searching her dirty face and black matted hair for any signs of recognition. I'd never let anyone see how many times I just stared at this girl when we were younger, secretly wishing it had been me she met first. My eyes traced over her dark arched brows, narrow cheekbones, and plump lips that were smeared in a gaudy red lipstick.

There was a spark of recognition, but she'd changed too much for me to know for sure. I reached down and lifted her wrist, turning it gently in my hand to inspect it in better lighting.

The breath was knocked from my chest in an instant. How could I have been so naive? So wrong? Now able to really see the birthmark, I could no longer deny it. It was so unique in the way it furled out like soft petals with dotting in the middle. Even on her pallid skin, which once had a lovely, tanned sheen to it, I could tell it still held that same dusty pink color mixed in with the usual darker pigments that generally comprised a birthmark.

It was Eden. No doubt in my mind, not anymore.

Releasing a harsh breath, I dropped her arm back to her side. I turned to leave the room but stopped short and glanced at the doctor. "Doc, get a blood panel to test for disease and toxicity and collect her fingerprints for analysis. With her obvious lifestyle, I wouldn't say it's a stretch to think she's been arrested at least once. I want irrefutable proof of who she is."

He nodded and immediately went to work, collecting what I'd tasked him with.

"You still don't believe it?" Vanni called out to me, frustration evident in his voice.

"It's not me that needs the reassurance anymore. Santos won't accept anything but physical proof. The birthmark won't be enough for him."

"You don't think he'll believe her even when she wakes up and admits who she is," Vanni concluded.

I shook my head. "He'd never listen. And who's to say she'd tell us anyway? She watched us shoot up the Finelli boys. Odds are she won't trust us, and we shouldn't trust her either. She may be Eden, but she isn't that same girl anymore. We need to be prepared."

There was a high chance her identity was recorded in a database somewhere. That would resolve problem one. Problem two would be figuring out if she could be trusted not to talk. Family came first. No exceptions.

Not even for Eden.

four
middle finger
Eden

Something wet and warm rubbed at my face, rousing me from oblivion. I wasn't cognizant enough to make sense of what was going on, but the trail of heat felt so good as it traveled over my neck and shoulders, down my arms, and gently around my hands. I'd have been content to drift back off, except the dull ache in the bend of my elbow turned into a pinch when my arm was shifted. The discomfort was enough to jostle the memory of my last lucid moments, resulting in my abrupt arrival at full panicked wakefulness.

"Hey, you're okay, settle down." The voice was deep yet calm. As for me, I wasn't interested in calmness.

"Get off!" My voice came out rough, my throat burning with the effort of forcing the words out. It set off a chain reaction of aches and pains from various parts of my body, an all-encompassing headache the most prevalent as I tried to sit up and scurry away from the form next to the bed I was in. When my eyes finally focused, it was to find a man sitting back with his hands up in surrender; he even had a white rag dangling from one. "Who the fuck are you?" The words came out slurred, mostly due to my dry ass mouth, but his answering dimpled grin meant he at least understood me.

His smile faded when I continued to stare at him, nonplussed. "You telling me you forgot all about me, Edie?"

I studied him closer, unease filtering through me at the use of the nickname. Not many knew my real name, and even fewer were familiar enough to shorten it. Honey-colored flecks shone prominently in hazel eyes under full arching brows that were a shade or two darker than the coffee-hued spiked out locks that would fall into a shaggy disarray without the product holding it up. I continued my perusal over high-cut cheekbones where a dark scruff was fast becoming the beginnings of a beard. I really hoped he didn't grow one. Those lips were too pretty to cover up. The instant interest in his *lips* of all things clued me into two things. One, I thought the dude was hot as fuck. Two, I needed my head checked if I was checking out a strange man while I sat in a strange bed in a strange room. *Okay, Eden, get your ass on track. Quit staring at the DSLs.* He looked familiar, but I was having a hard time placing him. He wasn't a recent john, that was for sure. I'd have remembered something this yummy.

"Come on, Paradise, it hasn't been *that* long. Although a decade sure does change a person." He pointedly looked me up and down, cocking a brow when he made it back up to my face.

"Marco?" I whispered in incredulity. I *had* to still be high and hallucinating.

"In the flesh, Lady Garden." The moniker threw me. It was a blast from the past and way too surreal to be believed.

"Fuck, I *am* seeing shit. I gotta get out of here." *What the fuck was in that blow?* The phantom Marco reached out to flick my nose, forcing the reality of my situation on my scrambled brain.

"No, Eden, you don't. Just chill the fuck out and listen for a goddamned minute." His switch from teasing to harsh was a familiar whiplash of emotion. "Tony and Vanni walked in on you coked up to the gills with the Finelli boys balls deep in both ends." He paused for a beat before adding, "But what a way to go, amirite?" His cheeky grin faded almost instantly, as if he'd just been waiting to deliver that line, and even bawling me out couldn't deter him. "Really though, what were you doing turning tricks in a backroom orgy with enough dope in you to blitz the entire chorus line of *West Side Story?*"

Tony? Vanni? Oh fuck, **Santos***?* My eyes darted

around the room, checking the nooks and crannies like my ex-boyfriend would be hiding in one of them.

"I, uh, I gotta go, Marco. Nice seeing you and all, but..." I completely ignored his question as I eyed the tubing in my arm. Surely it couldn't be too hard to get it out. *The movies make it seem easy...* But they also tended to squirt blood when that happened. Better just to unhook the bag from its hanger, take it with me, and figure shit out later. I didn't even want to know how I'd ended up dressed in a man's t-shirt. I just hoped I had some kind of bottoms on. If not, well, it wouldn't be the first time for a breezy walk of shame.

Marco startled when I gathered the gumption to move despite the pain and made a grab for the bag of saline.

"What the hell are you doing? Lay back down and knock that shit off." I'd made it to my knees and found that I did indeed have someone's boxer briefs on, but I only managed to get the bag halfway off of the pole before Marco's sinewy arms came around me to halt my progress. A swift jab of my elbow to his chest had him retreating for a moment, but he snagged my tube-free arm on the way, pulling me back down onto the bed. "Damn, girl, you're feistier than I remember."

"Let me go, Marco. I need to get out of here before—"

"Before what, Eden? Before you have to explain

what you were doing with the competition? Maybe you were hoping to escape and rat us out? Snitches and ditches, remember?"

I turned, wide-eyed, to stare at the man the rapid-fire questions had come from. The movement swung the ends of my dirty, snarled hair into my line of sight, making me internally cringe at how bad I must look. As there was nothing to be done at the moment, I pushed it back out of my face to see who had come in. Antonio stood just inside the door of the opulent but stark bedroom done in monochrome, glaring at me, daring me to refute any of it. He looked different than I remembered. Older, harder... *colder*.

"Nah, Edie wouldn't narc." My eyes darted to the next new voice. Giovanni was propped up on the open doorframe, a slightly less clean-cut, dark-featured bookend to his brother, just as matured, but softer. I would have grinned at the peacekeeper of the bunch if I hadn't been starkly aware of the precariousness of my situation. Down and out in the middle of the Carlotti boys. Well, that, and Tony's continued vitriol.

"You're right... The old Eden wouldn't have, but she's not that girl anymore, just like we're not those boys anymore." No, they definitely were *not* boys anymore. They'd all filled out and grown into the promises their adolescence had made. They were flat-out prime real estate now. Sexy, dark, suave—

assholes, my mind finished when the rest of Antonio's sentence was delivered. "I bet she's worried about Santos showing up and seeing she ditched him to turn out just like her mama. A thieving whore. But she went one better and added junkie to her résumé. *Angel*, my ass."

Bitter shame rolled over me. I was too hurt and pissed to address the thieving accusation. Who knew what my mother had done after she kicked me out. No, I was pissed at the high horse Antonio thought he was looking down on me from.

"Says the crime lord in training," I retaliated. My delivery was a bit off since I desperately needed a drink, but it didn't stop me from continuing. "Pretty sure prostitution and narcotics consumption is a lesser rap than a double homicide." I felt the blood drain from my face at the menacing mask that Antonio's visage morphed into. I was too scared to take my eyes off of him, worried he might strike like a viper if I broke eye contact.

"Alright, time out. You two knock it off. Vanni, go get the doc, will ya?" Marco broke in, again holding his hands up, this time for peace instead of surrender. "Tony, I'm grabbing some water. Don't move. You either, Edie."

Not sure who was more surprised at Marco for bossing his cousins around. Them, because he didn't immediately take Tony's side, or me, because he'd bossed the brothers around and they'd actually listened. Granted, I had been around them a lot less than Santos, but things really seemed to have changed since I last saw them.

"Um, actually," I ventured after Vanni disappeared, "if you could point me to a bathroom, I can get my own water."

"I'd really appreciate it," I tacked on to be polite. No need to aggravate the mobsters more than I already had.

"I'd rather you stay in the bed and wait on the doc before you get up." Marco's tone was polite but firm, while Tony just grunted from his post by the door. My bladder, however, didn't care how polite they were or not; waiting was no longer an option.

"Yeah, that's not gonna work for me. I feel like utter shit, have a bitch of a headache, and topping my night off by pissing myself like an invalid isn't on my to-do list. I charge extra for that sort of thing." Nice hadn't gotten me anywhere, so maybe blunt honesty would do the trick.

"Take her to the toilet, Marco," Tony barked out, disgust curling his lip. "She already puked on my shoes and got who knows what in my car. I'd rather not have my person or belongings subjected to any more of her bodily fluids." *What the fuck? Why is he being so awful? It was just a joke... mostly.*

It wasn't like I'd crashed *his* party and hijacked him off to parts unknown. Embarrassment burned through me, but it just made my resolve not to show it even stronger. Eyes burning, I pointedly ignored him while edging my legs out from the tangle of the sheet. I discovered they were bruised as the soft light from the bedside lamp hit them, prompting a glance at my arms. *Yep, bruises there too.* From the throbbing of other body parts, I assumed I was riddled with them.

Marco reached out to help me up, I think, but I shied away, not wanting him to touch me. There'd been enough manhandling for the night, thank you very much. I pretended not to see his frown at my reaction, holding onto the I.V. pole as I eased to my feet. Taking a few steps, I found my legs were a bit weak and wobbly but functional.

"Um, where to?" I asked, finally making eye contact with a tight-lipped Marco.

"Right over here." He indicated a door on the far wall of the bedroom. "I'll follow, just in case." I didn't argue, remaining silent as I shuffled across the unpleasantly cool, polished floor. I wouldn't be surprised if it were marble or some shit, but it was cold—and my shivering didn't help the fact that my borrowed shorts were trying to fall off.

"I can get it from here, thanks," I told him when we reached the door. A bathroom buddy was *not* necessary.

"If you're sure, I'll be right back with the water." He glanced at Antonio before saying, "If you have an emergency, yell. Tony will help if I'm not back." The man in question didn't agree, but he didn't disagree either.

I nodded before ducking into the bathroom and shutting the door as soon as the I.V. pole was in with me—only to realize it was pitch black, other than a thin glow of light on the floor from the threshold to the bedroom. Blindly running my hand over the wall, bladder screaming all the while, I finally encountered the nearly flat switch. The light came on, revealing the bathroom was as opulent as the bedroom had been, with the color scheme continuing in that space. The decor wasn't my agenda though, and I beelined it for the toilet as quickly as I could with the pole. Plopping down and letting go was instant relief, but as one issue was taken care of, another popped up.

All the movement had my stomach protesting. Not wanting a repeat performance, I silently hoped it was just still sore from throwing up. I didn't remember it but knew I had from the rancid taste in my mouth and Tony's scathing recap. Paired with the extreme dryness, it was on par with what I imagined a dirty litter box would taste like. Quite disgusting and needing immediate attention.

After the awkwardness that was wiping with my non-dominant hand to avoid jostling the tubing in my arm, I went directly to handle it at the sink. The sight that met me in the mirror wasn't quite as bad as I'd anticipated. My hair, while wild and tangled in a snarled black cloud, didn't visibly have anything in it. The bigger surprise was the lack of raccoon circles and streaks of mascara, though I now had my suspicions about what Marco had been doing with the washcloth. I knew for a fact that my makeup had run down my cheeks when I was blowing Arlo. I'd seen it in the mirror.

The reminder sparked the memory of his dick going down my throat when Oscar fell on me. It wasn't only bile that had made my throat burn, and it explained my sore mouth and neck. The thought that I'd had two dead dicks in me while I wore their owners' blood nearly had me gagging. Tony had killed the Finellis, not that I'd known their last name at the time. And Trixie. Tony had killed *Trixie*. Annoying, vacuous Trixie was gone for nothing. He didn't hesitate to put her down, like a varmint that rooted in your trash. He would have put *me* down like that. *He still might.*

The tears threatened hard then, but I pushed them down, just like I always did, and flicked on the water using the *fancy* handles above the *fancy* vanity. *I don't fucking belong here. I never did.*

The bending action made my back twinge, and I lifted the oversized shirt to check the damage in the mirror. My torso, front and back, was mottled with bruises. Not unexpected, but they were going to take a while to heal—I couldn't dance like this.

Stressing about the prospect of no money, I

dropped the shirt, allowing it to settle back around me before I turned my attention to what I *did* have control over. I opened the cabinet in search of toothpaste. Instead, I found mouthwash and made liberal use of it, and a finger, to scrub off what I could of the fuzz. I didn't want to snoop further, so I just used the hand soap to wash my face, patting it dry with the hand towel that likely had a higher thread count than my sheets back home. Murder paid well. *I need a fucking hit. And to get out of here.* Resolved to do just that, I tried to fingercomb my long tresses into some semblance of order, quickly giving up when a pounding came from the other side of the door.

"There's nothing to snort in there but Tylenol, Eden. You can hurry up now." Antonio's snide comment echoed my wish for something to take the edge off.

An argument ensued before a softer tap sounded on the door. "Edie, I have your water and the doc. Can we come in?" I'd already made use of my hands, guzzling water straight from the tap, but he'd at least followed through on his promise. Maybe I could convince him to get me out of here.

"Yeah, sure, come on in." The door opened to admit the water-bearing Marco and the doctor that had been mentioned, the latter carrying a bag of what I presumed was his medical kit.

The man was of average height, fit, and middle-aged with fine lines around his eyes and dark hair just starting to gray at the temples. He smiled kindly at me, and I wasn't sure if I could trust it, but whatever, I'd play along if it got me the hell out of this place sooner.

"Hello, Miss..." He looked at Marco, but I answered first.

"Moretti. Eden Moretti."

"Yes, well, Miss Moretti, I'm Carlos, but most just call me Doc. Would you like me to come in there with you?" I really didn't and said so. I'd had enough of being in rooms with strange men. "That's fine, then. If you'd like to come have a seat on the bed, I'll get you checked out and see about getting that line out of your arm."

I nodded and followed him back out, picking up Marco as the caboose back across the room and studiously ignoring Tony. Taking a seat, I held out my arm. That I.V. needed to go first. The doctor continued laying out his supplies next to me on a blue-backed cotton pad before he addressed me.

"Let's get your vitals and then see if we need to leave it in." The man was perfunctory as he went about his business, completely disregarding me. Obviously, the right to make my own medical decisions had been rescinded when I was brought into wherever I was.

"Let's not and say we did. Get this out of my arm. Regardless of what you find, it's still coming out." Despite my hard and resolute tone, the doctor still looked to Antonio for a decision. I didn't bother waiting to see what he'd say. I grabbed a cotton ball from the kit set out on the bed, pressed it over the entry mark, and had the tape loosened in a few short seconds. The doctor was too late, reaching to stop me as I slid the cannula free with a brief pinching burn, and then it was done. No muss, no blood gush. *Should have done that thirty minutes ago.*

"*Miss* Moretti, that was uncalled for," the doctor reprimanded, glaring at me with narrowed eyes and flared nostrils. Out of the corner of my eye, I noticed Marco was exasperated again, but I wasn't taking my gaze off the one that was irritated with me. That was usually a mistake, and if he was going to retaliate, I wanted to see it coming. He didn't do anything other than bitch at me though, and I was kinda surprised. "The area should have been disinfected before removal, and you don't have gloves on! You could have introduced all manner of things into your system." *Like I didn't just wash my hands.* I rolled my eyes as the man continued. "Just last night, you had two seizures, symptoms of an extreme overdose, and your blood panel shows—" I held my hand up, halting his tirade.

"*Last* night? As in a day ago?" I ignored the seizure part. Wasn't the first time I got a bad batch and had a bad trip. Maybe I was being flippant, but it was what it was. I needed the drugs to function, and risks like that came with the territory. "You've had me an entire day? What time is it?" I glanced toward the window but couldn't see any light coming from behind the curtains.

Giovanni spoke up, drawing my attention to his still boyish features. I swore I saw the barest edge of a dimple. Had I planned on sticking around, I might have tried to get him to smile to see if it popped out. As it was, his words barely registered through my distraction. "It's an interior room in case of a security breach, or ya know, if you need to keep a guest secure; they're just for show. It's been almost twenty-four hours since..." *Yeah, not so quick to volunteer exactly what they'd been up to, huh?*

The doctor continued his exam as if I hadn't spoken, cleaning my arm and putting a piece of tape over a clean cotton ball. Dude was pissed if his quick, methodical movements were any indication, not that I particularly cared. *Knew I shouldn't trust that smile.* But I had bigger issues than the grumpy physician— I'd left work with no notice and without my take. I'd be lucky if I had a job to go back to, and since I worked under the table, I'd play hell getting my money if Danny wanted to be a dick. I held my tongue, silently urging the damn doctor to hurry up so I could get down to getting out of here.

He was taking my blood pressure when an eerily familiar yet wholly matured voice rang out from another part of the house.

"Hey, what's up with a detective coming round,

looking for some hooker from Cherry Baby after a quadruple homicide?" I froze as I waited for the owner of the voice to come closer. *Fuck me sideways, maybe he won't notice.* But the man continued speaking as he moved closer, just outside the bedroom door now. "She's presumed missing and goes by the stage name Angel. You have to tell me if you need me to clean up a mess *before* I hear it from our contact at the precinct. Where the hell is everybody? Is someone hurt? I saw Doc's car out front." *Quadruple? Who the hell else did they kill?*

I was sidetracked from my question as Tony and Vanni hurried out to meet who I was certain was Santos, and my anxiety spiked further. They closed the door behind them, but a minute or two later, a shout came through.

"She was doing *what*? Where is she?" The man's rage was palpable despite the space between us, and the doctor didn't even finish or tell me anything before he was packing up and getting away from me to escape across the room. I didn't blame him. No point in doctoring a soon to be corpse. *Of course, I had to be fucking sober for this shit.*

"You tore him up pretty bad when you took off. You know that, right?" Marco volunteered solemnly. Solemn really didn't suit him, but the accusation in his eyes belied the calmness, and I had an inkling that Santos wasn't the only one unhappy with my disappearance. Or maybe with my reappearance? I didn't know, and the uncomfortable twinge it gave me pissed me off. Besides, Santos had been in the wrong, not me.

"Yeah, well, I'm sure he found a piece of ass to replace me soon enough." Marco had started to shake his head, mouth opening to respond, but he paused when the door popped open, bouncing off the wall to rebound into one heavily tattooed hand.

Santos stood in the doorway, scanning me from head to toe, while I did the same. I squashed down a twinge of concern as my gaze tracked over the scars that marred his once-perfect complexion. I didn't get a chance to catalog them all before Santos shook his head and slammed the door behind him on the way back out. His behavior, as if *I* were the one in the wrong, pissed me off. Didn't even say a fucking word. *Asshole.*

"Well, that went better than I thought it would." I could only stare incredulously at a grinning Marco, pretty sure the man needed his head checked. The doc was doing the same, so apparently we could agree on something at least.

five
miss you
Santos

I could handle a lot of things. I had just tortured the third Finelli for two hours about some guns they were running through our turf while Tony and Vanni took care of the other two. And that was a hell of a lot easier than walking in to see the girl who'd ripped my fucking heart out all those years ago casually sitting on the bed in Tony's spare room.

What the fuck was he thinking?

Now the unanswered calls suddenly made sense. After gathering what intel I could before putting that Finelli degenerate out of his misery, I tried finding out how the Cherry Baby thing went. The club sat in the buffer zone between the Carlottis and the Finellis, and I wasn't sure how well it would play out when Vanni messaged they'd tracked the other two there. No one answered, so I assumed they were still working, maybe waiting for them to leave the area, but after hours of nothing, I called them one by one, getting nothing but voicemails. I'd rushed to the manor, knowing this silence wasn't like them, after cruising by the club and finding police tape over the doors.

I had barely made it to the gate outside the compound when I was hit with flashing lights. What the fuck? Vincenzo Carlotti paid off a number of the force to stay out of our business, yet this guy was flashing his fucking bubblegum lights at me. He should know better, especially in an unmarked car.

I considered stepping out onto the pavement, but I didn't feel like getting shot today. If I was being stopped, then obviously someone didn't know who I was. Instead, I rolled my window down to yell at the approaching figure, "The fuck do you want? I wasn't speeding."

The man continued up into my line of sight before he stopped and grinned at me, his hand entirely too close to his holstered service weapon. Ballsy.

"If it isn't Santos De Luca... You happen to know anything about the quad murder over at Cherry Baby? Some Finelli boys and a couple club workers were found murdered last night. We also have a missing dancer. Goes by Angel."

Pissed that he knew who I was and stopped me anyway, I shoved my door open to get out and stand next to my vehicle, arms crossed over my chest. The man didn't balk like I'd expected, but he did take a few steps back until he was out of my immediate range. It didn't surprise me this guy recognized me. I'd made it a point to be known so they wouldn't fuck with me. Either this guy was new to the force, or he wasn't under Vinnie's thumb. Neither boded well, so I went with tried and true denial. Mostly accurate in this particular moment anyway.

"Don't know shit. Now, who the fuck are you?"

The middle-aged man tucked his hands into the tan trench coat he wore, his smile growing wider. "Detective Fields. Just transferred over from Chicago, and despite what you think you believe, I don't answer to you or your boss." He glanced pointedly behind me at the guards standing just inside the gate and pulled a card from his pocket, holding it out for me to take. "If you decide you suddenly know something, I suggest you give me a call. I'm not going anywhere anytime soon and will keep an eye out for any other late-night drives in the vicinity of crime scenes."

When I didn't accept the offered card, he flicked it at me and turned back to his car without a backward glance as the little rectangle fluttered to the pavement at my feet. That man is going to be a problem. I'd let Tony know and see what he thought we should tell Vinnie before we dealt with it.

After making sure the detective had disappeared down the road, I climbed back into my car and through the gates onto the property, the guards confirming that the brothers had come back. Anger and impatience rippled through me as I contemplated what the man had said. What the fuck had happened? There was only supposed to be two bodies, not four. And who fucking cared about some missing stripper? What did she have to do with all this?

My mind raced, trying to put the pieces together but coming up with holes instead, and the doc's car had fear coursing through me. When I entered the house and shouted about the detective, I'd expected the others to be in the den, but it was empty, and I was kicking myself for not coming to check sooner. If any of those Finelli fucks had hurt either of them, Vinnie better be prepared for a war. But my concern was short-lived as Vanni came out from the hall with Tony following close on his heels only a moment later. From their expressions it was obvious something had happened, but I didn't see any apparent injuries on the pair.

"I'm going to need you to keep your shit together for what I'm about to show you," he told me before I could speak.

My brow lifted with curiosity and concern now that I knew it wasn't either of them. "What'd you do? Is it Marco?"

"No, we found Eden tonight. She was fucking the Finellis when we went into the club."

"She was doing *what*? Where is she?" I didn't fucking believe him. We'd looked for Eden for *years* before we gave up, and now she randomly turned up in a strip club?

Tony didn't answer, instead he crooked a finger for me to follow him. Steeling myself for what I might find, I stepped into the guest room only to receive the shock of my life. I was glad I'd already schooled my features as it allowed me to outwardly give a cursory perusal of the bedraggled woman on the bed while inside I was cracking apart. Stiffly, I turned and left, slamming the door behind me to stalk back toward the front of the house, Tony following behind. As soon as I was out the front door, I turned and punched my fist into his fucking face, full force. The icy rush that overtook me when recognition hit had given way to white-hot fury.

Tony stumbled back but managed to keep on his feet. We sparred quite often, and it took more than that to knock him on his ass, but I was tempted to give it another go.

The warning glare he sent me as he swiped at his bloody lip with the back of his hand usually would have made me back down, but I was raring to hit him again. Tony was my boss, my future leader, and my best friend. I respected him and did anything he asked of me, but not this time. This time, he'd crossed the line.

"What the fuck were you thinking?" I roared at

him. "Why the fuck is she here, and who do you think you are, bringing her here at all?"

Tony barely blinked an eye at my outburst, but I knew he was seconds from retaliating if I didn't lay off. And after he got a gander at the already rising bruise on his cheek, he still might.

"You get one punch, Santos. One. If you don't listen to what I have to say, I will fucking put you in your place." Tony rarely pulled rank, but when he did, he was more like his father than I thought he realized. Both Carlotti men could turn cold and dangerous without issue.

I ground my teeth, hard. Granted, he deserved more than one punch, but I needed answers, so I nodded but kept my hands fisted at my side. Boss be damned. He couldn't drop this shit on me then hide behind the station being the eldest child gave him. He was my friend long before he ruled over me, and I would risk my life in this Family to hit him again if I didn't like what he had to say.

Tony sighed and raked a hand through his styled hair, messing it up as the hardassed demeanor fell off. "Shit went wrong last night. The Finellis were in a room with two girls. One we got rid of since she witnessed everything and was screeching like a fucking owl. When I dragged the second girl out from under a table to get rid of her too, Vanni stopped me after noticing her wrist. She had Eden's birthmark." He paused to make eye contact, his gaze warning me it wasn't good, though I wasn't sure what was worse than her fucking two men and my best friend almost killing her.

"She was drugged out of her mind and started to OD. I tried, man. I tried to convince myself to just shoot her and pretend I saw nothing. I should have made Vanni leave her convulsing on the floor, but the fact of the matter is, I couldn't shoot her. Not without making sure if she was Eden. We brought her here and let Doc fix her up. Honestly, I'm surprised you believed it with just a glance because it took a bit on my part. So now we have to figure out what to do with her. I can't kill her, Santos, but she saw everything. For now, she'll have to be locked in that room at all times unless someone is here to watch her. Just until we can figure shit out." And there it was.

It was a long-winded response, but it answered all the questions that had filtered through my mind. Except one. How the fuck had Eden ended up at Cherry Baby? Not to mention fucking our rivals. No matter how I wanted to feel or not feel on the subject of Eden fucking Moretti, that was a stickler and something I didn't care to think about despite it being burned into my mind.

I narrowed one last accusatory glance at Tony for hiding this from me then turned on my heel and jumped back in my car. I needed to get the fuck out of there. I needed to drink something, fight someone, and fuck. Anything to get the image of the girl who haunted my thoughts out of my brain. At the moment, her gaunt and pale face was etched into me like a bad tattoo. There was no mistaking it was her, but a few more years of whatever she was doing, and she'd be well on her way to unrecognizable. As it stood...

It had been almost a decade, and even though I barely had the balls for more than a brief look at her, I saw what time had done. She looked bad. The telltale signs of drug use had been apparent even without Tony saying anything, and it had dulled the glow that used to radiate from her. Yet somehow, she was still as fucking beautiful as I remembered.

And that just pissed me off more.

I started the engine, but Tony stepped up to my window and knocked before I could pull away. I growled but rolled it down anyway, not wanting to be rude to my best friend. He wasn't really the one I was mad at. He leaned down and rested his hands on the open windowsill. "I just want you to know that you come first. If you want her gone, I'll make it happen, and you don't need to have any part in it. You're my brother, and I know you're pissed off, but try not to do anything stupid, huh?"

I scoffed, not giving any further reply while burying the inkling of unease at his offer to dispose of the girl I'd loved. At my refusal to promise good behavior, Tony straightened and backed away with a sigh, allowing me to rev my engine and bolt out of there.

Without needing to think about it, I headed downtown to the dead zone, ironically the same area Eden had been hiding in. It was outside both Finelli and Carlotti territory and had the shittiest bars, so I could easily find someone to fuck up there without backlash from either side.

The drive was quick, and the partying crowd was out in full force when I reached my destination. Hell's Den was just the place to let off some steam. Filled with the filth of NYC, from thieves, to prostitutes, and other criminals of all shapes, sizes, and manners of debauchery, it was the one shithole in this city where nobody would think twice about finding me.

With my scarred-up face and tattered jeans, I was barely a blip on others' radar as I sat at the bar crawling with unsavory clientele looking to fuck, get fucked up, or both. The bartender eyed me dubiously before taking my order for a bottle of Jack. My goal was to finish it off before the end of the night, and I planned to see it done.

I'd made it halfway through the damn thing in peace before a pretty little thing came sauntering to my side. Her firm body was wrapped in the skimpiest of black dresses that dipped low between her breasts, and her dark eyes glimmered with lust as she eyed me up and down like a snack.

"You look lonely this evening," the red head purred in my ear. "Buy a girl a drink?"

I smiled wickedly at her for her blatant play, figuring it was fifty-fifty odds whether I was going to get laid or fleeced. I wasn't too concerned about the second option; my pockets were empty of anything but enough cash to get thoroughly fucked up. "My pleasure." I motioned for the bartender to make another of whatever froufrou concoction was nestled between her slender fingers.

She sat on the stool next to mine, crossing her long legs as she angled toward me to rub my ankle with her stiletto-encased foot. She was sexy, for sure, and an excellent distraction despite the copious amount of perfume wafting from her. For my purposes, she'd do just fine.

"What's your name, handsome?" she asked, not taking her eyes off me as she sipped her pink cocktail.

"Whatever you want it to be," I replied. I never gave my name and never bothered to remember anyone else's when it came to what passed for my one-night stands. This girl was here for a purpose, and that didn't require names. All I was after was a quick bit of relief. I never took them back to my place and rarely went to theirs. No, what I usually got didn't require a bed. I didn't want to know her or learn her secrets. I just wanted to forget about the abrupt reappearance of the dark-haired ghost from my past, and this chick looked just the type to not give a damn about that.

She let out a tinkling laugh. "Well, if I don't know your name, how will I ask you to take me somewhere and fuck me?"

See? Not one fuck given.

"You just did, sweetheart." I stood and held a hand out to her. She grinned like she'd just won the lottery and hastily shoved her hand in mine. Holding just tightly enough to not leave her behind, I had us through the crowd and in the back bathroom faster than I think she expected.

I threw her into one of the stalls and slammed her hard against the wall inside, my leg going between hers and my hands trapping her in on either side.

"I hope you like it rough because I have no intention of going easy."

Her eyes grew wide with excitement when she realized it was going down right here and now, and she nodded emphatically. "Tell me how you want it, darling, anything you want, then maybe we can take it back to your place—"

My mouth sealed to hers, distracting her from that line of thought, and I did my best to ignore the taste of too much sugar and cigarettes that slicked across her tongue as it tangled with mine. She lifted one of her legs and wrapped it around my waist, dragging me harder against her as she ground into me. Her arms came down, one hooking around my neck and the other diving into the back of my hair. I didn't like the attempt at dominance, and immediately knocked her leg away with mine.

She pulled back, surprise on her face before the sultriness took over again. "Oh, so you want to be in charge? What do you want, sexy?" I wasn't bad to look at if you ignored the pale lines marring my face, but this chick must have had a hard-on for scars because she hadn't flinched once, not like the bartender had.

I chuckled darkly. "Get on your knees." This part was always easy; I didn't touch them, and they didn't touch me. Not more than necessary anyway.

Without hesitation, she dropped and began unbuttoning my jeans. I groaned when her hand wrapped around me, her mouth following soon after. But as I went to glance down at the bobbing redheaded woman sucking me off, something caught my eye. Something I'd done my damndest to keep covered and out of sight for the better part of the last decade.

A peony tattoo peeked out from beneath the watch on my wrist. It had been a mistake I'd had to live with for years, having gotten it done after the one night I'd spent with Eden. A night of pure fucking bliss that set the standard too high for all the women I met after. Ones they couldn't live up to. Being with her that first time had set in stone the love I knew I'd never feel for another. I had gotten the tattoo done the next day, hoping to surprise her later that evening. I wanted her to see that she was mine, and I was irrevocably hers.

But she never saw it. That was the night I'd learned of her betrayal and subsequent departure from my life forever.

Seeing it now, after all this time of being able to ignore it, I was left empty and angry. This girl kneeling before me was nothing and would always be nothing so long as Eden existed. I couldn't do this. I was fucking ruined.

I abruptly shoved myself away from the woman, making her fall forward in surprise before she face-planted onto the disgusting bathroom floor.

"What the fuck?" she shouted at me, but I was already fastening my pants and stomping out of the bathroom.

I couldn't fuck anyone tonight. I never could. If I couldn't get sucked or fucked, I sure as hell was going to get some stress relief another way. I *needed* to feel something besides this oblivion of hatred and nothing else. I hated her for what she'd done, and now I hated her more for what she was doing to me once again. And someone was about to be caught in the storm of hellfire coursing through me.

I spotted the biggest bastard in the bar and rushed at him, slamming into his back. Poor fucker was caught off guard and pitched forward into a nearby table, smashing everything on it and cracking the cheap thing in half.

"You're gonna fucking pay for that, shithead," the burly guy growled as he rolled and straightened up, spotting who'd initiated the attack.

He came at me hard, swinging his fists with brute force though not enough speed behind them to catch me. I ducked each one, landing my own punches in his gut and face. I was about to give him another when a blow to my head from behind rattled me. Just like that, an all-out brawl broke out. Four were on me while others around the bar fought each other.

I'd severely underestimated my level of drunkenness since my usually efficient punches began to get slower and more fumbled. I'd just chucked a glass in the face of one of my attackers when I was tackled from behind and slammed into the ground. My head was lifted and smashed straight down into the unforgiving, sticky floor.

Then it was lights out.

six
prisoner
Eden

It had been two days since Santos stormed out and I'd been informed I was a 'guest' for the foreseeable future. Being locked in a bedroom in the heart of the Carlotti compound was nerve-wracking enough. Throw in the lack of drugs, and things were dire indeed. When I wasn't too tired to move, my time was divided between miserable cravings, raging at the situation, and dwelling on how Santos had got so torn up.

The scars on his face weren't red, so they had to be older, and a couple were vicious-looking, hinting at more than a close brush with death. The marks didn't detract from his attractiveness; instead, they added a rough and tumble, bad-boy element to it. It pissed me off that he was still hot as fuck with a curving line around one cheek near his ear and one through a brow that just made him appear rakish. I'd gotten the impression of other small marks decorating his skin, but I hadn't had a chance to get a good look in the brief time he'd stood there. That evidence of his violent life wasn't the only new addition. Tattoos had peeked out from around the collar of his shirt and run down his hands. I was curious about those as well, but I couldn't stop my yawn as I imagined what he could have hiding under his clothes.

It was irritating as fuck that I couldn't seem to stay awake. The lethargy was bad, making me want to sleep, but then again, when I was awake, I didn't care about jack shit unless it was food or yelling to be let out. Grumpy about it, but unable to fight it, I drifted off with the image of the adult version of the boy I'd known dancing in my head.

I'd thought I'd gotten through the worst of my withdrawals. Fuck. I was so wrong. I couldn't seem to pull myself out of the funk I was in, my forced confinement not helping matters. Upon waking, my mood was plain unhinged fury. The anger lent me the energy to utterly destroy the bedroom, but by the time Marco came in to check on me, I'd petered out and was bawling on the glass-strewn floor next to the mattress I'd managed to flip off the bed frame.

"Shit, are you hurt?" He was at my side in an instant, crouching down to brush my ratty hair away, looking for injuries. I shook my head and shied away from him, slapping his hand when he tried to persist.

"What the fuck happened, Edie? Who did this?" he asked, immediately standing and crossing the room to check the bathroom before coming back out to peek in the empty closet. Settling on the edge of the boxspring after surveying the mess, he rested his elbows on his knees before demanding an answer. "Was someone in here, or did you do this?"

With a watery laugh full of hysterical disdain, I lifted my head to glare at him. "So what if I did? I'm sick of being locked in like a criminal."

"Girl, Tony is going to flip his shit when he sees the mess you made in his house." He ran a hand through his spiked hair, muttering about how he was supposed to fix the room. It pissed me off, and the last of my tears dried up.

"*Fix* it? Tony can pull his dick out of the mega-douche, bring his mobster-in-waiting ass in here, and explain why I'm being held against my will, or let me the fuck out!" Marco appeared impressed and shocked in turn at my tirade, eyes wide and hands held out as if to ward off the slap he expected to be delivered any second.

"Do you have *no* sense of self-preservation? You

know Tony is still considering just getting rid of you altogether, right? The only reason he hasn't is the fact that the 'mega-douche' might have a problem with it, and you're *you*. Keep it up, and even me and Vanni might not be able to stop him."

"Maybe that would be best then. Save me the trouble. Although there's plenty here to take care of it for him." I reached out to snag a piece of glass off of the floor. Shards littered the room from the framed prints I'd ripped off the wall and broken, giving me plenty to choose from.

"Don't you dare," Marco snapped at me, slapping my hand to make me drop it before grabbing my wrist to check for cuts. I started to struggle, pissed at being manhandled, but he ignored me, picking me up and settling me onto his lap. I wasn't sure which of us was more surprised at the action, but it did quell my more violent impulses and changed my thought process to something a bit more personal. I smelled, and I knew it. *Should have showered.* Fuck, that was embarrassing. I might be a whore, but I wasn't a *dirty* one.

"Okay, just put me down. Unless you're trying to get a piece, then we're going to have a problem."

Marco grinned unrepentantly. "Yeah, a Santos-sized problem. But if I really thought it was an option, I might brave the mega-douche for you."

My mouth fell open before snapping shut again. Hadn't brushed my teeth, not that I had a toothbrush, but there *was* mouthwash. I covered my mouth with my hand before replying, "Nope, I'm good. I could maybe take you up on the offer if you brought me some blow... I know you can get some." *And now I* am *a dirty whore.*

Marco looked down at me, hazel eyes full of pity as he shook his head. "I'm sorry, Edie, but I can't."

Anger managed to push through the pain long enough for me to lash out. "Then let me the fuck out of here, so I can get my own," I snarled at him, throwing his arm away from me to get off his lap. He just hauled me back before my feet could touch the floor.

"That's not happening either. Give me something reasonable I can do, because you're not leaving, and you're not getting drugs." His features were set in stern lines that told me he wasn't going to budge.

The anger plummeted into an irrational sense of betrayal then on to bleak depression. "Just get out. If you won't give me what I need, then leave. Fucking kidnapping piece of shit! May as well call Tony in here to finish this bullshit right now."

"Eden, what the fuck? Knock it off. Getting off whatever you've been taking is a good thing. You'll agree when you're feeling better." He slid me off his lap onto the boxspring beside him when I crossed my arms and stared at the wall. After he stood up, he pulled my feet up to check the bottoms. "I don't know how you managed to avoid getting cut, but sit still until I can get someone in here to clean up. Seriously," he added with the point of a finger, "don't move." He backed out of the bedroom, completely ignoring my accusation about kidnapping, and left me to stew in silence.

I curled up on my side, tired after my hissy fit. Sleep was quick to come, and the thought that he'd vaguely smelled of cigarettes fleetingly crossed my mind. *The bastard is holding out on me. I'm going to hit him the next time he shows up.*

"Rise and shine, Lady Garden! You've got company coming. Might want to take a bath while they do their thing... You're looking a bit grungy, and that hair is bordering on the side of something the cat threw up."

I slit one eye to glare at the motherfucker. "Eat shit, you little Godfather wannabe. No wonder you aren't married if that's how you talk to women." I rolled over, putting my back to his rude ass. I knew I needed to bathe, but that didn't mean it was nice to point it out.

"Who said I wasn't married? Assume much?" *That* piqued my interest. I turned enough to pointedly glance at his left hand and its empty ring finger. "That doesn't mean shit, and you know it. But since you're so keen on my marital status, no, I'm not married." He gave it two seconds before adding with a leer, "Been holding out for the day you came back." The not so smooth line only got him a groan of annoyance and my head going back down into its sleeping position.

"Unless you brought a toothbrush and clean clothes, I'm not getting up. There's no point in showering only to put this dirty shit back on." I plucked at the side of the oversized black t-shirt without lifting my head or opening my eyes.

"I'll have you know that 'shit' is mine, and I was nice enough to loan it to you. Could have let you go naked. It would improve my day, for sure." A moment later, there was a soft knock at the door and the rustling of something before Marco asked the person on the other side for another minute. As soon as the door closed, I heard his footsteps crunch toward me, then a slap hit my ass. I'd shot up, ready to kick him, when a pile of black fabric hit me in the face.

"More clothes from moi, because you look sexy in them when you're clean, and... tada! Toothbrush *and* bubble bath. Now, who's your favorite?" The fucker wouldn't quit flirting, which was making me both uncomfortable and a smidge flattered. I was also kinda impressed he'd noticed the lack of oral hygiene tools, but maybe my halitosis had clued him in. Then I remembered...

"I'll go take a bath, but if you don't hand over the tobacco and a lighter, I'm going to get real unagreeable again. And don't even try to deny it. I can smell it on you." My arms crossed as my face settled into a mutinous glare.

"Tony doesn't allow smoking in the house," he evaded.

"Then let me outside and I'll have one there."

"Sorry, no can do." He moved as if to help me up, getting kicked as soon as he was in range. "What the hell, Edie? I've got people out in the hall, just waiting to clean up your mess. Get in the fucking bathroom before I put you there myself." With a huff, I got to my feet on the boxspring and leapt over the broken glass to the area of carpet that was mostly clear of debris, ignoring his extended hand. My muscles twinged with the effort, but it felt nice to stretch them. I was used to dancing most days, and being cooped up was making me nuts. I hoped it was a sign the bouts of lethargy from detoxing were on their way out.

Marco followed me into the bathroom, setting the plastic sack from the store on the vanity before he flipped the fan on and fished around in the pocket of his jeans. He gave me a stern glance as he pulled out a pack of cigarettes and a lighter, grabbing one from the carton and laying it and the lighter next to the bag. "Don't burn anything down or make me regret ignoring Tony's edict about smoking. Ya got me?"

I nodded in agreement before focusing on him for a moment, confused as to why he was so eager to help me. Sure, he'd been nice and accommodating when I'd first come in, but I attributed that more to curiosity than anything else. Marco had always been fiercely loyal to the brothers and Santos, so I'd assumed he would side with them. Well, I guess he had for the most part since he wasn't letting me out of here. Maybe he was playing me?

He had also been quite mercurial from what I remembered. He was the wildcard of the four when we were younger, usually the jokester or the one who would commiserate with the others over just about anything. But he was also a bit crazy underneath the happy exterior. Santos had recounted more than one story of the shit Marco had gotten up to in school. He could also hold a grudge to the end of time. *Seems he has that in common with the others.*

If any of them were going to show up and offer assistance, I figured it would have been Vanni. He'd never hated anyone, at least as far as I knew, so I thought he would've been the safer option... for me, at least. "Why?" I finally questioned when I couldn't puzzle it out.

Marco laughed. "I can at least give you a cigarette. It's definitely the lesser of two evils."

"No. Why help me?"

His lips softened into a smile, dimples peeking out to give him an irresistible mix of bad boy meets boy next door allure. I was sure more than a few pairs of panties had dropped when it was aimed their way. "Because despite the welcome Tony and Santos have given you, I'm happy you're here, Edie. That you're safe and away from the life you were living. So I'm going to help you through this because you were my friend once upon a time. If that's okay?"

As he left the room to let the staff in to fix my mess, I could only stare after him, incredulous that he'd just decided we were okay and that was it. I wondered if he even knew what Santos and his dad had caused. It was absolute bullshit if they all thought I'd been the one in the wrong and were pissed with me over it. They could just go fuck themselves if that was the case. And while Marco might be cool...

Santos definitely fucking hates me.

And there was the pain that the drugs usually dulled along with other haunting memories. I didn't even know why I still cared about what he thought. Damn me for thinking about him at all. I needed to get back to my own life and put this whole mess behind me. Maybe skip town and start over. If I had to accept this forced detox for the time being, maybe I could stay off the shit long enough to relocate and start my life over even though all I wanted was the tiniest amount to take the edge off. *Hope for another day, I suppose.*

Turning away from where Marco had gone, I

caught my appearance in the mirror and realized how truly awful I looked. It was probably worse than when I was actually on the drugs. I glanced away and stepped to the stall, starting the water and setting the garden tub to fill before putting the contraband on a hand towel on the wide ledge. After quickly washing my hair and scrubbing my teeth, I dried off just enough not to drip all over the floor before getting into the bath full of bubbles to relax.

I sank back and lit up, enjoying the bit of light-headedness that came from not smoking in a while. It wasn't the same as coke, giving only a short buzz. My smoke didn't last long; soon enough, I doused the cherry in the bath water before leaving the butt on the ledge to flush later. Idly rubbing the fragrant suds over my arms, I found myself staring at my birthmark. It amazed me that after all this time that had been the one factor that saved my life. If they hadn't seen it, Tony would've put me down like Trixie without blinking an eye about it. I felt a little bad that Trixie had been killed just for being in the wrong place. She was a shitty person but hadn't deserved that.

This whole situation was fucked. What were they planning to do with me? If Marco was helping me, maybe they didn't intend to kill me. Vanni would surely make a case against it, I hoped. As it stood, I didn't trust Tony not to bust into the room one night on a whim as he'd been quite vocal about his opinion of me. Santos was absolutely my biggest concern though because I didn't fully understand his attitude. Yes, I'd left, but *he* was the fucking reason. All of it had been his fault, and I split before I became just another victim to their way of life.

Stop thinking about Santos. It's done. It's over. Let's work on getting better and getting the fuck out of here.

After soaking until my fingers and toes pruned and the bubbles were little more than tiny islands of suds floating in the surface of the water, I scrubbed my hair one more time, doing a better job than the first. While the water drained, I turned the spigot on and stuck my head under it to rinse out the conditioner. I left it on while I dried off before rinsing the tub of any stray bath product or ashes on the edge of the porcelain. A quick flush eliminated all the evidence of my sneaked cigarette other than the faint lingering smoke scent. I felt squeaky clean and a *lot* better than before.

Marco hadn't only procured a toothbrush, toothpaste, and bubble bath. The bag also had a brush, a card of hair ties, a jar of moisturizer, and a new tube of deodorant, which was much better than the tiny hotel branded one I'd found with those little wrapped soaps under the sink. I figured it was from someone who had stayed here at some point, but at least I hadn't pitted out. I was grateful and knew I should at least say thanks for the supplies. Thankfully, the bathroom had already been stocked with cotton swabs and over the counter pain reliever, so I had most of the necessities now. It was a relief to be able to properly take care of basic hygienic needs. Surveying my less ragged appearance in the mirror, I decided to leave my hair down after brushing it, wanting to braid my long, wavy tresses once they dried a bit. It was much easier to deal with when it was out of the way

I stepped out of the bathroom to find a pristine bedroom. I'd heard the rustling around and low voices while in the bathroom, but they'd been muffled enough, besides the vacuum, that I didn't realize how much the staff had actually done. The bed was made, and even the pictures were fixed. Or maybe they'd gotten new ones that looked the same. *Something new to look at would have been nice, but at least the bedspread is a different pattern.* I immediately felt bad for my uncharitable thoughts; their replacement would hopefully deter Tony from noticing I'd wrecked his room and dealing out retribution.

A knock at the door drew my attention from the decor, and I watched as Marco came in with a tray-bearing Vanni behind him. Vanni didn't say anything other than hello as he set the tray of food on the bedside table and perused the room. *So he's in on it too.* He wrinkled his nose at the bathroom, and I wasn't sure if it was the flowery bubble bath or hint of cigarette smoke he detected and disliked. The pointed glance at Marco, who only shrugged unrepentantly, made me think it was the latter. Vanni just shook his head and left, closing the door behind him.

"Well, that was weird. Did he forget how to talk?" And there went my plan to say thank you first. "Umm... thanks for the brush and stuff. That was nice of you." I held up the item with a tie wrapped around the handle.

"You're welcome, Edie. Vanni is annoyed that I asked him to keep your *redecorating* to himself for now. He reluctantly agreed, but he refused to lie if Tony found out elsewhere and asked him about it."

That made sense, and I said as much as I sat down to inspect the tray of food. I probably should have said thanks to him too, but he'd been a bit standoffish, and it felt awkward since he'd always been nice when we were younger. Just another thing to add to the De Lucas' list of transgressions. The ice cream snagged my attention, and I ignored the grilled cheese and tomato soup to snatch the bowl up, Marco laughing as I popped the second bite in before swallowing the first.

"Iss udder acan," I tried to explain without getting the cold on my teeth. That shit hurt.

"Geez, woman, swallow first. That's giving me *very* naughty ideas." I nearly choked at his blatant innuendo, not because I wasn't used to hearing them, or even specifically hearing them from Marco, but from the image it inspired if it were him in my mouth. *You like it, you dirty bitch. Just admit it. You've always been attracted to him.* Externally, I rolled my eyes and finished the bowl while Marco typed on his phone. When I was done, he tucked the device away and cleared the worried frown from his face.

"So what's on TV today? Anything good?" And there went my good mood.

"Really, jackass? I haven't gotten to watch anything except the fucking walls. Although... they did do some interesting shit that first day, unless that was a dream. Didn't realize detoxing came with hallucinations."

"You're seeing shit? You're okay now, right? How come you didn't say anything? Damn it, Eden, you could have hurt yourself!" Marco went from surprised concern to worried anger in barely a breath. *And I'm the only one having mood swings?*

"I'm fine, as you can see. And what's this about a TV? Would have been nice, you know?"

"Promise you'll tell me if they come back," he demanded instead of answering. After I nodded, he went over to the wall with the curtain-covered faux window and pressed a spot on the wall next to it.

The fucking thing clicked open to reveal a cubby with a remote and a control panel. He took the remote and pushed a button, waiting expectantly. The curtains pulled back automatically, a portion of them receding into the ceiling to reveal a goddamned television.

"Oh, you've *got* to be kidding me! No one said jack shit about that." And now I was the one pissed off.

"Sorry, didn't think about it. We're all used to the setup of the house." *Isn't it nice to be so well off that you don't think of the 'little things' like electronics in hidey-holes for aesthetics.* I was just too damned poor and unsophisticated to consider such things. Hell, my car was a rusted out, busted up, piece of shit. The heat only worked on defrost, and the A/C meant rolling the windows down. The damned thing wasn't even registered to me; I bought it off one of the roommates for five hundred bucks. My expression must have reflected some of my thoughts because Marco began apologizing again.

"I'm sorry, Edie, just didn't think about it. But I have time if you want to watch a movie or something?"

He was hopeful enough that I felt bad saying no. Besides... I was bored stiff in here alone. "Sure, why not?" He jumped on the bed and settled against the headboard before I could suggest he sit in the chair.

A bit more sedate and slightly uncomfortable, I

settled on the opposite side, close to the edge, to watch the zombie show he'd chosen. Until the bad boy rule breaker pulled out a little silver contraption. "Is that a solo pipe? I thought we couldn't smoke in here." I eyed the all-in-one pipe, able to smell the pot from where I sat, and scooted closer to him in anticipation of lighting up.

"He said no cigarettes. This isn't tobacco, so it doesn't count." He gave me a wink as he held it up to his lips and clicked the button.

By the time we finished, the high was taking the edge off and I was too tired to braid my mess of hair, giving up after two failed attempts.

"Here, let me help."

I eyed Marco with skeptical surprise, unsure if I was comfortable enough for him to do something so familiar or not. *I guess I could always change my mind if it's awkward.* "You remember how?"

"Yep, and I'm practicing up for when Santos pulls his head out of his ass and takes me up on the bet that I can still do it. Although he hasn't taken one since the piercings..." He trailed off after that, scooting me forward so he could get behind me and start sectioning my hair. I couldn't say I wasn't curious about what exactly Santos had gotten pierced, but in an effort to stop thinking about him, I concentrated on the television while Marco took care of my hair.

That day and several more were spent watching movies, smoking pot, and having the sneaky occasional cigarette in the bathroom with Marco. He teased and cajoled and kept me occupied as much as possible. Vanni would stop by once or twice a day to bring food, and though he would eye the two of us as if he knew we were up to shit, he never said anything about it. His visits were actually fairly brief, and he only said hi and bye to me. If anything at all, I guessed he was busy or just didn't want to be around me. When I asked about it, or anything else, Marco refused to answer my questions, evading them or stating Tony would be the one to decide what happened next.

One afternoon, I caught him checking his phone for what seemed like the millionth time, and he must have gotten tired of me bugging him because he finally spilled that Santos had been MIA since he took off the night I arrived. Marco rapidly paced in front of me, practically wearing a hole in the floor, as he tapped on his screen every few seconds to see if he'd missed a notification. Despite enjoying Marco's company, I'd considered taking it more than once, and besides the guilt that told me it was a shitty way to repay his kindness, I didn't know who I would call. Then there was the problem of the passcode and me not really even knowing my actual location. I'd have to bide my time, for now I was stuck in here with the door locked from the other side unless I was supervised, so it wasn't like I had the power to easily change my situation. At the moment, I just wanted to take it to make Marco quit. His pacing had just about gotten on my last nerve.

"Do you really have to do that in here?" I asked, officially fed up when he kept on.

"You keep me calm. So yes."

I raised my brows in surprise. "You call this calm? You're causing so much friction that I swear I'm starting to see smoke billowing up from your feet."

He suddenly stopped and turned his attention to me. "Oh. Sorry. I just can't help worrying about what shit he's gotten into. I mean, it's not unheard of for Santos to go on a bender and disappear for a few days when he's pissed, but..."

Why does that not surprise me? "Okay, so if it's normal for him, why the sudden worry?" I asked, more to be polite than from caring where the mega-douche was.

Marco sighed, absently sliding a hand through his dark hair. "This isn't from just the usual things that piss him off. It's *you*. The girl who fucked him over and destroyed what little happiness he had inside him."

My jaw dropped in outraged shock at his audacity. "Fucking excuse me?" Marco's face twisted in complete horror as he realized what he'd just said to me.

"That's not what I meant."

I jolted up from the bed, and without any hesitation, I shoved him hard in his chest. "*I* fucked *him* over? Are you goddamn kidding me? How dare you! You don't know shit about what went down between us, Marco!" I pushed him again, furious that I'd taken all Marco had done for me as a sign that I could trust him. He was just as bad as the rest of them, and clueless to boot. He simply stood there, my shoves not moving him in the slightest. He stared at me hard, his narrowed hazel eyes burrowing into mine with laser focus. I couldn't tell if he was considering retaliation or pondering my words, but I guessed I would find out soon enough.

I shook my head at him, disgust showing plainly in my face. He didn't try stopping me as I wrenched the door open and rushed from the room. I'd almost made it to the front door, so close to sweet escape, when a large figure suddenly stormed through it. I crashed hard into the imposing chest, not able to stop myself in time.

Arms wrapped around me as I bounced backward, holding me in a vise-like grip.

"Where do you think you're going?" Tony's deep baritone growled in my ears.

I glanced up and sighed, knowing there was no

way I was going anywhere now. Figuring honesty was best, I answered, "Away from your stupid fucking cousin before I murder him with a pillow."

At first, Tony just stared at me blankly, but then a damn *miracle* happened. The barest of smiles crooked up the corner of his mouth. It was just the slightest movement, but it was a massive difference from his perpetual resting bitch face.

"Is that so? Guess I can't blame you for that. One of us regularly wants to kill him at least once a week."

Huh. Not the reaction I thought I'd get. It confused me to no end that Tony had magically found it in him to joke with me. I was pretty positive he hated my guts, so that was some kind of progress.

Tony turned me in his arms and guided me back toward the bedroom, not even taking me to task for my escape attempt. Frankly, it made me nervous. When we got back into the room, Marco was sitting on the bed, guilt written all over his face. He started apologizing as soon as Tony shut the door behind him.

"I'm sorry, Edie. I shouldn't have said what I did. I took my frustration with Santos out on you, and that wasn't right."

Seriously? If I hadn't seen Tony and Vanni outright shoot three people with my own eyes, I'd have a hard time believing these guys were mafia at all. I *did* know better though, and that was the truly scary part. That they could be nice and normal one moment and then off some dudes and any bystanders the next.

Seeing that he meant his apology, I grudgingly relaxed and nodded to him. I was still angry, but I needed to play nice. I had to gain their trust if I was going to get away from here. Then I'd disappear again, but this time, I'd go far enough that they'd never run into me again. Tony must've taken my calm state as a sign I wouldn't try to run again because he released me.

"I have no idea what's going on, but it can wait. Vanni found Santos, and he's in rough shape. One of our guys found him, belligerent and drunk off his ass, at Hell's Den and somehow convinced him to go home. He's there now, and we need to make sure he doesn't do anything stupid. *Again*."

"That's a terrible idea. You know that guy got lucky. If one of us tries to go there and talk to him, one of us is going to get shot. Again."

My wide eyes bounced between them. "Again? He's shot one of you?"

Tony shrugged. "A couple times. I got one in the leg for waking him up during one of his nightmares. Vanni got shot in the side when he got between Santos and a guy he was fighting. Marco got stabbed for trying to drag him out of a club one time when he was plastered. We've learned to be careful in how we approach Santos when he goes off the deep end."

They're crazy. All of them. And Santos is a goddamn psycho for shooting his friends. There was no denying that the sweet yet rough Santos I had once loved was now more dark and twisted than me on my darkest days, and that was saying something. I had managed to not kill, or even maim, a single person yet. I was afraid to ask how many Santos had.

"So... who's going?" Marco asked, standing and folding his arms over his chest. "We can't all go. One might be able to pull it off delicately, but all of us will spook him."

"You're right. When Vanni gets here, we're drawing straws." Tony pulled three blue coffee straws from his pocket before reaching behind his back and pulling a blade out of some hidden sheath beneath his shirt. I wasn't sure what he was going to do with it until he pushed the blade against the bottom of one of the straws and cut a small piece from the end.

"You're shitting me, right? You're drawing straws?" I'd waited days to get ahold of Tony, needing to convince him to let me out of here, and now they were *drawing fucking straws* because of Santos, and I couldn't even bring up leaving.

Marco snorted. "Trust me, this is the best way to do it. Visual proof is the only thing that can't be discredited."

"Let me guess. Rock, paper, scissors got violent?"

Marco threw his head back and laughed, that same small tilt appearing on Tony's lips again.

"Sadly enough, yes," Tony replied. "And we couldn't agree even then because someone always released their hands before we could see who got what, and they'd claim they won. It got messy."

I scoffed, blown away by how little these men had matured. Still a bunch of idiots. Except one of those idiots drank heavily then apparently shot and stabbed people.

"Hello?" Vanni's shout filtered through the door.

"Bedroom!" Marco shouted back, and I scowled at the volume. *Was that really necessary? Asshole could have opened the door.*

A moment later, Vanni came in, casting each of us a curious glance before noticing what was in Tony's hand.

"Shit. Straws again? I suck at this."

"It's fair, and you know it," Tony shot back.

"Whatever. Let's do this. But you're not holding the straws," he told Tony, snatching them from his hand and swiftly shoving them into mine.

"Uh, what?" I asked.

Vanni grinned, flicking his head to the side to get the bit of hair that'd fallen across his eye out of the way. *He used to do that when he was nervous.* It was cute then, and I wasn't fully immune now.

"Yep. Great idea, Vanni," Marco praised. "Tony cheats like a motherfucker."

Tony threw him an accusatory glance. "How? I let you assholes choose first!"

"I don't know, but you never get the short one when you hold the straws, so Edie is holding them."

"Just throwing this out there, but it's dumb as hell, and you're all five years old."

"She's just mad she isn't in the running to go calm the beast," Marco told the other two, acting as if I couldn't hear him.

I rolled my eyes at him. "Yeah, I'll take solitary confinement over that. Thanks," I snarked.

Vanni chuckled, and I took that to mean he wasn't about to throw me at a volatile, trigger happy Santos. *Fucking Marco and his big mouth.* "Solid choice. Now, turn around, make the tops of the straws even, then turn back to us so we can pick."

I did as he asked, ready to just get this over with. The guys quickly drew one each, with Vanni choosing the short one.

"Fuck. You have a bulletproof vest I can borrow?" he asked, eyes pleading with Tony to say yes.

"Okay. I'm done. Out, all of you. Go do your thing. Santos isn't my problem, and unless you're letting me out," I growled, glaring at Tony's shaking head and narrowed eyes, "then I'm taking a nap." Surprisingly, none of them argued over me shoving them out the bedroom door and shutting it behind them.

I heard the click of the lock before Vanni insisted more intensely from the other side, "Tony, I'm serious. Give me one of your vests."

Contrary to how I was behaving toward this situation, I didn't want Vanni to get shot by Santos. I also couldn't wrap my head around why Marco believed *I* was the one who had broken the maniac. He must have told the others what he wanted them to believe when in reality, the story of what had happened between Santos and me was the complete opposite.

Santos De Luca had ripped the heart from my chest and pushed me to become the dark abyss of misery that I was today. My life wouldn't be the cesspool it had become if it hadn't been for what he'd done.

After that day, I was no longer Eden Moretti.

seven
fireworks
Eden

E***ight Years Ago...***
He didn't know it yet, but today was the day. We'd waited long enough and pretty much done everything else. Today I wouldn't chicken out, the guys wouldn't interrupt, and Santos' dad was gone for the weekend, which meant Mom wouldn't be around until late the next day to tidy up before Rodrigo's return. It was just me, Santos, and a box of condoms. I'd gotten on the pill last month, just in case we went all the way, so we were doubly covered.

It took Santos a few moments to answer the door when I rang the bell. He was sleepy-eyed, in sweats and topless, and his dark hair was still deliciously disheveled from his pillow. My nerves reared up, but I squashed them down to give him a hello kiss before closing and locking the door behind me. That earned me a brow raised in question, to which I just smiled and took his hand.

"Your dad's gone, and the guys still have that thing this weekend, right?"

Santos nodded, confusion in his blue eyes. "Yeah, just me. Why? Do you not want to be alone?"

I shook my head. "No, I *definitely* want to be alone. I have plans." He really must have been asleep because he was slow on the uptake. "Bedroom plans," I elaborated with a grin.

It finally dawned on him, and he answered with one of his own before tossing me over a shoulder, my long black hair trailing down nearly to the backs of his knees. "Shoulda said so in the first place, angel." I still got the warm and fuzzies when he called me that. Him and Marco had an ongoing contest to see who could make the most Eden-related puns, but he'd threatened to thump anyone else that tried to use angel. It was for his use only.

"Well, you shouldn't have been so slow," I shot back, pinching him on his tight butt through the thin cotton. He jumped and swatted my backside in retaliation, but I was more interested in the lack of underwear I'd felt. Just to satisfy my curiosity, my hands slipped under the waistband of his pants to encounter smooth skin, stretched taut over flexing muscles. He didn't react other than to let out a husky chuckle and do a total dude flex, but my explorations were short-lived since he dumped me in the middle of his bed.

"Whatcha doing?" I asked as he pulled off one of my tennis shoes, then the other, before starting to work on the button of my jeans.

Arousal was already flaring in his crystalline gaze when he glanced up from his task. "I haven't eaten breakfast yet." He paused a beat to wet his lips, and I swore it was more for effect than any dryness. "Is that not what you were offering?"

My face flushed with heat at his teasing, and I was sure my cheeks had turned a dusky rose. I had anticipated being in charge, but I didn't mind the change in plans a bit. "Feast away, baby," I invited coquettishly, wriggling to help remove my pants. His grin was *definitely* devilish that time.

"Oh, I plan to. How many times did you have to bite the pillow last week?" He was playing dirty, reminding me of the last chance we'd had to fool around, hands and mouths more than enough to satisfy us for hours. My thighs tensed as my core clenched in anticipation, and I felt the beginnings of the telltale dampness between my legs.

Before I could get too sidetracked by my ever-distracting boyfriend, I grabbed my purse, unhooking the strap that was still over my arm and fishing out my surprise. When I tossed it on the bed, it was Santos' turn to flush, but his tenting pants made me suspect it was more from lust than embarrassment.

His pale icy eyes bored into my forest-hued ones with barely leashed excitement. "You sure?" At my nod, he finished stripping me down in a hurry before shucking off his sweats. My gaze ate him up. He was beyond gorgeous to me and likely anyone else with eyes, but if those people wanted to keep their peepers, I'd better be the only one who got to see him in this state. He still had hints of youthfulness that I imagined would disappear in a year or so, but the tone and definition was all there. "Tell me if you change your mind. You know I'm happy to wait as long as you're my girl, right?"

"I know, and I want to." My long, tanned legs bent at the knees, spreading in invitation, to expose the small strip of trimmed hair I'd left when I shaved and the dark pink of my center to Santos' hungry gaze. Propping up on my elbows for a better view, I bit my lip and glanced pointedly at my pussy before looking back up.

It was all he needed to dive right in, instantly wedging his shoulders between my thighs to lick and suck just the way he'd discovered I liked it, his scruff a rough contrast on my smooth skin. A moan trembled in my throat when he added a finger and crooked it inside to ratchet my arousal up before he worked in a second. It only took a few short minutes before my hips were rolling in sync with his movements, my insides clamping down on the digits as my impending orgasm came on hard. Santos took the opportunity to go farther than we had before, forcing in a third as every part of me seemed to twist with pleasure. The pinch of pain at the overwhelming fullness made me peak again before the first even abated.

When the sensations subsided, my legs fell limply to the sides as I collapsed bonelessly back onto the bed. A cloud of black strands fanned out around me, damp from sweat near my scalp, a few fluttering down to stick to my face. I was too languid to bother brushing them away, needing a moment or six to recover. A whimper escaped my lips when Santos stretched his fingers straight, angling them up to massage out the aftershocks of my release, before he leisurely withdrew them from my still clutching flesh.

"Again, Eden," he rasped out, "but you on top." My eyes slit open to watch Santos swipe the back of his hand across his glistening mouth and chin. I'd soaked them and the stubble that had undoubtedly left abrasions on my thighs.

"Not sure I can," I mumbled, not quite ready to move. But even then, Santos had had his own agenda, lifting and turning me until my knees straddled his head, my body facing his feet with my messy hair hanging over one shoulder.

"Want to take a bet on that?" he retorted as he leisurely toyed with my swollen and oversensitive center.

I huffed out a brief noise of mirth at his challenge. He and Marco were so competitive that a wager was only a moment's notice away at any given time. "No, but I'll return the favor," I offered in compromise. "Tap out before you get off though. I want you finishing in *me*, not my mouth."

It was his turn to chuckle, and the sound made me moan as it reverberated between my legs. "Unless you plan on thirty seconds, I should probably do just that. Besides, it's hot as hell when you try to swallow me down." He didn't wait for my reply before he pulled me down to seal his mouth to my slick folds.

The last few months that we'd officially been dating, I'd discovered giving Santos blowjobs got me crazy horny, and I'd been trying to take him all the way down since. Hadn't quite gotten there yet, but he would come so hard when I choked and gagged around him, getting teary eyed from my efforts. He always laid back to let me do my thing, occasionally tangling his hand in my hair but never anything rougher, and I thought I loved him just a bit more for it. Other girls at school had said their boyfriends or hookups would push their heads down or go too far on purpose just to get off. Santos wasn't like that at all, and it made me even more determined to engage in an act that we both enjoyed.

"Fine, but I'm holding you to that," I challenged, receiving a tap on my bottom that I took as an agreement. Apparently, he wasn't coming up for air anytime soon.

Stretching out, I wiggled my shoulders between his legs so I could get a good angle and took just the tip of his wide head between my lips. The first dart of my tongue picked up the evidence of his arousal, slightly bitter but not unpleasantly so. I'd started taking him farther in and adding suction when Santos locked his lips around my clit and speared my core with what I was nearly positive were the same three fingers as before. My moan was closely echoed by his in a chain reaction of mutual pleasure.

Taking him deeper yet, Santos hit the back of my throat, and I struggled to breathe through it and swallow as I pushed down. I managed to get just the head in before my gag reflex convulsed, constricting my esophagus and forcing him back out.

"Fuck me, angel, that's so good," Santos groaned, praising my efforts as he bit the inside of my thigh before sucking hard enough to leave a bruise. He loved marking me as his, especially where no one else would see. "You clamp so hard on my fingers when you choke on my cock. Promise you'll do that while you ride me, taking my fingers into your throat until you retch around them?" The imagery his dirty talk elicited had me wanting to try it right now, but even though I was open to trying anything, I wanted my first time to be a bit sweeter.

"One day soon, babe. You have to actually put your dick in me first though," I taunted.

"Soon," he repeated back to me. In the same breath, he slid a hand up my body to tweak one hard nipple as he resumed his task between my thighs.

Eager to get to this 'soon' he spoke of, I used one hand to gently squeeze and tug at his sac, the other stroking the portion of his erection I couldn't fit into my mouth. His dick hardened further, the vein along the underside beginning to pulse, and he moaned against me as his hips arched up. I wasn't quite there yet, but Santos was. As if to prove his dedication to getting me off again, his fingers slipped free while his other hand abandoned its twisting and pulling at the peak of my breast.

His tongue never let up, and as he chased his own orgasm with twitching hips, he worked fingers back into me. I had an inkling of his plans when a slick digit probed between my cheeks, but even though we'd briefly tried it once before it, that first touch was still a bit shocking.

I relaxed immediately, trusting him to go slow, and tried to take him into my throat again. He barely breached my ass before retreating, picking up a shallow but rapid pace with his finger while the others worked me into a sloppy, wet mess. My tight ring burned slightly, but it added to the myriad of sensations going on instead of inhibiting them, and I was quickly on track with my impending release.

Not to be outdone, I forced his tip back into my throat and swallowed fiercely around him while my hand jacked him to completion. He came in jets that went straight down with minimal effort, and seconds behind him, I screeched with the force of my orgasm, the sound muffled by his still-hard member between my lips. I immediately collapsed, sprawling on top of Santos as our sweat-soaked bodies cooled down together. Acutely conscious of where his fingers were and that my crotch was probably smothering him, I made an undignified effort to slide off to the side.

"You okay down there?" Santos' voice came from the head of the bed, husky and languid, but he sounded like he had a heck of a lot more energy than I did at the moment.

"Uh huh, think you broke my vagina though," I mumbled through still tingly and kinda numb lips. *Suckers are probably swollen from all the... sucking.*

He slipped the rest of the way out from under me, turning to lay so we were face to face. With a soft kiss that I could taste myself on, he pulled me close to cuddle. "That mean you want to wait? It's okay if you do. This was great and more than enough." He continued to pepper kisses over my face, being sweet and silly, making me giggle when we bumped noses.

I took stock of my body and decided that while I was extremely satisfied and more than a tad worn out, I was still excited and wanted to go that bit farther. "Yeah, give me five minutes, a bathroom break, and some water."

"Yes, ma'am. I think I need the same, to be honest. That mouth..." Santos hummed a pleased note in his throat and bit his bottom lip for effect. He was such a goof sometimes, but he was also sexy and sweet and a fiercely loyal boyfriend. My life hadn't been all fairy tales, just like his hadn't, but we wouldn't let it tarnish us or hold us back. No, I took us finding each other now as a sign we were meant to be.

It was more like thirty minutes with us tangled up together in a dozing catnap before I used Santos' bathroom while he pulled his sweats back on and went to the one down the hall. Feeling a bit awkward when I came back out naked, I slipped on one of the t-shirts he'd discarded on the back of his desk chair and debated whether to wait in the bed or not. That's where Santos found me, hovering next to the bedside, indecision creasing my forehead.

"What's wrong, angel?" he asked as he handed me a chilled water bottle, slipping his arms around me from the back to rest his chin on my shoulder.

"Nothing. Well, kinda nervous, but more awkward nervous, not not-wanting-to-do-this nervous." I huffed out a breath at myself, frustrated that I couldn't just be smooth like other girls. Or how other girls seemed to be. Deciding that elaborating wasn't going to help my lack of brain to mouth coordination, I unscrewed the cap and tipped the bottle up to my lips. The cold water felt great going down. I'd rinsed my mouth out in the bathroom, but this was way better, and I nearly emptied it before putting the cap back on.

Santos distracted me from everything else by sniffing me. "You like Marco's cologne, huh? I'll have to tell him, maybe steal it the next time I'm at his place. Can't have my girl lusting after one of my bros."

My head snapped to the side, face brushing Santos' to stare wide-eyed in horror. I'd put Marco's shirt on? It hadn't occurred to me that it might not be my boyfriend's; the scent was light enough I hadn't made the distinction that it wasn't Santos'. Not that I was around Marco enough to have his scent memorized. And what if they used more than one? Surely guys did that too? Marco was hot as hell in a bad boy way, much like Santos himself, but I'd *never* do that to him.

Freaking out, I stepped to the side, dropped the water bottle, and yanked the shirt off before tossing it back where I'd found it and trying to explain. "I swear I didn't know it was his! I thought it was yours —" Santos' laughter cut me off, and I glared at him for making fun of me. "It's really your shirt, isn't it?" I accused, crossing my arms over my now very bare chest.

He shook his head, finally getting his mirth under control. "No, it's really his. I just didn't expect that reaction, but I'm glad it got you naked again. Plus, I'm going to tease the shit out of Marco that these beautiful gals fill it out better than he does." Santos reached out a fingertip to hook into where my arms were crossed, tugging them down with little resistance from me. I liked where the subject had moved to, so I let the matter go.

I leaned in until I could just barely touch my lips to his when I lifted up on my toes. Santos assisted by tipping his head down to meet me, and I took his full lower lip between my teeth before sucking on it. The action had his arms curling around my back to pull me in tight while he groaned and ground his semi against me. "Lose the pants, De Luca."

"Yes, Miss Moretti, losing them now," he responded, only briefly moving a hand down to push at the already precariously perched fabric on his hips. The sweats pooled in a heap that he deftly toed off as he leaned forward to grab me behind the thighs, hoisting me in the air.

My still-sensitive core rubbed up against the thin line of rough hair on his abdomen when my legs wrapped tight around his back. Santos took the couple steps to the bed, supporting my lower back with one hand as he used the other to brace himself on the mattress. Reluctantly, I unhooked my ankles and loosened the hold of my thighs. On my way down I felt Santos' full erection brushing against my bottom until it slipped up to drag across my lower lips and settled against me.

We didn't speak as we took our time exploring each other with our hands and making out with deep, almost frantic thrusts of our tongues—all the while grinding against each other where we pressed together between my thighs. By the time we separated a bit, we were both out of breath, and the slickness of my arousal had returned. More than ready for him to finish what he'd started, I broached a concern I hadn't thought about before.

"Should I get a towel or something? What if I make a mess? Some of the girls I know said it was noticeable, and others didn't." I bit my lip, staring up at a distinctly unperturbed Santos.

"Angel, I hope it stains," he said in between kisses, surprising me with his answer. "Leave your mark on my bed, like you've left it on my soul. I'm yours, and you're mine, forever," he continued as his kiss-swollen lips trailed across my jaw and down to the sensitive flesh of my neck, leaving a wet path of love bites with a combination of little sucks and nibbles. I didn't even care that they'd have to be hidden from my mom and at school.

Santos' response alternately flooded my chest

with overwhelming affection and my pussy with a begging, insistent ache. He continued working his way down to my chest, only pausing briefly to speak again. "I'll go to bed every night, knowing I'm sleeping on the proof of our first time and that it will forever be branded on your mind. I'll *always* own that piece of you." His words were as drugging as his talented mouth, but one thing stood out starkly.

"You're a virgin?" My tone was high with disbelief as Santos met my wide-eyed gaze with his hooded one.

He didn't answer for a moment, taking the time to slide back up my body until he hovered over me, hips again nestled high between my legs. I thought he was going to just go for it, but he didn't even have a condom on yet. Instead, he notched the tip of his erection at the apex of my folds to bump that already oversensitive bundle of nerves as he slipped back and forth, further coating us both in my abundant arousal. Santos never broke eye contact the entire time, keeping up his slow and steady tease that was almost enough to push me to another orgasm.

I'd nearly forgotten what my question was until he finally answered, his hips coming to a halt, lessening my acute distraction. "Yes, I thought you knew." I shook my head, and worry started to take over the lust in his crystalline gaze. "I'll do my best to make it good for you, angel. I only ever made out with a couple girls before I met you. You've been the only one I've wanted since that first day you came here with your mom. You were all cute and shy, and I was done for."

It was my turn to be unconcerned. "I'm not upset about it. I'm actually kinda relieved it's not just me. Plus, even if the first time isn't the greatest, you've already gotten me off multiple times, and we can always try again later." I grinned cheekily as I added the last bit. I had every intention of practicing until we were perfect at it.

"If it sucks, I'll make it up to you now." He gave me a quick kiss, relief and anticipation written all over his face, before he retreated enough to open his bedside drawer. Where he had condoms. At my questioning and quite possibly accusatory stare, he explained, "I wasn't going to be unprepared for whenever this happened... and I may have opened them and stroked one out a time or two with one on. Just to see how it felt." He shrugged, grinning unrepentantly at my amusement with his candor on self-pleasure. I wasn't quite to the stage where I was comfortable sharing my forays in bean flicking. But I did have one question...

"Did I get the wrong ones?" I asked tentatively. It had taken a lot of courage to carry them up to the cashier after trying not to be embarrassed when other shoppers walked by as I debated the dozen different options. The entire time I had to repeat to myself what the doctor had said when I got on the pill. *If you aren't comfortable enough to protect yourself, your partner, or discuss protection with your partner, then you have no business having sexual relations.* And since I'd noticed the ones Santos had were different than what I'd picked up, that third part was giving me the courage to address it.

Santos was slightly bashful, and after he answered, I thought maybe it was because he didn't want to hurt my feelings. "Those ones are too snug. I got a bag of samples at my last physical for school sports, and the regular ones pinched, and uh, broke when I... The others are more comfortable," he quickly said after pausing. Then it dawned on me that the letters on the black box weren't a type, but a size. I tried to brazen it out and forced down my embarrassment.

"I didn't realize there were different sizes. There's that ice cream bar with the same name that I like... Apparently I have a type," I laughed at myself, realizing I was only making it worse when Santos folded his lips in, trying to keep a straight face. Then he was the sweetest boyfriend ever.

"If I have my way, you'll never have another dick to compare it to, but I know someone who can use them if that's okay?" At my nod, he ruined the perfect boyfriend routine. "Now I get to tell Marco you were naked in his shirt *and* you think he has a small cock." I reached out to grab my purse, fishing the small box out and throwing it at his head.

"You'll do no such thing, De Luca, or I'll tell him you want me to judge who's bigger." That shut him up, but my victory was short-lived when he narrowed his eyes and tackled me back on the bed.

"Only mine, angel. Remember that so I don't have to hit him. The dude is bigger than me now, and you wouldn't want me to get hurt, would you?" I knew he was teasing, well, not about Marco being bigger. Marco had sprouted up over the last summer and was gaining muscle by the day... not that I had noticed on purpose.

We didn't continue the conversation as Santos rubbed up against me, turning my thoughts firmly in his direction. He lifted up to look me in the eye before suggesting, "How about you grab one of those and let's find out what all the fuss is about, yeah?"

"Unless... you sure you wouldn't rather have the ice cream? I think there's a box in the freezer." I groaned in amused embarrassment at his teasing, but he shifted until he could reach the strip of condoms in the drawer, pulling me to him until he had me situated to his satisfaction.

My amusement fled when Santos ripped one of the foil squares open. My eyes tracked his movements as he pinched the tip and rolled it down over his length. I thought he was about to get back into position when he mumbled, "Just in case," and pulled out a bottle of lubricant to coat himself with.

When he was hovering back over me, he locked

his eyes on mine, reaching down to grip his dick and directing it to spread my slick nether lips with the tip. The wet coating on the condom was cool enough to make me flinch slightly, and he immediately tried to back up. I latched onto his biceps, my heels pulling up to press into his ass cheeks. It simultaneously halted his movement and gave him better access to notch his rigid member against my opening.

The steady pressure he exerted made my flesh burn as it stretched, and my breathing became shallow in nervous anticipation. Brows furrowed, Santos took his time, rocking into me until my body relaxed and softened enough to accept his intrusion. There was a sharper pinch of pain that had me jumping slightly with a squeak muffled in my throat, but I didn't stop his progress. A few short moments later, his pelvis met mine. The sensation of being stretched and filled was foreign and somewhat uncomfortable, especially with him bumping against something deep inside that gave off an ache that wasn't completely bad.

Santos rested his forehead on mine, his damp with sweat even though we hadn't really done much moving around. The muscles in his arms were rigid where I gripped them, reminding me that it was his first time too. He probably wanted to move, and here he was, waiting for my go ahead. Or maybe he was afraid he was gonna lose it already. Regardless, I wanted to reassure him that either option was okay, so I tested out a wiggle of my hips against him.

A zing almost like what I got when he pinched my nipple, but better, radiated from where I was impaled by him, the sensation trailing up into my abdomen, and I clenched around him. With a groan, Santos worked his hips in small, grinding circles, dragging against my clit with every revolution. The steady movements ratcheted my arousal back up until I could hear as well as feel it.

"Angel, can I move, yet?" *I thought that's already what he'd been doing?*

"Uh, yeah?" I replied, the question in my voice blatant, but I didn't think he heard that part. He just said "Thank fuck" and pulled almost all the way out before surging back into me.

The push and pull of our flesh together was something new but also enjoyable after I got used to the friction. It prompted me to meet his thrusts when he hit that spot inside and out each time he sank to the hilt. My arms slid up to wrap around his neck while my heels slipped down to dig into the mattress for leverage. Santos' hot breath puffed against my neck where his face curled down, punctuating his thrusts with frequent moans.

His rhythm stuttered after a few minutes of steady movement, becoming rougher and shorter. I could feel the pulsing throb through the condom before his erection got even harder and he buried himself as deep as he could get with a quick flexing jerk of his hips. A rush of muted warmth filled me as he stiffened, and I guessed that sensation was him coming in the barrier that separated us. A moment later, he slumped down on top of me, breathing heavily.

I didn't get anywhere close to an orgasm, but it still felt good. My fingers trailed through Santos' sweaty black hair, affectionately rubbing his scalp while he caught his breath and recovered.

When he remained silent, I started to worry, but when I worried, my mouth started to talk. "So, uh, we're not virgins anymore."

Santos let out a sharp bark of laughter and picked his head up to look at me incredulously. "That's it? Just 'we're not virgins anymore,'" he mocked in a falsetto that sounded nothing like me.

"Um, it was nice? I want to do it again?" I tacked on that last one before he could say anything. "Later, when I'm not sore, cuz now that I've settled some, things are telling me quite loudly that they need a break."

"Oh, crap, sorry, I didn't think." Santos shifted to pull back, but with my tightness still around his softening penis, the condom stayed, while he exited. "Shit, that's not supposed to happen." I was too horrified to ask what exactly wasn't supposed to be happening when he caught it, holding tight to what was left around the tip of him, and pulled the rest of the condom out of me.

His panicky eyes met my horrifically embarrassed ones. I wasn't sure which of us was more mortified, and I blurted out, "At least I'm not the only one that left a mess?" I did indeed bleed just a bit, but it was now smeared with what came back out of the latex sheath before he could completely stop it, and it all puddled on the sheets.

With a groan, Santos flopped his head down onto my stomach, and then we both busted up laughing at the absurdity our mutual lack of experience had caused. Note to self: hold the base of the condom when disconnecting.

After we calmed down and Santos disposed of the used condom, we both cleaned up and I helped him change his sheets. My mom was the housekeeper after all, and I definitely didn't need her finding that. She'd tear me a new one if she thought I was messing up her gig. She already didn't approve of me and Santos dating; only his dad talking to her had kept her from banning me from seeing him.

Not to mention I avoided all thoughts of sex and my mother if at all possible. I wasn't an idiot, and Santos had confirmed it when I asked— my mother was his father's mistress. For the most part, they were discreet, but the arrangement still squigged me out. I wasn't positive, and I *definitely* wouldn't ask, but I thought it had started after my dad passed and we were broke. Mom refused to tell me exactly what had happened, but she'd refused a lot of things since he died. Like being more than a perfunctory parent.

I switched that train of thought off as I cuddled up with Santos to watch a movie before I had to leave and head home.

It was late morning when my mother yelled at me to get out of bed. Rodrigo was on his way home early, and she wanted to make sure 'that boy' hadn't thrown a party and trashed the place.

"Mom, he didn't have a party, and there isn't even a mess! I was over last night and watched a movie before I came home." After last night, I really didn't feel like going to polish and dust everything at Santos' today. I was seriously sore all over, even if it did give me a little thrill from remembering why.

"You can come and help earn the money that pays for your food and clothes, not to mention that ridiculously expensive cell phone."

I didn't know what was up her butt today. The phone had been free with signing up, and we were on the cheapest family plan. If anything, hers cost more, but I knew better than to say anything else. The older I got, the quicker she was to fly off the handle and smack me for talking back.

When she left my room, I stiffly slid out of bed. It was slow going until my sore muscles limbered up, but the ache in my center was a novel thing that almost had me lost in the memory of the night before. Mom yelled at me to hurry up twice more before I managed to get myself into the car despite my daydreaming.

The drive wasn't too long, but the silence was tense and uncomfortable, and I couldn't wait to get out. I wasn't sure what her problem was other than maybe a ruined half-day off, but I bailed the minute she put the gear shift into park. Mom had a key, so we let ourselves in, and I discovered no one was home. Hoping to get done quickly, I got started with the vacuum. I wasn't ashamed to clean, but it was always a bit awkward when Santos was home and tried to help me. Especially if his dad or my mom caught him, then it was downright embarrassing. My mother would dress me down, or Rodrigo would explain, yet again, how that was why we were the help.

It was why I took the opportunity to make a quick grocery run while Mom finished up. I came in the back, loaded down with bags so I didn't have to make a second trip, and started putting it all away. I was storing the last of it in the pantry when Rodrigo came in, and I never would have expected what happened then.

Rodrigo walked up to where I was bent over, tucking the plastic sacks into the bin designated for them, and smacked my bottom. I straightened so fast my head nearly clipped a shelf.

"What the hell?" I shouted at him, furious that he thought it was okay to touch me like that.

"What's the problem, Eden? Your mom doesn't mind when I do it to her. I just thought with you and my son having done the deed, you'd be open to it." The jerk wasn't even slightly apologetic as his gaze raked up and down my body in a positively lecherous manner. He'd given me a few overly familiar glances a time or two, enough to make me uncomfortable, but I never thought he'd actually touch me.

"What Santos and I do isn't anyone else's business, and it's definitely not okay to behave like this. What would he say if he knew his dad was hitting on his girlfriend?" I wasn't entirely sure what to do. I couldn't cost Mom her job, but I wouldn't put up with this, and Santos wouldn't expect me to.

"You mean my son, the one you'll be set up for? Can't have his mistress hanging around when his engagement is announced."

"Wait, what?" I didn't understand what was going on or why his dad was saying these things.

"He hasn't told you yet, but after he turns eighteen, he'll be marrying one of the Carlotti cousins, cementing his ties to the Family. Why do you think the boys have always been friends? Don't tell me you thought that he would be marrying *you* someday." My mind reeled; this wasn't something we'd discussed. They were just Santos' friends when I was around, and I thought they were mine too. I never realized there was more to it than that.

Before I could form an argument, Rodrigo continued. "You'll still come by to clean, of course, but you'll have your own apartment for him to visit soon enough, and you'll need to earn your keep." I shook my head, refusing to believe it even as moisture welled in my eyes. "Why the tears, Eden? It's good enough for your mother, but not you?"

I couldn't answer as a sob caught in my throat at his callous comments. My mind told me he was lying, but I couldn't dwell on any of it when Rodrigo reached for me again. I blindly dodged back, but there wasn't anywhere to go except into the pantry. "Your mother was quite young when she had you, but she's getting up there in years. Soon enough, I'll be in the market for a newer model, and I think I can talk Santos into sharing or even giving you up after he's had his fill. He just wanted to pop that cherry first, and there's no doubt about that now, is there? Now come here and let me see what I'm paying for."

I lashed out, trying to hit him, to push him away, but he grabbed my arm, spun to face the shelves, and pinned me painfully against them. "Let go! I'll call the police!" My shout echoed in the space on the shelf in front of me, but all it earned me was a hand around my throat.

"You ever mention the cops again, girl, and I'll have both you and your mother gutted, starting with this." His hand came around my front, and he let up enough to slip it between my thighs to grip my still sore crotch before he squeezed. A whimper escaped me, and I shut my eyes tightly as I prayed my mom would come in and stop him or Santos would come home. I would never believe he'd allow this to happen.

Despite his threats, I still struggled against his bigger frame while his hand wandered to the waistband of my pants to force itself in and under my panties. The seeking fingers roughly prodded at tender flesh until they forced their way inside as choking sobs wracked my body.

"Such a hot and tight little pussy," he groaned, grinding his erection against my bottom, but he didn't make it any further.

Mom walked in, exclaiming, "Rodrigo! She's a minor." My heart stuttered in my chest. *She's not worried about what he's doing, but that I'm too young?* Instantly, I was hit with painful, crushing disbelief that those words had come out of her mouth.

Rodrigo released me, allowing me to turn and

cower back into the corner. My eyes darted to Mom's face, only to find it pinched in fury as she shook a black trash bag at me. "I didn't tell you what I found so you could trade me out for my daughter. I don't want her getting knocked up and having to support another mouth. I wanted you to put a stop to it."

We didn't empty the trash. I couldn't believe I'd forgotten the condom was in there. The thought was fleeting as Mom came forward and roughly grabbed my arm, yanking me through the kitchen and out the back door. She pointed to the car, and I nearly ran to the passenger seat while she threw the garbage in the bin in the garage.

She didn't say anything on the way home, only telling me to shut up when I tried to tell her what he'd done, then completely ignored the tears I couldn't stop and the sniffles that accompanied them. Without a word, she slammed out of the car when we got back to our apartment complex. It was one of the nicer ones, made affordable by *him*. I sat in shock, trying to figure out what to do. I was afraid to go to the police. And Santos? Surely, that wasn't what he had planned for me! He'd said he loved me... But would he go against his father? I just didn't know. And he knew all about what his dad and my mom got up to and had never said anything bad about it. I knew the boys he hung out with were essentially mafia royalty, but I didn't know them as well as I did him or if they would help me if I told them. Would they have hidden that he was supposed to marry one of their cousins? Or be on board with the situation? It was all just so hard to believe.

Thoughts spinning, I dragged my feet on the way up to our apartment on the second floor only to have a duffel bag thrown at me when I walked inside.

"Get your trampy ass out of my house. Trying to steal my meal ticket! Is the boy not enough for you?" she nearly screamed at me.

Shocked, I didn't even grab for the bag, letting it hit my chest and fall to the floor. "I'm your daughter, and that man was assaulting me! He was going to *rape* me!

"You probably asked for it, just like you spread your legs for that boy. Don't think I'll have you replacing me again, just like with your father. I won't have it!" I didn't understand what she meant about my dad, but she didn't care at all about what I'd gone through. It only left one conclusion.

"It's true, then? I'm supposed to be some live-in housekeeper slash whore? *Santos* said this?" I couldn't believe he would do something like that, despite what his father had done and claimed.

"You know damn well that boy is slumming it with you. He's practically part of the Carlotti family, nearly an heir himself. Where's your brain, girl? If you can't get in line and help earn your keep, you can get out." Mom's face was red, her eyes wild with rage, and she continued spewing hateful crap.

"Those weren't the first rubbers I've emptied out of that bedroom. Boys like him don't marry girls like you. We're the *help*," she sneered. But I knew she was wrong, and hope bloomed in my chest even if it felt an embarrassing betrayal to reveal why they'd been there.

"Santos said he was just trying them out. That he'd never been with anyone else before."

"And I suppose the girls that I've seen leaving his room were imaginary? Wake up, girly. You'll be better off when you accept reality."

"He has school too! When would you—" I didn't finish my question when it dawned on me as to what she'd be doing when I wasn't here. Doubt tried to creep in. He had all but told me he knew I wouldn't get off my first time. I'd thought it was something he'd heard from his friends after he admitted he was a virgin... and then the excuse about the condoms... But no, I wouldn't twist every unforgettable, amazing moment of our first time. Plus, I had one last trump card. "He said he loves me and wants us to always be together." My chin raised in challenge. Santos had been sincere, I knew it.

"Love and duty are two different things," she scoffed. "He'll do what he has to to secure his future, and that's marrying who he's told to." My mother's lips curled in disdain. "Let me tell you, even if he did marry you, chances are you'd still end up like me. Widowed with a brat to support." I started to deny it again, but she cut me off before I could. "I can't take the chance you'll spread your legs for them both. Pack your shit. You have an hour, and I don't want to see you again." She stormed off, leaving me heartbroken and lost in our tiny entryway.

I wasn't sure what to do, but I packed a bag with the essentials then added a few snacks and grabbed my birth certificate and purse. If she really followed through, I'd have to go straight to an ATM and pull out my savings. Maybe I could get a motel room for the night since I didn't have any close friends I could crash with. What would I tell them anyway? I really needed to talk to Santos, but I was afraid to do it where she might overhear.

My hour was almost up, and I was sitting on my bed, trying to get the courage to approach Mom's bedroom door. Surely, she'd let me stay if she had a chance to cool off; she always had before. I'd get a real job and help out until I graduated and then get out of her hair. I knew I wasn't her favorite person... She'd said more than once that she'd have gotten an abortion if my dad hadn't insisted on keeping me, but she'd raised me for seventeen years. A few more months shouldn't have been too hard to deal with. My phone buzzed in my hand, distracting me from my crappy internal pep talk.

Santos: *Hey, Dad said you were upset when he talked to you at the house. Are you okay?*

I wanted to blast him with accusations, but what if they weren't true?

Me: *So you know what he talked to me about? What he did?*

Please, no. I begged the universe to tell me that he wasn't in on it.

Santos: *Well, yeah, I didn't think it was that big of a deal. We're together anyway, right?*

Me: *Just to be clear, you talked to your dad about having sex with me?*

Santos: *Yes, angel, I did. Do you want to come over? Or I can call you. I don't want it to be weird between us. We don't have to. I wanted it to be a surprise and tell you myself, but he jumped the gun a bit. I thought you'd be happy about the arrangement, being independent from your mom and getting an apartment.*

Me: *What apartment?*

Santos: *The one I wanted to set up for when you turn eighteen. I thought that's what you were upset about?*

Me: *You thought I'd want you setting me up in an apartment? That was supposed to be a surprise?*

He really did plan to hide me away. All the times he'd had to go off for 'business' with his dad or friends ran through my head. Had he been with the girl Rodrigo mentioned? In my mind, his next response put the final touches on the destruction of our relationship.

Santos: *Can you just come over so we can talk about it? Or at least call me? I don't want to do this over text messages.*

Me: *You and your dad can both go fuck yourselves. I fucking HATE you! Don't ever speak to me again.*

More dots popped up, showing that Santos was typing, but I could barely see through my tears, and nothing he said at this point would make his intentions any better. *I was always the* help.

"Leave the phone when you go." Mom's slurred demand came as she slammed my door open. She must have downed quite a bit of her nightly wine to be this tipsy already.

Anger pushed the jagged remnants of my heart into a pile of blackened shards as I straightened my shoulders. They could all go fuck themselves; no one deserved what they'd done. I shouldered the duffel bag and brushed past the bitch that used to be my mother. The first spark of rebellious rage urged me to detour into the kitchen where I dropped my phone into the garbage disposal, turned on the water, and flipped the switch before I walked away.

I made it to the ATM and drained the account. I had to borrow a phone from a stranger and pretend to be her, but after a sob story about a made up emergency, made much more believable by my unstoppable tears, the teller took pity on me and upped the daily withdrawal limit. When I finished the multiple maximum draws, I had a total of fifteen hundred to start a new life.

I was seventeen and homeless, walking until I could find somewhere safe to stay for the night, the ache of false love pulsing between my legs with every step.

eight
ice cream

Eden

P ***resent day...***
Barely a month after what had happened, I was going by Angel. Broke and starving, I started hooking on the street corners in the heart of New York City for food and a shitty bedroom in an apartment I shared with three other working girls. I'd avoided it for as long as I could, but when your stomach is eating itself and the dregs of society took what they wanted even if you didn't offer it up, it was easier to give in and at least make a buck.

My trip down memory lane was brought up short by raised voices outside the bedroom door. Marco had rushed out a bit ago and failed to lock me in. Not knowing if they were still around, I was afraid to risk trying to escape yet. But with all of the commotion, I *did* risk cracking it open to peek out and see what was going on.

A slightly bruised Vanni supported a sagging Santos under one shoulder while Marco propped up the other side.

"Just get the door and the doc, Tony. We'll figure the rest out later. Dumbass about got his head kicked in. He's lucky he made it home on his own. Fucking idiots that called should have said he was injured."

Vanni's griping prompted me to look more closely at a nearly unconscious Santos. He did look pretty awful. When the light illuminated his face as they neared my door, I caught the days old bruising that masked some of his scars and the remnants of bloody streaks where it looked like someone had made a half-assed attempt to clean his head up. Having gotten a few overs the years, I knew scalp wounds bled like a bitch. My perusal was rudely interrupted when Tony spied me lurking. "Get the fuck back in there and don't come out unless you're told to." The straight up lethality in his voice and expression had me slamming the door shut and retreating to the bed. I didn't even wait to see if the other two would even bother to stick up on my behalf.

I didn't know what Antonio's malfunction was, besides his buddy getting fucked up, but I didn't want him taking it out on me. No, I needed a game plan to ditch the kidnapping fuck, get my money from Danny, and skip town, with a pitstop for some peace in a baggie.

※

I was getting more pissed by the minute, and my stomach hurt. They'd fucking forgotten to feed me like an irresponsible kid with a pet that wasn't interesting anymore. It wasn't the first time I'd gone without food. Hell, it wasn't even the first time this week, but I wasn't just hungry. I was bored too, and that made it harder to ignore burning acid coming up from the hunger cramps. Which made it all that much worse.

Without a way to tell time, I couldn't be sure what would happen if the door was still unlocked and I tried to sneak out and get something, but I needed food, and I was about to risk it— plus, the sugar cravings were real. With my ear against the door, I listened for any hint of noise to indicate anyone was around, but other than my own breathing, all was quiet. Testing the handle and finding it unlocked, I thanked whatever had them so preoccupied that I wasn't stuck in here. Cracking the door, I peeked out, trying to gauge the time of day. It was a bit déjà vu from earlier, sans the Carlotti boys, but I was nearly certain there had been daylight filtering down the hall.

Wrapping my little bit of courage around myself like the tattered shield it was, I crept down the carpeted corridor in the baggy men's clothes I was still forced to wear. I'd finally gotten some fucking luck. Everything was softly lit with recessed ambient lighting, but I'd found a clock when the hall split into a T. It sat at the intersection of the corridors, one of those fancy ass grandfather things, but it ticked away, reading one in the morning. Well, I assumed the morning part since there wasn't anyone around and the overhead lights were off.

A voice came from the direction I'd come, and I raced down the hall perpendicular to the clock as quietly as I could. I was ninety-nine percent sure the swinging double doors with their porthole windows led to the kitchen. A quick darting glance through one proved that yes, it was the kitchen. And it was blessedly empty. My slight frame barely made the right one open as I slipped inside.

I went straight for the gleaming, metal-finished, industrial-sized refrigerator. Pulling open the door, I immediately scowled at the plate covered in plastic wrap. I had a feeling the soup and sandwich had been intended for me. Taking it out, I removed the covering and started inhaling the ham and swiss while I figured out how to work the controls on the high-end robot masquerading as a microwave. Did it have to beep so fucking loudly?

I finally got it going with what I hoped was the

correct setting and went in search of silverware. Spoon in hand, I had every intention of eating the soup, but I really wanted some ice cream. The freezer side of the refrigerator combo beckoned to me, daring me to open its door. Which I promptly did. An unopened mint chocolate chip sat there like it had been waiting for me to discover it. Who was I to deny its last request?

Spoon in hand, I moved to make my escape, only to be thwarted by the voice I now recognized as it came through one of the doors. All I had time to do was duck behind the island in the middle of the floor.

"Yeah, thanks, Dad. I'll check in tomorrow and let you know what our plans are. Somebody apparently needs to be reminded that we allow the buffer zone and split the tithes evenly to keep the peace."

Aw, shit. He's talking to Vinnie. Vincenzo 'Vinnie' Carlotti was the head of the Family and not a man I wanted to fuck with.

"Yes, we're sure it's her. I'll send over what we have." A pause, and then, "I know, will do." I thought the rustling meant he was done with his call, and after that last tidbit, getting caught was gonna be bad, I just knew it.

Might as well own it. While Giovanni bitched about food being left in the microwave, I took the opportunity to pry the cardboard lid up and dig into my treat.

"Jesus, fuck, Eden. What are you doing in here?"

he nearly shouted when he came around the corner of the island. Of course, he went right to the worst case scenario. "Are you spying on me? You won't like what happens," he warned.

I decided to go straight for the pitiful truth. "I'm hungry, Vanni. No one fed me after breakfast, and I was too hungry to sleep."

"Uh huh, and ice cream is the cure for starvation?" he inquired with an eyebrow arched skyward.

"I ate a sandwich and tried to heat up the soup, but I heard someone and got scared. So I hid, kinda, and I'm craving sweets something awful without the drugs." I shrugged and tried to look pitiful. Also… not a lie. I was constantly starving and had even put on a few pounds in the last week.

"Fine, but hurry up before Tony decides he wants a midnight snack too." He went back to dumping the soup down the sink that was situated in the middle of the island while I dug into my treat. I mourned my soup for a moment since I would have taken it with me, but the ice cream would hold me over well enough. When he was done, Vanni turned, and from my position, I was nearly eye to eye with his crotch. Well, if I glanced up a bit, but whatever. It gave me an idea, one I wasn't above exploiting.

"So, what have you been up to all these years, Vanni?" I asked as I flipped the spoon and scooped the contents out with my tongue, all the while keeping my eyes on the fly of his trousers.

"Not sure that's something I should be discussing with you, Eden. How about you tell me what's been going on at Cherry—" He paused mid-sentence before blurting, "Are you eye-fucking my dick?" He sounded surprised at my boldness. *Idiot*.

"Mmhmm, that a problem?" My eyes stayed locked on his cock as I issued my challenge.

"Yes, it's a fucking problem. I saved your ass, and you're, what, gonna risk it by coming onto me?" He stepped closer, making me have to crane my head up to look at his face. I'd have sworn his dick twitched under the fabric before he moved, a hint of curiosity in his hard, dark eyes.

"Didn't ask you to save me, now did I?" I shrugged and added on, voice going sultry, "Do you have a big dick, Giovanni? I've always been curious." Total lie... almost. Back then, I had been too innocent and naïve, too much of a lovestruck bitch in heat, chasing after Santos, to do more than give a cursory notice that the others were attractive. It never would have crossed that Eden's mind, but Angel, well, Angel would contemplate just about anything if it was of benefit to her.

"We're not talking about my dick, Eden. Get the fuck back to bed before you cause more trouble than you're worth. And next time Marco doesn't lock that door, we're going to have problems." The usually staid peacekeeper was irate, about more than just me getting out I'd wager. And a bit horny if the slight bulge I spied was any indication. Then it dawned on me.

"You had a thing for me, didn't you, Giovanni? Mmhmm, I knew I'd caught you staring at me more than you should have been." Again, total lie, but from the flash of guilt in his eyes, I knew I had him.

"I was a teenage boy with a one track dick around a hot girl, Eden. Of course, I looked. Doesn't mean I would have betrayed my friend, my *family*. Not like you." Oh, and doesn't that burn when your family is the one that fucked me over?

Ignoring the urge to lash out, I rose up on my knees. The tiled floor was cold and uncomfortable, but I'd had worse, so I shrugged it off and persevered. "Ever had an ice cream blowie, Vanni? The cold can be such a turn-on, and the mint... bet that would tingle long after you blow your load down my throat. Whaddya say? For old time's sake? To satisfy your curiosity of what it would have been like if you had met me first?"

"Is that what you want, Eden? To choke on my dick? Because I'm not the gentleman you seem to think I am, and if your mouth gets near me, you're going to need that ice cream for your sore throat." He reached down to grip his hard-on, and I'd just found out that yes, yes he did have an above average sized cock.

Licking my lips, I scooped out a generous spoonful and held it out on my tongue in invitation, daring him to follow through. When his fingers deftly popped the button and lowered the zipper, I got a tingle of interest right between my legs. I was attracted to Giovanni Carlotti. Not. A. Fucking. Lie.

It was a novel feeling, the attraction to another person while being stone cold sober. I thought maybe it was something I wanted to explore more closely, but my subsequent idea to possibly retreat and change my approach after my revelation was dashed when Vanni fished his dick out of boxers. Holy fuck, that was going to push my jaw to its limit, nevermind my throat. I nearly choked on the melting ice cream in my mouth before he even got it near me.

"Do you know how pissed I get when Tony gets to say 'I told you so'? You can't bribe everyone with your golden pussy or your talent to suck the brass off a doorknob, Eden." It kinda stung that that was his and Tony's opinion of me, but really... they weren't wrong. "I'm going to enjoy this, you self-destructive bitch." That was all the warning I got before he crammed as much of his fat cock in my mouth as he could in one go, moaning while he used my trailing hair as a handle to pull my head back and forth, staring into my eyes the entire time. "You're right. This is definitely in the top ten blow jobs with the cold, but let's see if we can bump that number up, yeah?"

His stare bored into mine until his visage blurred with the involuntary tears he elicited from me as he did his best to pound through my throat. Even with the amount of practice I'd had, taking something that big down my esophagus was a struggle, and I reached up to tug on his balls and hummed around him just to try to hurry him up. When my lips finally met the skin at the base of his dick on every stroke, he picked up the pace until he stilled all the way down and refused to let up. When I tried my best to breathe through my nose, he pinched it off between two knuckles until my throat wildly convulsed around him in an effort to get oxygen.

That's when he finally let loose with jet after pulsing jet of cum straight down my throat. I heaved when he yanked out, coughing and gagging as I tried to suck in air. It was a miracle I didn't throw up everything I'd eaten onto the once pristine floor, now marred with the evidence of our tryst.

By the time I was able to breathe normally, the mortification had set in. When I was high, I never really had the presence of mind to dwell too much on how the clients treated me. Now that I was totally sober and able to appreciate every bit of this embarrassing interaction, I was getting pissed. And then a wet wad of something hit me in the face and slid off to hit the floor. "Clean up your mess, so we can go." I glared up at the previously mild-mannered Giovanni and shook out the paper towel he'd thrown at me. When I started to wipe my face, he snapped at me again. "I meant the floor."

He tried to glare me into submission, but my throat was too sore to even begin to give him a piece of my mind, so I defiantly scrubbed at my face anyway.

"You can wear what you asked for and clean the floor, or I'll try for a round two. Who knows how long that would take." The threat was enough to halt my efforts and abandon my half-cleaned face. Slowly, with death in my stare, I wiped up the splatters of ice cream, spit, and cum from where I'd choked and coughed.

I struggled to my feet, my knees protesting harshly from the abuse they'd sustained. Taking the spoon and tub of half-melted mint chip with me, I flounced out of the kitchen the best I could with sore joints.

Vanni followed me silently all the way back to my room, and the whole time I prayed no one would come up on us. I pushed my door open, only to be brought up short with a hand in my tangled hair. Voice low and growly, Vanni warned me off. "Don't ever fucking try your honey trap bullshit on me again, you understand me, Eden? Better yet, don't try it on *anyone* here. Not a one of us will fall for a whore's routine, and even if you didn't want me to save you, that boy that was infatuated with you demanded I try. He doesn't exist any more than the girl you used to be does, but from time-to-time his voice will echo with just a bit of a conscience I feel the need to listen to. Tony and Santos would rather put you down like the whoring bitch you just proved yourself to be. Don't make me turn on you too. Three against one, and the gardeners will be adding you to the mulch pile. Nod if you understand me." It pulled a few strands from the roots, but I managed a couple short jerks of my head.

After the door locked behind me, I went to the bathroom and threw up, sick with fear and with myself. When I finally finished retching, I washed my disgusting ass face in the sink, then I went and sulked in bed, drinking my now melted ice cream like a milkshake.

It was two days of mostly silence and staring at four walls, except for the new installation of an automatic lock on the outside of my door. Marco came to see me each day, bringing food with him, but he was cold and aloof the whole time. I'd heard shouting on what I thought was the morning after the BJ from hell, and I'd caught my name a few times, along with some other choice words I didn't care to remember—most of it coming from Santos.

After repeatedly begging for some clothes to wear other than the ones that were very obviously theirs, a couple pairs of black leggings and tank tops appeared, along with underwear and a sports bra. It wasn't fabulous, and I didn't have shoes, but it was a vast improvement. It was also the day of my first escape attempt.

T he guys were out again from what I'd overheard through my door, and the doctor had stopped by to check on me and bring me dinner. He sat and watched as I ate so that he could take the utensils back with him. Like I was gonna slit my wrists with a fucking butter knife or some shit. Who knows what the jackasses thought.

I ignored him as I made short work of my plate then got up to wash my hands. Waiting for the doctor to open the bedroom door with his key, I dropped the trash can of water I'd filled onto the floor and let out a screech that brought the older man running. With the light off, he blundered straight into the darkened bathroom, and I slipped out from behind the door and sprinted for the hallway. The doc yelled, but it was too late as I slammed the bedroom door shut, the lock immediately engaging behind me. He'd get it open soon enough with his key, but I'd have a small head start.

Unsure of which way to go, I chose farther down the hall in the opposite direction of the kitchen. At the end, it branched off into two staircases, one leading up and the other down. I was almost positive we were on the first floor, and the basement did *not* seem like an option I wanted to explore, so up it was.

I blindly ran, ducking into wherever my body could fit any time I heard someone. Somehow I ended up in a room with plants, a shit ton of plants. I was fairly certain it was a conservatory due to all the glass... and a balcony. The balcony didn't have a way down, other than the obvious that would likely end up with me breaking something, but it did drop into a courtyard that led off the grounds. I decided to chance the drop and hoped like hell that I landed okay. If I could backflip off a stripper pole in stilettos, a fucking twelve or so foot drop while flat-footed should be a piece of cake.

And it was. Unfortunately, I had a greeting party. "Hello, Eden, long time no talk. I hear the apple definitely didn't fall too far from the tree. You'd think OD'ing like your cokewhore mother and trying to drown in your own vomit would have been a hard pass." The dark voice was different, definitely deeper but still so familiar. And I wanted to hit him as his barbs struck true. Also, since when did my mother take drugs? I didn't really care about her much other than being compared to the cunt, but there wasn't a chance to ask before Santos continued. "Not that you'd know, but there are only a few ways out besides the front door. Doesn't do you any good to run. We have guards."

I went to blast him with the pent up rage stirring in my gut, only to be hoisted over a shoulder and marched into a side door. He unceremoniously tossed me into my prison and slammed the door, ignoring my taunts and epithets just as he had all the way back.

Several more days passed, but now Marco didn't even come in. Instead, he sent a maid while he stood watch at the door. On the fourth day, counted by the meals I'd received, if that was even accurate, someone new showed up. Someone I knew way more than I cared to.

He was a regular at the club and a frequent flyer for lap dances, never able to afford what Danny wanted to charge for free use of my body. My eyes darted to the door as it locked behind him. *No fucking way.* I wasn't sure if I'd survive whatever he had planned with the dark and intense stare he was giving me. There was a reason Danny wouldn't let him near his dancers. After the first couple that didn't make it out in one piece, we all became 'unaffordable.' Danny liked his girls to be largely unmarred with scars or defects, and to have all of their teeth, the ones that would be seen anyway. This man was a sadist and a wannabe, but he was loosely connected to a few of the high-rollers Danny didn't want to make waves with. Well, he *had* been a wannabe. Now, he was here, locked in with me, and from his demeanor there wasn't going to be a rescue this time.

"Hey, uh, you're supposed to wait outside." I tried not to let my voice bobble but was pretty sure I failed.

"Nah, I think we have time for some fun, right, Angel? You know, there are people looking for you, and they'll pay a pretty penny to know you've been taken care of. I'll be long gone before any of them make it back, on my way to a payday big enough to set me flush for a year." And there it was, we were alone in the house. My adrenaline spiked at the icy terror flashing through my body.

The hulking man advanced on me, and I tried to dodge off the bed, but I barely made it to my feet before the first hit came, landing solidly on my ribs and knocking the air out of me. I fought back the best I could, but I couldn't keep away from him indefinitely, not in the limited space with him between me and the door. My only reprieve was when I managed to brace the bathroom door against him until it broke under his onslaught. He dragged me out after an open-handed slap that caught me in my mouth, cutting my lip on a tooth.

"One for the road okay with you, slut?" I screamed as he bent me over the bed, getting my face shoved into the mattress for my efforts. "Shut the fuck up, or it's gonna hurt a lot worse." My leggings were ripped down, the sound of threads popping standing out starkly in the quiet of the room. I refused to open my legs, and they held firm until he started kneeing the backs of my thighs. Even a dancer's muscles can only take so much, and they eventually gave out.

Rough, blunt fingers dug at the soft flesh between my legs as the jangle of a belt being undone echoed in my ears. I took my chance, freeing one of my arms trapped under me to twist and scratch at the man's face. His weight came down over my body, pinning me to bed as he called me a slew of vulgar names, his hand wrapped around my throat until I ceased struggling.

Santos

The lead on who was attempting to orchestrate a coup didn't pan out, so I headed back to the compound early. My head was all sorts of fucked up, from Eden to the concussion I'd gotten myself to the bastards fucking with us, and I wanted to lie down to stop the insistent ache that still lingered two weeks after my bar brawl. If it wasn't for the masochistic need to be close to Eden, I'd have gone home to recuperate. As it stood, my housekeeper was taking care of things until I returned.

I started to walk to my room, the one I always used in Tony's wing of the house, the one I had to pass where Eden was stashed to get to. *And isn't that a constant reminder of the one time I allowed a bitch to get that close to me?* Regardless of the magnetic draw I had to her, the situation was still fucking with my head.

A frown creased my forehead and pulled at my lips at the absence of the guard we'd left posted outside her door. The man was newer and wanted to prove himself. He didn't have any permanent responsibilities yet, so we'd pulled him in to keep Eden locked up when one of us couldn't be here.

And he wasn't at his fucking post. With the mood I was in, he'd be lucky if I didn't kill him once I found him. Before I turned to head off in search of the wayward guard, the sound of a low masculine voice caught my ear. *No fucking way she's at it again.* Vanni and I had about come to blows when he confessed to what happened in the kitchen. As much as I'd wanted to beat his ass, imagining what he'd done made my dick twitch. The mental image of Eden on her knees, choking on a cock, was satisfying in more than one way. If I'd thought I could pull it off without maiming or killing her, I might have given it a go myself.

As I went to unlock the door, ready to blast the guard for incompetence, I heard the unmistakable sound of a slap and hurried to open it to put an end to whatever kinky shit she was up to now.

"Get wet, you whore, I don't want you chafing my dick." The sight of the guard spitting onto the fingers he was pushing back between Eden's legs boiled my blood. *How dare she pull this shit again.* Moans sounded out despite being muffled by the bedding, turning my stomach. And the idiot was so intent on getting a piece, he never noticed me coming closer. "There you go, knew you could do it." A squeal from the prone form in front of him preceded his statement, and that's when I saw the blood. The man, Roger or Ralph or some shit, was inches away from plugging his dick in and *raping* Eden.

My mind blanked out at the blatant violation she'd already suffered, and when I came back to myself, Marco was holding a dry-eyed Eden on his lap, wrapped in a blanket, as they both observed my handiwork. The man was dead, having been beaten until he was unrecognizable, and my hands were covered in blood and fleshier bits of gore. I was splattered in the mess like some gory, abstract painting.

My gaze went from Marco's satisfied one to Eden's, where I expected fear or disgust. The disgust was there, but it wasn't directed at me. No, she glared at the destroyed body on the floor before lifting her head and saying, "Thank you, Santos." After that, the energy holding her up seemed to cut off like a string being clipped, and her head lolled over onto Marco's shoulder while he protectively tucked her further into his body. I was struck by how quickly she'd gone to him and remembered the times she'd been in my arms. I stared at the pair, and after killing a man over her, I could understand Marco's instinct to wrap her up to keep her from harm. My head was a jumbled mess over my recent reactions and thoughts regarding the dark-haired woman. She was a mind-fuck named Eden Moretti.

I didn't know what to say for a long uncomfortable moment. Finally, I got out, "Get the doc and get her fixed up. Then find out what happened and teach her how to defend herself. He was scratched up, but that's about all I remember before I blacked out. Teach her how to use a gun too, if she doesn't know how already. Fucking rapist pig." I kicked the body again for good measure.

"She'd benefit from all of us helping her, I think... even you, Santos," Marco dared to broach. But his next revelation sealed the deal on my help. "When I picked her up to take her out, she wanted to stay even though I was concerned about her injuries. You know what she said? She said that she's fucking used to it, that she knew it would heal. She shouldn't be used to getting hurt and raped, Santos!"

The heart that I'd long thought dead and gone burned in agony for the abuse her thin frame had endured, now and in the past. No one was going to hurt her again, not if I could help it. Things weren't fixed or even tolerable between us, but beating defenseless women was even beyond the Family's purview unless you had a damned good reason.

I turned on my heel and left to clean up while Marco got on his phone to call the doc—again.

nine
alone
Marco

What the fuck is going on? I couldn't wrap my head around the events of the last few days. First, Vanni pulled that bullshit with the fucked up blow job from Eden, which pissed me off to no end. Vanni could've just called her out on the stunt she was trying to pull, but because he'd quietly carried a torch for her that burned as hot as the ones we'd all had at some point or another, he lost that normally hard to rouse temper. He desperately didn't want Tony to be right about her, but that was currently how it looked to be going. I'd been equally pissed at Eden for sinking so low, and giving her the cold shoulder was my way of coping with the fact that she was no longer the sweet, innocent girl we once knew.

There were moments I saw it—the old her. But it was just a passing flicker. You blinked and it was gone. I wanted to believe that she would see that despite us holding her here, we meant her no harm. Well, most of us didn't. I still wasn't convinced Santos wouldn't put a bullet in her if given the chance—and maybe Tony. Santos' bender was proof that her presence was fucking with his already fragile psyche. That guy has been holding onto his last thread of humanity for so long, and we had all been waiting for that pivotal moment when the thread snapped. The state he was in when Vanni brought him back had shown we were nearing that moment. Fast.

And we were right. That bastard who was supposed to be watching over Eden made the mistake of trying to rape her, and Santos had been the one to walk in on it.

The brutality with which he'd bludgeoned that guy with his bare hands was almost enough to turn my stomach with fear over the man Santos had become. Roy—or whatever the hell his name was— was just a slipping mess of human sinew by the time I managed to drag Santos from him. It had been a feat for sure, and Eden was a violently shaking mess that I needed to comfort. Santos' rage hadn't helped that one bit.

Eden's torn clothes, bruised body, and bloodied face were all I needed to see to know what that bastard had done to her and why Santos had reacted the way he had. I was only jealous I hadn't gotten there first.

I had half-expected Eden to cower away from me when I approached her, but to my shock, she launched herself into my arms. Lifting her into a bridal hold, I sat down with her in my lap, dragging the blanket up and over her shaking form.

After Santos said his piece about getting her seen by the doc and demanding she be shown self-defense, he left. I held Eden tighter, trying to convey to her that she was safe. The man was dead.

"I thought he would... but Santos..."

"Shhh. He's gone. I'm so sorry, Edie. We should've just left watching you to the four of us. This is on us for putting a new guy in charge of you. It won't happen again." That last part I delivered in a deadly serious tone.

No one will ever fucking touch her again. For the most part, I had made sure to show Eden the softer side of me while she'd been here. I wanted her to see she could trust me, and if she knew the dark and twisted shit I'd done, she might think differently of me.

Santos wasn't the only one to have beaten a man to death. He might be the enforcer when it came to our group in the Family, but he was far from the only one with blood on his hands. Torture a part of getting information from people like the guy who tried to rape her, and I'd volunteered more times than I could count, helping to perform such atrocities. But while Santos' approach was brutal and frenzied, I'd always been more calculated. I was the guy who took over after Santos had softened them up and needed a break before he broke his own hands. I was the guy who knew how to fuck with their minds and push them the rest of the way over the line. And I would use all of that expertise if anyone tried to take Eden from me again.

That was a fucking promise.

"Thank you, Marco Polo," Eden suddenly said to me, using the nickname she'd chosen for me after my countless ones for her. It was a terrible one, but it put the first smile on my face that I'd had in days.

"Anytime, Lady Garden. Are you okay if I leave you for a minute, so I can dispose of the trash and call the doc?"

She nodded against my chest, pushing herself off my lap and to her feet. "I'm going to go shower. I need to scrub off the feel of his hands on me."

"You do that. You don't need to see this anyway. Until we get all the blood cleaned up, you can stay in my room. I'll take the couch."

She stopped at the doorway of the bathroom and glanced back at me in surprise. "Not afraid I'll try to escape?"

I chuckled. "I'd like to see you try."

A small smile split across her bloodied lips, but she said nothing before entering the bathroom and shutting the door. Waiting until I heard the sound of the shower running, I reached down and hefted the dead body over my shoulder. I groaned in disgust when the man's blood soaked through my shirt, wondering how I'd gotten stuck with clean up. Knowing no one would think twice about a body in the yard here, I took him outside and unceremoniously dropped him on the front lawn. I shot off a text to Vanni and Tony, telling them to get back ASAP.

Santos was nowhere to be seen when I headed back inside. I assumed he'd either gone upstairs to cool off or taken a walk, and I had better shit to do than go chasing after him. After stripping the bloody sheets from Eden's bed and tossing them in the laundry room, I grabbed some fresh clothes for her and set them on the floor outside the bathroom.

By the time I was done talking to the doc, Eden stepped out from the bedroom, wringing the hem of her shirt tightly between her hands.

"Doc is on the way," I told her. She bobbed her head in acknowledgment but didn't meet my eyes. "You need anything?"

"Maybe just some sleep," she replied softly, finally lifting her eyes to mine. I nodded and motioned for her to follow me. Without hesitation, she trailed up the stairs behind me.

When we reached the top landing, heavy metal music was blasting from behind the door to the room

Santos stayed in when he was here. That answered my earlier question.

Eden glanced at it as we passed but said nothing. I opened the last door in the hall and gently nudged her in. She looked around for a moment before walking over and settling on the edge of my massive bed. She was so small, it seemed to swallow her.

I cleared my throat. "I'll, uh, wait for the doc. You should rest until he gets here. Just shout if you need anything."

Before I could turn and leave, she shot off the bed and wrapped her arms around my waist. The hug surprised me, so I ended up standing there awkwardly. Noticing my tense state, she released me quickly.

"Sorry. I just wanted to thank you— again —for being kind to me. This isn't the first time someone has done this to me, but it's the first time I was treated like a victim and not some whore who'd asked for it. So... thank you."

My blood boiled at the reminder that she'd endured this before. That someone had violated her and acted as if she'd wanted it or deserved it. I swallowed down the fury and pulled her back into me, taking control of the hug this time.

She felt so good in my arms, and there'd been so many times I wanted this, but the circumstances were tainting it for me. Whoever had made that asshole so confident he could do as he pleased was going down. I looked forward to inflicting some of the same pain and suffering that Eden had endured, and wouldn't lose an ounce of sleep over it.

I let her go and led her to my bed, dragging the blankets over her as she snuggled down. "No one will touch you like that again, Eden," I promised in a whisper before leaving the room. After closing her door, I went to Santos' and pounded on it. There was a loud curse before the music was turned down and the door flung open.

He glared at me, but I shook my head, warning him not to start shit, and pointed downstairs. He seemed to get what I was saying and nodded, following me without a word.

Tony and Vanni would be here any minute, and it was time we had a Family meeting to figure out where we would go from here.

I just hoped whatever Tony decided, Eden would be okay.

ten
blood water
Eden

I was woken up by a tapping at the door before it swung open. I felt like I'd just fallen asleep, and I probably had. When a member of the Family called, I was sure the doc came running. I sat up with a groan and threw back the bedding before trying to swing my legs over the side.

"Motherfucker, that hurts," I grunted out as my *everything* pulled and burned. It was a toss-up as to which body part hurt the most. I hadn't felt this bad, well, since I nearly starred in a snuff scene the night I arrived.

"Let me help, Miss Moretti," the doctor demanded as he hurried to the bed and sat his bag down on the foot of it. "I was told you were attacked and needed medical attention. You sure do manage to get up to a lot for a woman in your situation." The man clucked over my bruised face as he took my vitals and asked his inane questions. *Yes, everything fucking hurts. Idiot.* Although his saltiness might have been a bit deserved... I did lock him in a bathroom when I tried to escape. "I think it best to get some pain relief set up before I go any farther with the exam. Would you like one of the others to be present for the rest of it?"

It took a second for his meaning to sink in, and my eyes rolled of their own accord at his attempt at modesty or whatever the fuck his malfunction was with me getting naked in front of him. He must have gotten the drift because his lips pursed in what I imagined was disapproval, and he took out a syringe that had my heart about to skip a happy beat. Without even asking what it was, I stuck my arm out, fully on board with escaping the pain.

A couple short minutes later, the edges of the world went fuzzy, my favorite place to be. This was what it was like when I first started using, a soft bliss drip through my veins while I coasted through clouds of indifference.

Tony

I was sent to be the errand boy in my own damned house. Apparently, I was the only one that wasn't thinking with my dick or blinded by years of sorrow turned to rage. Hell, Vanni had been the first to whip it out, even if it was to teach the opportunistic bitch a lesson. "Fucking pussy-struck, the lot of them," I mumbled irritably as I came up on Marco's door.

My hand paused when the doc's voice reached my ears, the door unlatched enough to see through a slim crack.

"You want me to do *what*?" His incredulity had ice cold fury shooting though my body; surely, she wasn't propositioning him already. I wondered for a moment, but then I glanced up at the mirrored ceiling Marco loved. The man was a narcissist *and* a pervert, but it gave me a bird's eye view of the room.

The sight of Eden splayed out naked on Marco's bed with a towel under her, various white bandages littering her battered frame, and the doc between her legs didn't help my anger. Until she responded in a soft and slurred voice.

"I've had worse, man. Just glue the shit shut, it worked last time." I stood frozen, a voyeur to what was transpiring. My need to know exactly what was going on overrode my desire to bust in and start making accusations.

"You've glued your vagina shut before?" I couldn't see his face, but I could imagine his shock—it probably matched mine. *What the hell kind of kinky shit has she been doing?*

"Yes, well, no, well, kinda. See, when you're

seventeen and your mom kicks you out with whatever you can grab in an hour, and then you take the money you helped save out of her account, you can't really go to a clinic or hospital. Not for sexual assault anyway... they call your parents." I wondered if her story was true, or if she was trying to get sympathy from Doc, but he just made commiserating noises and waited for her to continue. My eyes narrowed at whatever his game was. It wasn't his place to interrogate anyone. I got sidetracked from my train of thought when Eden spoke up again.

"Marco was so worried about me being traumatized by nearly being raped, and it wasn't fun, especially being lucid when it happened, but I was more in shock over nearly dying. I didn't fucking do anything to anyone. For years, I've just been trying to *exist*. Why would someone want me dead for that? Anyway, Santos saving me was a serious mindfuck. Honestly, I thought he'd have been more likely to finish the job. Anyway, it was nice to have someone care too. It's been awhile for that." She raised her head up off the pillow, a wince crossing her swollen purple and blue face as she squinted at the doc. "Hey, you gonna do some maintenance down there or just get your jollies from staring at it? It's not free, and it's currently out of commission, so hurry up or I'm getting dressed."

That seemed to snap Doc out of his stupor and piss him off at the same time. "I was *waiting* for you to get to the gluing part of the story, *Miss* Moretti, but I can get started. You'll feel a couple pinches before it numbs up. I'm *not* using glue. It's a wonder your test came back clean after the shoddy medical care and habits you have."

"And exactly how would you know that? Not your damn business!" She'd learn *everything* was my business. *Ungrateful witch.*

"Antonio requested a blood sample be taken to check the overall state of your health. It's all clear, by the way, as I previously stated."

"It wasn't his place, nor yours, without my consent," she fumed.

"If I might suggest a consideration?" At her grudging nod, he continued, "Be happy you got the free healthcare and you have nothing to worry about besides some general malnourishment." Whether the pain meds were overcoming her or she'd decided it wasn't worth fighting, I didn't know, but she let it go. Almost, anyway.

"Do it again and I won't just shut you in a bathroom. No, it's going to be painful if any of you fuckers pull bullshit again. I'm a person. *Ask.*"

"Fine, Miss Moretti, I'll do my best to secure your permission if the matter arises and you're lucid. Now, you need a couple sutures for an external tear, and a quick exam at the least to make sure there's nothing internal. And I'm still interested in that glue." I had a feeling he wasn't, that it was more to distract Eden than anything.

"Fine," she huffed out as he got to work. As he pressed the needle to her flesh, I had a hard time concentrating on the rest of her story, pissed beyond reason that she needed stitches in such a sensitive place.

"Where was I? Oh, yes, I remember. I was broke and panhandling after the money ran out; fifteen hundred just doesn't get you far in the city. Anyway, these guys come up and want to know how much. Well, I'd only had sex once, and I wasn't quite hungry enough yet to take them up on their offer, so I tried to walk away with a polite refusal. Except guys like that don't take no for an answer. They dragged me off into an alley and pushed me down onto a pile of cardboard. I didn't even care about rats or needles or what I was laying in— I was just fucking terrified. Of course, it only got worse from there. They didn't even do more than expose the parts they needed. Two held me down while the third had his way first, then they swapped places. But the last one, he didn't like how loose it was, no matter that it was all sorts of fucked up and their fault to begin with. At least the blood and cum from the first one slicked the way of the second. The third... well, I learned how important prep work is for taking it up the ass. Ouch! The fuck, dude?"

The doc mumbled an apology, and I could see

his shoulders were set just as rigidly as my entire body. If this was some made up story for attention... I didn't have a problem with violence against women as a whole, like the hooker that had been with Eden, but undeservedly beating them or raping them in an alley *just because* wasn't something I went around doing. There was no honor to be found in those who did.

"Oh, the glue, that's right. Sorry, this is some nice shit you gave me, Doc. *Anyway,* the assholes finished and threw a wadded up twenty at me before walking away, ranting that I should be lucky they paid at all because my service sucked. I was nearly petrified that they'd given me HIV or knocked me up, and everything hurt... I got back to the dump I shared with a couple other girls, and they helped me get cleaned up. One of them used to give blow jobs to a paramedic on the regular, and he paid her in first-aid shit and pills when he could get them. Usually gave her syringes and whatnot for the drugs, but sometimes he'd give her other stuff... like surgical glue. So there I am, whisker biscuit all sorts of banged up, and my roommate pulls out this purple shit in a syringe. She tells me she's gonna put it back together like a shattered knickknack you don't want your mom to find out about. Burned like a bitch, but hey, it worked." She shrugged from her prone position, seemingly unconcerned that the doc was finishing with shaking hands.

I was about to announce my presence when he asked his next question, anger palpable in his voice. "And why did your mother kick you out, Miss Moretti?" He gave her another shot of something in the thigh that she barely acknowledged, then slipped her shorts back over her feet.

Eden launched into that story a bit more clearly and with bitterness coating every word while she slowly finished dressing. "She wasn't too happy when she caught my boyfriend's dad trying to put the moves on me since he was already fucking her. And although she was pissed at his suggestion that he'd trade her in for a new model, aka me, when said boyfriend got tired of me, she didn't give a fuck that my asshole boyfriend was apparently just setting me up to be his mistress all along. Like father, like son, I guess." Eden paused as if lost in the memory before she continued. "Anyway, she gave me an hour to pack what I could in a duffel bag. Come to find out, the boy I'd given my virginity to less than twenty-four hours prior had known all along and thought I'd be happy with it. Funny how I ended up being a whore anyway, huh?" She didn't add anything else, and when I looked closely, I could see she'd passed out.

"I know you're there, Mr. Carlotti. Please, come in."

"How's she doing? Anything that needs more than you can handle?"

"So no comment on what she just rambled out?" At my hard stare, Doc sighed and shook his head but moved along. "No, just going to take a while to heal up. I'm going to give her a couple vitamin injections to help bolster her immune system. They're somewhat like the banana bag I gave her before, but they should help her heal at least somewhat better. Her blood panel was low on just about everything, and this type of thing isn't helping. I can call in some prescription prenatal vitamins that will help more than a regular multivitamin, but she's going to need to lay off the narcotics and take them for at least a year to replenish what she's depleted."

He squared his shoulders, gaze defiant, before adding, "It's not my place to ask questions, but a bit of advice? If you plan on her sticking around, get her healthy. I can't say that the damage already done to her body from her circumstances or the chemicals won't have long-term effects. I'm going to leave some supplies in the bathroom." He muttered the next bit, scowling all the while. "At this rate, I'll be back tomorrow." The doc shook his head again and cleaned up his supplies, storing the extras in the cupboard under the vanity.

Admittedly, I was somewhat surprised he'd been so candid, but he *had* been around for years and was a friend of Father's, so maybe, in hindsight, I should have expected it. I followed him out when he left after a quick glance at a sleeping Eden. We'd have to wait until she woke to ask her exactly what the guard had said. Rafe Trillo, one of the newer soldiers wanting to work his way up the food chain, was definitely not going to be answering anything. I couldn't blame Santos for tearing into him, but it would have been easier to interrogate the source directly. And what the fuck was I going to tell him about what I'd overheard Eden say? I wasn't sure it was even worth bringing up. Rodrigo was one of our best money-men and had been loyal for decades. I'd hate to lose him over a ploy to garner sympathy. Best to run it by the head of the Family first. Mumbling again about the pussy-struck idiots that my inner circle had become, I headed back to them to figure out our next steps, my own nerves just barely buzzing beneath the surface of my skin. I was *not* looking forward to a trip to the manor to explain to my father how we'd let someone without loyalty onto the property.

eleven
get free
Eden

It took a few days for some of the pain to abate. Tylenol was pretty much my only choice for pain medication since the doc believed it was better I steer clear of anything harder. Couldn't say I didn't agree with him no matter how badly I wanted to fall back into old habits. The dead guard had been a stark example of what staying on my current path could result in, and since I was sober, it really hit home. On the brightside, I could move fine with the two stitches I'd ended up with on my inner labia, and the doc would take them out in a couple days if it healed quickly. My best guess was I'd caught a fingernail from the rapist asshole. Unfortunately, not much could be done for my throat; the damage just had to heal on its own. The rasp hadn't gone away, and there was still bruising. I'd tried to avoid talking much the last couple of days, but it seemed that my silence was about to come to an end.

Because I had an appointment with Vincenzo Carlotti. He'd been briefed on my attack and had questions for me. I couldn't very well say no to him either.

So here I sat in his office at the manor, anxiously bouncing my leg as I waited for the boss himself to come interrogate me. The few times I'd briefly met Vinnie had been years ago, with little words exchanged and the buffer of one of the guys with me. This time it was just me and Vinnie. No barriers, no escape. And I was terrified.

The door to the office opened, signaling the appearance of the head of the Family. I sat up straighter and kept my eyes forward as he walked past me toward a mini bar to my left. I snuck glances, watching him pour some dark liquid from a glass decanter and drop in a cube of ice.

The man had barely changed in the last decade, his presence just as imposing as it had been back then. The only noticeable difference was more gray in his otherwise jet black hair and beard. He'd not let his broad muscular figure go even though he had to be pushing sixty, and when his piercing dark eyes met mine as he settled into the large leather chair behind the desk, I felt myself involuntarily swallow in trepidation.

"Miss Moretti, it's been some time."

I nodded, avoiding full eye contact with him. "It has."

He let out a noncommittal hum in response, tipping back his glass and downing the contents while I waited. Once empty, he set the glass down and leaned across the mahogany desk, folding his hands together.

"How did you know the man that accosted you?" I twisted my hands into the hem of my shirt, anger searing through me. I knew before coming here I shouldn't say anything stupid or anger Vinnie, but I had never been one to hold my tongue.

"Accosted? Like I was out for a stroll and he just happened upon me? We both know I've been an unwilling guest, and I was locked up with the sick fuck set to make sure I didn't stray." I wanted to slap my hands over my mouth and pretend I'd said nothing. But I'd found my backbone and wouldn't back down, and frankly, I was over all the bullshit.

Surprisingly, Vinnie showed no reaction to my outburst. He simply leaned back and pulled a cigar from a drawer in his desk. After clipping the end and lighting it up, he took a puff and merely stared at me for a moment.

Finally, he replied calmly, "Do you think I'm unaware that you've attempted to flee more than once? What were your plans once you'd gotten away from the grounds, to run to the police?" The warning in his tone that was loud and clear. That I better not have even entertained the thought.

Before I could answer, he continued. "You didn't answer my question. And if I have to repeat myself, you'll find yourself needing Carlos' attention. Again."

Knowing defiance wouldn't be tolerated, I tucked a stray hair behind my ear and carefully answered, "He would come into the place I worked sometimes, Cherry Baby down on the strip. He couldn't afford me, and he didn't like it. Or that was always the boss' excuse. He gave me the creeps, and that's saying something with the types that I *entertained* on the regular."

He took another long drag of his cigar and looked at me with a contemplative gaze. "What did he want? I have a hard time believing he'd risk being beaten to death to get his prick wet. No offense to your... charms..."

I flinched a bit at the remark and felt that swell of anger rise once again. *Well, I've never claimed to be the smartest person.*

"He said there were people that have a price on my head, so he was going to have a go then get his payday," I spat, then added, "I don't know anything else. I was too busy getting choked and mauled. Can I go now? Talking hurts my throat." I just wanted to be done but wasn't sure what else he wanted from me or what more I could offer him.

"When I'm through getting the answers I need. I

believe you know nothing else about your attack, but that's not what you're here for. I want to know what went down that night at Cherry Baby when my boys brought you here without my knowledge."

Oh shit. This had never been about that raping bastard. That was a front to what he really wanted to know. If I would talk or not. Vinnie was not only a highly intelligent man, but he also had eyes everywhere. There was no mistaking he knew exactly what went down that night, but he didn't want the truth. He wanted to know that I had a story to tell that wouldn't blow back on him or the Family. If I ever wanted to be free, this was my moment to convince him that I wasn't a threat.

"Honestly, I don't remember much about that night," I deadpanned, my lie coming easily. "I had taken several narcotics and could barely stand without the aid of the men I was servicing. All I remember is the popping of gunshots and ending up on the floor beneath a table. There was blood everywhere, but my head was spinning. The guys were suddenly there, and they helped me. Apparently, I overdosed, so they had a doctor take care of me. I've just been detoxing and hiding out in case whoever did the shooting was still looking for me."

I mentally patted myself on the back, immediately knowing by his slight bit of smile that was exactly what he wanted to hear.

"Yes. I think that sounds about right. See to it

that your story doesn't change, Miss Moretti, or your problems will only multiply."

I bowed my head to him, noting that he was giving me one chance and one chance only to show I'd keep my mouth shut. Despite how horribly I'd been treated by most of the guys while here, I still would never be stupid enough to talk to anyone about what I'd truly witnessed.

"We're done for now. Marco will see you back to Antonio's. We'll discuss our plans for you at a later time," he said, much to my dismay, before he tapped a button on his desk phone. A moment later, Marco opened the office door, dashing my hope of being released.

"Uncle?" he asked, nodding his head respectfully at Vinnie.

"You may take Miss Moretti back now, then I'd like you to tell Antonio he's needed here."

"Right away. Come on, Eden." Marco held his hand out to me. Standing, I placed my hand in his, not offering Vinnie a backward glance as Marco pulled me from the room.

I tried to tell myself this was a good win for the day, that I was one step closer to freedom, but I knew deep down nothing would be that simple. There was still so much to do if I wanted to leave this place. Then I'd disappear again, this time far away from the reach of the Carlotti Family.

No Good Deed

For the first time in weeks, I found myself alone in Antonio's home. Marco dropped me off at the front door, stating he had to run a few errands and that there was a surprise in my room. Vanni was seeing to some business matters across town, and Tony would be at the manor meeting with Vinnie before he returned. I was also reminded that while I had the freedom to move around the house, I had best not leave it since armed guards patrolled the property. Santos wasn't mentioned, but I figured he was probably the type that came and went as he pleased with no one aside from Tony knowing his exact whereabouts at any given time. In all honesty though, after my talk with Vinnie, I knew it was in my own self-interest not to try and escape. At least not yet. I was lucky Vinnie had so readily accepted the story I'd concocted, but his lenience would only exist so long as I didn't cause trouble. I'd have to wait for an opportune moment to make an escape.

For now, I busied myself by seeing what Marco had left. I found a department store bag with jeans, a few tops, and *shoes*! They weren't anything fancy, but they were quality brand trainers, and I immediately tried them on with a pair of jeans. They were half a size too big, but I wasn't going to complain. It was just nice to have something on my feet. In the bottom of the bag was a compact makeup palette, mascara, and eyeliner. It all bore the name of the cosmetic line the store carried, and I was a bit touched that he'd gone to the trouble of getting it all for me. I put everything away, planning on trying it out after I'd gotten something to eat, but I got sidetracked by a show playing on the big screen TV in the living room, and the freedom of being out of my room won.

I watched the reality show until an infomercial came on, then I grabbed some yogurt and browsed while kicking back on the couch. Many channels were flipped through before I decided on a show about four old ladies that lived together and spent every waking moment making jokes at the others' expense. It was quite funny, and I ended up binging a few episodes before the hunger pains annoyingly crept in again. Having an appetite was a new thing for me.

My secret for staying skinny had nothing to do with good dieting, though all the dancing certainly helped. After years of drug use, I simply rarely felt hungry. Shockingly enough, I was starting to see some meat on my bones. It wasn't much, but I was looking healthier. Minus the bumps and bruises I still sported.

I nosed around the kitchen, familiarizing myself with what was in the cabinets and fridge before deciding a simple sandwich was best. Pulling out the turkey, cheese, and mayo, I went to work. I'd just finished putting it all together when the front door opened.

I turned, expecting it to be one of the guys, ready to greet whoever it was. But the man who walked in was the *last* person I wanted to see.

"Well, hello there. Came here to find my son but I find a pretty little thing like you instead," Rodrigo purred at me from the kitchen doorway.

Surprised, I dropped my plate on the counter and stepped away until my back hit the counter behind me.

His eyes widened in shock as recognition dawned on him, a sinister grin spreading wide across his lips. "I remember you. You look just like your mother. No wonder you've been hidden away from everyone here." He walked closer, and I gripped the counter edge hard, my fingertips pushing painfully against the underside of it.

"Santos isn't here. What do you want?" I demanded, trying to disguise my unease as anger. I hated this man more than I'd ever hated anyone.

"Still as mouthy now as you were then," he growled, stalking farther into the kitchen. When he reached me, his hand roughly snatched my chin between his fingers. "Tell me, has my son had his way with you since you've been here? He was your first after all and I bet the best you ever had. Like father, like son."

He pushed his body against mine, pinning me between him and the counter. Bile rolled around in my stomach, flashbacks of that fateful day when Rodrigo had his hands on me dancing through my mind. All at once, I felt sick and pissed off that he would dare touch me again. *Not again.*

"Get your fucking hands off me."

Rodrigo scoffed at my demand. "You don't have a say here, you little bitch. You think my son hated you when I told him how you came onto me and made off with his mother's jewelry? Just wait 'til I tell him you came at me for round two."

I shoved at his chest, but he had me blocked too tightly against the counter to be effective.

"I would *never* fucking touch you, you bastard. Not for all the fucking money and drugs in this goddamn world," I spat at him viciously. I might not be able to fight him off physically, but I was no longer that timid girl he'd intended to groom.

"Big words for some homeless junkie whore," he retorted. "Let me make this simple for you, you stupid bitch. Your miserable, pathetic life is a direct result of being an obstinate little girl that couldn't fall in line. I made sure Santos hates you, and if you think for one second I can't make your life even worse, think again. I'm part of the Family and have connections and loyalty. You have nothing, so I suggest next time I come to you, you bend that sweet little ass over and beg for it."

And there it was. Like lightning striking, the agonizing realization hit me. Santos had never planned to hide me away. He hadn't known what his father had done to me, and worse, he believed I'd stolen something of his mother's when I left. It was all becoming clear now that we'd both been lied to and manipulated. It also shed some light on why Marco had accused me of being the one to hurt Santos. Why he was now this darker, more violent version of the sweet and gentle guy I had fallen in love with so many years ago.

"You sick son of a bitch," I whispered, horrified at how easily I'd been entangled in something so horrific. How could someone do that to their son? My heart felt shattered by the betrayal that had been done to not only me, but to Santos. I knew Rodrigo had never been particularly fond of me, but Santos was his fucking kid and by all appearances, he had doted on him.

Only a monster could orchestrate something so hateful and cruel.

"It's you who's the bitch," Rodrigo growled, his lip curled in a ruthless manner. He savagely gripped my arms and turned me around so that my front was pinned to the counter, my hips mercilessly ground into it as he pushed his dick against my ass. He twisted his hand into my hair and yanked my head back. I hissed in pain as he angled my head, bringing my ear to his lips. "Now, be a good little whore and give me what I want."

My skin crawled when his fingers brushed my stomach as he gripped the waistband of my jeans, trying to yank them down. Suddenly, a deep voice shouted, "What the fuck is going on?"

I knew that voice without even having to look. Thankfully, Rodrigo had released me and stepped back, and relief rushed through me when I turned and found Santos' furious gaze planted firmly on his father. He stepped into the kitchen and moved to put himself between me and Rodrigo.

"Nothing she didn't ask for, son. You should know. You're the one who had your heart broken by the little bitch."

Fast as a snake, Santos' hand shot out, punching Rodrigo in the face. There was a definitive crack upon impact. He stumbled back, crashing into the counter on the opposite side of the kitchen with a bang. Blood spurted from his nose, which was clearly broken, and his breath whooshed out, the wind having been knocked out of him.

"Get the fuck out before a busted nose is the least of your fucking problems," Santos spat venomously at him. Rodrigo spit the blood that had run into his mouth onto the floor at Santos' feet, saying nothing as he left the house. After we heard the car leave, Santos turned and leveled me with a concerned stare.

"You okay?"

I nodded, not really sure what to say at the moment. Shock at both what I'd learned and that Santos had come to my aid left me at a loss for words.

"Go get some rest. I'll deal with my father." He pivoted away without another word, but then a thought occurred to me.

"Did you hear what he said?" I asked, unable to stop myself. He stilled, glancing over his shoulder.

"I heard enough. He won't be bothering you again."

I let him leave then and slid down to the floor. Exhaling, I began to process exactly what had just transpired and all I'd learned. This changed everything, yet it still somehow changed nothing.

What the fuck am I going to do with this?

twelve
break you hard
Santos

That fucking bastard.

My father had taken the one person in this fucked up world that I'd truly cared about and turned her against me. Why though?

No. This can't be true.

Even though I'd heard the words with my own ears, I couldn't accept them. My father was my mentor. My rock. He'd raised me on his own and given me everything—taught me about the world and how to survive in it. I trusted him as I did my best friends and Vincenzo. There was no way he would do this to me. No. Fucking. Way.

After my father rushed from the house, I made sure Eden was okay. Rodrigo was lucky all I did was hit him, because at the moment, I wanted to murder the bastard. But I had to do this the right way. He wasn't just some hired meat bag I could kill and bury like he never existed. Rodrigo had rank within the Family. I needed to get out of here and think it over.

Asking Eden if she was okay was about all I could manage to do before I left with the amount of rage coursing through me. Sliding into my car, I turned the ignition and headed down the drive. The conversation I'd heard burned through my mind, overtaking my every thought like a cancer. I'd barely made it inside my house when I lost it.

My fist went through the first wall I reached, scattering drywall and dust as I continued to punch over and over again. I screamed and cursed, out of my mind. Eventually, I tired myself out and slipped down to sit on the floor amid the mess I'd made.

I needed to calm the fuck down and figure this out. I needed to be sure that what I'd heard was the truth. Tomorrow, I'd ask Eden one time and one time only about what had happened all those years ago. And I promised myself that I'd believe whatever she said despite not having done so these last few weeks. Only then would I be able to come to terms with this.

Either she really was a lying whore, or my father was a manipulative asshole. Neither outcome boded well for me. On one hand, the guilt from how I'd treated Eden would eat away at me if she'd been innocent of anything all this time. On the other, I'd be losing my father and the role model that I'd looked up to since I was a child.

It was a lose-lose situation, and there was no way I was prepared for the resolution.

Tomorrow... tomorrow I'd finally know.

That morning I wasted no time getting in my car and heading back to Tony's. I'd spent the whole night pondering what I'd overheard, leaving me little room to fully relax. When my car slid to a stop in front of the house, I saw that Marco's car was there, giving me some relief that she wasn't alone.

When I stomped into the house, Marco looked up at me from his place on the couch in surprise at my abrupt entrance.

"Santos, what are you-"

"Where is she?"

"Taking a shower," he replied, pointing toward the hallway. He went to ask something else, but I held my hand out and left him staring after me as I went to find Eden. When I reached the bathroom door, I barged in, not caring what she was doing or that she was naked. This conversation was happening before I lost my nerve.

"We need to talk." I gave her the briefest of warnings before opening the shower door and stepping into the stall, not caring that I was dressed and already getting soaked. Eden shrieked and launched her fist in my direction, but I caught it before she could land the hit, using the appendage to keep her from trying to escape.

"What the fuck are you doing?" she demanded, trying to pry her wrist from my iron grasp.

Instead, I shoved her hard against the wall, placing a hand over her mouth. Water rained down on us both as we stood there with my body pressing against hers. A whimper of pain reverberated against my hand, and shame rolled through me. I'd gotten so wrapped up in my own head that I'd forgotten her injuries. I eased back, but the bastard that I was, I still needed answers.

"I'm only going to ask one time and don't fucking lie to me," I warned. She glared at me but nodded. "Did my father manipulate everything that happened with us? Did he really convince you that we were only together because I wanted you as a side-piece?"

Her eyes widened in shock then searched mine for a moment before turning wary. I released her mouth and waited as she formed her thoughts.

"You heard that part?"

"Yes, the tail end of it, and now I need to know if it was true or if I'm yet again being manipulated." My hand went to her throat, fingers wrapping around it firmly enough to let the threat speak for itself. "Again, don't. Fucking. Lie."

She swallowed hard, her throat moving beneath

my palm. "It was true. He told me I was there to be your mistress. When I texted you, asking about it, you acted as if you knew what I was talking about."

My brows bunched together as I tried to remember when I'd ever said anything like that. When I did, incredulous anger filled me at the gross misunderstanding of that long ago conversation. "I was talking about telling my father how I felt about you! That I was going to ask you to move into a place with me! You refused to see or call me, then you left a letter and ran!"

She shoved me hard, but it didn't faze me. I stood steadfast. "What fucking letter? I packed my shit as fast as I could then sat waiting and hoping for my mother to change her mind while your messages proved exactly what our parents had said." Did she really not write that letter? I didn't get a chance to ask because she wasn't done yet.

"And don't yell at me because your father is a disgusting piece of shit who lied and tried to fuck me in your kitchen! I gave you every part of me, and you let me go. He put his hands me and told me about how he'd arranged for me to be your fucking whore like my mother was to him." Her body trembled with every word. "Why the fuck would I stay if you were a part of that?! You crushed my fucking heart and treated me like trash when you saw me again! You turned everyone against me! So get the fuck off your high horse, Santos, before it throws you off onto your ass!"

Shock and a knee-jerk reaction to deny her accusations had me frozen in place. Her voice had become raspy from the yelling, reminding me again that she was still very much hurting from her encounters with both my father and the traitorous bastard that was now decomposing in an unmarked grave.

A gut feeling that she was being completely candid shifted my perspective on everything that had transpired up until now. Unsure of how I could ever repair the damage or the rift between us, I leaned into her, making her back up against the wall, but this time I was more cognizant of the bruises that marred her beautiful skin. My wet shirt rode up, putting my flesh against hers and making me increasingly aware of how much of her body was touching mine. Even years later, I could still remember how it had felt to have her writhing beneath me, her body rubbing sinuously against mine. Her skin had been so soft, so tempting. After the way I'd treated her, I was a bastard for wishing it hadn't only been that one time, but it was impossible not to.

"Listen to me, Eden Moretti, as I will only say this once. I had no idea what my father had done or said to you that day. After what happened with my father, if you say you didn't write a letter, then I believe you. I would try apologizing for the way I handled it, but I'm shit at apologies, and it wouldn't mean squat now. However, I *can* promise I will never treat you like that ever again."

I really did believe her, and I hoped my words were enough for now. Maybe someday we could sort out the whole thing if she ever forgave me. She had been a victim of my father's perversions, and I'd played right into his manipulation like the fucking idiot teenager I'd been. It had cost me the one woman I'd loved and resulted in years without her, leaving me stuck in an abyss of hate and vengeance.

No more. Rodrigo De Luca was dead to me, and if I had my way, he'd be banished from the Family. That was the last favor I'd give that fucker instead of killing him like I would had it been anyone but blood. Maybe I could even convince Vinnie to let me take his hands as punishment for touching Eden at all. Or at least a finger or two if not.

Eden's chest heaved between us, bringing me back to the reality that I was in her shower. However, the will to step away from her was lost. Her eyes bored into me, filled with obvious disdain, as if she wasn't sure what I was still doing in here, and honestly, I wasn't either.

"You expect me to take all of that as the truth, but what about the Carlotti girl you were supposed to marry? Is she hidden away somewhere, waiting on her erstwhile husband to show up whenever it suits him? Marco told me you have a room here, but you don't actually live here." I had no clue what she was going on about, but she continued, each word filled with hate and anguish.

"Even my mother was only pissed that I was offered to take her spot when you got tired of me. She at me, told me how naïve and stupid I was when I explained that you only had condoms as a curiosity. She said she'd seen the girls you were with behind my back." Utter disbelief coursed through me at the blatant lies that had been told. Paired with the abuse she'd suffered from my father on more than one occasion, I was devastated on her behalf.

"Never. None of that ever happened. There were no girls, to marry or otherwise." I swallowed thickly, the turbulent emotions bouncing around in me making me want to rage and at the same time to wrap up the woman in front of me and never let her go. My hand convulsed with impotent anger, her flinch reminding me that I still held her captive. I released her throat to slowly slide my hand downward until it settled over her rapidly beating heart, relishing the feel of her hot wet skin. She let out a light gasp, bringing my attention from where my hand had stopped between her breasts back to her eyes. "Ang— Eden," I corrected myself, "the only girl I ever planned to marry was you. The only girl I've ever really been with is you."

"Santos..." she whispered, my name a soft plea on her lips, as confusion and past hurt filled her gaze.

I wanted more. More *what*, I wasn't exactly sure, but I did know the brief touches between us, the ones not in anger anyway, weren't enough. But despite what I wanted, she didn't deserve my fucked up life getting in the way of hers. She needed to be able to move on from this, and I'd make sure Tony and Vanni stopped going at her. Marco had been a lost cause the minute she'd been brought in, firmly in Eden's corner. They were good men and could hopefully be there for her in ways my cold, black soul wouldn't allow me to, until she could stand on her own. She deserved that much at least.

I leaned forward and pressed a kiss to her forehead. "I'm sorry, Eden." Then, as quickly as I'd stormed in, I left and went upstairs to change into dry clothes. When I came back down, Marco stood at the end of the hall, his arms folded as he waited. Most likely wanting to make sure I hadn't hurt Eden.

"Everything good?" The sharpness of his tone wasn't lost on me. He was prepared to do anything to protect her. *Even if he's protecting her from me.* I wondered if he'd only bided his time until he found her again, if his anger on my behalf had been more out of loyalty than truly believing she'd been the two-faced bitch she'd been labeled.

"She's fine," I replied shortly, walking around him, wanting out of the house in case he went to her. I didn't think I could handle it. Not now, not when I knew my blind trust in a man I'd looked up to all my life had taken the only woman I'd ever loved from me.

Not noticing, or more likely ignoring my desire to leave, he kept pace with me. After a few steps, he spotted my wet hair. "Have a nice shower?"

I flipped him off over my shoulder as he stopped at the open door while I continued through it, ignoring his comment completely. He watched without further comment as I got into my car and headed for the main house.

Now that I had my answers, it was time to go see Vinnie about my father. I shot Tony a text, letting him know I needed him to meet me there. He'd back whatever I had to say and convince Vinnie it was for the best that Rodrigo was gone. And if he didn't honor my request, I'd leave myself.

The guards outside Vinnie's office avoided eye contact with me as they informed Vinnie I'd arrived. That tended to be the reaction most guys around here gave me, knowing full well exactly what I was capable of if they pissed me off. I was something I liked to perpetuate, so I didn't take offense at the treatment.

"Go ahead," one of them stated, opening the door and quickly stepping out of the way.

Tony sat in the chair opposite Vinnie, looking beyond pissed off. His eyes caught mine, and I knew whatever was going through his mind wasn't good.

"Santos, we've been expecting you. Sit," Vinnie ordered, waving a hand to the seat beside Tony.

I did as I was told and rested my elbows on my knees. "Before you tell me whatever it is you need to, I want to request my father be removed from the Family. I want him gone."

Neither Tony or Vinnie seemed at all surprised at my demand, which I found odd.

"What's going on? You don't seem shocked," I replied to their silence.

Vinnie sighed and stretched back into his chair before folding his hands into his lap. "We're not. Seems we wanted to see each other for the same thing." Vinnie glanced at Tony and motioned at his phone resting on the desk. "Antonio, show him."

Tony obliged, picking his phone up and flipping through his videos before landing on one that looked to be surveillance video from his house.

"The audio is shitty in spots, something I'll have Vanni look at, but I managed to catch all the video," Tony responded before pushing play.

At first, it just showed a viewpoint of the empty entryway and kitchen. Eden meandered around, looking through the cabinets then started making a sandwich. Tony fast forwarded the video until my father came into frame. Eden was visibly shaken by his presence and immediately took a defensive stance against the counter, not letting Rodrigo out of her sight. *Smart girl.* The video then showed him accosting her while she tried her best to get away. By the time he forced her to turn, I'd had enough of listening and had joined them.

Tony shut the video off just after I landed the punch I wished had been much harder then placed his phone back on the desk.

"I didn't see it happen until the video now, but I caught the end of their conversation. Rodrigo orchestrated everything that led to Eden's disappearance all those years ago, telling her she needed to submit to him and threatening to make her into his whore after feeding her some bullshit lies about being my future mistress. He had every intention of taking advantage of Eden if I hadn't come in. Rodrigo's a piece of shit and a threat to this Family. Who knows what else he's manipulated in his favor? And if he stays, I can't. I'm sorry, Tony, I just can't, I'll kill him."

I saw fire beginning to dance behind Tony's eyes as his rage surfaced. The same rage I was still feeling for this betrayal. He might not have been involved with Eden like I had been, but her leaving had affected all of us. This betrayal ran just as deeply within him as it did me.

"The fact of the matter is," Vinnie finally said,

"we only have your word as to what passed between them due to the majority being too quiet to make out. I trust you, and I trust your word. However, that tells us nothing about any wrongs he might have committed against the Family."

I glanced at Tony, but he said nothing. I couldn't believe this! He of all people should've been on my side.

I saw red and immediately shot up from my chair. "You mean you'll do fucking nothing? He's a bastard that deserves to be thrown out on his fucking ass!"

"Sit down, De Luca!" Vinnie roared at me. When I didn't move to follow the order, he slowly rose from his chair to stare me down. "Boy, you best do as you're told and let me finish what I was saying."

Despite wanting to protest, I complied.

"Good. Now, if you had waited, you would have learned that I still plan to grant your request. He's already going to be audited based off of the meeting we just had. I also wanted to get Rodrigo's side of the story regarding Eden. Normally, I wouldn't concern myself with it, but you were close before she left, and you know I've always kept tabs on my boys. Your mother and my sister were best friends; it's how you all met when you were infants." I nodded, already knowing this and wondering where he was going with it.

"Eden's mother was one of the working girls that

circulated through some of the lower ranks, and when she turned up pregnant, Joseph, her regular at the time, insisted she keep the baby. In turn, her mother insisted he marry her." Now that was a part I hadn't known about.

"So, you see, in Eden's case, we owe her. When Joseph was killed, Eden's mother became our responsibility to take care of. Our protection and support are what loyal members of the Family can count on. Your father offered Maria employment, and after your mother passed, it wasn't inappropriate for their arrangement to evolve. But when Eden left and was accused of theft, there was no longer any reason to continue the relationship with Maria. She was only under our care as long as she raised her daughter. With Eden's claims, my honor is put in question. She should have been protected, even from her own mother, and from Rodrigo's defensiveness when I asked if he'd ever heard from her, I began to have my suspicions. Seeing his actions on the video would be enough for me to question his association with the Family. You don't come into my house and disrespect anyone in it.

"But in light of the situation, Tony will have Vanni conduct a full accounting of his ledgers for the last year. I've sent men to collect his files and electronics. Rodrigo has worked his way up to overseeing most of our accounts and handling any legalities regarding them. It's unfortunate he has likely broken one of my most absolute laws. Never betray the Family. For that, and that alone, he will be removed.

"As for Miss Moretti, I still don't have full confidence in her ability to keep quiet regarding the circumstances she was discovered in, so she will remain here until I deem otherwise. If she can prove her loyalty, then we will let her go. I assume her past relationship with you all will work in our favor, so long as you protect her from any new threats while she's here. She is a prisoner, but she doesn't need to be miserable. The best we can do is prove we aren't a current threat to her despite the events of the last few days. Do you both understand?"

Tony and I bowed our heads in agreeance.

"Good. Tony, go keep an eye on her. Santos, you can be the one to tell your father of his excommunication if you'd like?" At my nod, he dismissed us. "Now, go. Both of you."

Without another word, we rose from our chairs and left the office. We stayed silent until we exited the manor, but Tony stopped me before I got to my car.

"So... she was a victim this whole time?" I could hear the guilt in his tone. It was a very familiar feeling that I'd experienced just as deeply since the moment the truth had come out.

"Yes. We fucked up. I can't change things, but there's still hope you and the others can get on her good side. If we want her to leave here alive, you need to gain her trust."

Tony scoffed. "I was more of an asshole than you were. What makes you think I deserve her forgiveness?"

My answer was simple. "Because you're not the heartless bastard who broke her heart."

Tony frowned, nodding before sliding into his car and heading back toward his house. I, on the other hand, had some business to take care of. Let's just hope I didn't kill the fucker.

thirteen
bad bitch

Eden

Sleep failed me after my impromptu shower visit. It had been both terrifying and exhilarating to have Santos so close to me, but I knew better than to entertain any further thoughts about it. He and the others were not the guys I once knew, and I needed to remember that. They were hateful and had wanted me dead when I first arrived. No. Santos didn't deserve my desire no matter how little the spark. I had a job to do—get Vinnie's trust and get the fuck out.

Nothing more and nothing less.

Except my body didn't seem to agree with that logic, causing me to toss and turn, still feeling the trail Santos' hand had taken down my chest. If I was being honest, I still thought about the night Vanni took advantage of my ploy to seduce him and shoved his dick down my throat.

No Good Deed

Between my twisted thoughts about the two men, the matter of a letter I knew nothing about, and the residual anxiety from Rodrigo, it took forever to fall asleep that night. Which made my wake up call the next morning all the more annoying.

"**G**et that fine ass out of bed, Lady Garden! It's training day!" Marco's voice trilled excitedly just before he laid his hulking body across mine on the bed.

"Ow! What the fuck, Marco? Get off of me." I tried to shove him away, but he'd sprawled sideways across me, and it took a moment before he remembered I was still sore. Most of the bruising had faded, but spots were still sensitive.

Marco instantly rolled off me with an apology. "Sorry, Edie. But come on and get up. Tony is waiting for you outside."

I growled and threw the blankets back over my head, wishing with all my might that he'd disappear so I could get a few more hours of shut eye. I didn't know what training day entailed, but it sounded way too early for that shit.

"Come on. Tony is gonna start getting bitchy if I don't have you dressed and out back in the next ten minutes." The shit jerked my covers away from me and wouldn't let them go.

"Ugh, why can't I sleep? Go train by yourselves!" Before I could yank the blankets back out of his hands, Marco swooped down, lifting me up and over his shoulder.

"We're not the ones who need to learn to throw a punch," he said over my instant shouts of irritation as he walked me toward the bathroom. He gently set me down on the bathroom counter and shoved a pile of clothes in my hand. "I had these picked up for you; the size should be better this time. Shoes too. You're so tiny," he joked, poking me in the ribs.

I jumped and swatted his hand away. "I should breathe on you for this," I threatened as I eyed his offering.

"Trust me, Eden, I'll survive, won't be the first time." My face heated at the reminder of my first days here, and he seemed to take notice of my discomfort, adding, "I'll get revenge one day, just you wait."

My cheeks cooled as I studied the mercurial man. I wasn't sure why Marco had suddenly become more chipper than usual, but I'd be lying if I said I didn't like it. He had this weird ability to make me feel comfortable without much effort on his part, and comfort was a rare commodity for me lately, so I might as well enjoy it while I could.

"Thanks, Marco. Now shoo, so I can get ready.

And it's going to be more than ten minutes. Bossy ass wannabe."

Marco snorted and backed out of the room. "I'll be sure to relay that. Just hurry up and come save me before Tony kicks my ass." It was my turn to snort, highly doubting Tony could take Marco one-on-one. Without a reply, I hopped down and closed the door on his retreating back before starting my morning routine.

"What the fuck is that?" I demanded as I came out of the back door. "Has that always been there?" I wasn't sure if the crazy I was seeing was normal or not.

There was a gauntlet of training exercises set up on the lawn that looked like it had come straight from some football training montage out of one of those feel good teamwork kind of movies. There was a rope attached to a high wall, tires set in a pattern on their sides, monkey bars that reached high up off the ground, and even a damn rope ladder resting at an angle. There was no way this was set up overnight; some of it was cemented in.

"This is where we work out when it's nice outside," Tony replied as he walked up to me. Well, shit...

It was then I noticed he'd forgone his usual suit and was dressed in a simple gray shirt with black sweatpants that—I had to say—looked damn fine on him.

"But why is it in your backyard? Isn't it a bit of an eyesore? And I thought I was getting a few self-defense lessons?" *Should have ignored Marco and gone back to bed.*

To my surprise, Tony nodded and grinned. I got a bit hung up on the transformation from stick up his ass dictator to dirty dark lord and how much he looked like Vanni when he did it. "Blame Marco and Santos. One of their damn bets later... they already had it halfway installed by the time I found out. They spent the better part of a week seeing who could get the better time on the drills." Tony's exasperation came through loud and clear despite the fondness beneath it. I almost felt sorry for him when I remembered the feuds they'd get into. "And you are learning some basic things, but I want to make sure you're actually physically able to pull it all off."

"How about we skip this and just move on to the rest," I countered.

"Show me you can do it, and I will," he challenged, dark eyes daring me to defy him.

I smirked as I shot his challenge right back, my sense of self-preservation likely having been shot all to hell. "You first." I thought he might deny me, but then his eyes raked up and down with calculating interest, and my nerves sent off warning bells.

"Fine, but when I win, you do what I say without complaint. No more tantrums, tearing my house up, or trying to run off." I winced under his knowing gaze. Fucking narcing Vanni.

My eyes scanned the course one more time before landing back on Tony. "I hate you."

Tony nodded his head. "That's fair. Now let's get started." He waved his hand toward the first part of the course which was the tires. "Stretch out, and I'll message Marco to come time us." Oh great, an audience.

As I bent over, a whistle sounded behind me. I looked over my shoulder to see Vanni and Marco walking out onto the back porch with a beer in each of their hands.

"Looking good, Moretti. Knew those clothes would fit you," Marco praised, eyeing the fitted black crop-top and stretchy pink capris that hugged my body. The two of them sat on the lounge chairs and opened their beverages, making it quite obvious they were here to watch the whole debacle that was about to go down.

"Seriously?" I asked, motioning at what they were doing.

"What?" Marco replied cheekily.

I flipped them both the bird. "You're both assholes."

Simultaneously, they shrugged. "Can't blame us for wanting to watch the show," Vanni argued, smiling at me. Which was fucking weird. What the hell was going on?

"Hey! Stop distracting her. Eden, move your ass! I have to take a call," Tony ordered as he pointed at Vanni without giving me a chance to argue that I would wait. "You make sure he doesn't cheat and let her win." Marco feigned being hurt by the accusation, but from the unrepentant grin that quickly returned, the warning hadn't been unfounded.

I let out a slew of expletives about stupid, reneging men as I stretched before starting the impromptu exhibition. At least I was used to all eyes on me. The tires were easy enough since all I had to do was run through them, planting my feet in each one. However, the rope ladder was a bit harder than it looked. I was used to a stationary pole, and this thing had more give than I'd anticipated. I tripped, slipped, and fell through the holes several times before making it to the end and hopping off the edge. I wasn't about to get skunked by Antonio Carlotti, no fucking way. Running as fast as I could, I leapt up and managed to grab the first bar on the long set. I swung hard, flipping my body to skip bars instead of taking them one at a time, using my feet to anchor me as I repeated the motion before gripping the second to last bar with my hands and launching off on the upswing to land nearly in front of the wall with the dangling climbing ropes. I heard a muttered "Damn" but didn't stop to see who it was from.

I'd gotten halfway up the rope when icy water hit me and I fell, landing flat on my ass with a screech.

"Tony!" Marco and Vanni exclaimed at once.

"What?" he asked innocently. "She looked hot." My mouth hung open at his blatant lie and the audacity he'd had to cheat.

Vanni groaned, rubbing a hand over his face. "And you thought Marco was going to add to your time? What the hell, Tony?"

"He's just a sore loser," Marco crowed. "You know he's the slowest out of the four of us. Bet he's butthurt he almost lost to a girl."

Unfazed, Tony just shrugged as he turned the hose on his brother and cousin. I started laughing amid their shouts and attempts to run and protect their phones from the spray.

I got to my feet when Tony went to put the hose back on its holder, glad for the warm day and the quick drying fabric of my clothes. My shoes weren't so lucky, but they hadn't gotten too wet.

"Happy now? That prove I can do your stupid obstacle course?" With a curt nod, Tony walked off, the direction to follow him implicit. I called out after him, "Don't think I forgot you chickened out." The sore loser flipped me off and kept walking. I followed and noticed Vanni and Marco had disappeared, probably to get dry clothes on.

We went inside to a part of the house I hadn't been to yet... the basement. Turned out there was a nice gym down there with mats laid out in the center of the room.

"Eat this." Tony tossed me an energy bar from the bowl on a small table right inside the door. "The techniques are easy to learn, but it might take you a bit to default to them." His tone was polite, not as cold as it had been. The change alternately relieved and worried me. I didn't understand it. I was sure Santos had shared some of what happened in the shower, with Tony at least, but regardless of the past, Tony seemed more fixated on who I was now with little bearing on who I used to be.

Regardless, I thanked him and immediately scarfed down the bar, my ever-present hunger letting me know it wasn't happy that I'd skipped breakfast. My body was quickly becoming used to regular meals and being taken care of, and now protested any deviation. While I'd found new motivation to prove to Tony that I could handle myself, I was still wary that he was about to hand me my ass.

"You got this, Edie. We'll make you a hot little

fighter in no time," Marco encouraged, coming into the room and giving me a quick swat on the ass.

I threw a knee at him, nailing him right in the crotch, before realizing what I'd done. He hunched over, cupping his balls with a groan.

"What was that for?" he managed after a few breaths. But I stood there, trying to get my own breathing under control. It had been a knee-jerk reaction, literally. After the visit from Rodrigo, my defenses were up, memories of being pinned by him sitting right at the surface of my mind.

"Sorry, Marco. Just after the other day... It brought up memories of the first time he tried... Are you okay?" Marco straightened, pain evident in his eyes, but also worry. Before he could say anything Tony barked out his own questions.

"Are you talking about Rodrigo? What first time? Has he been here before?" His tone indicated that had better not be the case. And now I wasn't sure if Santos had told him anything at all.

"Yes and no. I meant back then. You know, before?" Awkwardness had set in, and I desperately wanted to change the subject. "Can we just get on with this?" I waved my arm at the mat, no longer in the mood, but I guess I hadn't really been in the first place. Now I just wanted to go change and eat.

"In a minute. What are you talking about? Has Rodrigo attacked you before? Does Santos know?"

Tony was pissed, and Marco didn't look any happier, a dark frown marring his face.

I shrugged a shoulder, unsure of what to say. Finally, to be diplomatic and drop the subject I settled on, "I think so? At least I thought he knew." I evaded the rest of it. "I'd rather not discuss it if it's all the same to you. Nothing to be done about it now anyway."

Tony didn't appear to want to let it go, but after a shared glance with Marco, he motioned me forward, his features clearing into an indecipherable mask.

"I'm going to teach you three moves to get you out of different types of holds—from behind, if someone tries to choke you, and if you're pinned against a wall or other surface."

As he spoke, Vanni joined us. It was barely a minute before the distraction came.

"Five bucks says she gets out of each of his holds on the first try," I heard Marco say to Vanni.

"Pft. Right. You're on," Vanni replied.

"Quiet," Tony snapped at the idiots before moving me to face him directly. It wasn't lost on me that I'd been in all three predicaments he'd outlined just within the last week, which was probably why he'd chosen these moves specifically. It made me wonder if he knew about my encounter with Santos in the shower. I hoped not.

"We'll start with a choke." He moved his hand to my neck, his grip firm but not painful. "First, you'll step back to keep your balance. After, bring your arms up so your biceps are on either side of your ears." He showed me what he meant then had me do it. "Good. Next, you'll pivot your body to the side, away from your attacker, bringing your elbows down to break the hold. Once broken, bring your elbow back and hit them as hard as you can in their face, aiming for their temple or cheekbone. You're small and short, so you may have to put a bit of hop to it when you thrust your arm back."

He slowly moved my body the way he described then started the choke stance back at the beginning.

"I want you to repeat these three steps over and over, then we'll move onto the next one."

I nodded in understanding and began to mimic the moves. It was easy yet difficult all at once. Tony was a tall guy, and my elbow kept mostly grazing his collarbone or just the bare edge of his chin. I wasn't confident in the move, but he kept urging me that I would get it with practice.

We moved onto the next defense which was the one where I would be pinned against a wall or other surface. He used the wall as an example and gave me a searching look before carefully and slowly pinning me to it. I was grateful for his consideration and tried hard to get it right, my reaction to the close proximity of his body overriding any uneasiness the position might have inspired. The move was a bit easier than the first, just pushing against the wall with my hands while turning my body to swing my fist back into my attacker's ear or temple.

As we were about to practice the last move, Tony received a phone call and halted the session.

"I have to go do some things for Vinnie. Marco will take over since he's about my same size, so you can keep training. I should be back for dinner though," he told me, quickly heading toward the door. "Vanni, you're coming with me."

Vanni groaned. "But this is so much more fun."

"Now," Tony ordered, leaving no room for any argument before disappearing into the hall.

"Don't have too much fun without me," Vanni shouted as he followed after Tony.

I rolled my eyes and faced Marco. "I don't see how Tony thinks you're equal in size. I'd say you've got at least a few pounds more muscle on you and another two inches in height."

Marco threw his head back and laughed. "Nice of you to notice my muscles, Edie. You're in for a real treat now."

I was about to ask what he meant, but my unasked question was answered when he grabbed the hem of his shirt and pulled it off. I swallowed hard at seeing the tan, sculpted torso displayed before me. He had muscles on top of muscles, and each one begged for attention. And piercings... dude had shiny silver barbells through his nipples. I tried not to stare. I mean, it wasn't like I'd never seen piercings before, but it made me wonder what else he was hiding under his clothes. I firmly kept my eyes away from his junk, not that it helped much to stare at the eye candy masquerading as his chest. Marco had been hot as hell as a teenager, but as a full grown man, it took everything in me not to drool at the exposure of so much delicious flesh.

"Like what you see?" He cocked a brow at me and smirked.

I shook my head no, a very hard feat to accomplish since my head wanted to nod emphatically.

"Not in the least bit. Can we get on with it?" I turned my back to him and tried to catch my breath. Training just got a whole lot harder—in more ways than one.

Marco chuckled but got in position behind me. "As you wish. Try not to get too excited when I grab you."

I scoffed. "Think I'm good." *Liar, liar pants on fire.*

"For this move, since you can't reach my face with your elbow, I want you to bring it back into my stomach, stepping on the top of my foot. When I release you, turn and use your palm to hit me in my nose. Sound simple enough?" He slowly slid his arms around my waist, just as careful as Tony had been not to spook me.

His skin was hot against mine, and my anxiety perked up for an entirely different reason. I didn't want to broadcast that I was attracted to him. It felt too weird.

"Yep. Got it," I replied breathlessly.

"Okay. Here we go. Attack."

I did as he instructed, slowly at first—so I could get the idea nailed down. After I was sure I had it, I went at him harder and harder each time we repeated the move.

The last time I repeated the palm hit to his nose, he snatched my wrist at the last second and yanked me into him. It wasn't part of the moves we'd practiced, so it surprised me, causing my knee to fly up again in a panic.

But Marco was quicker this time, twisting his hips to let his hard thigh take the hit. He instantly fell back, dragging me down to the ground with him. We landed hard on the mat, my body firmly on top of his.

"Shit! I'm so sorry, Marco. You surprised me."

Marco's chest vibrated with strained laughter. "It's okay. Good strategy, but don't use it too often. It's your default, and that's okay, but we want these others to become just as intrinsic."

I tried to push up off him, but he suddenly rolled over, putting himself on top with his hips between my legs, somehow keeping the bulk of his weight off my body. My squirming immediately stopped at the contact as heat filtered through and my heart began to beat almost painfully beneath my chest.

Marco's expression went from playful to serious the moment he realized I'd stilled. The tension was palpable, but he just laid there, his hazel eyes scanning my own before falling to my lips. His mouth parted slightly, and a soft exhale slipped out.

Just as I was going to ask what he was doing, his mouth came down against mine, quick and hard. The kiss was searing, but it was over faster than I could comprehend it happening at all. It took me by complete surprise, yet the second his lips met mine, I knew I wanted more. Needed more. I couldn't remember the last time someone had kissed me without asking for something in return or paying for it. It confused the hell out of me.

One thing was for sure though—if he could make my body feel this way with just a simple kiss, I could only imagine what doing more would feel like with him. Marco leaned forward and laid his forehead against mine, closing his eyes and just holding me.

"I'm sorry, Eden. For everything." He lifted his head and began to stand, but I was too speechless to reply or even move. "Come on, Lady Garden. Let's get you some lunch." His moods changed fast enough to give me whiplash, always had, and it took a second for me to catch up.

He held his hand out to me, and without thinking twice, I gave him mine and let him pull me to my feet. Wordlessly, he led me back up the stairs, not releasing my hand until we reached the kitchen.

I watched him as he threw together some BLTs, saying nothing. I wasn't sure what was going on or what exactly *everything* had meant in his apology. I did, however, know that I would enjoy this peace while I could.

Because sooner or later, we'd go our separate ways, and Marco Carlotti would once again push Eden Moretti into the back of his mind. In the end, it was better that way.

fourteen
smoke and mirrors
Tony

"Tell me I'm not looking at what I think I am, Santos." My tone was as dark as the expression on my best friend's face as I stared at the decorative wooden box. I'd hurried over to Santos' place with Vanni when his call interrupted our training session with Eden. Frankly, I was glad for the distraction, and I was sure Vanni needed it too. While I was looking at this current clusterfuck with Santos, he was packing my car with any files and electronics Santos had gotten from Rodrigo's place.

"I'd say I wish I could, but I'm glad to have them back. This was sitting on the entryway table when I went in to tell him he was out," Santos relayed as I opened the lid to expose the pile of precious metals and gemstones. "She was telling the truth; she never took a damn thing either." Sorrow weighed heavily on me for my friend at the blatant proof a young woman's life had been destroyed, along with his relationship with the father he'd idolized, all because of lies.

"This is all he left?" Alina's missing jewelry had burdened Santos' mind for a long time, and its reappearance might have cleared Eden in his eyes, but I just saw a new potential problem. Now we had proof that the girl had been wronged, and in my mind, that was a stark reminder that the woman might want her chance at revenge.

"Besides the business records, some of the furniture, and my personal belongings, yes. I've been trying to track him down since I showed up to find the house nearly emptied. He had to have already been packing to be gone that fast. And when I started asking around, I got another bit of news I could have lived without... there really is an offer out for Eden. She didn't make up what that bastard said to her either. Everyone I talked to was clueless about who called for the hit, or they're at least doing a good job at playing dumb. When we investigated the guard and came up empty, I thought maybe she'd misunderstood. There are plenty of sick fucks out there. Now, I think there's a coup in the works, and we need to talk to Vinnie and figure this shit out before we're blindsided and left holding our dicks."

I sighed, weary with everything that just kept piling up and the knowledge that I needed to ask

Santos a more delicate question about Eden and Rodrigo. "Hey, Eden had a bit of an episode over Marco screwing around. Kicked him good over it. But it brought up that she's touchy after the other day in the kitchen, and that it might not have been the first time." I paused, hoping Santos wouldn't take offense and that he'd offer an explanation without me demanding it. Thankfully, he did.

"That was something I was going to confront him about. She didn't exactly say it, but I'm positive he tried to force her that day." His eyes dropped to his wrist before coming back up to meet mine. "He said a lot of bullshit, touched her, and her piece of shit mother backed it up then kicked her out. The story she told Doc?" At my nod, he sighed. "It was all real. Is she okay? Do I need to thump Marco for getting handsy?" His abrupt change of subject threw me for only a second, but it was long enough for anger to take over the sad bitterness that had been there before.

"No, she's fine now. And you know Marco is probably the person she's most comfortable with right now, period. He just caught her off guard, but it was kinda hilarious since we were giving her pointers on self-defense at the time." Becoming more serious, I leveled Santos with a direct stare and pulled my phone out to call my father. "We don't tell Eden that we've confirmed the hit. Not yet." He didn't hesitate to nod, but I could see he didn't agree with me, and I hoped I still had his loyalty over the dark-haired woman that had crashed back into our lives.

※

E*den*

Things were oddly peaceful for the rest of the day after we called it quits in the gym. After my shower, Marco and I had sat and watched some TV, laughing at the sitcom we'd settled on and acting like we didn't have a care in the world. It felt like old times, and I ate it up despite the bittersweetness. The kiss wasn't brought up, nor was another attempted, but he sat shoulder to shoulder with me on the couch even though there was plenty of room for us to both stretch out.

Vanni and Tony arrived later that evening, a tower of pizza boxes in hand. It still confounded me that they'd changed their demeanor toward me so much, but I was too afraid to look that gift horse in the mouth, so I kept my trap shut on the subject. I'd take the olive branch of nicety for what it was. For now.

We sat down at the dining table with Marco on my right, Vanni directly across from me, and Tony to my left at the head of the table. Vanni passed me a plate, and Tony pushed a box toward me, nodding at it.

"Still love pepperoni, olive, and bacon pizza with extra cheese?"

I couldn't stop the look of shock that fell over my face. "You remember what I like on pizza?" Tony just shrugged as if it were no big deal. My eyes scanned the other two who just grinned at me. The thoughtfulness wasn't lost on me though. I lifted the lid and inhaled the tantalizingly delicious aroma of my all-time favorite food.

"Thank you, Tony," I said, giving him a genuinely appreciative smile.

He bit into his own pizza and bowed his head. "You're welcome."

I didn't waste time diving into the box, it had been so long since I had pizza. Now that I had my appetite back, I had every intention of stuffing my face with as much as I could possibly fit.

Conversation was light as the guys ate, and Tony looked more relaxed than I'd seen him since coming here. He joked around with the guys and occasionally even smiled. It was a good look on him. I was starting to think this might actually be a decent night.

But then the front door opened, and a minute later, Santos walked in and sat down at the other end of the table. He avoided eye contact with me completely and snatched a box of pizza from the pile, simply deciding to just eat it straight out of the box.

He then directed his stare toward Tony, his expression blank.

Tony cleared his throat to get everyone's attention. "Now that we're all here, we need to discuss something with you, Eden."

I grudgingly set my third slice of pizza down and gave him my full attention. "I'm listening."

"We haven't told you this, but a detective has been sniffing around, looking for you and trying to get more info on the shooting at Cherry Baby. He knows you're with us as we've already contacted our lawyer and given statements on the matter of what happened and why you're here. But now we need you to corroborate the story we've given. We think the detective just wants proof of life from you and to see if you saw what happened. While a lot of the force is on Vinnie's payroll, he is not, and he's adamant that he speak to you."

I had a feeling this might happen, and I instantly knew that I would have a role to play.

"You want me to make sure none of you go down for the shooting." I glanced around the table at them all, making sure I'd guessed right.

Vanni was the one that answered. "At the moment, the detective doesn't believe our version of events. We hope your testimony will help get him off our backs. If you do this, not only will we be grateful, but it will go a long way with convincing Vinnie to release you. We don't want to keep you captive here, but we're under orders now. This is your chance to prove you're not a threat to the Family."

I let what he was saying sink in. If I played my part and took the heat off Tony and Vanni, there was a high chance I'd earn Vinnie's trust and he'd finally let me leave. It was a no brainer.

"Okay. I can do that. What exactly is the story?"

"Simple," Marco replied. "You don't know much of anything because of the drugs. You do remember there were two masked men who came in as you were performing for a private party. They started shooting, you fell to the ground, and they assumed you were hit as well. When they left, you ran out for help and ran into Tony and Vanni. Fill in some blanks from there. Use as much of the truth as you can without implicating Tony or Vanni."

I nodded along, "I can do that, no problem." I shrugged, picked my pizza back up, and continued eating.

Santos snorted out an unamused chuckle, still avoiding eye contact with me. "We'll see. Fields is a piece of work. You're going to need all the luck you can get."

It wasn't exactly a snotty remark, but it certainly held no faith in my ability to get them out of the situation.

"I've handled my fair share of pieces of work, Santos. This detective will be off your backs in no time, then you can thank me for saving your asses for once." Santos finally glanced my way, and I was surprised to see a hint of amusement flash across his face.

Maybe there was a chance for us to be civil to one another after all.

The next day was the day I'd be meeting Detective Fields. I wasn't particularly excited to have so much riding on my shoulders to make sure this interview went well. If I fucked it up, I was as good as dead. It wouldn't matter what I once meant to the guys. Vinnie would have me killed and disposed of the second shit went sideways. My life literally depended on this.

I tried not to let the nerves get to me. Tony had woken me up early to go over my story one last time, then he presented me with a new outfit to wear when Fields showed up. Marco had only picked up basic clothes like simple shirts, a couple sweaters, leggings, jeans, and yoga pants. This outfit, however, was a fancy version of casual, made up of shorts, black tube top, short black blazer, and strappy wedge sandals. The high-waisted mauve shorts were pleated with a bow on the front of the waistline. The tube top left only a few centimeters of skin showing between the bottom and the waistband of the shorts. It was on the verge of being a bit too risqué with the sandals added, but the blazer covered up more skin and gave it a business flair. I had to admit, it looked pretty damn good on me.

I barged into Marco's room and borrowed his razor and hair products. His propensity for styling his hair came in handy, and since no one thought about hairy legs and shorts, he could deal with me using his razor. I might not care much what people thought of my appearance, but I did occasionally enjoy looking nice and fixing my hair. Having only been able to brush it and pull it up or deal with it being frizzy had been a nightmare. My wavy locks needed the product to lay properly.

I went to work immediately, excited to prove that I could accomplish a happy medium between overly made up hooker and bedraggled hobo. A grimace crossed my face as I denuded my legs of their hairy forest.

When I'd finished, I looked like a completely different person. For the first time in well, a really long time, I actually enjoyed my reflection in the mirror. I smiled, loving the healthy sheen of my skin and the orderly natural waves in my hair as it cascaded perfectly down one side. I'd pinned the other part back so it wouldn't all fall into my face. I wanted to maintain eye contact and not hide behind the curtain of dark tresses like I was wont to do. In every crime documentary I'd watched, being direct seemed to be the best course of action.

Ready to go, I proceeded down the hall to meet the guys for the trip over to the manor. The detective was due within the next hour, and Vinnie wanted a run down of our plan before he arrived.

As I neared the living room, my stomach twisted into knots. Not because of what I was about to do, but about what the guys' reaction would be. It was silly to be nervous, but for so much of my life I'd been treated as if I were nearly worthless, and now I had the chance to prove to myself and them that I wasn't. Taking a deep breath in, I rounded the corner and headed into the room. They were all sitting around on the couches, waiting for my arrival.

Santos was the first to look up, and I swore I saw a twinkle of pride and lust shimmer in his gaze instead of the usual anger or disdain. Tony, Marco, and Vanni noticed Santos' diverted attention and turned to look at me.

"Well, you cleaned up nicely, Eden," Vanni ventured, his eyes roaming up and down my entire body.

Tony nodded, also seeming satisfied with what I'd done.

"We wanted the detective to trust her, not be attracted to her. Damn it, Tony, you're going to get me arrested if he hits on her." Tony reached over and smacked Marco hard in the back of his head. I thought I saw Santos throw a glare at him as well, but it had happened too fast for me to be sure. Vanni just laughed and shook his head. As for Marco, well, he was Marco and completely unfazed. He seemed to realize he was being kind of a dick and grinned at me. "You look like a dirty slice of heaven over there, Paradise."

"Can we get this show on the road?" I asked Tony, doing my best not to act like the appraisal hadn't filled my stomach with butterflies. Wanting any appraisal at all from them was such a bad idea. In my defense, it had been a long time since I'd gotten laid because I wanted to and not had to. Being in a house filled with men who were sexy as sin made blood rush to all the naughty bits in me, creating an all too tempting situation.

"Yes. Let's," Tony replied, throwing a look of warning at Marco and Vanni.

We all loaded into a black SUV and drove the half mile to the manor. I went over my story in my head, preparing myself for both Vinnie's pre-meeting powwow and Fields' imminent arrival. Positive I had it down, I held my head high as we reached the manor and went inside.

The guys led me toward a room off to the right that was closed off with double doors. When they opened, I found myself in a fancy parlor where Vinnie stood next to a marble fireplace. He smiled and nodded approvingly, and I released the breath I'd been holding in anticipation of his reaction.

"Miss Moretti, you look lovely."

I bowed my head. "Thank you, sir."

"Right, let's run through it. I want to make sure you have everything planned and ready," he said, getting right down to business. After explaining it to him as thoroughly as possible, Vinnie nodded, appeased.

"Very good. If you pull this off, Miss Moretti, I may just owe you a favor. Don't mess this up."

I swallowed thickly, hearing the warning in his tone. "Loud and clear, sir." Not even a few minutes later, a guard came into the parlor and announced that the detective had arrived. Early.

"Shit. He really was adamant to get to you," Vanni remarked, worry evident in his tone.

"Relax boys," Vinnie instructed. "I have faith in Eden to get us through this." I had no idea why, but that statement scared me more than any threat could. I knew everything rode on me and how bad this would be for everyone if I didn't deliver.

"You got this," Marco whispered in my ear, taking a seat right next to me and squeezing my knee gently. He had no idea how much I had needed that.

Without thinking, I leaned over and gave him a quick peck on his cheek. "Thanks, Marco Polo."

Marco glanced at me in surprise at my public

display, but he grinned as if he'd just won the lottery all the same.

"Am I missing something?" Tony asked, eyeballing Marco and me suspiciously.

"Not the time for this," Santos groused at Tony, not seeming to care about my actions in the slightest.

Vinnie watched the exchange with a mix of amusement and concern yet said nothing. We all fell into silence just as the doors opened once again and the detective came striding in.

I had expected some old, grumpy-looking guy with graying hair and a bushy mustache. What I saw instead was a smoking hot guy, who resembled a broodier version of a popular actor. He had deep black hair that was cleanly shaved on the sides with the top left slightly longer, and deeply tanned skin. His jaw was angular, strong, and only the barest hint of a mustache grew above his upper lip. His slender yet toned frame was clothed in black slacks and a white button-down that hugged his frame nicely. The badge hanging around a chain from his neck gave him less of a formal feel, making me think that homicide wasn't always his specialty. This guy used to work the streets for sure, and he wasn't going to mess around when it came to this case. I had to play this right... Attitude would get me nowhere with him.

His dark eyes found me quickly, and he headed for me instantly. I stood and stretched out my hand to him. *Polite and reserved, Eden.* He accepted my handshake and returned it in kind.

"You must be Angel," he said in a deep baritone.

"Eden, actually. Eden Moretti. Angel is my stage name," I replied, letting a smile curve my lips.

"Ah, I apologize. We haven't had your real name given to us even though we asked for it several times." He aimed that last part at Vinnie.

"I'm sure it was provided. It's likely your personnel didn't pass it along properly," Vinnie taunted, hinting that the detective wouldn't receive any information the Family didn't curate. I'd bet there were filed memos waiting at the station if only the detective knew he had to look. Vinnie wasn't green and knew how to play the game.

Detective Fields eyed Vinnie with a hint of disdain, giving him a tight smile that was clearly fake. "Right." He turned back to me. "Now, Miss Moretti, I don't know if these men told you, but I've been looking for you for a few weeks now. It wasn't until a couple of days ago that I was made aware you were here and well. I need to get some details from you about what happened that night at your place of employment." He consulted his notebook. "Cherry Baby." There's no way he didn't know that without looking. The man was starting shit already. Guess we'd both be liars and smile all the while.

I grinned and motioned for the detective to sit in the armchair across from me. "Of course! I'd be

No Good Deed

happy to. I warn you, I don't remember much, but I will give you all the detail I can."

Fields sat and pulled a notepad and pen out from an inside pocket of his coat, flipping it open then leaning forward on his knees to give me his full attention. "Anything you can give will be greatly appreciated." He looked around, pointedly stopping on each of the guys and Vinnie as he went. "But can we do this in private?"

Before I could reply, Tony jumped in to answer for me. "This is our home. It's a courtesy that you're even here at all. Eden still has a hard time telling anyone what happened and wants us here to support her if she needs anything during her testimony."

Fields' jaw clenched, but he must've decided having them here with me was better than not speaking with me at all. "Very well. Fine. Miss Moretti, from the beginning, what happened that night?"

I put on a very fake thoughtful expression as if I was remembering. "Let's see... I had been told by my boss Danny that there were two men who requested a private session from me. Of course, I agreed. Us girls didn't say no to Danny, plus, he claimed the men had a lot of money. Anyway, I went in there with another girl I worked with, and we were about halfway through the session when these two masked men came rushing in. It's a bit blurry because I'd taken quite a few drugs that night."

Fields held up his hand to stop me. "What kind of drugs?"

"Blow, meth, and some pills... I think. You have to understand, while I know it's illegal, drugs are about the only thing that make servicing the bastards worth the money. No hooker enjoys her job, well, in my experience anyway, but it's good money."

The detective made a humming sound as he jotted down quick notes of what I was saying. "Understandable. But I don't care about the drugs, Miss Moretti. I care about the four dead people in that club. Don't be worried about the other stuff." It was obvious that he was trying to lull me into trusting him with his false politeness and easy "forgiveness" of crimes he could most definitely pursue. Well, two could play this game.

"Of course. I'll continue then," I replied, trying to sound sympathetic even though none of those deaths bothered me one bit. It was heartless to say, but none of those people had ever given two shits about me, so why should I let their deaths weigh on me? Except maybe Trixie, but only the smallest bit. She was just a victim of circumstance.

"As I was saying, I was fucked up. When the shooting started, all I saw were two men with these black masks on. Stupid masks, really. I thought they only used those stretchy cloth masks with the holes for your eyes and mouth in the movies. Anyway, there were loud pops that I'm assuming were gunshots. I don't know how many, but the guy I'd been servicing fell onto me, and we toppled onto the floor. His body covered mine, and I blacked out. When I came to, the men were gone, and I pushed the guy's body off me and got out of there."

Fields continued writing, his brows pinched in concentration. When he finished, he looked up at me. "So you think these masked assailants thought you were dead, and that's why you're still alive?"

I could immediately tell the detective wasn't fully buying my story, so I had to think fast. "There was a *lot* of blood, Detective. I was covered in it from the guy on top of me, so it's entirely possible that's the only reason I'm still alive. They were probably trying to get in and out as quickly as possible. It was a busy night, after all."

Fields leveled me with a suspicious look but waved his hand. "Alright, continue."

I relaxed a bit, hoping that was a good enough save. "The last thing I remember is making my way toward the front, but I started feeling dizzy. I'd taken way too much shit and was struggling to continue even moving. That was when Vanni and Tony came upon me. Everything went black again after that."

Fields turned his attention to the two in question. "And how did you two just happen upon her? What were you there for?"

Vinnie stepped forward. "My boys gave their

statement to your superior already. Why do they need to answer your questions?"

"Just getting the scene fresh in my head, and they may have remembered something that isn't in the report." Vinnie didn't look pleased, but he motioned for Tony to go ahead.

Tony folded his arms and sat on the edge of the couch next to me. "My brother and I were belatedly celebrating his birthday since we'd been apart on the day of. Vanni had a bit too much to drink, so I helped him find the bathroom. The main one had a line, but I knew one of the bouncers, and he told us to use the one down by the private rooms. We ran into Eden, looking terrified and on the verge of passing out. We tried to ask her what happened, but she collapsed. It was then we realized we knew her and that the symptoms she exhibited indicated a possible overdose. So we took her through the back entrance at the end of the hall and drove her to our family doctor. We didn't stop to question anyone; all we cared about was getting her help as soon as possible."

Fields wrote something on his pad before continuing. "You say you knew each other? How?" he asked, glancing at Tony and myself.

I smiled, letting the warmth of the memories of good times with them filter through me. It was the first bit of this interrogation where I didn't feel like I was acting. "We all go way back to our teens. I dated Santos and regularly hung out with the others. After my mother kicked me out of the house, I left and tried to find my own way through life. She was Santos' dad's housekeeper, and she didn't want me around. I was embarrassed to ask them for help and thought I could do it on my own. Things obviously didn't work out for the better considering my career choices. They saved my life that night though." I glanced between the guys, eyes begging them to just play along. In truth, most of my memories were absolute shit when it came to them. There were good ones, of course, but they were tainted like they'd been sprinkled here and there with the bad like stray confetti. Thankfully, they got the gist to go with it and smiled back at me.

"Right," Fields replied drolly. "So why bring her to your family doctor and not a hospital?"

"I don't have health insurance," I supplied quickly, but Tony held up a hand to forestall anything else.

"Look, Detective, she'd obviously had a bad time, and that place isn't exactly on the up and up. Anything goes for the right price if you get my drift? For all we knew it was animal blood and some fetish scene. Eden wasn't in a state to explain. Besides, if something had gone down, surely the security would have been on it, no?" The detective flattened his lips as if he was holding in a retort, but he nodded anyway. "We thought to save her the embarrassment and possible repercussions of any paid activities." All eyes moved to me, and I flushed with shame at the implications. Luckily, it was just that reaction that sealed it for the detective. Or at least it appeared that way.

"Okay, so why did you not come forward sooner with what you witnessed?"

I composed myself before leaning forward to look dead on at the detective as sincerely and innocently as possible. "I've never seen anyone die before, Detective. And I was in no shape to do anything, let alone march down to the police station. Not only that, but I was terrified that those men might have come back and noticed I was gone. Would they be looking for me? Would my boss come looking for me when he realized I was gone? I didn't know. Coming down from the drugs I was doing also instills a lot of hysteria and paranoia, and I spent several days not knowing what was up or down. Even if I'd gone to a hospital and likely ended up in a rehab center, I wouldn't have been lucid enough to interview." I shot a glance at the guys before continuing. "The Carlottis took me in and watched over me as I came down from the withdrawal and the emotional trauma. When I was feeling better physically, they asked me if I wanted to go talk to you. I was afraid to leave just yet, so they contacted you, and here we are."

"Miss Moretti, do you expect me to believe it's taken this long for you to be well enough to have a simple meeting?" The detective's brows dipped as he frowned, his lips tightening and turning down at the corners, he was getting pissed, and I knew I had to do something to cement my story.

"I-I had a bad time a few days ago." I dipped my head as if struggling to find the courage to continue then whispered, "I'm sure you've noticed some of the marks on my body. I wasn't in a good way and tried to harm myself. The guys had to restrain me, physically." I looked up at him, holding his gaze for the rest. "Did you know that it can take weeks for the mood swings and other symptoms to abate, Detective? I've been an addict for the better part of a decade, so my symptoms have been quite severe." The few tears that fell weren't all an act, but no one else needed to know that, and the detective looked more than uncomfortable for forcing the admissions from me in front of an audience.

I took a shaky breath, and a hand gripped my shoulder just before a tissue came down in front of me. I glanced over at Tony and thanked him, grabbing it to blot delicately at my eyes.

Detective Fields sat forward and placed a hand on my arm. "I understand, Miss Moretti, and I thank you for your testimony. I only have a couple more questions, then I won't bother you with any more."

I nodded slowly and exhaled. "Of course."

"Can you remember any other defining details about these men other than their masks? Eye color?

Height? Race? Tattoos that might've been showing? Any detail could be important."

I sighed lightly and shakily replied, "I couldn't tell you eye color. It was so fast when they came in. I'd say they were both maybe between five foot eleven or six feet tall. Something like that. I'm pretty sure they were white, but tanned, maybe? That's it though."

"And what about the bouncer, Samuel Brothers? His body was reported outside by a passer-by."

The bewilderment wasn't hard to fake as I shook my head. "I have no idea, I didn't even know he was dead. Last time I saw him was after my set." I shrugged and left it at that. Other than being told, I really hadn't seen anything.

Detective Fields patted my arm. "That helps a lot. Thank you, Miss Moretti." He finally stood, tucking his notepad and pen back into his coat. He then pulled out a card and handed it to me. "If you feel up to it and can think of anything else, you have my number. I hope you continue to heal both physically and emotionally from this. Truly."

I stood and held out my hand. "I'm happy I could help. I promise I'll call if something pops into my head." Fields shook my hand and gave one last look around the room at the guys surrounding me before heading toward the double doors.

"I'll walk you out, Detective," Vinnie called after him. He stopped next to me and put a hand on my shoulder, leaning down to quickly whisper, "Well done, Miss Moretti." Then he swept out of the room after Fields.

I blew out a long breath and fell back into the couch.

"I think you convinced him," Marco ventured.

"I don't know," Vanni argued. "It was a good performance, but only time will tell if it worked or not, I don't like the odds of 'thinking it worked', something more concrete would be comforting."

Scoffing, I turned a glare on the lot of them. "You're welcome for possibly saving you from going to prison, assholes. I said what you told me told me to say, and did the best I could," I replied, angry that I couldn't get at least a fucking thank you for my efforts. It wasn't my fault they'd shot up some Finellis in a public place, yet here I was, covering for their ungrateful asses. Even after they'd threatened my life.

"I think he suspects you weren't telling the whole truth, so I'm not so sure you saved us just yet," Tony interjected callously, infuriating me even more.

"Well, how about *you* deal with him next time? Cause I'm fucking done trying to help if that's how you want to be about me putting my ass on the line to lie for you." The nerve of them. Vinnie had seemed pleased, so why weren't the others convinced? Yeah, I might have laid it on a bit thick, but what the hell else was I supposed to do? Didn't they see that it didn't bode well for me to not get the detective off of their backs? I had just as much stake in them staying out of prison as they did.

"We know you tried," Marco added, trying to placate me, but his praise fell on deaf ears. I folded my arms across my chest and chose to ignore him.

Vinnie came back into the room a few moments later and stopped right in front of me, his hands in his pockets. "I believe I owe you now, Miss Moretti. That was some performance. A Carlotti never forgets a favor done or a favor owed." *Finally, someone who appreciates what I'd done.*

"I'll remember that."

Vinnie gave the slightest bow of his head. "I'm sure you will."

I knew he wouldn't release me as the favor, but I had to come up with a way to use this to my advantage. Come hell or high water, I wouldn't give up until I was free.

fifteen
problem

Eden

It was raining outside, and I was tired of watching television, so Marco and I were practicing some of the self-defense moves on the mats in the basement gym.

"Again, Edie," Marco commanded when I broke his hold and made it past the mats. The floor was the 'safe zone' I had to reach. In theory, I'd run my ass off once I managed to get away. For now, the mats were a marker to practice with.

I tried to throw myself down and away, but I'd gotten too close, and Marco had underestimated how hard I could pull. The air was knocked from my chest when Marco landed on me, the two of us pressed to the padded floor. He immediately lifted up, but I was already at that moment when you're about to panic because you're not sure you'll ever get your lungs to fill again.

"Oh fuck, are you okay? Breathe, damn it!" Marco's reaction was starting to edge toward the same panic I was beginning to feel. Before either of us could fall over that edge, my lungs remembered to do their job, and I sucked in air between bouts of coughing.

"I'm not sure whether you're trying to scare me to death or get me killed by the others." Marco stared at me, exasperation taking over the worry in his hazel eyes.

"Not my fault your fat ass landed on me," I panted out as my breathing regulated. "Besides, they still like you more than me. I doubt they'd do more than shave your head for a punishment."

His eyes narrowed while his nostrils flared in annoyance. "Fat? Shave my head? You even *suggest* touching my hair to one of them, and it's not going to be pretty."

"Nah, I think you could pull it off." I grinned when he shook his head.

"Not what I meant and you know it. And as for fat, you've seen me, not an ounce of it." He was smug for all of two seconds.

"Yeah, you hide it between your ears." I couldn't help the breath of laughter that escaped.

"You're just being a shit now. I'm warning you, your skinny butt can't cash the check it's writing." Retribution shone bright in his gaze, and I wondered

No Good Deed

if I was going to regret it. But I was still bored, and this was fun. So...

"Looks like you shaved this morning." He looked down at me warily and nodded. I brought one leg up and managed to push the bottom of his t-shirt up to rub my slightly prickly leg on his lower back, making him squirm against me. *Well, I didn't intend for that to happen.* I brazened through and pretended I didn't notice what the shift in position had done.

"Ack! Stop that. Damn porcupine." His twisting rubbed us together, making it harder to keep up the teasing.

"Notice anything?" My voice had become huskier, drawing Marco's attention to my lips.

"You mean my dick about two seconds from dry humping you or the sandpaper on your legs?" *Oh, he's going to address that elephant then.*

"I was referring to the fact that none of you bothered to give me a razor but expected me to wear shorts yesterday." It dawned on him then, and horror briefly crossed his face until he grinned and looked down between our bodies.

"Happen to shave anything else?" I bit my lip in indecision, hesitating just long enough that Marco started to back off. I tightened my leg around him then added the other when he continued to move back. "Sorry, Edie, I shouldn't mess with you after everything." I appreciated his concern, but Marco had been the steady in all the crazy, and I was comfortable with him and wanted to take the chance to explore the fun and pleasurable side of sex because I wanted it, not because it was being forced on me or paid for. I was fully confident that if I panicked or wanted to stop, he'd let me go in an instant and proceed to take care of me.

My decision made, I used my leg muscles to pull me up tight against his growing semi until my ass left the mat.

"Would you be disappointed if I said no?" I hadn't shaved there. It didn't occur to me that I might need to, and I was now definitely contemplating borrowing his razor again soon.

Marco shook his head. "I'm good either way, but I'll tell you a secret. I use the one in the shower for my man grove." He gave me a wink before adding, "My version of a lady garden."

Well, he won that round. "You're gross, you know that, right?"

"Matter of opinion, I think. Don't be hating on my manscaping." He pretended to be affronted until I reached between us to flick his nipple, earning a slight flinch from his pec and a pleasure-filled noise from his throat. "That's going to get you in trouble if you keep it up. I only have so much restraint. If you're not interested, then best let me go now." All sense of play was gone from his face and voice. He was dead ass serious, but I wasn't ready to fold yet.

"I am. Interested, that is." That was all I had to

say. Marco's eyes lit with anticipation as his weight settled firmly against me, pressing my hips into the mat. When they met, his lips dominated mine until I allowed him entry, then it was deep plundering kisses while he settled his weight onto his elbows, cradling my head in his hands.

I was impatient and so turned on that I didn't even care where we were or about getting undressed. I just wanted him to touch me and not stop. Twisting my head to break my lips from his, I demanded, "More, Marco, please." An upward grind of my hips paired with my heels digging into his ass told him exactly what I wanted.

Marco reared back, reaching his arm over his shoulders to drag his t-shirt over his head, baring his ripped torso and the shiny piercings on his chest. "You too, Edie." He didn't give me a chance to remove my tank, sliding his hand down my stomach to grip the hem and push it up until his hand was high enough to catch the sports bra underneath. With a quick movement, he tugged them both up and over my breasts. I had to help a bit at that point, but then I was topless in front of him, arms limp above my head with my top twisted around my wrists and nipples pebbling in the cool basement air.

His eyes flicked up to mine as he arched his back to lower his head to one pointed tip. A tentative touch of his tongue came before he took it into his mouth to suck hard. My back rose off the mat, and a high-pitched moan came from my throat until he switched sides. He teased that one, licking and nipping at the bud until it was red and swollen, and I gripped his head in my hands with my fingers tangled in his hair.

Finally lifting up, Marco propped himself to the side on one arm, the other beelining for my yoga pants. His hand slipped beneath them, unerringly finding my core between already slick lips before sinking his fingers home.

"I want you, Eden. Badly. Tell me stop if you need to, and I will, but I'm dying to get in this hot pussy." He punctuated his statement by curling his finger up to rub at that flat, rough patch inside as he ground the heel of his palm on my clit.

Panting moans echoed in the room around us, and the need to reciprocate drove me to seek the erection tenting his sweats. When my fingertips found his hard length, they encountered something not wholly unexpected. Well, several somethings. "You pierced your dick?"

The question barely slowed him down. "Yes. That a problem?" His hooded gaze met mine as I shook my head.

"No, it's hot. I just didn't expect more than one." That got a chuckle from him.

"Yeah, lost a bet." He didn't elaborate, and at the moment, I didn't really care how he'd gotten them. Taking him in hand, I traced my thumb over the warm metal balls on either side of his shaft and the bar just under the surface of his skin then moved down to the tip where more sat behind the flared head, one above and one below.

I was getting close from the motions of his hand, and I wanted more than his fingers in me. "Marco."

"Hmm?" he replied, eyes closed as he kept up his ministrations and thrust his hips against my grip.

"I want you in me. Please." My request was embarrassingly breathy, but I couldn't help it. It had been a very, very long time since I wanted sex just for the sake of chasing my own pleasure.

His movements stilled, his features set in indecision. "Are you sure? I don't have anything down here. We could go upstairs to get something?"

Mortification and shame flared in my face and clawed deep at my chest, but my chin jutted up. I refused to hang my head even if I dearly wanted to. "I'm clean, if that's the problem. If it's my past, well, I can't do anything about that."

"I hate that you had to do that to survive, but even if you had done it because you wanted to, it wouldn't make any difference. And I know you're clean. I am too if you're wondering." My forehead creased in confusion. *What is his problem then?* "I don't want to be a distraction. This means more to me than that. Also, I don't want to accidentally knock you up if you're going to take off on me." Now my face flushed for an entirely different reason. Partially from imagining having a little Marco and partially because he knew I didn't plan to stick around. But the fact that he seemed to want me anyway tugged at the strings of my heart until I reminded myself that there was just too much history there. I needed a fresh start. *Don't catch feelings, Eden.*

"No to the knocking up and no comment on the other." His brows lowered as he opened his mouth to say something, but I quickly cut him off. I didn't want to ruin the mood any further. "Birth control is still good for a few weeks yet, but I think you can handle pulling out to finish elsewhere." Marco's mouth snapped shut while a challenging glint flashed in his eyes.

"Remember you said that, Edie." He punctuated his words with a twist of his fingers, eliciting a chirp of surprise from me before he withdrew, sitting back far enough that he could shove his pants down and stroke his straining dick with his coated fingers.

I started to shimmy out of my leggings while he was busy, but he gripped the center of them just as they were down to my knees, lifting up and bending my legs back. It was an unexpected and awkward move with my shoe-clad feet hovering above my head until he dove into the opening to settle over me, trapping my legs behind him at the same time.

"What in the world are you doing?" I questioned him.

"You can't escape this way," he replied, and I

wondered what the hell *that* meant, but his mouth was on mine before I could push the issue further. His hips settled between my thighs, his length close enough to tease me with the piercing but too far away for me to arch up and take him inside me, especially with my legs trapped as they were. Trying to catch his evasive cock was too much to concentrate on, so I relaxed back onto the mat and enjoyed the make out session he seemed intent on.

As soon as I relinquished control, Marco notched his tip against my decidedly wet pussy, never letting up with the onslaught of his lips and tongue as he slowly pressed forward until I stretched to accommodate him. He made it partially in, the ring rubbing nicely across my sensitive spots, only to stop and angle his hips to rub the barbell on the top of his dick against my clit. Short, shallow thrusts was all he allowed, no matter how I twisted and bucked, and he broke away from my mouth to chuckle against my lips when I growled at him in frustration. He was using his rings to stimulate me to the point that it was driving me crazy, but his movements were too slow to get me where I wanted to be, and he wouldn't go past that invisible line of demarcation.

"What's your damn problem? Are you torturing me on purpose?" I was grumpy and turned on and about to reach down to finish myself when Marco halted my movement, using the fabric tangled around my hands to pin them down onto the mat above my head.

"Uh-uh, Edie, you want my dick, you get it my way." My eyes widened in shock that he planned to continue his sensuous torture, then narrowed in consternation when his words echoed in my head. *Remember you said that, Edie.* His trademark grin popped up as he delivered his unwelcome news. "You only want to let me have part of you, then you only get part of me." At my apparent confusion, he elaborated, "Just the tip, Paradise." My look of disbelief only got an eyebrow wiggle in return before he dipped and rolled his hips against me. Then my expression matched his, filled with carnal expectation.

The devilish man took pity on me, speeding his movements until he leaned down to swallow my cries of release with his kiss-swollen lips.

Tony

I knew I should have closed the screen on my laptop when I checked the cameras to see what Eden was up to. I wasn't a hundred percent sure of her yet, but I also felt a strange compulsion to make sure she was okay throughout the day. I'd managed to hide my twisted, disdain-laced desire from the others so far, but watching her with Marco, open and happy, was a temptation I couldn't resist. When things turned heated, the proper thing would have been to stop watching. Instead, I watched, and several minutes into my foray of voyeurism, I found myself unfastening my slacks to free my throbbing erection. A quick search through my desk drawer came up with a tube of lotion I'd never used, and soon enough, my hand was rubbing one out as I watched Marco above a writhing Eden. I came a moment after he pulled out to paint her pussy with his ejaculate, rubbing it in like the possessive bastard he was. Her hips arched as he drove his fingers back into her used hole, and I thought I was going to go for round two when my dick tried to immediately twitch back to life. But my door busted open after a brief knock, Vanni appearing with a shit-eating grin on his face.

"You'll never guess what I just caught Marco and Eden doing in the gym... Bro, did you just jerk it in here?" Vanni's tone and face were full of disgust as I tried to surreptitiously tuck my junk back into my pants behind the shelter of my desk.

"None of your fucking business, *bro*. How about waiting for an answer before you barge in?" I was mostly embarrassed, but also a bit pissed that I'd been caught with my dick out, and I was now stuck holding a handful of cum.

"How about you lock your damned door? And

did you hear what I said? I went to go work out and got an eyeful of Marco's ass as he was banging Eden." I'd been so wrapped up in watching the couple, I'd completely missed the door to the gym opening, but apparently so had Marco and Eden. When I didn't say anything, Vanni tried to peek around to see my screen, but I slammed the lid shut, hoping I didn't break the fucking thing when I used a little more force than I meant to. "You were watching them, weren't you? Antonio Carlotti, whacking it in his office to surveillance videos. Wait until I tell—" His crowing cut off when he had to duck, avoiding the stapler that flew at his head.

"You tell anyone and I'll use that to tack your balls to your asshole," I yelled at him as it crashed into the door behind him. The fucker just gave a salute as he cackled his way back out of my office and down the hall. *Caught with my hand on my dick like a teenager*. A groan echoed in the room as I used tissues to clean up then zipped my fly, feeling slightly guilty that I'd so thoroughly enjoyed myself over my best friend's girl. *But she's not his girl anymore, is she?* The thought didn't do anything to alleviate my guilt, but it did make my feelings on the matter even more confused.

sixteen
bulletproof love
Eden

That night after my rendezvous with Marco, a plan formed in my head. Even with Marco's new purchases, I was still lacking some serious amounts of clothes, and Danny owed me a paycheck from the last two weeks I'd been at Cherry Baby. With everything that had happened with the detective, I figured there was a good chance I might get away with an hour or two of freedom to collect my things from my shitty apartment and my earnings from the club. Vinnie had said he owed me, and after getting Fields off their asses, there was a chance he'd let it happen. If the guys said no, I'd march my ass all the way up to the main house and find a way to ask him myself. It was worth trying at least.

Plan in mind, I decided to help sweeten my pitch by cooking everyone dinner. Maybe playing nice would help them see I was trustworthy enough to make the trip there and back.

After checking through the contents of the kitchen to figure out what I had to work with, I realized the options were slim. Especially given my limited comfort as a chef. In the end, I settled on tacos because it was familiar and something I could easily handle. I was sorely tempted to say the hell with it and maybe drug the guys' food with some sleeping pills I'd spotted in Marco's bathroom, but the idea was quickly struck from my thoughts when I realized that wouldn't blow over well. My trust with them was already on thin ice. Well, maybe not so much where Marco was concerned. A frisson of arousal had my thighs clenching over the reminder. I could still feel him there, between my legs and driving me crazy. I shook my head to clear the haze of lust trying to convince me to track him down for another round. *Food, Eden. Food. No dick.*

In the end, I was a good girl and made the food sans drugs. The guys, except Santos who was still avoiding me, had been surprised when they noticed me moving through the kitchen, but they stayed silent, observing for a moment before leaving. Marco came in a few times, stealing bits of chopped toppings from their bowls and commenting on how good it all smelled. He even snuck in a few overly casual touches that had me itching to either slap his hands or jump him and ride him down to the floor.

The man was a menace, and I finally had to shoo him out before I did something about it in the very public kitchen. We were lucky we hadn't been caught earlier, although Vanni's smirking glances were making me wonder if Marco had overshared.

When I got it all done, I called everyone into the dining room. Tony, ever the observant one, immediately grew suspicious as he took his seat.

"Not that I don't appreciate you cooking, but what do you want in return?" he asked, eyeing me dubiously.

"You didn't say anything, so I assumed it was okay," I responded before biting into my taco.

"It is. Okay, that is. But I'm wondering what your angle is. Marco is still alive, so I doubt it's poisoned since he ate the most." *How the hell does he know that? Does he have cameras on me?!* My suspicion must have shown on my face as I glanced up to inspect the ceiling. Tony hurriedly took a bite of his own food, making a production of chewing, while Vanni started laughing for no apparent reason. Santos quietly started making his plate, ignoring all of us. Obviously the most mature one, I sat my taco down and crossed my arms to glare at them both.

"Spit it out, Eden. I'm hungry and want to know if I'm going to get the shits or something if I eat it."

I rolled my eyes with a sigh, knowing full well I was caught. "Okay, fine, and not that it didn't cross my mind, but it would have been something like sleeping pills, not anything gross I might have to witness." They all paused with varying expressions of anger and horror, the latter from those with food in their mouths. "Oh, for fuck's sake, I didn't put anything in it. I'm eating too! Idiots. I want my stuff from my place, and I would really like to get my last payout from Danny. The fucker owes me, and I could use that money to pay off the last of the rent I owe my roommates." Not only was my appetite gone, I was pissed I had to go to such lengths for a temporary furlough on my sentence.

Tony finally nodded and picked his taco back up, the others slowly following suit. "Okay, that's no problem. Tell me what you need and I'll go get it for you." *Seriously? That's it?*

"No. I want to do this on my own. Vinnie said he owes me, and this is what I want. I'll go straight there and back, I swear." I needed to get out of this house and feel free for five damn minutes. They could at least give me that much.

The guys didn't look convinced in the slightest.

"You know how shady this sounds, right?" Marco asked. "You just admitted you considered drugging us to get out of the house, shame on you by the way. In any other scenario... Atta girl, but this looks like you have plans, and I'm not sure I like that."

I groaned at his accusation, my glare promising zero chances of repeating our earlier tryst. "Look, you can call it shady all you want, but the fact of the matter is I really do just want my belongings and my own money. I don't like feeling kept. I'm not meeting someone for a hook-up." I pointedly stared at Marco who *still* didn't look the least bit repentant. "You want me to prove you can trust me, well, here it is. If I'm not back within a few hours, feel free to hunt my ass down." I was annoyed as fuck after trying my damned best to behave and be cooperative. Well, within reason anyway.

The room grew silent for a moment, then Tony wiped his face on a napkin and excused himself from the table. I thought that was it and dejectedly began to consider just saying fuck it and going back to my room. No one spoke a word, probably figuring the same, until Tony returned a few minutes later and settled back in his chair. He folded his hands together on the table, his eyes locked on mine.

"I called Vinnie, and he agreed so long as some terms are met. I don't like it, but he said it was a fair trade. You have two hours, but you will take my car and a phone with you, so we can keep in touch. If you are not back in this house within two hours, he told me to say that you will regret it. Are we understood?"

I couldn't believe that I was actually getting some freedom. It wasn't much, but I'd take what I could get. It was highly likely both the phone and car had trackers, but neither bothered me. I had no intentions of doing something stupid like running. Not yet, anyway. Not until I knew for sure I wouldn't be picked up by the cops or some rival of the Carlottis. I had no intention of being collateral damage. And now I was thinking it might not be a good idea to go, but if I backed out, who knew how long it would be until I would get another chance…

"Fine, deal. Two hours."

Tony nodded in approval then continued eating as casual conversation resumed around the table, but I heard none of it. I was too damn excited and worried about having a couple hours to just breathe without someone watching me.

"Tony?" I waited until he looked at me to continue. "Can I borrow your car, please?"

Marco and Vanni snorted out a laugh.

"Fifty bucks says she runs," Vanni chimed to Marco.

Annoyed, I interjected, "A hundred bucks says I come back with my stuff and two middle fingers just for you."

Marco found that hilarious, and Vanni smiled, extending his hand to shake on the bet. Tony fished around in his pocket, holding out a set of keys before slipping a phone into my hoodie pocket. The fact that they were readily available led me to believe he'd already decided to let me take his car, but as I moved to grab them, he pulled back his hand.

"One single scratch on my car and your ass is mine, Eden," he warned.

"You promise?" I joked, not at all worried about his threat. I was actually a fairly decent driver when I was sober. Tony blanched at my retort while Vanni snickered, and Marco's and Santos' eyes met in confusion. I didn't get it, but whatever.

"Seriously," Tony barked. "Not a single scratch." Finally, he handed me the keys.

I jingled them in my hand and gave him a two finger salute. "Yessir." Before anyone could say anything else to hold me up, I slipped on my shoes and rushed from the house.

Tony's black Audi was a sexy, sleek car that was as comfortable as it was beautiful. I slid into the leather driver's seat and ran my hands along the steering wheel. It was without a doubt the nicest car I'd ever driven, purring like a panther when I started it up. I shifted it into gear and headed sedately down the long driveway toward the gate, reveling in the feeling of being absolutely free—if only for a short time.

I switched on the music and flipped it to a rock station, happily singing along as I drove. It was kind of thrilling to drive past the armed guards at the gate, waving at them as I went. If it weren't for the situation, I wouldn't have had a care in the world.

Unfortunately, the twenty-minute drive into the city went by too fast. I found myself in front of Cherry Baby, almost wishing I had forgone coming here entirely, but the money Danny owed me would be a huge help in disappearing once I was released from Vinnie's watchful eye. I was marginally concerned that the detective would be lying in wait to return and pick me up, or someone with a more nefarious intent like that rapist guard, but I planned to be in and out as quickly as possible.

"Here goes nothing," I muttered to myself before opening the blacked out double doors and stepping back into the club that had been a huge part of my life.

The smell of the place hit my nostrils hard, reminding me that I really had been here too long if I'd become nose blind to the mixed scents of booze, sweat, and industrial cleaner. I pushed through the drunken crowd, searching out Danny. Several waitresses and dancers passed, most of whom waved, but a few acted as if they didn't recognize me at all. The attention on me was unnerving, but it served in helping me find Danny more quickly.

He'd been coming out of a back room when he spotted me winding through the crowd, and the excitement on his face immediately had me on edge. I put on a stern expression and made my way over to him.

"Angel, baby! You're back!" he shouted over the music, his arms going wide as if he were coming in for a hug.

I sidestepped him, not in the least bit interested

in acting like we were old friends. "I'm only here for the payout that you owe me. Nothing else."

Danny chuckled and lit a cigarette. "Right down to business, eh? I wasn't even sure if my prize dancer was alive. Good to know those Carlotti boys are taking care of you. You look hot as shit, Angel."

Knowing full well it was a terrible idea to even acknowledge the guys around the obvious eavesdroppers, I shook my head.

"No idea what you're talking about. I've just been laying low. Now, my money?"

Danny sighed. "Fine, fine. I get it. Your lips are sealed. Come with me." He motioned for me to follow him toward the office.

I did so without a word, not wanting to say a damn thing else concerning the Carlottis or anything related to them.

"So, where you been staying and when you coming back?" Danny asked as we entered the office. He sat at his desk, opening a locked drawer to pull out a wad of cash.

"Here and there. And I'm not. Moving on to other things," I replied vaguely.

Danny scowled, his hands stilling. "What? But you're my best girl!"

"Why the hell would I come back after what happened with Trixie?"

Danny's scowl deepened. "Damn shame what

happened to her. But business ain't the same without ya, kid."

I shrugged. "You'll figure it out, Danny. You always do."

He bobbed his head and finished counting out my money. Standing, he walked around the desk and handed it over. "Well, if you change your mind, you know where to find me."

I quickly took the cash and shoved it into my pocket. "Not likely. Thanks anyway, Danny." I turned to leave, ready to finally close the door on this chapter of my life. As much as it had done for me, keeping me off the streets, it had also been the catalyst for my descent into addiction.

As I went to close the door behind me, Danny said, "Take care of yourself."

I didn't acknowledge him and kept my head down as I made a quick detour to the dressing rooms where my locker was. Luckily, the key to the locker was still hidden behind an old wall socket that no longer worked. I snatched it up and quickly unlocked it, retrieving my items with a small measure of surprise. I'd thought Danny would've broken into the thing, clearing out anything remotely valuable. *Guess he really had expected me to come back to work.*

I hugged my slouchy faux-leather purse to me and dug through it, finding my phone down at the bottom. The thing was useless, completely dead after not having been charged in so long. I stowed it in my pocket, putting the money Danny had given me into my wallet, then stilled when I saw my glass pipe still sat in the back of the locker. It was tempting to take that with me as well. Figuring I could always ditch it later, I began to put it in my purse, but the shitty lighting happened to hit just the right spot to illuminate the barest amount left in the cusp of the bulb. My hand automatically reached for a lighter, and only the sound of a door opening and voices approaching had me hiding it in my hoodie pocket. After they left and the moment of weakness was gone, I warred with myself for a few moments before I decided I needed to take a step in the right direction and get rid of it. Grabbing the pipe, I walked it over to the trash can and threw it in. I nodded my head, proud of myself for making the choice even if I'd been tempted to keep it for emergencies.

Locker thoroughly cleared out, I hurried through the club and back out the front doors. I had no idea how freeing it would feel to say goodbye to the place even though it had featured so prominently in my life, but as I drove away toward my apartment, it was like a weight had been lifted. I wasn't sure where I'd end up in the future, but I promised myself I'd do better than Cherry Baby. I deserved that much at least.

I arrived at my apartment in record time. The building wasn't anything special, but it was mostly serviceable, and the occupants tended to look out for each other.

A few neighbors recognized me and said hello as I made my way up the steps. Digging out my keys, I unlocked the door and walked in to find my two roommates bent over the coffee table. A mirror was situated on it with lines of blow all cut and set pristinely on top. Sugar, a fellow dancer at Cherry Baby, wiped at her nose as she finished one then squealed upon seeing me.

"Angel! Where've you been, honey? Bless your heart, you look horrible in that outfit." Her thick Southern accent grew thicker anytime she was the least bit high. Her comment didn't bother me though; she preferred her attire to be quite a bit more revealing than what I currently wore.

I welcomed the hug she greeted me with and shook my head. "Finding a new gig, one with less..." I waved my arm, at a loss for polite words that wouldn't insult her choices. "I just came to get my stuff and give you guys my last part of the rent. I won't be coming back." I fished a couple hundred out of my wallet and handed it to her. It was a bit more than they needed, but they'd been there for me when I needed help, and I wanted them to be covered until they could find a new roommate.

Diamond, our other roommate and fellow dancer, finally seemed to notice I was there, stumbling as she stood. "Oh, Angel! Wanna do a line? It's soooo good." She sucked off the bit of powder that coated her finger and smiled, holding out the little straw to me in invitation.

Everything in me wanted to say yes. The temptation of feeling the effects one last time was enthralling, but another part of me knew that I needed a new start, and getting fucked up and blowing my cash on drugs would inevitably happen if I gave in now.

"No thanks, D." I offered her a smile in return, then excused myself to do what I'd come for.

I didn't have much to really pack together. All of my clothes, shoes, makeup, accessories, and some other small personal belongings filled a black duffle, the same one I'd left my mother's apartment with that day, and a kitchen trash bag. It was a bit surreal that everything had come full circle, and I briefly wondered why I'd kept it. It was definitely a reminder of what not to do, and I shook myself out of the memories trying to suck me down before hefting it over my shoulder.

Satisfied I had everything I wanted to take, I went back out into the living room and pulled Sugar to me for one final hug.

"I left the bedding. Sorry, I don't have time to wash it, but maybe the next girl can use it. And you two take care of each other. I don't know if I'll see you again, but look out for yourself. Okay?"

She squeezed me back before pulling away. "You

too. Wherever you've been, it's done you good. The outfit is still up for debate, but you look healthier."

I laughed and stepped back. "See you around, Sugar. Bye, Diamond," I said to my other roommate who had resumed her position at the table. She giggled as she waved, more interested in chasing her high than anything else. *That won't be me again,* I vowed to myself.

"Bye, Darlin'. Be good," she said when it finally registered that I'd spoken to her.

"Never," I snorted out, then wiggled my key off its link and set it on the edge of the table before I left without another word.

Before returning to the compound, I made a pit stop at a nearby gas station, stocking up on snacks and cigarettes. When the clerk handed them over to me without issue, I was relieved I didn't have to try to use my old expired license. Having to put them back or try to get them to take it usually caused a scene, and that was the last thing I wanted. I was already uneasy enough being out by myself, the thrill of freedom having slightly dulled, and Tony's car was getting more attention than I felt comfortable with. I was ready to get back to the protection of the gated and guarded property. It felt surprisingly okay having to return to the guys. I still wished for my freedom, but for now, I could handle playing nice and doing what I needed to until that time came.

Feeling chipper from my small dose of alone

time, I finally arrived back at Tony's and was greeted by three of the guys gathered in the living room. Of course, Santos was MIA.

"Any scratches?" he asked sternly, standing up and holding out his hand.

"Nope! It's a dream to drive." I dropped the keys in his hands then pulled his phone from my pocket and handed that over as well. I hadn't needed it because I had my own, but I wasn't about to tell them that, besides it was dead anyway. I had started to head back to the bedroom when he stopped me.

"By the way, we're proud of you for turning down the blow."

"How the fuck do you know that?" I was instantly irate.

Tony pointed at my hoodie pocket. "Check that."

I shoved my hand inside and felt a tiny, hard plastic object brush up against my fingers. Pulling it out, I raised a brow. "You bugged me? Seriously?" I'd figured they'd track the car or his cell, but this was too far.

He shrugged and held his hand out once again, this time for the tiny device. *Oh hell no.* I dropped the offensive thing onto the floor at his feet and stomped on it until I heard a satisfying crack beneath my shoe.

"Whoopsie." I bared my teeth in a facsimile of a smile and made my way toward the hall, ignoring the look of contempt on Tony's face as Marco erupted into laughter. Vanni, however, looked crestfallen at what I'd done and went to gather the pieces. I felt a twinge of guilt, now knowing that it had apparently belonged to him, but I squashed it down. *He was in on it with the rest of them.*

Which reminded me...

"Oh!" I stopped to turn around and flash Vanni two middle fingers. "You owe me a hundred bucks."

I ignored Marco's laughter as I stomped down the hall to unload my stuff in my room. *Not your room, Eden.* Just like not catching feelings, I knew I couldn't get too comfortable or start thinking of anything here as *mine*. Getting away from this city had to stay a priority.

seventeen
sociopath

Tony

After Eden made her grand—and frankly childish—exit, I turned to Vanni, who was glaring at me over his broken toy.

"Have a feeling we'll need more of those."

Vanni frowned down at the shattered pieces, fingering them in his palm and shaking his head dejectedly. Tech was Vanni's area of expertise, and destroying it would not win Eden any points from him today.

"Might need sturdier ones, actually. These are expensive," he finally replied, anger lacing his tone.

I patted his shoulder. "I'll pay for that. It was my fault. Shouldn't have told her we bugged her." I walked over to the coat hanger by the door and slid my suit jacket on.

"Where are you off to?" Marco asked as he absently flipped through the channels on the TV.

I straightened my shirt cuffs and slipped my phone back into my pocket. "Seems I need to pay Danny a visit. I don't like how he brought us up to Eden. Now's as good a time as any to see if he's holding out on us over any news on Eden as well. I don't trust him to stay neutral, and I'll string the little shit up if we get any flak because of him."

The guys nodded their agreement, eyes hardening at the mention of the threat against Eden. Had Santos not been ready to quietly follow behind as she went about her errands, she wouldn't have stepped foot out of this house. As it stood, he was pissed at me for using her as bait and had gone downstairs to beat the shit out of the heavy bag in the gym. He'd gotten here just enough ahead of her for him to sneak into the house without her noticing he hadn't been here the entire time.

"Need backup?" Marco inquired seriously. I considered the offer but finally decided to decline.

"I think I've got this. Keep an eye on Eden. She may not have played into Danny's hands, but I still can't trust her. Minus the mini tantrum, she's being entirely too cooperative." By their expressions, neither of them seemed convinced, but they didn't outright dispute my orders, nodding when I waited expectantly. Feeling like an ass since I wasn't committed to Team Eden yet, I tried to explain. "Last time two of us rolled up in there, we left a pile of bodies and kidnapped one of Danny's girls. I think a low-key warning from just me would go over better, especially when the Finellis hear about it. You know they have their eyes out just as much as we do." As an afterthought, I added, "And drag Santos out of the gym."

I glared at Vanni as he opened his mouth, but all he said was, 'You got it, boss." With a one-fingered salute.

Cherry Baby was the last place I wanted to be, but there were appearances to uphold unless we wanted to lose face by letting small transgressions slide. I strode into the club, drawing immediate attention from the hired muscle, and tried to ignore the fact that my shoes were sticking to the floor as I walked. Why we'd played nice with this guy despite our suspicion that he was letting the Finellis run product through here was beyond me, but Danny and my father went way back, and Vinnie wanted concrete proof before he caused a rift in the neutral zone.

Danny was well paid, by both the Carlotti and Finelli families, to hold his tongue, so his comfort in talking so openly about us to Eden had put me on edge. Mission firmly in mind, I instructed the first bouncer I saw to take me to him.

Not surprisingly, Danny got up as soon as he spotted me coming his way and motioned for me to head back to his office. He stopped a passing waitress on the way, leaning in to whisper something in her ear, but he caught up quickly and silently, not brave or dumb enough to attempt discussing anything out in the open.

I was as familiar as he was with the layout of the building but did him the courtesy of letting him open his own office door. As soon as we were enclosed in the modest space, I got to the point.

"Were you trying to get information from Eden?"

The crow's feet near his eyes became more prominent as a line appeared between his salt and pepper brows. His confused tone matched his expression when he asked, "Angel? Not really, I just asked how she was doing and when she was coming back to work. Angel's not the type to open her mouth. She's a good girl when she's not doped up. Looked like she was clean earlier too. But if you tell me who was telling tales, I'll take care of it. I admit I was somewhat excited to see my best draw walk in the door. Girl's always been reliable, not like these flaky shits that come in here now, all thinking they can shake their asses and be headliners overnight." His deflection was missing a few details, but I'd been expecting as much. The man hadn't stayed in business this long, or kept his tongue, by not knowing how to read a situation.

"I'm specifically talking about you asking her about us." My pointed stare at his desk chair had him sighing and taking a seat. I leaned against the wall to the side of the door, thinking I should have brought Marco or Santos with me given how busy the club was. Danny wasn't much of a threat on his own, but the number of bouncers out on the floor told me something was going on.

"It was just a friendly question. Maybe I was fishing a bit to see if I should be watching my back after..." He trailed off, knowing we were both aware what he was referring to. Could never be too careful with your words unless you were willing to stake your life on the chance of being recorded. "I assumed that was within my boundaries, but since you're here, I suppose not. It's a shame that Angel quit, although if she's picked sides, it's probably for the best." The last was said politely enough, but the underlying threat to label Eden as a snitch didn't sit right with me at all.

"Whatever it is you assumed, you assumed wrong. The Carlotti name is not to leave your mouth. Not a whisper, not a word. Neither is Angel's. She didn't say shit and had no idea that we were keeping eyes and ears of our own on her. From your attitude, I'm wondering if you know who has a hit out on her."

I smiled coldly and shifted to expose the gun at my side, more than willing to fuck him up on Eden's behalf. I might not fully trust her, but she was under our protection, and I'd be damned if I didn't do my best to honor that.

"Antonio, you know I'd tell you if I knew." The man held his hands up, finally getting the direness of his situation. "All I know is there's a new player in town, one that wants his own piece of the pie, and he's managed to pull in defectors and turn those ambitious enough to cause problems to his side. I didn't know why the Finellis were here that night until they hit me with their pitch to run their product through here. I turned them down and offered a night with their choice of the girls on the house. I already told Vinnie all this. Why are you asking now?"

I was definitely confused. My father hadn't said shit, but maybe he was playing it close to the vest for now. It wasn't out of the realm of possibility that he was waiting for something concrete before sharing; he *was* still my boss after all. Before I had to make something up, he snapped his fingers and pulled a phone from his drawer. "Cops asked, but I told them it must have been stolen. Sam was supposed to take video that night. I was hoping those boys would talk while they were fucking the girls, and I could let Vinnie and Edward know what was up, but I can't get in it and don't know anything else. You can have it, a show of good faith. And no hard feelings about Sam. He was an asshole, loyal but an ass. As for

Angel, she's always welcome back. If you don't mind letting her know."

I wouldn't but nodded anyway then stepped forward to take the banged up device, checking that it was off before I pocketed it. I didn't know what the hell was going on lately, but we needed to figure it out before shit got worse. As it stood, both the Carlottis and Finellis looked like they were being poised to try for a takeover and start a war. At least a third party would better explain the guard at the house. I'd been worried the Finellis were infiltrating us in preparation for a takeover attempt, but now that I knew there was a likelier option, I had a hunch that if we found the culprit, we'd also find who had it out for Eden. I hoped like hell Vanni could get into the dead bouncer's phone, and regret crossed my mind when I admitted it might have been better to execute Santos' suggestion of taking the men for interrogation. It could all be over by now if we had, but then Eden would probably still be here, dancing and fucking or dead of an overdose, and I couldn't find the will to truly wish we'd done it differently.

"Glad we understand each other then. In the future, it would be best to remember that you're allowed to operate here under the grace of both Families. Neutral means neutral, and letting one faction get a toehold into this territory over the other is against the truce my father and Edward set up decades ago.

"Of course, Antonio. Just like I told your father, and Edward when I had to explain why two of his own were dead, I only want to run my business in peace and pay my dues."

I left Danny's office after a curt nod and headed out of the club. Now, it was back home to deal with more pressing matters like getting into the phone burning a hole in my pocket and ending the fuck that was disrupting everyone's lives.

eighteen

black sea

Eden

The next few days were about as exciting and stimulating as watching paint dry. I spent most of the time working out or watching TV by myself, stuffing my face with whatever I'd raided from the kitchen. More and more options were showing up in there daily, and though I rarely saw the staff, I knew they'd been around cleaning and restocking the bathrooms and kitchen. I knew they'd cleaned because I was getting restless with nothing to do and hadn't even been able to occupy myself that way. Besides boredom, there was also this feeling in the pit of my stomach that this was the calm before the storm. The guys had started acting dodgy as fuck around me, even more so than usual. As far as I could tell, their disdain had completely disappeared, except for maybe Tony, but I didn't see him enough to be sure. Despite the rest of them also being curiously absent, the sudden distance from Marco was the hardest to take.

When I did see them, happening to walk into a room where they were talking in low voices, they'd fall silent then change the subject. It was obvious they were hiding something from me, and while it wasn't unwarranted for them to expect some privacy, I was extremely uncomfortable. Every time I brought up leaving, I was shot down.

I knew some of it had to be about the men they'd killed the night they took me from the club, but I couldn't figure out why. I did find out that Rodrigo's car had been found torched, and all of his belongings had been put into a long-term storage unit. Apparently, they weren't sure if he was dead or on the run. I didn't much care what happened to him as long as he was gone for good and never came near me again. Santos had been salty that day, snapping at anyone he encountered until Tony sent him off to the gym to cool down.

With the tension in the house ratcheting up, I'd also decided that I needed a last ditch contingency plan to help me disappear. I didn't have any compunctions about playing Detective Fields to get my way if it came down to it, so I texted the number from the card he'd left, using the cell phone the guys still hadn't discovered.

The detective wasn't so eager to talk to me this time, which only made me more suspicious that there was something else going on. Either he had bigger issues to deal with, or I'd really sold that shit story just like I'd told Tony. I'd rub it in his face, but then I'd have to explain how I'd contacted the detective, and I wasn't keen on having my phone taken away.

With that avenue opened, I settled into day to day life in limbo, hoping something would give before I had to take drastic measures. That action would make enemies of the guys and likely the entire Family. I wasn't sure what I wanted from them yet, if anything, but if my track record was any indication, burning those bridges might come back to bite me in the ass.

It was one evening later that week when I came into the den to find Tony and Santos whispering amongst themselves yet again. As soon as they noticed me, they clammed up and looked over.

"Planning your next kidnapping?" I deadpanned.

Tony's lip twitched as if he found my taunt amusing but refused to let out a laugh. "Not quite. Santos and I have some things to do tonight, but Marco and Vanni will be here."

That was all I was getting, as usual, and Santos quickly averted his eyes when I glanced at him, proceeding to walk past me without a word. "Fuck you too, asshole!" I yelled after him before muttering to myself about mafia twats and mood swings. He didn't have to talk to me. I mean, it wasn't *necessary*, but he could at least be civil when we encountered each other.

No sooner had Tony and Santos left than Vanni and Marco came through the front door, arms full with bags of snacks and drinks. At Marco's mischievous grin when he passed me by, I grew curious enough to follow them.

"You like games, Edie?" filtered back from the front of our little procession to the kitchen.

Not sure if I wanted to stew in my irritation from earlier or let it go to find out what these two were up to, I answered noncommittally, "Depends on what it is."

Vanni turned to me as he sat his load on the island, and I studiously avoided eye contact. Kitchens seemed to be where I got into the most trouble, and I didn't feel brave enough to tempt fate tonight. "Tony and Santos left us home to babysit tonight, so we're getting drunk and playing cards. You in?"

My annoyance reared back up at his griping over having to watch me, while Marco punched him none too gently in the shoulder. "Fuck you, Giovanni, I'd be gone already if you'd let my ass out!" My choice of words had been just as tactless as his, and I felt bad when Marco straightened abruptly and turned his back on us to put away the drinks with a bit more force than necessary.

I glared at Vanni while I tried to figure out a way to apologize to Marco without outright lying. "I didn't mean to sound ungrateful..." I didn't know where to go from there. He'd been great for the most part, but I wasn't happy with his change in demeanor since we'd hooked up. It *could* be circumstantial, but that wasn't my fault either.

"Don't worry about it, Edie. We all know you want as far away from us as you can get." Subdued and resigned, Marco forced a dimmer version of his usual grin before adding, "Come on and play with us. The billiards room is stocked with just about everything, but we're doing cards tonight. And alcohol." He jerked a thumb toward one of the bags Vanni had set down. "Wasn't sure what all was on hand so we picked up the makings for margaritas and Coke for the Jack."

"Fine, as long as Vanni can behave." I turned my gaze on the man in question who nodded and shrugged. It wasn't much of a reassurance, but I'd take it. Better than watching the same shit on television again.

We were on our third round of drinks, the atmosphere considerably lighter, when Marco went for a bathroom break, leaving me and Vanni alone in the posh game room. I considered using a cigarette break as an excuse, but it hadn't been that long since I was out on the balcony with Marco, much to Vanni's disapproval about the bad habit. He'd shut up when I said it was better than smoking crank.

After a moment of awkward silence, he moved over to sit in the chair next to me at the card table and sighed. "I'm sorry," he mumbled.

I let out a snort. "I'm not really sure what exactly it is that you're apologizing for."

Vanni smiled for a moment at my snark, then his face grew serious. "For everything. Well, not for saving you that night, I'm glad about that part, but the rest of it... After hearing what really happened with Rodrigo, I realized that I let my own anger at you leaving and wrecking Santos get the best of me. It wasn't just him that was affected, ya know?" I opened my mouth to respond but couldn't find the words, which was just as well because Vanni wasn't finished. "I wanted you to know that after everything is all said and done, if you want to stay, I can talk to Tony."

"Stay?" I questioned, surprise filtering through me. "Here? As in, with you guys?"

"Yeah. I know we haven't been that great to you on the whole, besides Marco, and don't think I don't know about that," he said with a wink, much to my consternation, "but I wanted to clear the air. Let you know there's a place for you here if you need it. Or, if you really want to leave, I'll help you disappear. The others don't even have to know if you'd prefer it that way. I can make that happen. You just tell me what you need for *you*, and don't worry about the rest."

To say I was shocked was an understatement. *Is Vanni really trying to make peace with me? Is his offer genuine?*

"That's— really sweet, Vanni. I'm not sure what to say." Unbelievable was what actually came to mind, but I didn't want to sound like an asshole when he seemed like he was actually trying to make amends with me.

"Also, I should probably apologize for the kitchen incident, but I won't. That was hot as fuck... Although maybe the aftermath shouldn't be repeated." He seemed to realize what he'd insinuated and tried to backtrack. "Not that I'm asking for a repeat. I mean, I would, but... Fucking hell, you know what I mean."

By the time he was done fumbling, the normally unflappable man was holding his head in his hands and groaning self-consciously.

"Oh, um, thanks? I think?" I tried not to laugh, I really did, but I couldn't help it when he lifted his head with a glower aimed at me.

"Thanks for what?" Marco asked, suddenly appearing and plopping down on the other side of me at the table. "You kids getting along in here?" The fucker had to have been eavesdropping; he was entirely too smug.

"I was apologizing for being a dick to her. About the babysitting," Vanni answered awkwardly, rubbing his hand on the back of his neck. Smooth.

Marco smirked and began shuffling the cards in his hand. "Right. Sure. Glad you two are getting along now. Do you want to play something else?" He bumped my arm with his elbow when I didn't respond, and I raised my brows in question.

"I'm tired of poker, and if you don't care..." He glanced slyly between me and Vanni. "I say we do something a bit more... fun."

Vanni looked just as wary as I felt, and I sensed a bet or something more nefarious coming on. "Like what?" I drew out.

"Go Fish," he deadpanned.

Both Vanni and I busted out laughing. I was relieved yet highly confused at Marco's agenda. I knew there had to be one. Marco could try the patience of a saint, and his antics regularly had someone pissed off at him.

"Are we seriously going to play a child's game?" Vanni finally asked after his laugh sobered.

"Wait, wait, wait." Marco held up his hands. "We'll make it interesting." He went to the sideboard and came back with shot glasses and a bottle of whiskey.

"That sounds like a terrible idea." I grimaced, knowing how quickly it would devolve, likely ending with someone puking. And I wasn't cleaning that shit up.

I glanced between them warily, feeling like I was missing something, but I was honestly afraid to ask. Unfortunately, my reluctance was the galvanizing force behind Vanni accepting the challenge. "Deal me in, Marco. You're going to be hanging over the toilet before the night's over."

I sighed, seeing no other option at the moment. At least if I started to lose, I could always go to bed, right? With one more sigh, I gave in. "Fine. How does it work?"

Marco began dealing out cards. "Simple. Same rules as the regular game, but with a twist. If someone asks for a card and you have one, you take a shot. If you have two or more of that card, you take two shots."

I nodded along, already gathering that there was no way any of us were walking away from this game sober, even with one round, and planned to quit after it was done. "And if we go fish, no one drinks?"

"Exactly," Marco replied as he finished dealing. "Ladies first," he declared with a grin.

"Wait, I'm not getting alcohol poisoning. Recovering here, remember? I had to take one of those fucking horse pills Carlos prescribed earlier, and I'm not puking that shit up. Grab the margarita pitcher instead. It's at least diluted." *Look at me, being all responsible and shit.*

They both froze at the mention of my addiction, as if they'd forgotten, and maybe they had. They'd been busy. Add in that I wasn't a screeching rage monster anymore now that the physical cravings were gone, and I could understand how it might've slipped their minds. It was easy to remember someone was an addict when they were in withdrawal or so far gone they couldn't remember basic hygiene. It was always harder to spot the cracks once someone was clean, well-fed, and acting like a normal, functioning human being. I probably wouldn't have been drinking on my own, just in case, but I knew these two wouldn't let me out of the house, and I had no access to any drugs here.

"We're assholes, Edie. I'm sorry. I wasn't thinking." I stopped him there with a raised hand.

"I'm a big girl, and I can say no. Honestly, other than thinking I want it, mostly when shitty memories plague my sleep, I'm good. But I'm not shooting whiskey. Besides, if we have to call Carlos again, he's probably just going to put me out of my misery." My joke fell flat, neither of them laughing, and Vanni got up and grabbed the melting pitcher filled with neon slush. Marco started the game, a bit more subdued than he had been moments ago.

I surveyed the cards I'd been dealt. I didn't have anything particularly good, and no sets of four, but I did have two aces.

I turned to Vanni first. "Got any aces?"

He checked his cards and shook his head. "Go fish."

I groaned and picked a card up from the deck on the table.

"Do you have any twos?" he asked me, grinning.

"Fuck. I knew that was going to happen," I lamented, handing over the one I had. Marco poured the icy liquid into my glass and pushed it closer to me.

"Drink up, Lady Garden."

I tipped the shot glass back, emptying the contents, and turned to Marco.

He winced as he asked, "Got any aces?"

"Ohhh, you're an asshole," I teased him, feeling bad when his expression went from cautious to crestfallen. "Dude, chill, I'm just teasing. Although, the margaritas are a tad like the ice cream if you want to up the ante." Vanni choked while Marco blinked at me, for once failing to have a snappy comeback. Slyly, I added, "It might be interesting to see which of you has the skills to deep throat." When they blanched, I couldn't hold it in and busted up laughing. It relieved the tension, and Vanni beat Marco to the pitcher, filling my glass once more.

"I think I'm good with the drinks, Edie. You know you're kind of a shit when you want to be, right?" I shrugged unrepentantly and spun my finger in a circle for the game to get going again. It was slightly ridiculous that two of the Carlotti men were playing a game of Go Fish, like one of those bad jokes that always started out with two men in a bar, but it was also kind of perfect. Despite growing up in the Family and officially being part of the business now, they could still shut it off just enough to have a small moment of normalcy. I wouldn't tell them this, but I kind of thought this was just what I needed right now.

I'd lost track of time *and* the amount of shots I'd taken when a very drunk Vanni had proclaimed we should change the rules up some. Instead of taking shots, he proposed, we should strip a piece of clothing off. Strip Go Fish sounded like a way better idea, especially since I'd absolutely reached my limit of drunkenness. At least, I thought it was a good idea when I pictured the two of them butt ass naked and displayed for my viewing pleasure.

After a while, I realized that drunk me was much better at this game than sober me because both of the guys were in only their underwear and socks. Well, Marco had one sock on. I, on the other hand, still sported my underwear, shirt, and bra. Socks had been the first thing to go. I had gotten down to my underwear, but that was more of a relief than anything. The temperature in the room had risen dramatically with both the alcohol and my libido.

"Do you have any fives?" Marco slurred, shooting me a large grin when he saw my face fall.

"Shit." I handed over the five I had, but I knew something they didn't. How to remove my bra without showing a thing. I set my cards down and leaned forward to twist my arms behind my back.

About the time the guys realized what I was doing, both of them groaning about it, a figure appeared in the doorway.

"What the hell is going on here?" Santos asked warily as I paused with a strap and one lady cup hanging out of my shirt-sleeve.

"Just some fun," Marco replied with a snort of laughter.

A scowling Santos came to stand next to me.

"How much did you let her drink?" he demanded of the other two.

"Hey!" I smacked his chest, getting his attention back on me. His head snapped in my direction. "Not your damn business!"

Santos' lips quirked upward at the corners. "It is now. Say goodnight, boys, and put your dicks away before you poke someone's eye out." It was the first time Santos had said more than two words to me in days, and I was torn between arguing with him over his high-handedness and seeing if I could win another round to get a better view of the goods.

Before I could do something stupid, like choose either of my options, he ducked down and threw me over his shoulder, heading out of the room amid the guys' hilarity and ignoring my demands to be released.

"Put me down!"

"Nope. Say goodnight, Eden. You've had enough," Santos ordered, not stopping his progression down the hall.

"Goodnight, Eden. You've had enough," I snarked.

He ignored my sass and continued to carry me until we reached my room where he tossed me onto the bed. "Go to sleep. You're going to need the rest to get through the massive hangover you'll have in the morning." I didn't get a chance to give him a piece of my mind since he immediately left the room, shutting the door behind him.

I considered tracking him down on principle, but then a yawn hit. Easily deterred, I dragged my drunk ass to the bathroom to wash my face and brush my teeth, then chugged as much water as I could before changing and climbing into bed.

My head barely hit the pillow before I passed the fuck out.

My ready-to-burst bladder woke me up. I vaguely remembered Santos dumping me into bed, and my raging headache reminded me of the amount of alcohol I'd consumed. With my thighs clenched together as much as possible, I awkwardly shuffled to the bathroom and swore my poor abused organ cramped in relief and retribution when it was finally empty.

The mirror was *not* my friend, and I ignored my reflection as I brushed my teeth then downed some pain reliever and copious amounts of water before going to shower. By the time I was done, the realization hit that no one had popped in on me yet. After the camaraderie of the other night, I'd thought things might have gone back to what passed for our normal, but I must have been wrong. A small part of me was disappointed, and then an even larger part mentally kicked myself for being disappointed that Marco wasn't up my ass when I had a hangover. Although I would be both surprised and impressed if he didn't have one too.

Feeling better now that I was clean and the Tylenol had kicked in, I wandered down the hall to get something to eat. Somehow, I still didn't encounter anyone. Shrugging it off, I went for the cereal, and that was when I found a note on the refrigerator. I scanned it once, then reread it again. The fuckers had ditched me to go handle 'business.' I was hit with an unexpected bolt of worry. *What if it's dangerous?* I told myself it wasn't because I cared, but because I wasn't sure what would happen to me if they didn't come back. Flimsy excuse, but whatever, I was sticking to it. Annoyed at being left out of the loop again and feeling dumb for it, I took my cereal back to my room and pulled my phone out.

I hadn't expected any messages, checking more out of habit now that I had it back than anything else, but there was a text and several missed calls. The text and the phone calls were all from Danny, saying he needed me to call him ASAP.

Curiosity won out over my better judgment, and I hit the icon to return his call. He answered on the first ring.

"Angel, girl, am I glad you called. I need your help. Please, I'm begging you." Alarmed at the seemingly genuine panic in his voice, I responded.

"What happened? Are you okay?"

"Nothing happened. Not yet, anyway. I've got high rollers coming in for a private party tonight, and they want entertainment. Your type, if you get my drift."

Angry, I almost hung up but decided to chew him out first. *"That's* your emergency? I quit, Danny. Told you I'm not doing that shit anymore, and you have me over here thinking you're gonna die."

"Angel, you don't understand. I might. I agreed to the party before everything happened, and most of the girls that do the private shows up and quit after that. I have three girls. *Three*, Angel. I need at least one more for the fourth satellite stage. I can explain the main one being shut down, but not if one of the seating areas is lacking a dancer."

"What type of high rollers are we talking about?" My suspicions were mounting, and I was pissed.

"The kind that I can't talk about, non-disclosure and all that. You know how it is." I did, and I'd bet my tight ass that I knew where the guys had gone. Actually, I was about to bet it.

"If I took it on, what would I be required to do?"

That's when Danny hedged. "All of it," he finally muttered.

That's what I was afraid of. But did I really care? It was just a job, and the Carlotti men obviously didn't give a shit since they'd left me here, passed out and in the dark after they'd been so congenial the night before. We'd almost been naked for fuck's sake. Not to mention that Vanni had offered to help me disappear. I was definitely doubting the validity of that drunken promise. Again, the worst of it was Marco and his apparent willingness to disappear on me. *And to go to a strip club, no less*, a strangely bitter part of me whispered.

Admittedly, Cherry Baby *was* a standard, neutral meeting place, but it just didn't sit right with me. I could have helped them, but they'd completely disregarded me as anything other than a reluctant guest and damsel in need of rescue. *And to think I've worried about and missed their rude asses. Jerks.* I'd had enough of waiting around for them to trust me or at least give me proof that the jackass guard hadn't been talking out of his ass when he said someone wanted me dead. With what I had saved and the pay day I could bring in on a night like this, I could jet out of town and not have to involve anyone else. It would also show the high-handed assholes that I wasn't some simpering female that couldn't hold her own.

"Fifty-fifty. Paid out the instant I'm done, so you'd better keep track. And I want a fucking guard this time. Won't be the first time they've seen me indisposed." Danny started to whine about the cut, but I refused to listen to it. "Only offer I'm giving, Danny. I want enough to jet and not look back. Make it happen, or I'm not making a pit stop there."

That sealed the deal, and I got off the phone to figure out how I was going to get off of the property and what the hell I was going to use to prep for what I hoped would be the last time I ever played the whore.

nineteen
you don't own me
Eden

Turned out, the guys didn't have random things like douche kits sitting around in a cupboard. Well, not where I felt comfortable searching anyway. Cognizant of the fact that there were cameras Tony could tap into at any time, anywhere, severely limited my options. I hit pay dirt when I found a bag of saline and tubing under my own bathroom sink. Locking the bathroom door just in case anyone came back, I used a bit of conditioner to slick the first several inches of tubing and squeezed the solution to the tip before clipping it off. Sitting on the toilet with my heels propped on the seat, I began inserting it until it was deep enough for my purposes then released the clamp to let it start to flow.

About half the volume was in when it started to become uncomfortable, so I squeezed the bag to hurry it along. It wasn't my favorite activity, but it beat far more embarrassing mishaps that might occur if I didn't do it. By the time I was finished and in the shower, the nerves hit. It would be the first time in forever that I wouldn't be high for a performance, and I wasn't sure how the guys would react to what I was about to do. It worried me there could be a very public scene in my near future that would blow my plans to hell. Pondering their reaction and my feelings about it, I finished getting ready and devised a plan to get off the property.

Leaving was a lot easier than I'd anticipated. After checking that there were guards stationed outside, I crossed my fingers, grabbed my purse and duffel, and went past the kitchen to the back hall that led to the multi-car garage. There was a mudroom that sat between the two with a box mounted on the wall holding spare keys for the vehicles. Opening the door didn't set off any alarms, and I prayed my luck held and Tony was too busy to check and see what I was up to. I pressed the unlock buttons on the fobs until an SUV with nearly blacked out windows lit up, took the set from the box, and pulled on an oversized hoodie that had been hanging on one of the wall hooks. I couldn't pinpoint whose it was, but Marco was the likeliest guess based on the size. It hung down to my knees and would hopefully do a decent enough job of concealing my identity until I was off the grounds.

The remote in the SUV opened and shut the garage, and besides a cursory glance, the guards didn't move as I drove by. The gates were opened by the same remote, and that guard eyed the vehicle a bit harder, but he still didn't stop me. I was fairly certain they'd been told to watch for me, but no one had anticipated I'd take one of the guys' cars. It made me feel vaguely guilty that they'd be blamed for my escape, but hopefully they could use the valid excuse that they'd normally catch hell for stopping one of the guys. I knew the vehicle was likely trackable, but it wouldn't matter once I'd made it into the city. I had an idea to ingratiate a certain detective to me and a safe place to temporarily store the SUV where someone could retrieve it from later.

Blindly fishing around in my purse at the first stoplight I came to, I pulled out my phone and tapped the call button on the detective's icon. I put it on speaker as I waited for him to answer, hoping I wouldn't have to leave a message. Even if Vanni's offer was genuine, I'd already inadvertently caused rifts in their lives once before. I didn't want to knowingly do it this time.

"Fields."

"Detective, it's Eden. Is there any chance I can

hitch a ride to the club?" I figured direct was still the best approach with him.

"Miss Moretti. You blocked your number." His annoyance came through the line, and I winced at the shaky start.

"Yes, I thought there'd be a fifty-fifty chance that it would work. I'd rather there be as little trace of our association as possible. I'm sure you understand."

A grunt sounded over the line that I took to be an agreement. "How'd you ditch your keepers?" At my silence, he sighed and tried a different route. "Can I assume that your sudden desire to go back to Cherry Baby and the rumblings I'm hearing about are related?"

And there was the rub. I couldn't, and wouldn't, actually share anything that he'd be interested in. Especially if the attendees were who I thought they were.

"Honestly, I have no clue. I'm doing this as a last favor to my old boss. A thank you for taking me in when I was broke and nearly starving to death. After this, we're even and I'm moving on. But I thought if I heard anything, I could pass it along on my way out. You know, wrap up any loose ends?"

If it weren't for the small rustling noises I could hear in the background and the timer still going, I'd have thought he hung up as he took so long to reply. I was almost to the diner where I wanted to leave the SUV; it sat on the fringes of the neutral zone, and it was unlikely anyone would fuck with it there.

"Send me the address. If it's close to the club, I'll be there in ten minutes," he finally replied.

I hung up and contemplated the fact that he was either watching the club, the guys, or both. My uneasiness became full-on paranoia. I started adding shit up in my head, and it all pointed at me or the Carlotti brothers, and since I was small potatoes compared to them... *Unless you're bait.* A frisson of fear worked down my spine, and I wondered if Danny had really sent the messages. I was kicking myself for being an idiot, about to bail on the whole thing, when a car pulled up next to me, facing the opposite direction. The detective motioned for me to get out while he pulled a ball cap lower over his face.

Hoping like hell I hadn't just fucked myself, I exited the car and locked up before settling into the detective's passenger seat.

"Miss Moretti," he started as he pulled out, "you look quite a bit different than when I saw you last."

I assumed he meant my clothing, but something was bugging me about him commenting on my appearance, and I thought it was deliberate on his part. "Did you actually need the address? Even though I'm *so* unrecognizable, you pulled right up to my vehicle, so you had to know which I was in. Is it me or the guys that are being monitored?"

"I'd suggest you trust your instincts, Miss

Moretti. Things have... changed." I stared straight ahead, refusing to react, as we neared the club.

The fucker was either trying to warn me, or he was fishing. Neither boded well, and again I wondered what hell I was walking into. Needing at least *some* reassurance, I pulled my phone out of my purse and hit the number for Danny, turning the speaker's volume as low as it would go.

"Angel, where the fuck are you? We've got early birds arriving." The thump of the music in the background and Danny's characteristic non-greeting had me relaxing enough that I didn't demand the detective turn around.

"I'm coming up in five. Have one of the bouncers meet me at the back. I'm not dressed to be coming through the main doors." Danny assured me someone would be there to let me in, and I turned to Fields. "If you pull through the alley, I can go around the corner to the door there. No sense in being seen together. I appreciate the ride by the way."

He nodded but didn't offer anything else, and I was seriously getting weirded out by his demeanor. We remained in an uncomfortable silence the rest of the way there, but he pulled in where I indicated and cut the lights.

I had opened my door to get out, glad the experience was over, when he quietly called out, "Miss Moretti, you dropped something." Turning to look, I watched as he laid a matchbook onto the seat, the front emblazoned with another club's logo. Warily, I picked it up, noting it felt heavier than it should, and flipped the cover open.

Use this if you're in need. Text only.

I was confused until he flashed his phone screen at me and tapped his finger before pointedly looking at the battery-like object in my hand. Not sure I was following, I pressed the smaller recessed portion and felt an almost indistinguishable click. Almost immediately, a notification hit the phone screen, and when he tapped on it, a map popped up with a dot on it. Right outside Cherry Baby.

Eyes wide in shock that he'd slipped me a fucking tracking device, I nodded and clicked it again, watching as the light disappeared from the map. Since he was being so careful, I was afraid to say anything and tucked the coin-sized device into my purse, pulled a cigarette out, and used the single match to light it before touching the flame to the corner of the empty matchbook to burn the note.

"I'm going to have a quick smoke before I go in. Thanks again for the ride." I dropped the burning note onto the pavement, tamping it out when the flame died down. "Oh, and detective? I'll be leaving town soon, just FYI." I added on the last so whoever was listening would know I didn't intend to hang around. A flash of guilt bombarded me at that. I hadn't intended to cause more problems. I didn't know which of us was being watched him or me, and

I couldn't exactly ask, but really, who the fuck would bug a detective?

"Take care of yourself, Miss Moretti."

I nodded and shut the car door before rounding the front and heading around the corner of the building to reach the rear entrance. Crushing my cigarette out in the sand-filled ashtray next to it, I rapped my knuckles on the door. A man I didn't recognize, wearing the club t-shirt under a jacket, answered to usher me in.

"Angel?" he asked as I passed his large frame. He was clean-cut and better looking than most of Danny's recruits. The boss had always been adamant that the girls' attention needed to be on the paying customers, not eye-candy like this guy. I decided then and there not to rely on the new hire. Too many things were off with the whole situation.

"Yep, that's me. You shadowing me tonight?"

He nodded and gestured down the hall toward the dressing room. "I'm Steve, and Danny said he's waiting for you on stage four."

I made an annoyed sound in my throat at the impatience of my former boss, but I picked up my pace to go prepare. When Steve made to follow me into the dressing room, I put my hand up.

"I got it from here. Give me a few minutes, and I'll be right back." Steve was shaking his head before I even finished.

"Sorry, boss' orders that I don't let you out of my

sight. It's my second week, and I'd rather not get canned tonight, Miss Angel."

I opened my mouth to argue but decided it wasn't worth it. Maybe Danny was simply taking my request for security more seriously than he had in the past. Shrugging, I opened the door and went straight to my old locker. It was still empty, so I stowed my purse inside before stripping down and shoving my clothes in as well. Steve watched the empty area instead of me, which I appreciated, while I went to the racks of clean costumes to get dressed.

By the time I was done darkening my makeup using one of the other girls' cosmetics, I'd transformed from fresh-faced and casual to sultry and seductive.

"I'm ready. Is Danny on the floor?" Steve nodded as he opened the door, holding it out of the way for me, and I walked toward the main area with him following closely behind.

"So, you've done one of these parties before, right? You know what all can go on, and unless I signal, you're to stay back?"

"Yes, ma'am. Understood." I gave him a half smile and took a breath for courage as I pushed out through the door leading to the main floor.

The music was set to a low thumping rhythm, and the lights were dim enough to hide the imperfections of the room despite it having been cleaned until it was a definite step up from its usual condition. The room was littered with men in suits and muscle packing heat. Ignoring it all, I kept my eyes on my route to Danny. He currently stood near the stage I'd be working, talking to a group of men. Arriving at my destination, I took a moment to survey the room's occupants.

There were few women besides the dancers and waitresses, and those that were there were seated or hugged up tight to the men they'd come with. I gave Danny a nod when he glanced at me, and then, as I stepped up onto the small stage and gripped the pole in preparation to begin a simple routine, the attention of the room shifted. A familiar group of men dressed in varying styles of black and white made their way across the floor... heading directly for the seating area nearest my position.

Choosing to ignore their presence, I lazily twirled around the pole and set out to perform a slower, more sensual routine than I usually did. It would allow me to keep a better eye and ear out for the goings on but wouldn't wear me out so quickly. If all went according to plan, I'd need to leave immediately after the club closed, and I didn't know how long it would take to get out of range of everyone's radar. Not to mention I'd need to be awake and alert in order to handle any unexpected issues. I had hoped to talk to Danny before I started, but I was fairly certain I could get him to give me a ride to pick up my duffel before dropping me at the train station.

Santos was the first one to recognize me, eyes widening in shock then quickly narrowing in anger after a brief flash of appreciative appraisal. His intent was clear as he stalked toward me, but Tony caught up and gripped his arm, pulling Santos to a halt as he leaned over to speak quietly into his ear. The anger in Santos' gaze banked, but it didn't fully disappear, and I studiously avoided making direct eye contact with anyone after that. I didn't want to know what their reactions would be. I didn't require their approval, and it would piss me off if I started to feel guilty over sneaking out. I was done being a prisoner.

Tony turned to greet the men at the table, shaking hands and slapping backs, while Santos took a seat against the wall and observed. Vanni followed Tony's lead, and I noticed he was getting more attention from one of the women than the man she was tucked up against. A burning sensation set up residence in my gut, and it took a moment before I was able to identify the emotion. I'd vowed not to catch feelings, and now I was fucking jealous of some twat that had chosen the route I'd gone to such extremes to avoid. In an effort to prove to myself that I didn't care a bit about any of them, I turned my attention to the rest of the room and pretended they weren't there. Until Marco came up...

The room had started to clear, the main players of the night gradually making their way over to Tony's table while others left after whatever business they'd come to discuss was finished. The other stages shut down, one by one, until the dancers were congregating near the guys as well. I was sure they were waiting to see if their services were required as was par for the course at these events.

I'd made a few hundred, mostly from those I thought to be mid-ranking members of one faction or the other as they waited for their leaders to get down to business. It wasn't enough for my purposes though, and I was preparing myself to do what was needed to earn enough to make the night worthwhile. The problem was... despite some of them being attractive enough, I wasn't interested in any other than the four that I was trying my best to ignore.

Marco sauntered up to my stage right about the time I caught sight of a guest perusing one of the degradingly familiar menus used to offer extracurricular services. He edged out one of the few men watching the show, not that I was putting on much of one since getting naked hadn't been a requirement. *Not yet, anyway.*

"Hey, doll, does this cover the rest of your night?" He produced a wad of bills and fanned them out on the edge of the stage. I nearly swallowed my tongue at the money and hated that I had to turn him down, but his expression was full-on mischievousness, and I knew he was up to no good. Unless everything he'd said when we hooked up was a lie, I also doubted that he'd come in with what appeared to be several thousand dollars to tip the dancers or buy a piece of ass. To validate my suspicions that Marco had paid for my favors, I shot a glance toward Danny to find him already waiting to give me a nod.

Scooping up his cash and handing it back over, I resigned myself to a very different situation than I'd planned. I accepted Marco's hand when he held it out. With a sharp tug, he had me toppling into his arms, and I barely managed to tone my shriek down to a yip of surprise. I caught sight of Steve straightening from the corner of my eye and turned in Marco's arms to give him a discreet shake of the head while gesturing for him to collect my tips. I wasn't the only one that noticed, and as I wiggled for Marco to let me down, Santos' gaze met mine, giving me the opportunity to glare at him for shifting toward my guard.

"Tell him to stop it," I hissed quietly at Marco. "He's there to protect me if I need it." Marco's attention went from playful to serious in an instant as he glanced away from my earnest stare to assess the bouncer. He tucked me under his arm to guide me over to the table and gave Santos a pointed glance before flicking his eyes back at the man watching over me.

Santos eased back, likely familiar with the signal, but his glower didn't lessen a bit, making the pale, curving scar stand out starkly against his darker complexion. I wasn't sure if it was in disapproval that I was here entertaining, or here in general, but it stung to witness his disdain. This was me. It was what I did to survive after him, and if he didn't like it, that was too damned bad. I wasn't here for him anyway.

Turning to Marco, I whispered, "What did you do that for?" When he looked offended, I realized he thought I meant calling Santos off, so I nudged the pocket the cash had disappeared into.

"Don't worry, Angel. I only put down a deposit on a cocktail called Angel's Kiss. From what I gather, it gives me first dibs but allows me to spend some time in your company, no?" I nodded and silently sent Danny a thank you for leaving me an out if I needed it. I could turn it down, but when that option was selected, which wasn't often, the patron's credit card was charged for a round of drinks to prove they had the cash. After that, I automatically earned a thousand as the down payment to hold their spot until the end of the evening. The patron received the other four thousand if the offer was accepted, at which point it was carte blanche. Normally I hated the situation, it either ended with getting shorted for the night, which was incentive to seal the deal, or they wanted things that even I cringed at. With Marco, I knew the latter wouldn't be an issue, but I needed to earn more than the deposit he'd put down, which meant fucking him, or finding another client.

I flashed Marco a grateful smile as well, knowing he didn't have to do that. A slight bite of guilt hit me since he obviously didn't realize I'd have to put out or try for another offer too. Danny would expect to make more than I had so far, especially as the split was fifty-fifty. It felt greedy and slightly scummy to think of it like that, but I tried to steel myself for the inevitability that I'd be Marco's whore, or I'd likely take his money and go fuck someone else.

His face cleared of annoyance as he winked back in response before he took a seat next to Vanni and pulled me into his lap. Both Tony and Vanni gave me quick glances, but they didn't pause in their conversation to say anything to me.

Coming in on the middle of the discussion, I was a bit lost but eventually gleaned that they were discussing the escalating rush of products being run through both territories and the neutral zone. Products that hadn't come from either side. Seemed like whoever was attracting and amassing a veritable army of members had set up to run guns, drugs, and girls right under the Families' noses.

Midway in the conversation, Vanni leaned over under the guise of feeling me up to speak softly in my ear. "I don't know what game you're playing at, but it ends now. You'll be returning home with us as soon as this is over."

Before he could pull away, I murmured with heat in my tone, "Isn't everyone here playing one game or another?"

He sat back like I hadn't responded, signaling the waitress for another drink. "Another, please, and get the lady a water. I'm sure she's parched, and I wouldn't want it to affect her... performance."

The woman gave me a round-eyed glance at the vitriol in Vanni's tone despite the attempt at politeness and scampered off to collect his order. One of the men leaned over with interest in his eyes. He apparently wasn't important enough to be directly involved in the current conversation, but he certainly thought enough of himself to question a Carlotti's claim.

"I thought Marco had you for the night?" He pointedly glanced at Vanni in question.

"I do, or is that not apparent?" Marco had stiffened under me and tightened his arm around my waist as he dared the man to contradict him.

"No offense meant. I was just told that it's her last night, and I've seen her around here and heard she's up for anything. Can't blame a guy for trying, right?" His demeanor didn't quite match his words, as his tone and forced smile betrayed his true feelings, but Marco didn't pursue it. Instead, he twisted me further to face away from man.

Unfortunately, it put one of the other guests directly in my line of sight right as they leaned over a silver tray to snort their drug of choice. I closed my eyes and leaned into Marco, suddenly ready to abandon my plans and regroup tomorrow. The club was too full of temptation and bad memories, and the guys were intent on taking me back with them anyway. Life had been simpler in some ways when I only had my next fix to look forward to. There weren't any budding feelings to process or old hurts to try to forgive. There was only doing what I had to to survive and blissing out the rest of the time. The compounding complications of my current circumstances made me crave the bleak simplicity of my former life, even if it was only for a moment. It would be a welcome reprieve from the angst and uncertainty I suffered from now.

Needing to get away, if just for a moment, I turned my head to tell Marco I had to use the restroom. He seemed reluctant to let me go, so I reminded him, "Steve is my shadow for the evening, and I'll be right back."

He searched my face for a moment before

nodding with a sigh. "Don't take off, I mean it. I'll come after you if you aren't back in five."

Not wasting any time, I slipped from his lap and back onto my spiked heels. My feet were sore after the break they'd had and protested my weight being on them. I might have also needed a minute, but I really did have to use the bathroom. My guard in tow, I beelined for the one nearest the bar.

Being it was a single room without any other exit, he stayed outside, taking up a watchful stance with his back to the door. I quickly did my business and washed my hands, only to come out and get waylaid by the man from the table.

"Hey, I'm Jasper by the way. I got to talking with Luna over there." He tipped his head toward the redhead who sat with a smug grin on her face aimed in our direction. She'd been a friend of Trixie's, and I couldn't imagine she'd had anything nice to say. "She said you don't mind multiples and can pick your date for the evening. Also mentioned I'd have a better chance if I sweetened the deal." He pulled a miniscule, white powder-filled baggie out of his pocket and held it up in front of my face.

My willpower was waning by the second until Tony appeared to lay his claim. "I believe you were told that she's taken for the night." The cold finality in his tone had a shiver coursing through me, and Jasper's expectancy turned to offense.

"I believe the house rules state the whores are fair

game unless they're in a prior arrangement. You can't exactly pull rank here either." I didn't think Jasper wanted to go that route, but it was his ass, *not* mine.

Marco joined Tony to add his two cents. "I put a deposit down, so she's mine until I say otherwise." That wasn't quite how it worked, but I wasn't about to argue as he gripped my elbow and steered me back to the table.

Only to find Luna making a move on Santos. The anger came, hitting me in the gut then traveling up to my chest, and I shook off Marco's grip to stalk up to the bitch.

"Sorry, he's already occupied for the night," I blatantly lied. Santos, the asshole, didn't seem to be on the same page, raising his brows at my declaration.

"I don't know, Angel." He paused for a second after uttering the long ago endearment that I'd turned into my shield against ever getting involved with anyone again. I knew then that whatever he was doing, it was on purpose. He hadn't tried to address me in that manner, or in any manner at all lately, since he'd saved me from his father. The bastard had the audacity to check Luna out, as if he'd just now noticed her ample assets on full display. "Those lips probably suck like a vacuum. I might have to try them out."

Hurt ate at me as memories assailed me at the triggering word.

"Get on the table, Hoover" echoed in my head as sightless eyes stared at the ceiling beneath the neat hole in her forehead. My skin prickled with gooseflesh as I clutched my throat, phantom sensations of Arlo's dead dick ramming in and the pain that followed bombarding me. I was thrown back into the memory of being dragged about by my hair to face my death. Happenstance had saved me, but the fragility of my mortality haunted me as I confronted the ghosts of my past, leaving me to quail in terror.

With a whimper, I turned to flee, only to run into Tony's arms. Grateful for any place of refuge, I turned my head into his chest and held on tight.

"Santos is busy. Get lost." Tony's demand brooked no argument, causing Luna to blanch and back away until she was flush with Jasper. "Dick move, bro. Let's get this shit wrapped up and go home." Tony led me away, and I had to pause to shake my hair back from my face after I nearly stumbled from the wayward strands.

I'd have thanked Tony, but as we passed the table with the blow, one of the girls I spotted was a friendly face. Diamond giggled as she waved, and I did my best to muster up a smile for her. This time, when he took his seat, Tony pulled me down to perch on his knees as he resumed his conversation.

I did my best to hide my feelings about the way shit just went down with Santos, waiting for the guys to finish up so we could leave. Even without the mention of the night that everything happened, he had been deliberately cruel.

So it wasn't surprising that when Diamond came over and slid a tray in front of me with a commiserating squeeze of my shoulder, I snatched up the glass straw and snorted a line up each nostril, ending my sobriety. *Fuck this.*

Marco

She did not just do that. I stared in disbelief as coke disappeared up Eden's nostrils before anyone could stop her. Fucking Santos, he just *had* to open his mouth. And damn her for giving in. I'd drag her ass out of here and back home if I could talk Tony into ditching out.

Other than the tightening of his hand on Eden after he shoved the tray away, Tony seamlessly continued wrapping up the meeting. We'd gotten nowhere as far as figuring out our shared enemy's identity, but we had cemented an alliance, at least temporarily, to find the bastards that seemed to be planning a coup.

When he finished, we found the night's festivities weren't over yet, not by a long shot.

twenty
never be the same

Eden

"What the fuck are you doing?" Tony had hissed at me when I'd taken Diamond's offering. He hadn't been able to do much else in front of the group, but I knew he was biding his time until he could unleash on me.

I didn't give two shits as the drugs did their job just enough to take the edge off, and I spent the rest of the meeting in my old familiar happy place. It was like slipping into a warm bubble bath with an espresso chaser.

As it got to be time to go, Tony passed me off to Marco while he said his goodbyes. My high had mostly worn off, or maybe I still had a tolerance for it, and I was contemplating finding a chance to get more. But Luna had opened her fat ass mouth to point out that I hadn't fulfilled my agreement with Danny, and the man from earlier, *Jasper*, I remembered after a second, took the opportunity to make it public.

"I knew I recognized your name! You're the bitch that should be dead with my cousins, yet here you sit with the Carlottis' claim on you instead while we make a truce over it." He immediately had everyone's attention.

"Danny, what's he talking about? Jasper, sit down." Peter waited for an explanation from Danny, who seemed at a loss.

"I'm not sure what he's getting at other than Marco paid for Angel's services for the evening." The older man shrugged, brushing off the accusation. But Jasper wasn't about to drop it, letting loose with a rant that had more than just me in hot water.

"Luna here told me this one," he spat, hiking a thumb in my direction, "is up for anything, and I thought I'd try her out, but Marco said he wouldn't share and not to mention it again. I'd have left it at that, but then Luna tells me that this is the bitch that was there that night. Despite being there, she's definitely not dead like Luna's friend Trixie. This bitch should have been taken out too, but here she is, not even having to do more than shake her ass because they're on their way out the door and taking her with them."

"Is that true, Danny?" Peter's tone warned it had better not be.

Tony intervened before Danny had to admit

anything. "Since when does Danny answer to one of us over the other? And who the fuck said we're not fucking her? I had Marco pay for her because, as you said, anything goes with her, but I didn't realize it was a requirement for it to happen here."

"If she's not putting out now, then why was she here at all? She was promised to be part of the entertainment, but maybe she's just here to rub it in our faces that our guys are dead while the Carlottis and their bitch are alive and well. Seems sketchy on your part, Danny, since she's the only survivor from the night we lost two of our own. For all we know, you setting up tonight's truce was a ploy to get the heat off the brothers here. After all, you *did* let them waltz in here to take out our men without repercussions. Funny that my cousins just happened to be here trying to set up a deal, with only your word to say they'd tried to cut the Family out—" Jasper didn't get any farther with his tirade as Peter, the second in command for the Finellis, cuffed him in the back of the head and motioned for two others to take him out of the room.

Marco's grip had tightened on my arm until it was nearly painful, while Vanni and Santos closed ranks around Tony, prepared for shit to go south.

Tension holding him rigid at the defensive move, Peter offered an olive branch. "My apologies for Jasper, Antonio. He's taken the passing of his cousins hard, and the news of their betrayal has only made matters worse. I wouldn't have brought him along tonight, but he's one of the few that we can trust in our inner circles." His words might have tendered the apology, but his eyes drifted in my direction, letting on that he thought there was more to my presence as well. I doubted it was enough to wreck the agreements that had been made, but it made me leery nonetheless. Especially when I remembered what I hadn't had a chance to tell anyone. I'd been so pissed off that I'd completely spaced, and now it might be an issue. I needed to get alone time with one of the guys ASAP.

"I won't say no offense taken because we both know that had the situation been different, we'd be at war by now, but I do understand and can assure you Angel isn't in collusion with anyone. Her being spared was only by coincidence." *Tony, you idiot, shut the hell up. I'm so fucking dead.* I started to inch away from Marco, only for him to drag me back tightly against him. Then I was frozen in place as Tony dropped a tidbit I hadn't been aware of. "She was a childhood friend, and her father was one of us. It only stood to reason that we would have taken her with us, hence this being her last night as a favor to Danny, and us taking her home."

Peter stared at me with renewed interest and didn't comment further, but from the way he stared between us he still seemed skeptical of Tony's explanation. It wasn't enough to stop the party from breaking up though. Everyone was eager to leave or get their 'promised entertainment' and they all started to pair off to leave, move to the bar, or take one of the dancers into the back. But I didn't have the luxury of waiting until we were alone to drag Marco out of earshot and hiss a demand at him.

"Edie, if you know what's good for you, you'll just come along and keep your mouth shut. It may have worked out for now, but we need to get the fuck out of here." Marco was no nonsense and tried to pull me toward the nearest exit, but I dug in my heels as best I could and jerked back.

"There's no time! We need to talk *now*." He stared at me for a moment before giving in and signaling for the guys to come over. When they were huddled around me and we weren't getting more than a cursory bit of attention, I spilled the beans. "I got a ride here from Fields." They all started cussing me out, but I held my hand up to stop them. While they shut up, they still glared at me, but I glared right back. They shouldn't have left me desperate and in limbo. "When I asked for a ride, his answer indicated that he was already here, and he warned me that something's changed. I don't know what that means, but while Vinnie and Edward aren't here, all of you are. If there's something going down, where's the best place to make it look like a rivalry gone wrong?"

They didn't even pause and I suspected that they knew all of this, and hadn't bothered to fill me in at all, but there wasn't time for me to chew them out about it before Danny came up, looking pissed as hell.

"You showed up with the cops? I didn't believe Luna when I was about to hand her her pink slip and she told me to check the feeds. And of course Peter already knows. Luna probably whispered something about it to his men before she even came to me. I told Peter that he's an occasional client of yours, but with everything else, he's not buying it." Danny didn't give me a chance to answer before he turned to Tony. "Finelli is demanding proof that I'm not taking sides by letting you sneak a snitch out of here. He's prepared to end the truce *now*. I don't want my club to become a bloodbath, Tony, and that's what he's threatening. What would you like me to do? Because the other option is to turn her over."

Five pairs of eyes landed on me, filled with varying levels of betrayal and anger, and I hoped like hell they weren't about to leave me here. Tony, pinching the bridge of his nose, finally made the decision.

"I'd prefer to send them the way of the two others, but a war isn't in our best interest right now with everything going on, and it makes tonight pointless. Until we take out the new problem, the neutral zone stays neutral." He glanced at me before turning to the others. When they didn't add anything, he told Danny, "We'll take care of it."

"Take care of it how, exactly?" I nearly groaned out loud at Peter's voice, but turned to face him with as pleasant of an expression as I could muster. "Are you handing her over then? Is her pussy the bait and then you kill them off while she's got them occupied? How does this work?" Peter looked like he was two seconds from pulling his weapon, and I feared that the guys would have to give me to him to keep the peace.

"Usually, it works when I shove my dick in one of her holes, but if you think I'm doing it wrong, I'm open to pointers. As for the two that she was fucking? Look..." Tony grabbed my arm to hold up my wrist, exposing my birthmark, then he reached for Santos, but he shook his head and backed away. Adamant about who knew what, Tony grabbed Santos and pulled off the bulky watch that he wore. I barely heard the rest of what Tony said as I stared at the tattoo. *When did he do that?* I looked at the others, but they all ignored me, and I only came back to reality when Tony shook my arm. "This is what saved her. Giovanni saw it and stopped me when he realized the coke whore was Santos' old girlfriend that disappeared. There's some private shit going on that you're not entitled to know, but here's the proof. It's not new, so you can't use that excuse."

When Peter saw the tattoo, he glanced between us before nodding, but he didn't quite let it go. "If she was with him, then why are you all fucking her? And why is she here tonight?"

Tony sighed, obviously annoyed, and ticked his points off on his fingers. "Because we chose to share her. Danny asked for a favor since he was short. We paid to hold her spot, so Danny gets paid *and* she gets paid. Is that good enough now that we've discussed my sex life? I'd ask about yours, but honestly, you're not my type." I almost laughed at that one, but the dark flush in his cheeks was not a laughing matter.

"Look, I believe you, but Jasper has sway with the others and my father. If he decides..." He shrugged, and we all knew what that meant. "Maybe if he knew she really is just a whore with a streak of good luck, he'd cool off. You can always loan her out for an hour. It's a small price to pay for goodwill."

"No one else is fucking her." Santos' statement and its accompanying glare had Peter taking a half-step back.

"Maybe a demonstration then? That *is* her job." We'd gathered more attention by then, and it was only a matter of time before this became yet another public issue.

"We're not monkeys to perform for a rival Family. You can't seriously tell me you'd be willing to do so," Tony scoffed.

Before the situation could devolve any farther, Danny spoke up with a suggestion. "Why don't you gentlemen just make use of one of the rooms? Make it good and Jasper can get his thrill with it. Really, is this the point to contest with someone out there undermining both Families?"

I looked to Tony, as did Peter and Danny, to await the answer. They couldn't very well back out anymore than I could without causing more trouble. But it was Marco that stepped up, and with one of his cocky grins, he threw me over his shoulder so that my nearly nude nether regions were in Peter's full view.

Then the man had the audacity to slip a finger under the scrap of fabric covering my crotch and run it up my center. A moment after he withdrew, I saw Vanni's brows go up and heard the unmistakable sound of smacking lips. "I already called dibs on this pussy. Sorry, man, but my dick is calling. I gotta go answer." Marco turned to cart me off toward the back hall, leaving me to view the group as I was taken away. I tossed my hair out of my face and gave a little finger wave and wink to Peter, the man seeming more amused than pissed at this point. The others... Well, I didn't think they were quite so amused, but they were definitely interested.

"You're an asshole, Eden. You know that, right?" Marco didn't sound quite so gay any longer, and I hid a wince as I ducked my head down to his back. "And we're aware that we're under surveillance since we're not idiots, but you butting in isn't helping matters. You should have stayed at the house."

I kept quiet until he sat me down in one of the rooms, thankfully not the one they'd found me in, and walked over to the mini bar to get a drink. I was chugging a bottle of water while I decided that I wouldn't bring up the tattoo, but at the click of the door, I spun to face it, inhaling my water instead of drinking it. By the time my coughing fit was under control, all the guys had come in and shut the door behind them.

"Oh, look, my dick isn't even in her mouth yet, and she's already choking." My eyes widened in disbelief at Vanni's crude comment. *So much for a truce.*

"Fuck off, Vanni. I'm not screwing her, so I'll take her mouth. You'll have to wait your turn or pick a different hole." Hurt filled my chest at Santos' retort, and I realized they were all furious with me. And I fucking *cared* what they thought. *Goddamn it. There goes not catching feelings. Dumbass.*

Rounding on Santos, I demanded, "What is your goddamned problem lately? You wanted to make amends and now this? After giving me the silent treatment for days? What the fuck?!"

"I was giving you space and protecting your ass. This isn't the place to discuss it, but you better understand you're coming back with us tonight after this bullshit move, Angel." With that declaration, he pulled me over to kneel on the deep bench seat of the booth that lined the wall. Before he unfastened his pants, he leaned over to whisper in my ear, "We know we're being watched, so make it good." I couldn't figure out if he was being a dick for whoever was observing or if he was genuinely pissed. Either way, I lost my train of thought when he pulled his dick out, half-hard and sporting enough hardware to make my tonsils lodge an immediate complaint with the management. On the other hand, my more intimate parts perked up, only to pout when I reminded them that they weren't getting any of that.

"Um, those are new." The inane comment was all I could form as I stared at the crossing barbells, one horizontally through the tip, the other vertical and slightly behind the other. Farther up his shaft, there were more silver balls peeking out from the underside and another one near the base of his dick that would rub against a clit on every stroke. My shocked gaze traveled up to his smug one.

"Won a bet."

I glanced at Marco, who shrugged, and wondered what the fuck the bet had been for. My thoughts were cut short when Santos gripped my chin to return my attention to him.

"Open up, angel," he whispered, and I felt a pang of guilt for pushing this on him. His erection had grown while I studied the piercings, so he was clearly interested, and that helped at least a little.

Doing my best to forget we had an audience, I leaned in to take him into my mouth, wetting his shaft as I went, until he hit the back of my throat. Santos let out a hum of pleasure as he pressed against my throat until the jewelry was too much to take. I'd given head to guys with piercings before, but never so many at once, and I had to pull back before I gagged. I was about to attempt it again when Tony interrupted.

"Danny offered a present. I know how much you like it, so I took it. Turn your ass around here and take it."

I'd used my hair as a curtain to block the others out but now tossed it over the other side to see what Tony was going on about. When I found him with his dick out, my 'present' on top, my body flushed with embarrassed shock. A moment later, I was hit with the realization that they *knew*. The comment from Santos about Luna's sucking abilities, them knowing about the room, and Vanni calling me an asshole. And now this. *Sam had made a video. Fucking Danny.* With eyes wide in trepidation, I glanced around to find them all with hard or blank expressions. I briefly shut my eyes before opening them to find Tony even closer. Resolution settled in me. They were pissed, and I'd gotten us into this mess. Now I had to put out or deal with the fallout... and so did they.

My high had left me, and with the guilt and

shame building, the thick, white line on his dick beckoned to me even as I cringed. Still, I pinched one nostril and snorted the powder in one go, dragging my nose up his rigid length until it was clean of all but the residue.

"Suck it off," he demanded. "Take it deep. I want to feel you gag as I go down, your throat closing around my dick until your makeup runs, and you can't help but choke on it." It was like he was reenacting the scene from that night, using the reminder of the finale with the Finellis to punish me. All it needed was for someone to come from the back to fuck me while I blew him.

I didn't have to wait long before fingers prodded at my barely wet pussy around the strip of thong. I'd have turned my head to look, but Tony was impatient, already shoving his dick at my face. My mouth opened to take it in as one of the others pulled my panties off, and a cool slick gel was rubbed at my entrance then slid inside to coat my walls. The coke was working its magic, and my inner muscles clenched around the digit working me as Tony hit the back of my throat and kept going, not letting up until his balls hit my chin. He wasn't quite Vanni's size, but it was still a chore to swallow him down.

"Damn, Lady Garden, that's hot. Tony, do that when it's my dick, not my finger." Of course, Marco had to be the ice breaker.

"Shut it. *I'm* fucking her, then you can have a go.

Pulling rank, Cuz." Vanni's broad headed erection, wet with lubricant, pressed at my entrance until he gained entry then surged forward with a snap of his hips. The force bottomed him out, eliciting a cry from me, but he didn't hesitate to take up an immediate skin slapping rhythm, making me clench around him every time he bumped against my cervix. Vanni gripped my hips hard enough to bruise, holding me in place while Tony pistoned his thick length in and out of my throat, irritating my gag reflex and giving them both the spasming grip they desired.

Soon, my eyes ran with tears as saliva trailed out of my lips around him, but he didn't finish there. No, he pulled out to allow Vanni to shift me up onto my knees, yanking my head back by my hair until I arched with my ass sticking out to his satisfaction. With my head resting on his chest and my hips at such an extreme angle, Vanni pulled me down onto each brutal upstroke, dragging the head of his cock roughly along my front walls until I was drunk with lust and doing my best to work my hips against him in pursuit of my own pleasure.

Tony's body blocked my view of the others, and I was grateful for it as short gasps of air and soft sounds of my growing passion left my lips each time Vanni came to my end deep inside. The drugs helped dampen my mortification, but they didn't eradicate it. As if he knew just a bit of stimulation would push me over the edge, Tony reached out to pinch and twist my clit until it was sore and throbbing, but the deed was done. I reached completion, clenching around the thick member embedded inside me, until Vanni pumped his hips in an erratic rhythm, grinding hard against me. He set his teeth into my shoulder, biting down as he came with a groan.

When he pulled out and I somewhat came back to reality from the chemical-induced haze of post-orgasmic bliss, it was to view Marco's hooded hazel eyes staring at me with stark arousal. I was afraid to look at Santos and see the condemnation that I was sure was there. Even if he'd known exactly what was going to happen, planning to fuck other men wasn't the same as snorting coke and sucking off his best friend while fucking his other one.

Tony didn't let me off so easily, using his own grip on my trailing hair to turn my ravaged face directly toward Santos. He beckoned for him to come forward to take his place, and when I looked up at Santos, his eyes were steely, his face blank of all expression. I knew he wasn't as unaffected as he pretended. He was hard and leaking just a bit of clear fluid from the tip of his engorged dick.

"I'd consider banging that hot little hole, but I don't fuck whores, so I'll let the others occupy themselves with it. I do remember how much you like to

No Good Deed

give head though, so this should be a treat for old time's sake, right?"

I still wasn't sure of the agenda behind his repeated comments, but I knew if we really were being watched, I couldn't ask or balk. No, instead of getting pissed, I tugged my head back until Tony let go of my hair, then fell forward back onto all fours. I taunted Santos with a challenging stare and parted my lips, licking the bottom one. Without hesitation, he pressed his tip between my lips, and when he reached out to guide my head, his grip at the nape of my neck was gentle. He let me take him at my own pace instead of forcing it down. It reminded me of when we were teens and he'd been my world. It was hard to shut it out and focus on the here and now, but I just couldn't take the mental whiplash. Not here, not where we couldn't have the privacy to speak freely.

Preoccupied with blowing Santos, I was mildly surprised when Tony got behind me and ran a finger through my dripping slit only to pull it out and wipe it on the back of my leg.

"Well, this is a mess, isn't it? I don't do sloppy seconds, especially after my little brother. Guess we'll have to use the cleaner hole. Hopefully it *is* clean. All of Danny's girls are supposed to be clean, right, Angel?" I froze at Tony's crudeness, and for a heartbeat, so did Santos. His hand tightened briefly before relaxing again, and my eyes flicked up to see his jaw clenched in anger. I was getting tired despite the pick me up powder and hoped to hurry Tony up. But even having anticipated the possibility of anal, I wasn't quite prepared to take someone of Tony's girth and length. I hadn't done anything more than clean up.

Marco, ever helpful, tossed Tony a pack of lube from the bowl of condoms, the ones Vanni hadn't bothered to use. "Don't want to get dick rash, right, boss?" The bastard was enjoying this! "Or would you like me to warm her up?"

I started to pull back to blast the ass, but Santos took that as his cue to keep me quiet, and I considered biting him. When Tony told Marco to be his guest, I nearly growled, causing Santos' slow and steady thrust to jerk forward and push past the resistance in my throat. The metal balls were uncomfortable as they went down, and Santos pulled back out at a snail's pace, as if he really didn't want to, but I needed to fucking breathe.

Coughing once he popped out of my mouth, I glared at them all. Tony had joined his brother at the mini bar, the latter fully dressed and hair straightened, although there was still a bit of color high on his cheekbones from his exertions. I was going to be feeling the pounding the next day; jackass hadn't even attempted to take it easy on me, but he at least he'd gotten me off. Well, the two of them had anyway.

The rasp of a packet tearing open signaled Marco getting ready, and Santos resumed pumping lazily in and out, never doing more than touching the tip of my throat after the mishap. It was easy enough that I was on autopilot, able to pay attention to every other thing in the room— like the cool liquid that dripped on my puckered hole, causing me to clench with the anticipation of being breached back there. It was always a shock at first, and I had a feeling Marco would be merciless. He circled around, gently spreading the moisture, probing but never entering until I started to relax. The instant that I did, he pressed forward all the way to the second knuckle and then out again.

Another rip, and more fluid hit my skin to drip down my crack. This time, the digit came at an odd angle as another joined it, and they crooked inside. I realized they must be his thumbs when he pulled them apart, earning him a high-pitched yelp muffled around Santos' dick. He nearly lost his rhythm again at my slight sound of discomfort, but he stayed silent while Marco let my hole retract as much as it could around his joined thumbs, only to swivel them and stretch in the opposite directions again.

Marco continued his onslaught of twisting and pulling at my ass until it was loosened enough for his approval. After he removed his hands, I could feel the slight gape he had left, and as more lube hit my opening, he pushed it in with a corkscrewing motion to spread it liberally.

"All yours, man," he told Tony with a light slap to my leg after he pulled out.

Tony came over to inspect Marco's handiwork, spreading me apart to stare at it. Just as I was about to complain about my sore jaw and tell them both to hurry the fuck up, wet heat hit the rim of my hole before sliding in and around the clenching ring of muscle. *He just spit on me.* I couldn't believe how dirty the eldest Carlotti heir was.

"You do good work, Marco," he praised his cousin. "You should make sure she thanks you when I'm done because I would have gone in with just enough lubrication to keep the skin on my dick intact." My back stiffened at his callousness, and I vowed that it better be an act or I'd be seeing how well he could take a beating. I was half convinced that Santos would help me.

"Thanks, but I didn't feel like listening to her scream around Santos' dick while you railed her ass. Plus, I didn't go very far in; I just stretched that cute little star out. The rest of her should be nice and tight still. Oh, and she's clean, but you might want to glove up just in case."

Out of the corner of my eye, I could see Marco holding up his hands as he went to the sink behind the bar to wash them.

"Well, Angel," Tony said while he came into my

line of sight, rolling a condom on. "I guess you're getting all of your holes filled tonight, definitely earning a pretty penny. Should be enough, I think." My high was mostly obliterated from all the activity, so the anticipation of taking Tony's oversized rod up my ass and wanting him to get it over with had me arching my back and spreading my knees a little further apart to present a more willing pose.

"Eager for it, are you? I hope you remember this when you can't sit down tomorrow."

I leaned into Santos, taking him farther into my mouth until he poked at my throat, trying to distract myself while Tony lined himself up with my back door. He pressed just the head of his latex-covered tip into the slackened ring, resting there until I started to worry about what he was going to do.

"What are you waiting for? My dick won't fuck itself."

Wishing he'd stop with the reminders, I braced my arms better before bearing down to help open and accept the intrusion. I forced myself backward, steadily impaling my ass on his thick and rigid prick. It burned and ached until I got past the head, where I paused, breathing heavily through my nose. The moment I moved toward the root, the wider he got, and not having taken anything in this manner in quite a while, a whimper escaped my throat as I went on.

My progress continued regardless of the discomfort, though Santos was beginning to be less than enthusiastic, and I worried that I would lose him altogether if I didn't step up my game. Relaxing my throat as much as possible allowed him to gain entry, especially with his flagging erection. When he twitched as I swallowed around him, he started to participate again, and I hummed around him in earnest for encouragement. Every time he surged into my throat, I allowed it to push me back to take Tony to the hilt. My ass was on fire, but giving Santos head and enjoying it was fucking with mine. It reminded me too much of the past when it had been new and fun, only to be tainted by all that followed.

A side glance showed Marco and Vanni watching the scene with rapt attention, but Tony didn't last long with me taking it slow and steady on the back and forth. He grew impatient and snapped his hips forward on a downstroke, burying himself before spreading my cheeks wide. My skin above and below felt as if it might split while he adjusted himself to angle down before he started driving in and out with rough, slapping strokes, stabbing into my bowels like he was trying to run me through.

My breaths came erratically as I tried to take the domination without complaint. I groaned in relief as hands slipped underneath me and helped turn the burning ache into a tolerable discomfort. Thick fingers slid into me, pushing deep before hooking up to touch a spot that made me clench around them. I thought Tony was being nice at first, but the angle was wrong. Then more came to rub my clit, and my eyes opened to notice both Vanni and Marco had come up on either side of me, each with a hand buried between my legs as they watched the show. The four of them worked me to a fever pitch; even Santos wasn't immune to the tableau, coming down my throat in hot jets, and when I chanced to glance at him, his eyes were focused on the activity below my waist.

He slipped free from my lips, cleaned of all but my saliva, as I felt my orgasm coming on, causing me to buck back into the men who were working me over. I briefly wondered if they had done this before since they were so in sync. A moment later, I cared about nothing but screaming out my orgasm while clenching around the dick and fingers inside me. I came so hard that I gushed around the fingers in my pussy, peaking over and over until I was wrung out and sated.

But Tony wasn't done just yet. He pressed down on my shoulders until I was ass up with my sweaty cheek resting on the seat while he proceeded to destroy my sore entrance. After getting off, the stimulation was almost too much, and now that I was done, it bordered on the verge of agony. With every downstroke, he hit a point that was resistant to his advancement, causing a stomach ache to build until it began to make me sick. Tony finally reached his peak, hips stuttering until he pressed deep with several aborted thrusts and the telltale pulsing that heralded his completion.

He stayed where he was for a moment, catching his breath, before he pulled out. With my face hidden by my wild and sweat-dampened hair, the others couldn't see my wince, but Tony seemed fascinated by the wreckage he'd left behind. He ran his finger around the abused flesh before doing much as Marco had, stretching me until I buried my head against my shoulder and let out a grunt of protest.

"Damn, Angel, that ass can take a beating. I might have taken you up on it sooner if I'd realized. I bet Vanni could slip right in there, or something more..."

At the end of his patience, Santos snapped at his best friend and boss, "Enough! Put your dick away so we can go home."

"Almost," Tony replied as he let go of my ass. I attempted to push the hair sticking to my face out of the way with mixed results, but I did manage to ease onto my side without jarring my tender parts too badly. I didn't want it all hanging out there if Tony wanted to poke at it again. "Marco needs his gratuity first."

I stared at Tony in dismay, watching him clean himself up and straighten his clothes, waiting for him to say it was a joke. *Surely, he can't be serious.* Vanni started to speak up, but his brother glared him into submission.

"You look like you're ready for another go as well. Why don't you two take her together while Santos and I go settle up with Danny."

The guys glanced at each other, but Santos was the first to break, shaking his head with his lips mashed into a flat line. He shouldered his way past Tony before slamming out of the room.

With a shrug, Tony zipped his trousers and reached for several packets from the depleted bowl on the bar. "Here, I'm sure she'll need that." And then the bastard followed his pissed off enforcer.

"We don't have—" I cut Marco off with a forced laugh, flicking my eyes pointedly at the mirror on the wall. He shut up but didn't look happy about it.

"You heard the boss, boys. Who's first? And if you don't mind, I'll be on top." I considered cleaning up first, but since they'd both had their hands on me after Marco left a mess, I doubted they cared now.

Marco reluctantly came over to take a seat, ready for me to climb over him. They might have acted like they didn't want to, but their dicks were hard and still half out of their undone pants. I waited for Marco to put a condom on and climbed over his hips, immediately settling down over his hard, accessorized length. My ass might have been done for, but a moan worked its way out as my hips undulated over the big man.

Vanni came up against my back, and I signaled for Marco to scoot down a bit so he could have better access, fully prepared to take him in my extremely sore ass and hoping that he was quick about it.

But that's not where Vanni pressed. No, his slicked-up fingers shoved their way into my pussy until I was suspended over Marco, gasping with the overfull sensations that set off all my nerves inside. Satisfied with what he found, he pulled back before the blunt head of his dick pushed on the flesh his hand had just left.

"Fuck, Edie," Marco exhaled in a whisper. Vanni forced himself harder against the resistant ring.

"Relax," he commanded while reaching around and between me and Marco to rub firm circles on my clit. The stimulation helped, as did Marco joining in to wrap his arms around my thighs so his fingertips could help stretch me to take the massive intrusion.

I buried my face in Marco's chest, biting down on it to muffle my cries of pain-laced pleasure. Without the dulling effects of the drugs, every touch was registered, every feeling magnified, including those that I had to admit I felt for the two I was with. Until Vanni's super-sized member breached me, then I screeched at the stretch and tried to escape the overstuffed sensation, not so sure I even liked them anymore.

"Hold on, give it a second," he cajoled as he rocked back and forth in tiny increments. I complied, but it took several minutes before I could get my muscles to unlock. And then he gained more ground while Marco groaned and tried not to move.

"Fuck me, girl, you don't know how fucking tight and incredible this feels." I could definitely attest to the tightness, but I wasn't at the incredible part unless we were talking about incredibly uncomfortable. I seriously doubted that was his meaning, so I kept my mouth shut. For about three seconds.

"Tell that to me after you two wreck my cunt like Tony did my ass. Someone is carrying me out of here."

Marco chuckled, shaking me on his chest only to make all three of us moan at the resulting sensations. Vanni hooked his hips under me, not caring that his junk was all up in Marco's, and wiggled his free arm across my chest to grip my opposite shoulder before he relentlessly pushed up while holding me down in place.

A scream came out before he bottomed out and then blessedly held still until my panting ceased. He pulled back and abandoned my clit for a moment to smear more lubricant on me, and Marco took over working into my flesh. When Vanni pushed back in, more easily this time, it was with an abundance of the cool slickness that soothed my tender insides even as his rigid flesh stretched them to their limits.

"Now, Marco," Vanni commanded. Marco's hands slid to my thighs, gripping them tightly and levering me up until only his tip remained in my straining cunt. Vanni curled his hands around my shoulders and pulled me back down onto them as he leaned in, sandwiching me between their chests.

Our sweat-slicked bodies aided the carnal push and pull they inflicted between my legs. As we slid against each other, they did all the work. I was exhausted and hung from Vanni's neck, nearly boneless. It was all I could do to keep my arms looped behind him as he used his strength to impale me over and over on their engorged pricks.

The gasps and moans that permeated the room echoed the softer noises our writhing bodies made, and the scents of sex and clean sweat filled the immediate area around us. Marco gave up lifting me to slip one set of fingers around my clit, the others prodding at the rim of my tender back entrance. Vanni shifted to allow Marco's arms more freedom then picked up the pace, rubbing against both Marco and I with every thrust. I came first, though it was nearly agonizing to do so with my protesting muscles trying to clench around the men inside me. A high-pitched, stuttered keening accompanied my orgasm, and I didn't notice the guys had come until Vanni slumped against me with a groan. We were all a panting, sticky mess, and I didn't even care.

A slow clap startled me enough to turn my head so that I could glare at the jackasses in the doorway. "Good form, little brother. I'm amazed you both actually got in there." *I'm going to kill the fucker.* From the astonishment on his and Santos' faces, they really hadn't planned on us going another round.

"Get off me, Vanni. I have money to collect." I'd damn well earned every fucking penny they'd paid, and if I had to, I'd crawl there to get it. With the way my body was protesting at the thought of moving, it was a definite possibility.

T he guys cleaned up, leaving me limp and ruined in the booth, and filed out to let me straighten myself out in peace. I wasn't sure it was a blessing since I struggled to even sit properly, but I did manage to get to the bar. Some wet napkins helped wipe off the worst of the mess, and I drank an entire bottle of water. I really needed to pee and knew from the beating all my nether parts had taken that it likely wouldn't be a pleasant situation, but there was no way I was going to end up with a bladder infection from waiting. While I righted my skimpy clothing, considering just walking to the dressing room naked, the last person I expected to show up came into the room.

"Miss Angel, I have your things from your locker. I thought you'd like to get changed in here." Despite the sympathy in his gaze, Steve didn't look away from my face, and I imagined he had been at least one of the voyeurs. He'd likely recorded it for Danny, because why would the man pass up the chance to get dirt on the Carlotti heirs?

"Thank you, I appreciate it. Were you the only one?" I asked quietly as I took the bundle of clothes from his hands. My fucking jaw and throat hurt; my voice was husky and felt swollen inside, likely from the high-demand performance that had been required from it. Either way, it was unpleasant to speak.

"No." Flags of red appeared high on his cheeks while his lips flattened into a line. Either he didn't approve or he wasn't cut out for his job. Maybe a bit of both.

The door opened without even a fucking cursory knock. I had opened my mouth to chew out whoever it was, but I stood with wide eyes and my mouth open as Santos advanced on my guard.

"De Luca! Get your ass back here!" Tony's shout came a second before he appeared in the doorway, and he rushed to grab Santos as Steve got between me and the pissed off enforcer.

"Get away from her," an enraged Santos snarled at the bouncer while he tried to shake Tony off, his friend refusing to budge an inch.

"Goddamn it, Santos, he's protecting her!" When that didn't have any effect, Tony gave me a look between pleading and demanding I intervene. His wide-eyed, jerking head would have been hilarious any other time, but the genuine strain of holding his friend back left no time to dwell on the awkward motions.

"Hey!" My hoarse shout brought all eyes to me as I stepped to the side of the man tasked with defending me. Funny how they were both after the same thing. At least I thought Santos was anyway. Regardless, it pissed me off to walk or talk because I *really* needed some ibuprofen before I stoved up and couldn't move at all. "What's the damn problem?"

Santos jabbed a finger in Steve's direction. "Your *bodyguard* broadcast the entire thing to the Finellis in Danny's office." *Well, that's new.* "We agreed to maybe a quick peek to prove it, but the bastards shared it to prove a point. *Vinnie* probably saw all our asses plowing you." *Ah, so they lost face.* Honestly, it really could create a problem. If there wasn't a healthy amount of fear-driven respect, things could turn dicey in an instant. Some men just didn't have the right amount of respect for another guy after they saw him fucking a woman while his friend was balls deep in the other end. *Or the same one, I guess, considering what Marco and Vanni put me through.*

I edged away from Steve, the man having the audacity to look hurt at my retreat.

"You know I was only following orders," he defended.

"Just go. I get it, really, I do, but that wasn't part of my agreement. Thanks for stepping in though. At least Danny didn't lie about *that*." Steve's expression shuttered, then he stepped over to the bar to set my purse down and went wide around the guys.

He'd barely shut the door when it opened again, and I'd have stomped my foot in aggravation if I'd thought I wouldn't keel over from the attempt.

"It's taken care of unless he lied, and I'm not sure he's brave enough for that." Vanni went straight to Tony with a thumb drive held up. *Not sure why he'd keep it instead of deleting it.*

"Good. Santos, go watch the hall. We'll be right out." Tony came over to take the clothes from my arms then helped support me as I pulled them on over the lingerie. The stark difference in his demeanor was startling enough that I really wanted some fucking answers before I left with them. Unfortunately, leaving with them was the only way I might get them because the club definitely wasn't the place to have that conversation. As soon as my shoes were on, Tony stepped away to head for the door. "Let's go," he demanded, and Vanni swooped in to pick me up, collecting my purse on the way out. I was grateful enough for the ride that I didn't even try to put up a fuss or act like I didn't need it.

Santos silently fell into step beside us as we headed for the back entrance, and I started to struggle, wanting to get down.

"I need my money," I called out, voice pitched low to avoid unnecessary strain on it.

"Marco has it. Don't worry." Vanni's explanation was enough for me to calm down, and I let him carry me out to Tony's car. Marco had it idling in the alley with Santos' directly behind it.

As soon as I was curled into the back seat, Tony took the front, and Vanni went to ride with Santos. I was having a hard time fighting off my fatigue in the warm, dark car with its soft, cradling seat, but I managed a humming noise as I kicked lightly at Marco's seat to get his attention.

"Did you just put your foot... You know what, never mind." Tony's outrage was enough to get a laugh out of Marco, and I even smiled a bit until Marco dropped his news.

"Hey, Lady Garden." I managed to slit my lids open enough to catch Marco waving a stack of cash. Immediately, I found enough energy to shift forward and grab it. Fatigue always took a back seat to self-preservation.

"Not that I'm complaining, but where did this all come from?" And then it was Tony's turn to chuckle.

"If you thought Santos was pissed, you should have seen this one. When he found out what went down, he stalked in and pinned Danny down on his desk face first after slapping him with one of those laminated lists. Then he made him pay the fee out for every person that Vanni was able to determine had viewed it or was in the room. *Then* he demanded that Danny pay an additional fifteen percent for breach of contract." Tony sounded impressed at the last part, but I just smiled and tucked the *Gone with the Wind* thick stack of bills into my purse.

I didn't even want to know how many people watched me get gangbanged by the guys. Likely, I wouldn't have cared before, but having a viewer or two that I *knew* about, or at least suspected, was a lot different than being an unaware porn star. "Thanks, Marco. I really appreciate it."

"Anytime, Edie, anytime. And I'm sorry we didn't come right back. I stayed to cover Vanni as he combed through the files. Apparently, after that night, Danny set up a network to stream live and record. I guess he figured that was a more secure bet than using a phone like last time. Too easy for phones to fall into the wrong hands."

"You *did* see what happened that night, didn't you?" I ventured. At the silence that enveloped the car, I decided it wasn't worth pursuing at the moment. *For my own mental health.* There was one more thing I hadn't fessed up to though... "Um, we need to stop and pick up your SUV. I might have borrowed it."

Marco cracked up at the *borrowed*, but Tony only sighed and asked where it was. I wasn't going to question the boon and let my head tip back against the seat before I could get myself into any more trouble.

❦

I must have fallen asleep pretty hard since I was barely conscious of being taken out of the car and into the house. The motions of my clothes coming off managed to rouse me, but when I opened gritty eyes, it was to a concerned Marco and a waiting bath.

"Come on, we're getting in. Help out with the hoodie." My arms had started to pull out of the sleeve when the *we* part registered. I eyed him dubiously, noting that he was in a t-shirt and boxers.

"Uh, I don't think..." I didn't want to assume he was after anything, but there was *no fucking way*. Thankfully, he got it and didn't take offense. No, he gave a small wince of his own.

"Bath, Edie, not bang. Get your B words right. Anyway, yeah, there's a bit of friction burn there. Shouldn't have done that with the rings in... or maybe just not with dong-zilla." He shrugged before dumping a small carton of epsom salts into the bath then helped me out of the rest of my clothes. Carefully, he propped against the wall while he stripped down. I didn't mean to look. My eyes were just so tired they kinda fell in that direction and then sort of focused on the fact that I didn't see the silver jewelry. "Edie! Eyes up here, woman. I said my dick hurts. That wasn't a dare for you to stare at it. The fucker doesn't know what's good for it and might try to rise to the occasion." He was a bit salty there at the end, like his wayward dick habitually had its own agenda, and maybe it did. After all, I didn't have one.

When he was sans clothing and had towels on standby near the tub, Marco pulled me to him. He supported most of my weight as we sank down into the tub, my back settled against his front, sore patches stinging at the heat and salt in the water. He helped me rinse off and wash up where it was necessary, but I floated in a haze of sleep and heat through most of it.

I startled when arms hauled me up and wrapped my body in an oversized towel to dry me off before sitting me on the closed toilet seat. It vaguely registered that it was Santos tugging a t-shirt over my head and slipping panties over my feet, but I couldn't muster the energy to protest, especially not when he took a brush to my hair without yanking the shit out of it. His touch on a sore spot on my neck made me flinch, but Santos just murmured for me to hold still as he spread ointment over it so it wouldn't get infected. I'd have to check in the morning, but guessed that Vanni had broken the skin when he bit me.

Marco had disappeared; the sound of his

goodbye and impression of lips on my forehead was fuzzy, and my body stretching out under the sheets was enough to have me rapidly sinking toward oblivion.

"Can I stay in here? Please?" I turned confused and tired eyes on Santos. "Damn it, angel, I could have lost you tonight, and there wouldn't have been a fucking thing I could have done without starting a war. Just let me sleep here so I know you're safe?" Awkward and conflicted were only the tip of the iceberg that was our issues, but I was too goddamn tired to care. So, against any kind of better judgment, I patted the spot next to me and promptly shut my eyes.

A moment later, the bed dipped on the other side and Santos' warm body slid behind me and pulled me in close. It felt good, so I didn't protest, but the thought that it would change things niggled at me as I fell asleep.

twenty-one
she talks to angels

Tony

To be woken early the next morning with a demand for entry from two police officers made my mood less than pleasant. They should have known better than to dare set foot on Carlotti property without an express invite. Needing some kind of back up, I went to find Santos. My ire was somewhat tempered by the sight of my best friend wrapped up with Eden in the guest room, sound asleep.

"What?" he mumbled quietly, letting on that he was more aware than I'd thought.

"We have a problem at the gate. A couple cops are insisting on speaking to Eden or getting a warrant to do so, and I'm not getting a call back from our contact there to find out why. I'm going to have to let them in. You know we can't risk the warrant."

"You fucking serious?" At my nod, Santos' expression went from disbelieving to livid. It matched my feelings exactly, but we were stuck, and he knew it. "Vinnie is on board with this?"

"He's being cautious, so he suggested we cooperate until we can find out what's happening." I wasn't any happier with my father, but again, we had the Family to protect. Though it didn't sit right, we had to do this.

"Motherfucker, I can't believe this shit. Eden," he gently called out, shaking the still sleeping woman in his arms. She complained and tried to snuggle in further. "Go ahead," he sighed as he pulled away from her to sit up. "I'll get her up and be out in a minute." With a nod and no small measure of guilt, I left the bedroom.

Eden came into the den in sweats and a hoodie, followed closely by Santos. The rest of us, including my father and the cops, were already in the room, waiting. Despite the dark circles under her forest eyes and the ratty mess she'd twisted her hair up into, she was still as captivating as ever. If it hadn't been for the worry that had her hugging her arms to her chest, and our current company, I'd have chanced saying something to her. Last night had been wild, and I wanted more. More crazy, more sex, more *Eden*. But this wasn't the time or place for it, so I bit my tongue and patted the seat next to me, placing her between my father and me.

She complied, but the set to her face let everyone know she was less than happy to be here. "Is there something I can help you with?" Her question was directed at Vinnie, and I had to smother a smile at her disregard of the bristling men in the room.

"We're the ones that requested your presence. You are the same Eden that goes by the stage name Angel, correct?" At her wary nod, the solidly built, light-haired officer stood from his seat, followed closely by his thinner and taller partner. "We got a report from a Jasper Finelli that his wallet was taken last night while he attended a private party, and one of the other employees we interviewed remembered seeing you putting an item that matches the description in your locker. We found nothing when we searched it, but we were informed that you had your locker cleaned out before you left the premises. Is that correct?"

She seemed confused, her forehead creasing as she thought about it, but she nodded in response. "One of the bouncers brought me my purse since I was already on my way out, but I was only in the locker room before my set." Her voice still hoarse from sleep, or maybe from the activities of the night before. "I didn't meet the man until later in the evening, and I wasn't close enough to him to take anything. I wouldn't have had a place to hide it anyway; it's not like we're there to wear clothes."

"Was there a reason you wouldn't have returned to the locker room? Isn't that your normal routine?" The slimmer of the two joined in, and from the expectancy on his face, he was expecting to trap her. Whether he was trying to force her into admitting something about us or make her fumble and give them some detail to latch onto, I wasn't sure.

"It was a long night," she hedged. "I think the bouncer might have had a bit of a crush on me. He's new and probably not used to everything yet. It *does* happen even though the girls know better than to act on anything like that. He was only being helpful because my feet hurt after my shift."

Both men nodded knowingly but refused to let it go. "To clear things up, would you mind showing us your bag? Just so we can say we checked?" *They've set her up.* My gaze shot to Santos when he started to move, and I shook my head minutely. They had an agenda, and with them in the house, we couldn't chance a damn thing. With our luck and track record, we were being recorded by body cams.

Marco stood while Vanni nonchalantly positioned himself between Santos and the rest of the room. "I'm sure Edie's feet are still sore. I'll run and grab it." He was closest to the exit and slipped out before they could protest, but the effort was short-lived.

"I'd prefer that my partner escort him to be thorough in our investigation. Unless we need a warrant?" That pissed Edie off, and even as I stood to motion the one to follow me, she started in on the asshole cop.

"For one, I didn't fucking consent to having you snoop through my shit, and your *investigation* was instigated by a tiny-dicked man that was pissed I wouldn't pay him any attention. His wallet would have been *impossible* to get to because I was *avoiding* the jackass. Who the hell claims they saw me take it? This is harassment!" The anger was sharp, her voice cracking as it rose, making me worry her throat was really hurt, but underneath, I could detect the faintest hint of panic. We all knew this was a farce, but all we could do was wait for them to show their hand.

As we neared Eden's room, I made sure my voice carried to clue Marco in that we were coming. "Officer, I didn't get your name."

The man glared at me, but I waited expectantly with my hand on the knob to the guest room. "Evans. It's Deputy Evans. Now, if you don't mind, I'd like to see the evidence before it's tampered with." The knob twisted under my hand, and I reluctantly pushed the door open.

"Marco, did you get it?" He wasn't in sight, but the light was on in the bathroom.

He popped out, face blank and shoulders set in a

manner that I didn't like at all. "Yeah, she must have left it in there, so it took me a minute to find it. Guess I should have asked her where it was." I knew damn well he'd carried it in for her but kept my face carefully blank.

Officer Evans held his hand out, and Marco reluctantly turned the purse over. We were so fucked.

"Thank you, Mr. Carlotti. If there's no more stalling, perhaps we can return to the den to do this properly?" *Properly, my ass.* I kept my reaction to a curt nod and led the way back to a fuming Eden.

"Well?" she demanded, arms crossed and now on Santos' lap. I suspected the change had been a strategy on Vanni's part. Hopefully, the seating arrangement would keep the two from doing anything regrettable. Santos was much more likely to keep his ass down if it meant he got Eden on his lap.

Officer Evans held up the oversized bag. "I waited to do it in here, so you could see for yourself that it hadn't been tampered with. Although," he emphasized, shooting a dark glance at Marco, "it would have been best had it been collected with witnesses." It was apparent that we were screwed either way. If the wallet was there, it was a problem. If it wasn't... Still a fucking problem. Eden reached for the bag, but the officer dumped its contents on the coffee table instead. Amid the debris lay a *fucking cell phone* and a wallet, but not the one they were wanting. After a brief flit of relief crossed her features, Eden paled and reached for the bag again.

"Where's my fucking money?"

"Not so fast, Miss. There's something else in here." While the man flipped the lining out, Eden turned her glare from him to Marco. He winked at her, but the wry tilt to his lips let on that while her cash was fine, the rest was not. Eden turned her attention back to the search and watched as a tear in the lining was exposed and a man's wallet fished out. She swallowed hard when Evan flipped it open to show Jasper's driver's license, and a cocktail napkin with the Cherry Baby logo. Underneath was the red imprint of lips with 'Luna' scrawled underneath.

"That fucking bitch! Was Luna the one that 'witnessed' me putting that in there? Because she fucking hates me and was with Jasper last night. *She* would have had plenty of opportunities to take it." At the hard stares from both cops, Eden lost her temper. "I didn't fucking take that. She planted it!" Her eyes darted to us, one by one, but there wasn't a fucking thing we could do. Dad sighed, resignation in the sound, as the officers stood.

"Eden Moretti," the bulkier of the two stated as he pulled out his handcuffs, "you're going to have to come with us." He started his spiel, reading her her rights, while my father clamped his hand down on Santos' knee. He'd leaned forward, a hungry and slightly insane look in his eyes, when the officer pulled Eden up by her arm, and we couldn't afford for him to get arrested as well. Evans scooped everything back into her purse and declared it was being taken for evidence.

As they led her out after letting her slip on a pair of shoes Vanni retrieved for her, I turned to my father. "Call the legal team, please." I didn't say more as I didn't know if they'd left anything behind, holding a finger to my lips when Santos would have spoken. At Vanni's nod as he left the room, I knew he'd get it checked for any bugs.

E*den*

They'd let me get arrested. They *knew* I hadn't taken that fucking wallet, but there I was, cuffed and stuffed because some bitch had a vendetta. *And isn't that their fault too?* As the first wave of anger and disbelief waned, logic began to push in. The image of Luna scurrying after Jasper resurfaced, as did the cryptic warnings from Detective Fields. I didn't know if the two were related, but the Families didn't call the police, not unless it was for a favor. Either there was a serious breach of the code of conduct, or more was at play here. Neither of those options boded well for me.

I tried to see it from the guys' point of view.

They had barely reacted, other than Santos, but that seemed par for the course with him. The others had remained calm, much like they had when dealing with Detective Fields, and I knew much of that was because they owned a great number of the cops on the force. With the power they had in the police department, they should have been almost untouchable. There was little reason they couldn't have told the cops to fuck off, leaving them to confront Danny since the 'theft' had happened in his club. *Which is what Jasper should have done in the first place.* Santos' comment last night floated through my head. *Damn it, angel, I could have lost you tonight, and there wouldn't have been a fucking thing I could have done without starting a war.* Other snippets from the previous night came back, all adding up to one thing. I didn't know what the fuck I was doing.

Without more information, worrying was useless, so I turned my attention to the scenery as we neared the downtown area. When we went into the neutral zone, I started to get uneasy.

"Hey, what precinct are you guys from? I thought we'd be going to the one on the other side of town."

The officer that had arrested me met my eyes in the mirror before smirking and ignoring me. It was a few more minutes of my increasingly loud demands before the other one turned around and smacked the metal grid separating us. The sharp bang made me jump in my plastic bucket seat, painfully grinding my spine against the raised center between the wells where my cuffed hands rested.

As the buildings became increasingly familiar, I realized I was completely fucked. The neon of the Cherry Baby sign was turned off this time of day, and the street was mostly deserted. Not that it was likely anyone would interfere in this part of town no matter what happened, but they sure as fuck wouldn't intervene with the police.

I'd been correct in my assumptions. The instant they'd parked in the alley and dragged me from the car, I started screaming my head off, sore throat be damned, but it hadn't done a bit of good. The club was a fucking bloodbath. I didn't know whose blood it was, but it was splashed down the hall leading to the private areas.

When we'd gotten into one of the kinkier rooms outfitted with a mounted sex swing, I found Luna hanging in it, missing a chunk from the backside of her head, and Danny in much the same condition but with his pants around his ankles. I gagged at the sight and tried to breathe through my mouth to avoid the scent of death.

"Do we have to do it in here? This is fucking gross, bro."

"Shut up, Evans, and get the bitch down. Boss gave his instructions and wants this one left as an example. We'll haul these two out if it's bothering you so much. Fucking pansy," the older cop muttered.

"Damn, Duane, you don't have to be a dick about it." I was frozen at the sight of the horrific mess, memories of cleaning this room out once before petrifying me into place. "We need to change, or we're going to get this shit all over our uniforms."

Evans' pragmatic attitude about his fucking uniform getting dirty while they plotted my end pissed me off enough to snap out of it. Not that it did me much good seeing as my hands were cuffed behind my back. All of the shit Tony had shown me was basically useless unless I could get loose. Even then, getting away would prove a bit harder since they had guns. I couldn't exactly outrun those.

While my thoughts spun in circles, discarding one scenario after another, the two dirty cops used a second set of cuffs to attach me to a metal eye bolted into the corner of the room. They left me there while they changed into street clothes and dragged the bodies out into the hall before using the hose to spray the worst of the mess into a drain near the wall farthest from me.

When they finished clearing the room, they uncuffed me, and I tried my best to use what I knew to get away, but my muscles were stiff and my arms were mostly asleep from the awkward angle I'd been stuck in. My fucking shoulders wouldn't even cooperate after being twisted backward for so long. I was utterly useless, and I was going to fucking die in here.

Hanging from a sex swing is all fun and games until you're beat to shit in it.

I'd made the bastards work for it when they took my clothes, only giving in when Duane pulled out a knife and started cutting them off of me, not trying to be too careful with the pointy end. I had multiple shallow cuts, nothing too serious, but they stung like a bitch and had made a hell of a mess. If they didn't quit bleeding soon, I might be in trouble, but I figured I'd be dead by then anyway.

Wish I could say my life flashed before my eyes and all that sentimental shit, but besides a brief hope that the guys would come save my ass, my time wasn't spent reminiscing about the glory days. Honestly, there weren't that many, but even so, there wasn't time for it. No, happy memories were hard to hold onto when you're methodically hit over and over to send a message. *Enough to bruise, but not to make me unrecognizable.* The fuckwads had repeated their instructions enough times that I had them fucking memorized too.

It was pointless asking them questions; they just ignored me, paranoid that there were recording devices in the room that they hadn't found. It was a legitimate concern, but I'd eat shit before I told them where to look, or even that I might know whether they existed. If this was being recorded, at least someone might eventually be able to bring me justice. Again, it was a cute thought, but justice was for the living.

I groaned as another hit came, this time to the ribs. They hadn't fucked with my face too much. It had gotten tenderized on the cement wall when I fought back, and I was pretty sure my cheek was cracked, much like my ribs were about to be if they didn't lay off.

"Hey, look what I found. Better than leaving marks on our hands. Mine are getting sore anyway. Bet this sucker can do some damage quick." Evans, I'd determined, was a sick fuck. He'd already incessantly complained about the fact that they weren't allowed to stick their dicks in me until Duane told him to go take a piss and jerk one out while he was in there.

"That wasn't what we were told to do. If you can't follow simple instructions, then why are you here?" Duane was exasperated with his juvenile partner, but I thought it was fucking hilarious.

"Yes, Evans, why *are* you here? You hit like a little bitch anyway. Have to get big brother to do all the work for you. Bet you have a tiny dick—" The scream was completely involuntary, as were the panting gasps I took, trying to ride out the agony that used to be my left leg. *Motherfucker, that backfired.* The solid thud of the aluminum bat hitting my thigh felt like it had broken the bone in half. When I looked down, I really thought there would have been bloody and jagged pieces sticking out with just some skin and tendons holding it all together. Instead, there was a livid purple bruise already rising. *Won't do that again. Fucker could have at least aimed for my head, then I wouldn't have to be awake to feel this shit.*

"What the fuck did I just say? I'm not taking the heat for you. Knock it off." Duane was pissed, but Evans was a psychopath. I could hardly believe he'd been the sweet one this morning.

"I just want to have a little fun! This is boring. We hit her, the bitch screams, and we hit her again. Blah, blah." He made a jerking motion with his hand near his crotch, and if I'd been braver, I'd have rolled my eyes. "Say, did you see the vid with her and the Carlottis last night? Fucking hot. I've wanked off twice to it. I'm shocked her shit doesn't look like it's been tenderized after taking two at once. Probably just as well we can't fuck her. Hot dogs and hallways, right, my man?"

"Evans, if you don't shut the fuck up, I'm going to take that bat to you." Duane didn't take his anger out on his partner though; instead, he hit another rib, and that time I felt the pop as I screamed hoarsely. At this rate, I wouldn't have a voice at all by the time they finished.

"That one hurt, huh?" Evans came forward to poke at the spot, making me moan as my head fell forward and my hair stuck to the tears I couldn't stop.

"You know what? I need a break. You're driving me nuts." My heart dropped into my stomach as he left, simply tossing back a "Don't kill her yet!" as the door closed behind him.

"Betcha didn't see that coming, amirite?" I don't know how I'd ever thought that crooked grin made him seem nice. Now, all I saw was leering destruction waiting to happen.

Okay, so when the end was imminent, maybe your life did flash before your eyes. At least pieces of it. I swore I could see Marco as if I once again sat on the bed that night. *But what a way to go, amirite?* "Yeah," I wheezed, my throat and ribs doing my voice in, "what a fucking way to go."

"What was that? You want me to fuck you?" He held a hand up to his ear as if he couldn't hear me. "Sorry, no can do, but I bet my friend here can. Nothing about him being off limits. Don't worry," he said as I tried in vain to close my legs through the agony of my injuries, "after I saw what you took last night, this baby should slide right in."

The first touch of the rounded aluminum head was icy, and he was right. It might not look tenderized, but it definitely fucking felt like it. When he realized it was going to take some effort, he pulled the bat back and swirled the tip through the still bleeding cuts on my abdomen.

"Hope this helps! The stick in the mud will be back soon. Gotta hurry." I didn't know if the blood actually helped or if he just got a better angle for leverage, but while the first touch had been ice cold, the second was a burning inferno of agony as my flesh stretched and tore to unwillingly accept the unnatural intrusion.

I found out that I could indeed still scream even though it sounded more like a rooster with laryngitis than anything human. Tears and snot ran down my face, dripping off my cheeks and chin as the unforgiving object traveled inside until it came to the end of me.

"Damn, I thought you could take more than that," he said as he stepped back and left the metal weight hanging out of me. "You know I had to use two hands on the thing? Like plunging a stopped up toilet, but in reverse." He started jabbing the bat up in the air as he cackled at his obscene joke. I took the opportunity to push back against it, trying to get some relief, but my contrary snatch decided to let it go altogether. It hit the cement floor with a clatter, leaving dripping trails of blood behind. "That wasn't nice."

The gleam in his blue eyes scared me, and I silently begged for Duane to come back. Evans stalked toward me and picked it back up, and when he was this close, the rage that filled his face was impossible to ignore. Now, I begged for real.

"Please, don't do this. Please!" The last came out as the bat hit my hole with more force than the first time. Off-center, it briefly caught on the edge of my opening before plowing in and coming to an abrupt stop with a grunt from me.

Evans gripped the handle like he'd mimed and started plunging away amid my wails of terrified agony. On the fourth jab to my sides, I lost control of my bladder. Piss ran down the bat, causing him to leap back in disgust, and he went to rinse his hands with the thin hose.

"Fucking nasty, girl. Now you need a bath." He turned the hose on me, spraying off the worst of it, and was about to start again when Duane finally came back.

"What the fuck! Are you insane?" He stood there, appalled by the bloody bat poised at my opening. I wouldn't have looked, but it was too hard to hold my head up for very long anymore. The metal rod of destruction had been rinsed too, but my cunt was bleeding more than the absolute worst of period days. "You know what? There isn't time for this. We have to go. There's an APB out on us. I moved the car a few blocks away then came back here, but it won't take them long to track us."

"Well, *Miz* Moretti, it's been fun." Evans raised the bat to hit me, presumably in the head this time, but his partner stopped him.

"Get your shit together, I'll take care of this."

I thrashed my head as much as I could and yanked against the duct tape holding my arms to the straps that connected to the ceiling. It had torn a bit when Evans had started with the bat but hadn't given out entirely, and it still didn't.

The roll of plastic wrap spun round and round until my air was cut off and the panic set in. By then it was thick enough that it was hard to see or hear through. Duane hitting the floor, and the subsequent scuffle was a curious thing, but it took a backseat to my oxygen-starved lungs as my torso jerked and twitched like I was being electrocuted.

V*anni*

"What do you mean she's not here!? How do you lose an entire person?" Tony was ready to kill the desk sergeant, and I wasn't far behind him. Had it not been for the building full of armed officers, it would have been a done deal. "Did you spell her name correctly? M-O-R-"

"Sir, I've told you, it's not coming up. You'll have to wait for her to be booked before she shows up in our systems." The man was getting testy as this was the third time he'd given his blanket statement that pretty much meant 'go sit with your thumb up your ass and try again later.'

"I'd like to speak with the officers then. These are their badge numbers."

"And I've already told you they're not here."

"Then neither is Eden because they fucking left with her in handcuffs!" Tony's shout drew more than one hostile glare, and I gripped his shoulder tightly as I tried a different approach.

"Could you please page Captain Erickson then?" The desk sergeant turned his haughty ass stare on me next.

"No, I cannot. He's unavailable."

"Until when?" Tony demanded.

"That's undetermined at this time."

"You're fucking useless, you know that, right? You're incompetent, and I'm going to sue this entire precinct for losing her—" I clamped my hand over his mouth and dragged him from the building. Several officers appeared to be heading our way, reaching for handcuffs or tasers, and I was damn sure avoiding both.

"Come on. Before we're *lost* in their systems too.

Let's see if Dad got anywhere." I released his arm as we made it to the bottom of the stairs and headed for Tony's car.

"I have a text saying the Captain isn't answering his cell or home phone. Wait, there's another. He's on fucking vacation." Tony dropped his head into his hands after shutting himself in the car, and I was starting to worry that big brother was finally cracking up over a woman. Granted, it was the same one I was after, but I was the younger sibling. I was born to share.

"Check in with Santos and Marco, see if they're headed back from the hooker's place yet. Why the hell she lives so far from the city, I don't understand."

Tony picked his head up to stare at me, earning an irritated shrug in a universal 'what the fuck' gesture for his trouble. "They went to Jasper Finelli's house where the hooker stayed last night." His words were slow and deliberate, pissing me off more. Mostly at myself though.

"I'm not an idiot. You don't have to talk to me like one. It slipped my mind that was his address. Just see if they're coming. I'm calling Fields. Fuck this shit."

He kept staring as if *he* wasn't the one comprehending basic English. "Now, Tony!" Okay, so maybe I'd lost it over a woman too, but at least I could admit it.

I pulled up Fields' contact information and hit the call button. It rang until I thought he wouldn't answer before he picked up with a sleep-roughened voice.

"Fields."

"Detective, this is Giovanni Carlotti. I need a favor." No sense in beating around the bush.

"Sorry, I'm on administrative leave after giving your girl a ride last night. Not that I'd help you with anything that I wasn't legally bound to anyway. So have a nice day, Mr. Carlotti."

"Wait! It's about Eden. She's gone."

"That was her intent. She's a big girl; she'll be fine. Good for her on getting out too."

"No, she was arrested this morning and never showed up at the precinct. We can't get any answers from the police there."

"So she didn't just split town?" Fields' skepticism came through loud and clear. Trying not to lose my patience with the man for failing to understand the direness of the situation, I attempted to explain *again*.

"No, she didn't. Two cops came and took her in for the theft of a wallet belonging to someone who wouldn't have called the cops in the first place. It's been hours, and we're not getting anywhere. She's not there and neither are the officers that took her."

Fields sighed before mumbling something about regrets. "Look, I'll see if I can find her and call you back."

"Wait! She has a phone. They took her purse, but

I didn't know she had it until today. I'm going to try to find the number for it—"

Fields cut me off with, "They took her purse?"

"Yes, searched it then took it all. If I can figure out her number, we can hopefully find her."

"Don't worry about the phone. It's pre-pay and not under her name." *How the fuck?* He kept rambling on, only increasing my urge to kick his fucking ass. "If she has access, she'll signal me. Just give me a minute."

The call was on speaker, and now he had Tony's attention too. "Fields? Antonio. What did you do to Eden that she would allow you to track her?" Cold lethality exuded from him, likely already plotting the many ways to make the man disappear.

"I didn't do a damn thing but help her. Girl's good at games too. She isn't stupid, and she tested it out first. Okay, it's not broadcasting, but it was briefly this morning. Several times... what the fuck?" His confusion was blatant, but he needed to hurry up and sort it out. "I don't know if she ditched it last night or not. The signal still says it's at the club." Immediately, Tony started weaving through the few miles of downtown traffic that made the trip twice as long as it should be on any given day.

"Thanks, Fields, we'll owe you one, yeah?" I was ready to get off the phone, needing to ready myself for whatever we were about to find.

"I'll meet you there. If it's not her, I want that back. It's expensive."

"I'll get it for you if that's the case," I hedged, not wanting him there.

"I'm off duty, and it's not a police issue device. Plus, I'm closer." He hung up in the midst of my cursing, and I wondered if we were about to commit a crime, like murder, in front of a cop.

I sent off a text to the others, telling them to meet us at the club, and hoped like hell Eden was there and that we'd find her safe with Danny. My gut told me I was being overly optimistic, but hope was all I had at this point.

We all arrived at roughly the same time, but Santos managed to be the first in the door. I raced forward, trying not to fucking get shot as I ran toward the sound of gunfire instead of away like a sane person. One of my least favorite things to do. Going from the light of day and into the darkness of the club hallways, I was blind until my eyes adjusted. What greeted me when they did was not what I'd expected.

I found Luna and Danny laid in a pile, still contorted in their death throes from the rigor mortis. That explained where she'd disappeared to and why he hadn't answered the phone. There wasn't time to assess the situation before Tony came barreling in behind me, completely losing his shit. I barely managed to pin him against the wall before more gunfire came our way.

"Where is he? Santos?!" my brother yelled, frantic that he'd taken off without us. Tony was used to being the one to hold our friend together, keeping him from getting himself killed when he made rash decisions without thought for his own safety. But now we also had to contend with Marco, the idiot appearing determined to tie with our enforcer in the hothead department. He barely waited for a lull in the shots before taking off ahead of us.

"Fuck! Come on! We've got to catch up before those two get themselves dead. Goddamn pointless not to wait for backup." Tony shot me a look I interpreted as shut the fuck up, so I did.

We made our way through the hall toward the cacophony, rapidly but more carefully than the others had. By the time we made it, the shooter had moved on to the main floor and Marco and Santos were yelling for Eden as they sprinted from room to room.

A figure came out from in front of them only to dart back into another room before I could tell if they were friend or foe. *Fuck, there's got to be an easier way to do this.* "Tony, I'm going in the tunnel." He glanced at the concealed entrance and nodded, telling me to be careful. "You too, big brother."

I slipped in and made my way as quickly as possible to where I thought the guys were pinning the other guy down, checking each peephole as I went. At the last one, I yelled frantically for Santos, hoping he could hear me. Eden needed help *now*, and this wasn't one of the rooms I could get into from the passageway. I ducked and shouted out a warning as Evans shifted near the door, angling his body to take a shot in my direction. With my attention riveted on Eden, I hadn't noticed him. *Fuck, did I just send them into a trap?*

When I chanced another look, Santos had shoved into the room, closely followed by Marco, but the gangly man had darted around them and out into the hall. They turned to follow, but Evans' gun was already trained on a thrashing Eden, freezing them in place with the threat to her life. Each time they made the slightest movement, Evans fired a shot much too close to her.

I pressed around the wall, hoping it would give, but nothing happened. All I could do was watch as Eden's bloody and brutalized body stilled, her plastic wrapped head falling forward. Feeling like a fool for choosing to take the hidden corridor, I rushed from one alcove to the next, back the way I had come, desperately hoping that I wouldn't have to take the long way around, until I found a door that opened.

After a cursory check through the peephole, I went through the room and into the hall in time to hear more gunfire and Santos shouting for Marco. As I took a quick peek around the door jamb, I caught sight of Evans disappearing around the next bend.

"Tony!" I yelled for my brother, not knowing where he was but not wanting to get hit by going out into the hall. Figuring I'd already given my position away and would have to chance it, I gave a last warning that I was coming then ran out of the room.

The macabre sight that greeted me when I skidded to a halt in the doorway of the room would haunt me for a very, *very* long time.

Santos

Vanni's call to help Eden guided me directly to her and one of the bastards that had taken her. Getting to Eden was the priority, and even though I knew better than to take my eyes off the threat, Evans slipped past us enough to get the upper hand.

With Marco and I now trapped in the room with Eden, Evans immediately turned to fire on us. I'd instinctively fallen back against the wall, staring in horrified disbelief as the cop targeted Eden. Her body hung limply from the ceiling, and there was so much damage to look at that my eyes couldn't focus on one spot. It took precious seconds to process what was around her head, and even as I lunged for her, Evans popped another round off, trying to keep us away from her body. But Marco was already there, shielding her as he returned fire and forcing Evans to retreat. I could hear Vanni shouting from the hall and trusted him to have our backs. As I reached Eden and started tearing the tight wrapping off of her, Marco gave me a wry grin and buckled to the floor.

"I'm good. Get Edie," he mumbled as he held his thigh, the pant leg rapidly soaking with blood.

I took him at his word, pulling out a knife to cut her arms loose from their bindings and gently lowering her to the floor as fast as I could. Not knowing what else I could do, I tried to resuscitate her. Eden's eyes were bloodshot and vacant, and she was fucking bruised everywhere. Rage burned in my chest alongside almost paralyzing fear at the taste of blood on her lips when I forced air into her lungs. With each chest compression, I could feel the shifting of her ribs, but I couldn't worry about what new damage I might be adding to what those fucks had already done. I just needed to bring her back to us. *To me*.

"You jackass, you weren't supposed to get yourself shot." It only vaguely registered that Tony was working on Marco. My world was centered around the woman I'd loved and hated for over a decade, fearing I'd now have to call her angel in an entirely different way.

"*Santos!*" I turned my head as Vanni shouted my name, glaring at him for making me lose count. "Paramedics are coming, which means cops. I need your piece. Didn't want to startle you." As he reached out to unhook my holster, I swore Eden made a noise, so I stopped the compressions. "Is she breathing?"

"I think so." The guys looked at me like I was dense, but the barely there, choppy movements of Eden's chest didn't really give me any confidence that she was actually getting much oxygen.

"Is he gone? The shooter?" I asked as I monitored Eden. Vanni nodded, guilt written all over his face as he took in the room.

My gaze followed his from Eden's slack face to the gore that came from between her legs and a bloodied aluminum bat not far away. I was barely holding my own shit together and needed him to snap out of it; we couldn't afford to freak out yet.

"Hey! Not now. We'll deal with it later, alright?" He nodded again, then squared his shoulders and got back to business.

Vanni collected our weapons and took off to stash them as police swarmed the building, followed by paramedics that took Eden and Marco out on stretchers. The rest of us, including Fields, were detained and taken in for questioning.

By the time we arrived at the station, our attorneys were already waiting to work on our release. It took a couple hours, but we were finally let go without being charged due to Detective Fields' story supporting ours and Tony's memorable outburst from earlier in the day.

Now all we had to do was wait for news on Eden and find the fucks that had hurt her.

Eden

I woke to a world of hurt and opened my eyes with a groan. I nearly panicked until it registered that I was on a bed and not tied up. And that the doc was checking my crotch out...

"Miss Moretti, we need to stop meeting like this," he deadpanned with what I thought was the strain of worry around his eyes.

"That's my line, asshole," I whispered back, all I was capable of doing. "And I'm going to charge you if you keep finding excuses to get a peep show. I told you that shit isn't free." A laugh turned into a cough as a pained groan came from the side of me.

My eyes shot over to inspect the source of the sound, but Tony didn't appear to be in actual pain, just exasperated. The doc shot him a glare, but I was lost on the significance, plus the haze of detachment made things difficult to process. I was grateful for that familiar floaty, out of body sensation though, because I knew it was keeping the worst of the discomfort at bay.

"Wanna share with the class, boys?"

"Not particularly, Miss Moretti. Now, hold still. This could take a bit. I've already numbed the area and checked your other injuries. We can go over those shortly. I'd hoped you'd remain unconscious a little longer, but it's good you're awake too." He smiled kindly at me, and I sorta trusted it now.

He held up a curved needle and got another groan from me. "You know, it would be faster to—"

"I'm not using glue, Miss Moretti!"

"Not that shit again," Tony whined.

"Ha, knew you tattled, Doc," I teased as I adjusted the cannula in my nose, trying to ignore the marks and bruising from struggling against the tape.

"Antonio, the commentary wasn't necessary. I need her to stay still."

"It's me or one of the others, Doc."

The doctor looked pained for a moment. "You can stay, Antonio."

"How come he's Antonio and I'm Miss Moretti? Surely, this is our third date... or is it the fourth? Fifth? Well, whatever number, by now you can call me by my first name. I know you're from the last century, but get with the times, man."

Even the doc let out a bark of laughter at that one. But Tony...

"What the hell did you give her? Eden, you'd think you'd have a better tolerance for narcotics."

The doc shot Tony a dark look that had him grimacing. "Nothing more than was needed. Besides, pharmaceutical grade morphine is expensive and not as easy to obtain as it once was."

It was then that I realized we were in an actual hospital room and the doc had on an honest to goodness lab coat and name tag.

"Oh my god, you're a real doctor!" My whisper was triumphant.

"Yes, Miss— Eden, I'm a real doctor. What did you think I was?" he asked, affronted.

"Well, I thought maybe it was like in those shows where you had your license revoked or some shit for malpractice, and now you have to work off the books and get black market supplies—"

"Oh dear lord, maybe I did give her too much."

Tony stared for a moment, open-mouthed, before my wild imaginings had him laughing. And then of course the door opened, two men barging in, a third supported between them. They all looked like they'd been hit by various stages of exhaustion, and Marco sported a limp from some unseen injury. I was about to ask what had happened when I noticed that they'd zeroed in on my exposed vag and made a noise of objection.

The doc, taking immediate notice of my predicament, ordered them to leave. "Out, all of you. *Now.*" His tone brooked no argument, and Tony sobered to usher them out, but Marco refused. After Carlos whispered how he'd injured his leg, I let him stay, carefully ignoring the almost glare from Santos and frustrated grumble from Vanni.

epilogue
safe inside

Eden

"What do you mean, I *have* to go?" I stared in hurt and confusion as Vanni started laying out I.D. and debit cards.

"You have to go where we can't find you. We'd be tempted to check in on you, and that might be a fatal decision. Until we know who's behind the hit on you, you have to disappear."

"I thought I was safe here?" I whispered, stomach dropping out at the thought of leaving the property... Or, if I was being honest with myself, the guys. Marco and I had spent days in bed, recuperating and being waited on by the others. I was pretty sure Marco was fine to move around sooner, but I wasn't, and I appreciated the company. Those first few days, even taking a piss had been miserable. The first time had brought the guys running into the room, guns drawn. The other thing didn't bear mentioning, and I'd prefer to forget that mortification had ever happened.

The others came into my room, and then I understood that they'd sent Vanni as the proverbial canary. Since I hadn't killed their sacrifice yet, it was safe for the rest of them to come in.

"You *are* safe here, but there are things that are out of our control." He waved an arm to encompass my still healing body. Three weeks had done a lot for the surface injuries, but there were many that would take a bit longer to heal.

Looking to the others, I could see Marco was upset, but Santos and Tony were stony twin statues. Other than their doting and their reactions in the hospital, there had been no overly familiar interactions. Marco was a whole other story, cuddling with me at every opportunity, and even though Vanni had kept his distance somewhat better, he didn't shy away from casual touches at all.

"So you're kicking me out."

"No, we're keeping you alive." Tony's response drew my attention, and really, all I could do was nod. I couldn't force them to let me stay, and honestly, if they were to the point of telling me it was time to jet, then shit was going south. I might be nervous, and I hated leaving them after everything, but getting away could be good for more than just my physical well-being.

Deciding not to make a fuss, I asked, "Fine, when do I go?" When they remained silent, glancing between each other, I got the drift. "Right, I'd better pack then."

E*den*
One Month Later...

The needle of the tattoo machine dragged painfully across the skin of my inner hip, eliciting a hiss of pain when it hit a particularly tender area.

"Sorry," my artist, Kelly, apologized, wiping the area with her green soap-soaked paper towel before continuing on. "You've been doing awesome though, and we're almost finished."

A grunt of pain was my only response. *Thank fuck.* This was the second and final session to finish the tattoo I'd decided to get. It had been a whim after I'd seen an article about the shop and their specialties.

Originally, I'd come in curious about the different types of piercings they offered. After seeing and experiencing the ones Santos and Marco had, I'd kind of wanted to get something done, and when I found out there was a female version of Santos' called a magic cross, I'd booked an appointment. The vertical bar and small hoop through the hood of my clit was still a bit sensitive, and it would take a while to fully heal, but it wasn't like I'd be having sex anytime soon. Prostitution wasn't necessary with being flush with cash, and being on the run wasn't exactly conducive to hookups. At least temporarily. I'd eventually need to get a job, but that could wait until it was safe to go back or at least stay in one place long-term, and I didn't have any plans to return to either of my previous professions, so I'd have to figure out how to get my GED at a minimum. In the meantime, I was enjoying sightseeing, and apparently body modification, while trying not to dwell too hard on what the guys were doing at any given time.

They'd saved me in more ways than one, helping me kick my worst bad habit, even if, in a sense, they were one as well. The thing was, bad habits had a way of coming 'round, again and again. I'd once given up the Carlotti boys, only to be captured and consumed by their web of dark bliss years later. Those boys had come back to me as men and forced me to trade my other vices for them, whether I liked it or not.

And now that I'd quit them both, I wasn't sure what was left. So here I was, going wherever I wanted until it was safe for me to return. If I wanted to return.

The buzzing of the tattoo machine suddenly quieted, and Kelly made a pleased humming in the back of her throat, drawing me out of my thoughts. "I think we're done."

I lifted my head from the seat I'd been lying on for the last several hours and looked down. I was completely enamored with how she'd taken a distorted idea from my head and turned it into this beautiful art etched into my flesh.

Five playing cards fanned across my abdomen; four were black kings, a twist on the real deal being as there was one from each suit, with a red queen of hearts in the center between them. The script underneath it all read, 'The GAMES we play.'

"It's great, thank you."

Kelly grinned and applied an ointment over the area before covering it up.

"I'm glad! You know, you never did tell me what it means," she commented, taping down the edges of the protective film.

Instead of giving her an answer, I smiled and hopped off the chair to throw my shirt back on.

"One day you'll tell me, right?" she asked hopefully.

"Maybe," I replied with a shrug. I chuckled at her exasperated look then followed her out of the curtained off station toward the front of the tattoo parlor.

"Don't forget the first touch up is free if you end up needing it," she told me as she grabbed a piece of paper. Handing it over, she went over the aftercare instructions listed on it.

After making sure I knew what to do and thanking her, I paid my bill and was about to leave the shop when I caught the muted screen of the television by the reception area.

Images of very familiar faces flashed across it before video of them being cuffed and taken away in police vehicles was replayed from an earlier broadcast. I stood frozen as I read the ticker tape at the bottom.

Sons of prominent New York businessman and reputed mafia don Vincenzo Carlotti, along with two others, have been arrested and charged in the murder of two former police officers, along with being suspects in the disappearance of a dancer from a gentleman's club.

Another snippet showed Vinnie encircled by bodyguards and what I assumed were attorneys, forcing their way to his town car in front of a police station.

I rushed out onto the sidewalk, heading for the bed and breakfast where I'd been staying, and without thinking twice about it, I slipped my hand into my purse and pulled out the phone Vanni had given me should I ever need to reach out to them. As I waited for it to boot up, a little voice warned me that if I used it, there was a chance I'd never come back from it. My life was at a crossroads now, but I still had a choice. Reveal myself and help them, or walk away and never look back.

Decision made, I pressed the speed dial for Vinnie and brought the phone to my ear.

After only two rings, the call was answered.

"What can I do?" I asked.

"Come home."

Looked like my bad habits were already coming 'round again.

TO BE CONTINUED…

Read No Bad Deed, the epic conclusion of the Bad Habits Duology here now:
No Bad Deed

Or

Continue reading for a sneak peek of The Degradation of Shelby Ann by Emma Cole!

A huge thank you to the betas, ARC readers, Michelle for edits, and of course to all of you for reading!

Every review counts, so if you're inclined toward reviewing, here are some handy links. Thank you!

Amazon https://books2read.com/u/b505DR
Goodreads https://www.goodreads.com/book/show/57756401-no-bad-deed
Bookbub https://www.bookbub.com/books/no-bad-deed-a-dark-mafia-romance-bad-habits-duology-book-2-by-emma-cole

About the Author

Emma Cole is a multi-genre romance author covering everything from dark and light contemporary to paranormal and sci-fi. Almost all of her stories are, or will be, from the reverse harem subcategory, and none of them skimp on the heat. Emma lives in the mountains in the Northwest U.S with her kiddos and fur babies where she only puts on 'town pants' when absolutely necessary.

Follow Emma Cole

Newsletter Sign-Up

https://www.subscribepage.com/emmacole

Facebook Reader's Group
Emma's Author Stalkers

Other Works By Emma Cole

Remington Carter Series
Echoes
https://books2read.com/Echoes
Requiem
https://books2read.com/u/47EZy8
Clarity
https://books2read.com/Clarity-3
Resonance
https://books2read.com/u/4ERVXE

Dark Duet
Lark
https://books2read.com/u/mv2V1V
Nightingale
https://books2read.com/Nightingale-Dark-Duet

Blackbriar Academy

Other Works By Emma Cole

The Order: Hit and Run
https://books2read.com/The-Order-Hit-and-Run
The Order: Ascension

Twisted Love Series
The Degradation of Shelby Ann
https://books2read.com/DOSA
The Redemption of Shelby Ann
https://books2read.com/ROSA2

Excerpt from The Degradation of Shelby Ann

"I told you not to run. I took it easy on you before. Now, lick her. I'll stop when she comes."

Despite trembling with fear, I still turned my shocked gaze to my husband's cruel one as I tried to cover my nude form from the two women who climbed onto the bed. They moved into position in a well-rehearsed routine that caused fury to cut through me. *How long has this been going on?* Too busy staring at them while one laid on her back, legs splayed out to put her smooth pussy in front of me while the other straddled her face, I didn't notice Winston taking his belt off. But I sure noticed the lick of fire across my hip, yelping in pain and surprise.

"Get your face in there. *Now*." His tone warned me to comply as much as the second strike that came almost on top of the first did. My head bowed to the task— he knew I'd do most anything to avoid the agony of a belting.

Revulsion churned in my stomach when the heat of her flesh and musky female scent hit my nose. Screwing my eyes shut, I stuck my tongue out, tentatively touching it to the soft petals of skin. It was clean, but it was not an idea I'd ever entertained, and I tried to think of anything but what I had to do. A rough finger prodded at my own dry entrance, forcing its way in a small bit before retreating while my mouth worked at its first attempt to eat pussy. My pace picked up as the steady hits came, not as hard as before but still enough to sting like the devil.

I must have been doing something right because the woman's hips started bucking up to cut my air off at intervals, and her nether lips became slick with her arousal. The belt stopped only for the finger to return again to rub at my slit.

"You're not wet, slut. I thought you wanted me to come to you for my needs?" Terror at what he might do in retaliation coursed through me, making my skin flush with heat then prickle with cold. He always made me regret every word out of my mouth, twisting them to lay the blame at my own feet for whatever fit his agenda.

"I'm sorry," I croaked, but the whisper probably didn't even reach him with my face buried as it was.

"No matter, I can make you like it. Just like I do with the other whores who refuse to obey." He

Excerpt from The Degradation of Shelby Ann

moved away, and a moment later, the rattle of a pill bottle reached my ears. "Reach back and spread your cheeks." With a whimper, I slowly complied, fully expecting to get his dick in my ass. Instead, he commanded me to push out, causing my face to burn in mortification. As soon as I managed it, fingers held me open while another pushed in a small, jagged object followed with the instruction to relax. The finger wriggled its way into my dry rectum, burying deep beside it before retreating. He repeated the uncomfortable process again and again until four of the hard bits were buried in me. "That should start working soon enough. Next time you want to be my slut, I'll have the girls clean you out first to give you a good reaming. I know how you feel about sucking on a dick after it's been in a dirty hole, and yours, my dear, is filthy."

Tears of embarrassment welled in my eyes as he went into the adjoining bathroom to wash his hands. The promise of a future punishment already in place made me question a whole new avenue of escape. A permanent one—*no one could live like this*. The water shut off, and my pulse skyrocketed. I hadn't made the woman orgasm yet, and the unexpected reprieve from the lashes had me resuming my task with gusto in an attempt to thwart his ire. I should have known it wouldn't matter what I did; he was never satisfied until I was in a broken heap, whether it be emotional, physical, or his favorite— a combination of the two. The other woman, riding the face of the one I was servicing, started moaning, and I flicked my gaze up to watch as my tongue continued to work. The woman on top ground down, smothering the one below as she cried out with her own release.

"See, Shelby?" Winston started as he came back up behind me. "Sasha knows how to give good head. You take Marigold's place, but lean down and keep working at it. I want you to watch and learn what you asked for when you tried to betray me."

Limbs jerky with my movements, I crawled up the bed and turned around to settle over the woman with a knee on either side of her head. Sasha didn't even wipe the cum off her face before pulling my hips down to attack my pussy, while I leaned forward until I was on all fours so I could reach hers. I was slower to resume my task, but Winston didn't notice, being he was busy burying his dick in Marigold from behind. With the squelching slap of skin and the sly smile she gave me, I assumed he wasn't in her ass.

To my confusion, I began to enjoy the sensations elicited between my legs, and soon enough, I was in a detached haze, not caring about my situation. My body relaxed into the movements, a moan escaping my lips while my hips worked to get closer to the tongue underneath me. Sasha met my motions with her own, her legs stiffening, and I watched her empty hole clench on nothing as she came.

Excerpt from The Degradation of Shelby Ann

"There's my dirty slut. I knew you'd enjoy it." Winston's voice prompted my heavy eyelids to lift in an attempt to focus on him. "A little bit of Molly plugging always helps. Sasha, give her the gift in the drawer." He never stopped his steady thrusts into Marigold as he waited for his demand to be met.

Sasha patted my hip, and when I didn't immediately lift up, she pushed me to the side until I lost my balance and fell over, allowing her to roll across the bed to get to the nightstand next to it. The abrupt motion gave me vertigo, making my stomach turn briefly before it settled and then the euphoria returned. Sasha came back with a thick, tapered, clear glass rod to resume her position, and I reluctantly and clumsily climbed back over her. She didn't waste any time giving me my 'present', the dildo was cold as she twisted it between my legs, wetting the tip of it in my arousal. The burn of its entrance stretching my inner walls penetrated my fog and continued until it was fully seated, hitting the end of me deep inside.

"Give it to her hard." My pleading gaze met my husband's hard one as he delivered his order. "I want to hear her scream when she comes." Sasha immediately pulled the glass nearly all the way out just to ram it back in. I hadn't anticipated the pain of that unforgiving tip coming to an abrupt halt when it bottomed out with such force behind it, and Winston got his first scream.

Excerpt from The Degradation of Shelby Ann

Sasha bent her head to tongue and suck at my clit while she kept up the destruction inside my channel. Despite the pain and humiliating situation, I'd already been close enough to completion, and that, paired with whatever he'd given me, kept my unwilling arousal going.

"You'd better get off before I do, Shelby, or that's going in your ass next." The mixed sensations of fear, lust, and stimulation pushed me over the edge into a blinding climax. My throat hurt from the drawn out wail of pleasure and pain colliding in my body. "That's a good girl," he praised before he addressed the woman he was fucking. "Marigold, open my hole."

I watched, still hunched in pain after my orgasm, as the woman lowered her face into the bed sheets and used her hands to part her ass cheeks. "Get over here, slut, and watch." Sasha started to move, but Winston shook his head. "Not you, *her.*" I struggled into position, leaving the dildo where it lay after slipping out, glistening with streaks of blood and cum. When my focus was centered on the gaping anus with the pink insides showing, Winston pulled his thick erection from her pussy.

It was slick and shiny, wet with Marigold's juices. He teased her rear hole with the head of his dick, pushing until the crown was nearly swallowed only to retreat again. Each time, he pressed in just a little further until half his length was disappearing with each thrust and Marigold's dark tunnel was revealed bit by bit. "See, that's a clean hole. My girls know how I like it." Despite my detachment to the situation, it still stung that I'd never really been his *girl*, his dishonesty had trapped me in his web of depravity with no way out. A sharp tap to my face brought we out of my wandering thoughts. "Pay attention, slut." Abruptly, he plunged in, seating himself fully, before pulling back to repeat the motion, and other than her rapid breaths, the woman never moved away or complained about the lack of adequate lubricant.

Winston, appearing at the end of his patience, railed her swift and hard until he bit his lip and pulled out. Furiously jacking himself inches from my face, I prepared for him to ejaculate on it, but what he did was so much worse. He put just the tip back into her stretched hole and let loose with a grunt before demanding, "Clean it up, slut."

My gaze fixed in horror directly at the puddle of cum that sat at the opening, a bit dripping toward her pussy. I couldn't do it. I just *couldn't*. But Sasha, she had no issue eagerly licking and sucking at his waning erection while he stared me down. When my first knee slid back in an attempt to escape, Winston gripped a handful of my hair to jerk me face first into Marigold's well-used ass. "Clean it up— or I'll let the guards have a go at your holes while she sits on your face with your tongue up her ass."

Sobbing and too afraid to call his bluff, I opened my mouth to press my lips around the puffy, abused ring and began to lick. When I could work my tongue no further, Winston pulled me back to check my work.

"It'll do. Now, go shower. You're a mess. Don't forget, we have dinner with my father in the city at eight."

Not one of us moved until the door clicked shut behind him.

Get The Degradation of Shelby Ann Here Now!

Printed in Great Britain
by Amazon